A SONG OF SKY & SACRIFICE

A SONG OF SKY & SACRIFICE

LANA PECHERCZYK

Copyright © 2022 Lana Pecherczyk
All rights reserved.

A Song of Sky and Sacrifice
ISBN: 978-0-6454994-7-6

This is a work of fiction. Names, characters, businesses, places, events and incidents are either the products of the author's imagination or used in a fictitious manner. Any resemblance to actual persons, living or dead, or actual events is purely coincidental.

Text copyright © Lana Pecherczyk 2022
Cover design © Lana Pecherczyk 2022
Structural Editor: Ann Harth

www.lanapecherczyk.com

This book is for all the people told to sit down and shut up.

You're the voice.

PROLOGUE
PRESENT DAY

Melody slid blouses across the rack in one of the few remaining stores in Vegas.

"You don't think the war will arrive here, do you?" asked Shonda, Melody's backup singer, as she held up a shimmering skirt. Another two of her entourage were further in the store rummaging through the luxury items. They didn't think Melody noticed, but they glanced over with worry.

"Y'all shouldn't think about it," Melody replied. "We're here to offer escapism. We're not cancelled yet, so the show must go on. We'll deal with anything else when we must. Don't worry, sugar."

"Okay, what do you think about this?" Shonda pulled a distressed and torn blouse from the rack and held it against Melody's body. She made a duck face at the mirror. "Does it scream apocalypse chic, or is it trying too hard?"

Melody stared at her reflection but couldn't look at the blouse. Although her words had been brave, in her stomach, butterflies crawled with broken wings. Dread gnawed at her, but she put on a brave face for her fans. Someone had to.

The moment she gave in to her fear was the moment it became real.

Shonda jiggled the blouse against Melody's bust. "Marilyn Monroe, eat your heart out."

"I like it." Melody laughed. She had always been curvy, and since she'd started performing, her agents had encouraged her to use this and her natural blond hair to her advantage. But lately, she'd lost weight with all her partying, chain-smoking and stress fasting.

She was past caring what the public said about her figure online. She still sold albums, and money didn't lie.

"So, what are you wearing?" Shonda asked. "Your old wardrobe won't do for the next performance, considering the state of the world."

"And why on God's green earth wouldn't we? Ignoring the state of the world is—" Melody's voice died in her throat as something strange on the mirror caught her eye.

A snowflake formed at the edge of the glass. From there, the lacy frost webbed out. And continued. The temperature dropped, and fog left their lips on a breath. Melody's teeth chattered. Her breath bloomed into a white cloud. She hugged herself against the drop in temperature.

Shonda lowered the blouse as she, too, focused on the forming icicles over her reflection. The same frost cracked along the glass double doors looking outside into the street. Melody scanned the street and gasped.

Snow.

In Vegas.

She faced Shonda to share her amazement, and terror struck deep into her soul. Shonda was no longer nubile but frozen solid. A dusting of white frost gathered over her eyelashes and brows. Icicles formed in her hair. Death haunted her eyes.

She was a lifeless human-sized ice sculpture.

Melody wanted to scream, but when frost formed on the back of her hand, all she could think was that she didn't feel the cold. Maybe it was because she was already numb.

CHAPTER ONE

CIRCA 2000 YEARS LATER

"That's a good girl," Forrest crooned and stroked the feathered neck of his favorite *kuturi* at the Order of the Well stables. The flying animal was as big as a horse. It had an eagle's head and wings but a mythical lion's legs and tail. The only reason he knew this association was because he'd seen the ancient animals in picture books at the Autumn Court library he'd hidden in as a youth. But that was half a century ago.

As one of the elite Guardians in the Cadre of Twelve, it wasn't technically his duty to care for animals. He could psychically connect with animals. He felt more at home here than in the twelve-bedroom house he shared with the other burly and brooding soldiers. His brows lifted. He supposed more than twelve lived there now. Six had mated with *mana*-filled women from the old world. One couple even had a child together.

Rush and Clarke's daughter Willow was the perfect blend of

wolf shifter and human. She was also intelligent, incorrigible, and recently kidnapped by the human enemy. It was for her that he said goodbye to his beloved animals.

The kuturi he'd named Princess nuzzled into his palm and then made a demanding clicking sound with her beak.

Food, she said to him, mind-to-mind.

You've had three sugar sweets already, he scolded. *Don't be greedy.*

She huffed but bowed, somewhat mollified by the soothing strokes he gave her feathered neck.

Although he spoke to her using words in his mind, it was his intent that the animal read, just as he understood hers. *Lesser Fae*, like the kuturi, were still creatures of the Well despite having no mana to manipulate. They lived longer than the average human, but most were still animals and primal beings communicating in simple urges. Eat. Sleep. Shit. Fight. Fuck.

If only life for Forrest was so simple.

He'd tried it once—living like an animal. His hiatus in the wilderness hadn't lasted long. As the seventh child of the Rubrum Dynasty, his sole purpose was to be the family's sacrifice to the Well.

Back then, once a year, the Order of the Well went from town to town demanding "tributes" to replenish their ranks since being a Guardian had a high mortality rate. The initiation ceremony to become a Guardian also had a high mortality rate. Most didn't survive, so the appeal of the Guardian role was less than optimal. The Rubrum Dynasty wanted to remain in power at the Autumn Court for as long as possible, so they believed a promise to offer one of their blood as a tribute would endear the people to them.

It worked.

Because they risked one of their own, just like the general public had to, apparently, it meant the royals understood the suffering of the common people. The people didn't see the way Forrest was treated behind the scenes. The indifference, the snubs, the cold-hearted neglect from his own family was a direct order from Forrest's father, the Autumn Court King.

The only reason Autumn Court soldiers had fished him out of the woods as a child was because his presence was a visual reminder to the public of the family's gracious upcoming sacrifice to honor the Well. The fact they continuously called it a sacrifice meant they never believed one of their corrupt ilk would survive. After events, he'd promptly become a part of the woodwork again. Forgotten and invisible.

Forrest's Unseelie mother had emptied her womb, and she'd been encouraged to empty her heart of him too. Not even a name graced his birth documents. He'd simply been known as Sacrifice until the day he emerged victorious from the ceremonial lakes, a Guardian—much to his family's utter horror, surprise, and bitterness. They'd hoped to put his inconvenient existence to bed but had to congratulate him formally—the invisible child they'd rather forget—as being the only Rubrum royal ever judged *worthy* by the Well.

The Order of the Well was above the law of the courts... as long as it came to protecting the integrity of the Well.

Shaking the memories away before they took hold, Forrest forced himself to straighten, and, because he was a sucker for a good girl, he gave Princess one last treat before shutting her stable door. He looked at the stables and shook straw from his long auburn hair. He sent a *goodbye* to his animals and turned his back, wincing at the sudden brays and whines following him as he left.

They would only miss him because he fed them.

Tension crept into his posture as he strode away from the stables. The wind gusted against his face. He tucked flyaway strands of long auburn hair behind his ears, lingering just a little at the pointed elfish tips. Soon they would be cut off so he could pass as a round-eared human in the Well-forsaken city Willow had been taken to. As usual, since he'd agreed to the mission a few weeks ago, an unsettled feeling churned in his stomach when he thought about it. While he understood Willow was a child, not even a decade old, he couldn't shake the feeling this mission would change things. Losing signs of his ancestry was only the beginning.

Fae rarely volunteered to enter the human's Untouched land for long periods. Losing that connection to the Well would be like having his soul ripped out by one of the Sluagh. No one in their right mind would volunteer for the job. Only two Forrest knew of had visited the desecrated city in his lifetime. Three, if he counted Silver, the Well-blessed human now mated to the vampire Shade.

Forrest forced his boots home with a long, shuddering sigh of resignation. He crunched across the limestone path through the Order campus. At his feet, on either side of the way, culverts of water trickled along for company. He passed the time by reviewing the information he'd learned about the old world. To masquerade as human, he would have to act as if he'd freshly woken from a time after the Nuclear Winter and needed sanctuary, so he had to know a thing or two about their ancient way of living.

Sports, for one, were one strange human pastime. They seemed to have little to do except toss around a ball of various shapes and sizes. Watching television was another. For long periods, humans would sit unmoving in front of a screen that showed other humans dressing up and pretending to be others as they told a story.

It all sounded like nonsense, and he didn't think he'd prepared enough, but he couldn't put off the mission any longer. Willow's parents were becoming increasingly frantic, as they should be. Their daughter was in the hands of the enemy.

The sun sank below the horizon, and the sky turned turquoise. Twilight was the busiest time of day for the fae. Both nocturnal and day-walkers bustled about, greeting each other and catching up.

The closer he walked to the Cadre of Twelve's house near the barracks, the more Forrest noticed Guardians leaving their quarters and heading in the same direction. *Odd.* At first, he guessed they were eager to catch a sparring match between members of the elite Twelve on the field opposite their house. Two high-powered fae clashing was a sight to see. But since the battle that stole Willow, that field had been off limits. Tiny metal bullets had to be mined from the ground and adequately disposed of. Any metal, even small fragments, could block the flow of the Well and disrupt their harnessing of the magical energy.

A fae with fur-tipped pointed ears clapped Forrest on the back and said, "You Twelve are the best." He rushed away, his casual shirt flapping open in his haste.

Casual attire?

Forrest frowned as he continued to walk. His concern deepened upon hearing a flute melody punctuated by rhythmic drums drifting over the barracks roofs. When he cast a net of awareness out to the animals nearby, he sensed a disturbance near his home. Birds had been ousted from trees and rooftops where winged fae gathered.

Steeling himself for battle, half wondering if the Unseelie Queen had backtracked from her recent peace treaty with the Order, he arrived at the lawn doubling as a second training field. His jaw dropped. He blinked. Fae everywhere. But not in battle. No. Male shirts were off. Mage robes fell haphazardly off shoulders or dragged in the dirt. Elixirs and stubs of smoking mana-weed were in hands. Drooping, intoxicated eyelids. Raucous laughter.

This was wrong. The Order of the Well did *not* party. They worked. They protected the integrity of the Well. Guardians eliminated mana-warped monsters. They policed forbidden substances so the Well continued to flow. They executed raiding, Untouched humans when they dared enter their blessed land. They did *not* party.

His eyes said otherwise.

Blue-robed Mages and those without identifying uniforms —*civilians*—danced. Guardians, both rookies and experienced, caroused loudly—some had set up a game of manabee roulette at the base of the steps leading up into the Twelve's house. Manabeeze were physical manifestations of the Well. The balls of light only came from a fae lifeforce and were not to be trifled with.

Forrest's brows lifted when he caught Ash, the crow shifter and member of the Twelve, watching the game with a devious look in his dark eyes. The tall, quiet Guardian usually stayed away from gatherings. But there he was, starkly identified with his shoulder-length dark hair held back by a leather band at the brow. He wore his Guardian leathers, which meant he was heading out on a mission or just returning.

Probably hadn't intended to stay.

Two Guardians released a single glowing manabee from a jar and shoved a third Guardian toward it. Ash caught Forrest watching and winked before leaning back for the show. He'd probably tampered with the manabeeze before the drunk Guardians started playing the game.

This isn't good.

A floating manabee hit the male participant. His limbs loosened, his lashes lowered, and everyone watched with bated breath. Manabeeze were not only a power source but held memories from its original host. The intoxicating substance made the recipient relive the host's memory if ingested. The problematic part was what kind of memory. Would it be something benign like a *warada* foraging for food or something horrific like a fae being eaten by a Well Hound in the battle Ring pit at Cornucopia.

The wingless Guardian tried to flap his arms. When that didn't help him fly, he bolted for the trellis and tried to climb up to the roof. He would jump and break his neck and do it all thinking he was the person or creature the manabee belonged to.

"For Crimson's sake." Forrest scrubbed his face. This was not what he needed on the night he had to leave.

He was hoping for a quick bath, a quiet word with Aeron, his half-brother, and a swift exit through a portal to the cabin where Rush and Clarke had based the operations for their rescue mission.

"Fuck, yeah!" A loud shout came from the clay-tiled roof of the two-story house. When Forrest glanced up, the silhouette of a crow shifter in angel form stumbled drunkenly. The twilight halo around his blue-black hair and wings marked him as River, the rowdiest of the Twelve. A pretty faun had her hand shoved down his open leather breeches while he raised a cup to the sky and mumbled a prayer of gratitude to whichever goddess he favored at the moment.

Power-enhancing tattoos over River's naked torso were why he and the other crows were exempt from the rescue mission. The tattoos glowing like a prismatic oil slick were decidedly *not* human.

Bitterness rose up Forrest's throat as he glared at the tattoos. Selfish, power-enhancing marks courted the inky side of the Well. Without them, the crows would have made better candidates for the mission. Their round ears made them easily passable as human. But crows didn't have a selfless bone in their bodies.

"Nice of you to show up!" River shouted down, a gleam in his eyes.

The female attached to him scowled at whoever had stolen her partner's attention. River pouted when he realized she'd removed her hand from his pants.

"Who said you could stop?" He shoved it back.

She giggled and started stroking.

"Much better." River fisted her hair, pulled her lips to his, then shoved his tongue down her throat.

Forrest headed inside, but the crafty crow vaulted from the roof, minus his female this time, and landed deftly despite the state of his intoxication. He fixed his pants and lifted his chin when he straightened before Forrest.

"Password," he clipped in all seriousness.

Clearly, he was pissed that Forrest didn't take his voyeuristic bait. "Get out of my way, River."

River slammed his palm on the open doorframe, blocking Forrest from entering the house.

"What's the problem, elf?" River leaned in. "You gonna narc about our little gathering to the Prime?"

The Prime, the leader of the Order, must be off campus.

Forrest snorted. "Some of us are a little busy with actual missions."

"Do I detect a note of sarcasm?" He wrinkled his nose and looked down at Forrest's shirt. "I definitely detect some kind of shit."

Making fun of him because he worked with animals? Forrest leaned in closer until the two of them were nose to nose. "The bats are away, so the crows will play, is that it?"

River's blue eyes flashed. Forrest wanted to say so many things, but what was the point? These shit-stain crows were just as Unseelie as Forrest's biological family. Waste of energy.

"Our fearless team leader has a stick up his arse," River drawled. "But I'm sure he'd join in if he were here." River then cocked his head, studying Forrest. "Like your brother has. At least those elves don't run from the sight of a man getting his cock pumped by a pretty female. You should stick around; you might learn some pointers. Crimson knows you need them."

River smirked at the unavoidable tension tightening Forrest's expression. Then he gestured into the house where the music was loudest.

"Your brother is inside," he drawled casually before strolling back to where his faun waited at the porch steps, pouting at the interruption. River gathered her into his arms, snapped his wings out until their breadth stretched wide and blocked all from view, and then took a vertical leap into the air. The beating of feathered wings momentarily drowned out the music and conversation, kicking up dust and dirt. A few angry curse words were tossed his way until revelers realized it was one of the Twelve who'd caused the disturbance. Some even apologized. Crows were loose cannons at the best of times, but when they were drunk?

Fucking impossible.

FORREST

CHAPTER TWO

The lights were dim inside the house. Smoke from mana weed consumption gave the air a sweet taste. Forrest tried not to breathe in. He needed his full wits about him for the rest of the night. Still, as he walked into the front hall and passed the living room crowded with strange fae, he half wished he had the guts to sit and forget about the world for a while.

Waving smoke from his face, he entered the living room. He stopped at the threshold and let his senses adjust. Through accessing mana and calling upon the traits of animals, Forrest heard better than most elves. Mana pumped into his system, sharpening his senses.

What was grey became a full-color spectrum.

Sex. Drugs. Sweat. Soft feminine moans. Grumbling men in conversation. Voyeurs and exhibitionists mingled. It wasn't uncommon for Unseelie to behave morally loose in public—an apothecary from his own royal family had created the popular aphrodisiac, *divilixr*. He'd been exposed to its debauching effects way too early and seen things a child should never see.

Despite what River had claimed, when Leaf returned from wherever he'd gone, he'd be furious at this invasion. Forrest turned toward the staircase leading up to the bedrooms, but then two sapphire eyes glinting in the darkness caught his attention.

Cloud stared at Forrest from his spot in the center of a couch, squashed between fae. His leather Guardian uniform seemed to absorb the darkness like one of the vampires soaked up shadow. His butterfly knife moved so deftly; one would be forgiven for believing it was another limb. Power-enhancing tattoos covered every scrap of skin except Cloud's face. They twinkled in the dim light. A dark spatter of something Forrest assumed was blood covered one side of his face. Cloud was the Prime's private assassin and unofficial leader of the three crow shifters in the Cadre of Twelve.

Like Shade and Leaf, he was also a Council member, so he pulled rank in the Order.

Cloud stared at Forrest across the room like a homicidal maniac, uncaring that the world turned around him.

Nothing phased him unless he wanted it to. Not the female Mage flicking her hair into his face as she listened to another's conversation, nor the couple with their tongues down each other's throat on his other side, nor the group behind him laughing jauntily and poking each other in jest.

Then Cloud's eyes flicked to the right in a deliberate move.

Forrest followed his gaze to another couch where Aeron sat with a female straddling his lap. Disappointment trickled through Forrest. Out of everyone here, he'd hoped for a bit of empathy from his half-brother tonight. But during the same battle that stole

Willow, the Unseelie High Queen's monstrous demogorgon had let loose an eardrum-piercing shriek that deafened Aeron despite their best healer's efforts.

Aeron had no clue Forrest was there. His head rested back on the couch. The female's robes gathered around her thighs, but from how her hips rocked, it was clear what occurred beneath.

Aeron wasn't usually so reckless with his time. This party would have repercussions when Leaf or the Prime caught wind of it. Aeron was the most organized of them all. The most educated. Some would even say he was uptight and rigid in his efforts to stick to the rules. But since the accident, he'd spiraled into depression. He'd spent days in bed mourning his loss and now clearly was doing anything to forget about it all.

Unlike Forrest, who'd spent his time in the Autumn Court invisible, Aeron had been the King's bastard. People hated Aeron, but they never saw Forrest. The two of them had kept their blood relation a secret until recently. Now Forrest wasn't sure why.

There was nothing left to protect.

Aeron's hand slid up the female's front until his fingers wrapped around her throat. He was probably trying to hear with his touch, sensing the vibrations of her pleasure-filled moans.

Cloud smirked at Forrest. *What was his problem?* Was he waiting for Forrest to judge Aeron's actions, or was it that, like River, they all assumed because Forrest was a virgin, seeing this kind of debauchery would unsettle him?

He didn't have time for this.

He left and made his way up the staircase to his room, shoving past unwelcome fae in the hallway, most of them drunk or high. He clenched his teeth as he approached his door, hoping to avoid confrontation if anyone was inside.

Forrest entered his dark room and shut the door behind him. The music dimmed. He checked to ensure he was alone before sitting on the edge of his bed with his head in his hands.

One turn of the moon ago, he thought he'd had his life in order. But now, he had no idea what was happening. For decades he'd had a routine. The Twelve may not have always meshed, but they worked together well. They knew how to fight and what they were fighting for. And they had each other's backs.

Now, the Order was in chaos. The Unseelie and the Seelie were at war. Aeron was spiraling. The Well was tainted, and they didn't know why, but any time they used mana, they ran the risk of spells backfiring and injuring. Leaf and the Prime were looking into it now.

He scrubbed his face. There was no use dwelling on the changes, especially when none of it would matter to him once he was behind the walls of Crystal City.

He went to pack and remembered he needed nothing for this trip. He couldn't bring his weapons, bow, arrows, or sword. Couldn't bring mana stones or anything that marked him as fae. He was masquerading as an escaped prisoner from The Unseelie High Queen Maebh's dungeons. He glanced at the items he'd collected over the past few decades and wondered who would take his room if he failed his mission. Would Aeron pack Forrest's belongings away? Would he hold a mourning rite for him? Or would Forrest fade into invisibility again, like in the past?

After putting his fur-lined cape on his shoulders, he collected the portal stone sitting in a bowl by the door. Clarke had given it to him the last time they spoke. It was keyed to Rush's cabin in the woods. One way ride.

They'd assumed he'd either be with them on the way back or not be there at all.

The door blasted open. Aeron stumbled in with sweet-smelling smoke. He collapsed back onto the bed, face up, eyes closed, a self-pitying groan coming from his lips. His breeches were still open at the placket. His gaping shirt revealed fresh scars healing across his abdominals.

Forrest rolled his eyes. The *warada-tail* didn't realize this wasn't his room. He considered shoving him out, but instead took pity. Aeron had suffered in his youth, just as Forrest had. And now, his ability to be a Guardian was most likely gone. No one could be a warrior without all his senses. Even if the Prime and Leaf did fix the taint on the Well, even if they couldn't heal his ears and found another vocation for him in the Order, he'd not be the same.

Forrest plucked the boots from his brother's feet and then put the blanket over him before leaving and closing the door.

When he walked past the front living room, Cloud stared from his couch. Pensive and deep in thought, oblivious to the female still flicking hair at him—oh, strike that. Not oblivious. Instead of ignoring it for the umpteenth time, Cloud yanked her down to his lap, where he held his knife to her exposed throat. Her expression morphed from pouty to aroused.

Over the theatrics, Forrest kept walking. He was outside and across the field, barging through the stupid revelers when Cloud caught up.

"You fucking miss me?" Cloud asked as he shoved Forrest between the shoulder blades. It didn't bother him. He knew this was Cloud's version of a love tap. The psycho shifter had no idea how to make friends.

"You've been making eyes at me all night," Forrest drawled as he walked ahead. "Just spit it out, Cloud."

The shifter's feathered wings snapped shut, displacing air. Forrest stopped and faced him just as the scowling Guardian spoke. "You're headed to the human city now, aren't you?"

Forrest checked to see if anyone eavesdropped. This mission was secret. For the Twelve only. Cloud was one of them, but he wasn't the first fae you'd ask to go on a mission with you. He'd instead steal, pillage, and stab.

"Why do you care?" Forrest returned.

Cloud had hesitated when the humans arrived via portal. Forrest recalled it had something to do with the woman who'd kidnapped Willow. Cloud recognized her being related to the Unseelie High Queen Maebh. And if he recognized her, he must have crossed paths with her during his unfortunate time behind the Crystal City walls in his youth.

From the hate billowing from Cloud's eyes, Forrest guessed that history wasn't good.

"What's the plan?" Cloud's words seemed involuntarily wrenched from his mind.

"If you want to help fix your mistake and rescue Willow, come and find out."

"I don't give a flying fuck about the kid," he spat. "Why do you think we're having a party? Finally, no runts in the house. No parents telling us to pipe down because she's asleep."

And that was the real reason Cloud had not been asked to go, even if they could hide his tattoos and deal with his vicious tendencies. He cared sweet fuck all about whether or not the kid survived. She was a thorn in his wing.

"That's cold, Cloud. Even for you."

"I changed my mind," he said. "I want in."

"In what?"

"The mission."

Didn't he just admit to not caring about the child? "The mission?"

"Did I stutter?"

Cloud couldn't enter enemy territory. Those power-enhancing tattoos saw to that. Even if the Well was flowing correctly, and they found a healer capable of removing the tattoos, Cloud wasn't the sort to give them up. He lived and died by his power.

"You can't come, Cloud."

"Why the fuck not?"

"You insult both of us if I have to spell it out for you."

Cloud's leather creaked as he folded his arms and arched a brow, waiting.

Okay then.

"You don't give a rat's ass about the kid," Forrest pointed out. "You just want to get there to kill as many humans as possible. Probably, no—especially—the female you stared at for a little too long when Willow was kidnapped. What was her name? Rory, or something?"

Of course, Forrest knew. He just wanted to see Cloud's reaction.

Cloud's eyes narrowed. "So what if I want her dead?"

"You know we struck a deal with Maebh for her to call off her demogorgon... we have to bring Rory back alive. She's a direct descendant of Maebh's line. *You're* the one who told us that."

Forrest cocked his head, inspecting the crow shifter with a storm brewing in his eyes. Cloud seemed to want to say more from the grinding of his teeth. This was the way he worked. He'd sow dissonance and chaos until nobody knew his true intentions, but he always came out on top. Did he want to kill this human-fae hybrid, the queen's heir, or was this something else? Did he give a shit about anything? Or had whatever happened to him in Crystal City destroyed every ounce of his soul?

"Fuck it. Whatever." Cloud stalked back into the throng of fae.

"He's nuts," Forrest mumbled under his breath and continued along the lawn, intending to find an open space where he could activate the portal safely. With a heavy sigh, Forrest pulled out the stone from his pocket as he neared the edge of the training field. The crowd had thinned on this side because it was close to the Six's house.

Made up of Sluagh, the Six were the second and final set of elite Guardians in the Order. They were also the fae boogeymen and fed on the souls of humans and fae alike. Forrest had only ever seen three of them emerge from that house and only at night. The other three were still a mystery.

The portal activated, a light flashed, and the scent of ozone filled the air. Before Forrest stepped through, the hairs on the back of his neck stood on end. *Danger.* He was being watched. The snowy landscape through the portal billowed with a storm, promising a swift haven from what watched Forrest, but he wouldn't be in the

Twelve if he failed to search his surroundings—the dead bushes near the Six's house... their dilapidated porch, the party further back. He couldn't see a soul, but it didn't mean no one was there. The Sluagh separated from their bodies and became invisible wraiths. One of them could be standing right next to Forrest, and he'd have no idea.

A shiver shuddered down his spine.

Crunching behind him. Forrest whirled and found a stumbling, drunk fae with feathered wings moving to a bush to relieve himself.

"I'd get back to the party if I were you," Forrest warned, a wary glance cast at the Six's house. He could have sworn he saw the curtains twitch.

The winged fae flipped Forrest the bird and then belched loudly.

"Your funeral," Forrest muttered.

There weren't many alive who could fight a Sluagh and win. Forrest wasn't one of them. The sooner he left, the better. The electrical current of the portal kissed his skin as he passed through, and a foreign male voice slithered into his mind.

Tell Clarke the longer she fights her daughter's fate, the worse it will be.

The last thing Forrest saw as the portal closed was a tall, lithe shadow creeping on the winged fae in the darkness. And then the disturbing silence as whichever of the Six paralyzed the winged fae and fed.

MELODY

CHAPTER THREE

Melody surveyed Crystal City from the safety of the performers' green room on the ninety-ninth floor in Sky Tower. The world had changed so much since her time. Not only did the nuclear winter catch up to Vegas, but it destroyed everything. But then, twisted magical beings were born out of the icy ashes.

The barbed wire web reaching from the tower's pinnacle to the large opaque crystal boundary wall was a testament to the danger they faced daily. The deadly mesh was a security measure preventing winged *Tainted Ones* from invading—fae, they called themselves. They could enter, but if they tried to leave, their wings would be butchered by the razor blade wire.

Under the waxing moon, the dull, cloud-smudged sky depressed her. Now and then, she'd see a swatch of greenery, but apart from the president's garden, not much grew within those high crystal walls.

"Fifteen minutes," the stage manager warned as he poked his head into the room.

Melody gestured over her shoulder to let him know she'd heard. He'd be back again in five minutes. She was almost fully dressed and ready to go for her nightly performance.

She took a pot of red nail polish and sat awkwardly in the tight dress. Never before had she had trouble reaching her toes. She hated it.

With every stroke of red, a memory from her childhood climbed to the forefront of her mind. She finished her toes and stared, waiting for them to dry. The memory took hold.

She was eleven years old and with her mother at a gas station in Arizona. The weather was hot—gasoline stank.

They were moving to a new town for her mother's new job. It was the fifth time they'd moved in as many years. Melody tested how sunglasses looked on her face in the mirror by the cashier. Then she perused the nail polish collection in the spinning rack while her mother counted out pennies to the attendant.

Hot sun baked her skin through the dirty windows. Trucks rumbled outside.

"Just a minute," her mother said. "I'm sure it's somewhere here." She desperately emptied her purse, hunting for spare change to pay for the nail polish Melody put on the counter.

"Hurry up," called a trucker behind them in the line. "We don't have all day, darlin'!"

Melody put the red nail polish and sunglasses back on the rack. The trucker who'd yelled suddenly stepped forward. He had a pot belly sticking out of the bottom hem of a ketchup-stained T-shirt. A handlebar mustache collected crumbs. He rubbed his exposed belly button as he slapped a fifty on the counter and eyed Melody's mother.

"I'll cover it, darlin'."

Her mother gaped. Melody grinned and grabbed the items. But then the trucker added in a slow, southern drawl that made her skin crawl, "I'm sure we can figure out some kinda repayment outside in my cabin."

The attendant stopped chewing her gum. Her eyebrows lifted sky-high. Even Melody, at her young age, picked up the insinuation. But Melody's mother never showed her disgust. Her gaze flicked to the goods, and she thought about it. She actually thought about it.

"It's okay, mom. I don't need them." Melody felt like puking all over the trucker's flip-flops.

Her mother seemed to gather her wits and gave a polite smile to her supposed knight in shining armor. "Bless your heart, but we'll be fine."

"Your loss." The trucker took his money back and stuffed it in his pants.

Ew.

"I'm so sorry, sugarplum." Her mother sighed and packed all the items she'd removed into her purse with trembling fingers. Her following words seemed deliberately loud. "Sometimes, what you want ain't worth the cost." Her loose sandy curls bounced as she nodded to the attendant. "Just the gas, then. Thank you."

On their walk back to the car, her mother's sadness radiated into Melody more than the sun. Melody squeezed into their beat-up station wagon that smelled like baked leather and sticky sweet soda pop. The back passenger seats overflowed with every item they owned, which wasn't much. The radio was broken, but that didn't deter Melody from reaching into the back seat and finding something she could use to make a sound.

A wooden grade school ruler. Perfect.

When her mother sank into the driver's seat and closed her door, she turned to Melody with a sad smile.

"Don't worry, honey cakes. One day you'll have everything you want, and it won't just be red nail polish and glasses. It will be your heart's desire and won't cost a thing. Just you wait and see."

She smiled back. "I don't need it. It's okay."

To prove her point, she picked up that empty soda can and tapped her ruler to make a familiar beat her mother loved.

"My grandma and your grandma... were sitting by the beach," she sang, changing the words from the song Iko Iko to something they could have fun with.

Her mother turned the engine and smiled, thrumming her fingers on the wheel. "My grandma told your grandma gonna eat a giant peach."

Melody burst out laughing but never skipped a beat. They were well into their own version of the chorus when the car sputtered out of the lot.

Clearing her throat, Melody tested the nail polish. Dry. She slipped on peep toe heels and went back to the window. Now there was nothing left to do but wait. The anticipation didn't bring the buzz it once did. Only on special occasions did President Nero allow her to perform renditions from her time. Only then did she feel that tingle in her fingers and flutter in her stomach.

Suddenly, her dress felt too tight. She tugged at the low collar and wished it covered more of her breasts, but they spilled out bigger than ever. She couldn't hit the deep notes like this, and to let out the seams any more meant there would be no fabric left.

Melody's gaze switched from the scenery outside to her reflection in the window as light rain drizzled down the glass. She tugged at the laces down the front of her gown.

Maybe if she loosened them just a little...

But as her fingers twitched over the laces, she forced them to smooth over her stomach and hips. *Ugh. Bloated.* The silk dress hugged her curves in what she supposed was flattering for a woman of her body type, but she'd rather not feel like a stuffed sausage when she walked. At least her platinum finger waves were styled perfectly in her hair, and the red lipstick on her lips was classy. With any luck, Sophia wouldn't notice the darker circles beneath her eyes.

Since thawing in this time, Melody had been fed sugary food and locked in this tower with little chance to exercise or explore. Nero said she represented the abundant past, so he wanted her to look the part. He also said she was a precious commodity and must be kept safe. She only left the Tower to visit the president's private gardens for fresh air, which weren't far.

She glanced again, searching beyond the barbed wire web and city walls, trying to catch an impossible glimpse of the other world in the darkness.

Mystery consumed life beyond the walls, despite the stories she'd been told, which were the same ones she sang in her performances. For a moment, her mind drifted and wondered... what it would be like to indeed be out there. Would it be as terrifying as they said? Lord knew there were always two sides to a coin. What if—

The door opened, and Sophia bustled in with the rest of Melody's entourage. Sophia was born in this time, like the rest of the musicians.

Melody didn't know many like her who'd survived the Nuclear

Winter. There was an inventor dubbed the Tinker, but Melody had not spent much time with her.

"Oh good, you're here," Sophia said. "We will do the final wardrobe check together."

Sophia lined up the other three musicians on the brocade sofa and gestured for Melody to join them, but instead, Melody went for the ashtray on the stand near the dresser and lit a cigarette. She put it between her lips and returned to the window with all the entitlement her previous vocation had gifted her.

She was still a star and an integral part of Nero's propaganda machine. She could get away with more than most so long as she performed her nightly duties. A shudder wanted to travel down her spine, but she forced herself to inhale smoke and exhale until the room turned hazy.

Sophia gave a laborious sigh and then checked the musicians on the sofa. The two men on the outside were immaculately dressed in cream silk suits and frilly shirts that reminded Melody of renaissance times. The woman in the center—Caroline—wore something similar to Melody but less revealing. Much of the fashion in the Tower had taken a step backward in time. Most of the women wore dresses down to their ankles. Only the soldiers and workers wore pants, while the elite men wore garish and ridiculous suits. She supposed the backward fashion matched the backward ideals.

But if you looked closely at the clothes, you'd find threadbare hems and patched patterns. Supplies were running thin in this human settlement. There was only so much recycling one could do.

Sophia clicked a disapproving tongue at Melody's dress.

"I told you not to touch," Sophia snapped, tightening the laces again, yanking them harshly. Damn it. "This is how Nero likes it. This is how the Captain likes it. It's how you must wear it."

Mention of the Captain's name was like fingernails down a chalkboard. Melody exhaled her last drag into Sophia's face. Smoke billowed over her skin, but to her credit, the petite brunette only pursed her stained lips before mumbling, "I don't make the rules."

"But y'all police them," Melody replied. "Don't matter if you make them."

"Two Tower Guards outside say I don't have a choice."

"There's always a choice, honey."

Sophia looked at Melody like she didn't know which way was up, then screwed up her nose in disgust at the smoke and returned to fix the dress. Sophia tugged and pulled, trying to stuff Melody's "abundance" back into the seemingly shrinking attire.

"We'll have to let it out again," Sophia murmured more to herself than anyone.

It still hurt. Melody was sick of letting out her dresses. She wanted, for once, to not feel sick. When the weight gain was of her own volition, she couldn't give a rat's ass, but when it was forced on her... *ugh*. Unable to hide her irritation, she brushed Sophia away from her with a scowl not befitting a music icon.

Sophia looked at the three on the sofa and left in a huff. As the door closed, Melody caught the curious eye of one of the guards outside and flipped up her middle finger.

She waited for two beats of her heart before putting the cigarette out and waving the smoke away. The two men on either side of Caroline launched across her lap to get to each other and kiss.

"Goddammit," Caroline cursed and tried to push them off her. "You could have waited until I wasn't in the way."

Melody offered her hand to Caroline and tugged her out of Timothy and Andrew's path as they reunited.

"Don't blame them," Melody said quietly. "You know it's the only ten minutes they get to be themselves all day."

"It's still polite to wait," Caroline grumbled as she joined Melody by the window.

They turned their backs and gave the two lovers the only privacy they could afford. Supporting them not only warmed Melody's heart, but it felt like a secret middle finger shoved at the patriarchy of this new world where a certain few elites arranged marriages. She would rather rage against the system but had to rein in her urges. Even though this world was but six months new to her, it was millennia old to them.

Melody had asked around about arranged marriages. The story went that after the nuclear fallout, to avoid contamination and to survive the radiation they blamed for the mutations of the Tainted, a group of about three hundred had locked themselves in an underground bunker some billionaire doomsday prepper created.

Few humans left in the world meant they had to carefully arrange the intermingling of bloodlines to avoid genetic problems. Even though the population of Crystal City was close to a million, if not more now, this archaic practice still existed. The elite in the Tower didn't mix with commoners in the city, so they peddled their fear-mongering like heroin to keep this practice alive.

"Y'all learned the lines to the new song?" Melody asked loudly, although she didn't expect the men to answer.

Caroline shrugged as she picked up a cup of water from the dresser. "Of course."

"Good."

They stared out into the abyss for a while before Caroline asked, "Do you think it's true?"

"What?"

"They're part beast, like... down *there*, too."

Melody snorted and smirked at her friend. "I know I didn't write anything about beastly appendages into the song. Where did that come from?"

Caroline shrugged. "Just heard some things. So... do you?"

"Well, honey. I don't know. Maybe they're as crooked as a cat downstairs, or maybe they ain't much different to us. All we know is what we're told."

"Isn't it all a glamor designed to fool us, but they're really monsters underneath?"

Melody hesitated. "Right."

She picked up her glass and wet her dry throat. She usually saved the cigarette for a post-stage celebration, so her voice stayed true, but risking vocal chord damage was worth it to hear her friends happy.

"Oh, I don't know," Timothy drawled, coming up behind Melody, giving her a quick kiss on the cheek before tucking his shirt into his trousers. "There's nothing wrong with a bit of monster dick."

Melody caught Andrew's eyes. He gave her a cheeky wink as he finished straightening his attire and smoothing his messy brown hair. Big brass rings glinted on his knuckles.

"Is that the name of your next song, Mel?" Andrew joked.

"Beware of tainted monster dick?"

"Ooh, ooh." Caroline jumped up and down, her eyes bright. "You could sing it to the tune of Tainted Love. You know, the song you taught us the other week."

Melody smiled quietly as the three took their joke to new levels, volleying between themselves. It wasn't the subject matter but the mood of her friends. Being locked in this tower had its good and bad days. Mostly bad. And even though her friends weren't from her time, they embraced the knowledge like natives. Every day they practiced. And as often as Melody could, she taught them music from her time.

It softened that little homesick kick in her gut.

She finished her water as the door opened, and the stagehand called out that it was time to leave. Two Tower guards entered to escort them to the dining theatre. Their navy blue uniform had metal epaulet details identifying rank. The metal on them looked tarnished. Probably low rank, then. As far as Melody knew, the leaders like the president had gold. His daughter was copper. And others were less shiny.

Gus, the tall mustached guard, went straight for Caroline. She flinched as he grasped her elbow and guided her out the door. The second guard had long blond hair tied at his nape and a hand in a plaster cast. Sid had joined her security detail a week ago and had been her latest source of anti-fae content for her shows.

Sid was a handsome, private man who had ghosts in his eyes. Didn't talk much. There was a pinch to his expression as he noticed her looking at his cast. He used his good hand to take Melody's elbow and direct her, much the same as Gus had. But he clenched hard.

Melody shrugged out of his grip.

It was one thing for the oligarchs and high-ranking military men to grope at Melody, but another for the guards. Not that any of it was okay. Since awaking in this time, her body wasn't her own. She existed for the cause... and sometimes that cause thought it was entitled to manhandle her.

The shame on Sid's features made Melody curious. He flexed his good hand at his side and then gestured for Melody to walk ahead of him out the door. The men had already trailed after Caroline, and, of course, no guard manhandled them. Melody lifted her chin and walked on heels with as much dignity as she could muster.

"Sorry," Sid said quietly as they walked. "Old Reaper habits die hard. I seem to go from zero to one hundred without thinking."

A chill ran down Melody's spine. *Reaper.* They were the mercenary team the president's daughter managed. They scouted fae land, assassinated, and sometimes infiltrated. The emotionless man walking next to her was probably deadlier than anyone Melody had met, yet he was the only one who'd ever apologized for grabbing her too hard.

When Sid gave Melody fae information a week ago, he did not mention why he'd been in Elphyne.

"I've never seen a Reaper in the Tower before," she remarked. "Apart from Rory, that is."

"Never been here." He grunted and then lifted his plaster-covered hand.

Her brows lifted. "What happened?"

"Fucking vampire." He suddenly blushed. "Sorry."

"I've heard worse cussin', honey. Don't you worry about that." Melody assessed the man as they continued down the dark hallway to the dining hall. She was about to drill him for more information when he stopped and stared at her.

"Boss said your content is getting stale." He had the decency to look ashamed of the criticism he was forced to impart.

Her gaze snapped back to his. "Oh, he did, did he?"

"Not my words. His."

Melody wanted to laugh. She sure as shit was a long way from her past career as a world-renowned musician.

She glanced down at his damaged hand and sighed. "It's probably true. Even with you telling me about that, I've learned all I can about vampires. They don't scare anymore."

Don't scare me *anymore.*

"They should." He continued walking down the hall, and Melody had to hurry to catch up. "The only reason this one didn't kill us all was that he was in lo—"

He cut off suddenly.

"He was in what?" she pressed, suddenly positively alight with the illicit knowledge there were things Sid had kept from her. The damned tight dress made it impossible to walk fast. She couldn't catch up.

As they crested the hallway, the stage came into view. The decorations and musical instruments made her smile, despite knowing she was far from home.

She thanked Sid and promised they'd continue their conversation later. Her last sane thought as she took her place by the piano was that her mother would be disappointed in her. They might have laughed and joked about the fae earlier in the green room, but it was because, deep down, humans were terrified.

And it was Melody's job to keep them that way.

CHAPTER
FOUR

Forrest stumbled through the portal and landed on the snow-covered shore of a lake. He turned back but only glimpsed revelers through the portal as they partied on the distant lawn. No Sluagh was standing there, thinking Forrest was his next meal.

Where had it gone?

Its message still burned like fire in his mind.

Tell Clarke the longer she fights her daughter's fate, the worse it will be.

What in Crimson's name did that mean? Were the Sluagh threatening a child? He knew they didn't discriminate when they fed on souls. They fed on humans, fae, children, elders, and anything with a soul. But he'd always thought the Six were different. They would never have survived the initiation ceremony to become a Guardian if they were utterly evil.

No one understood precisely how the Well Worms judged initiates, but they knew that most of those who failed and floated were bad fae. Only the worthy carried the extra burden of being able to access the Well and hold forbidden materials at the same time.

Forrest always thought it was a defense mechanism of the Well. It had been snuffed out by industrialism of the past and now only gave itself to those it knew would take care of the land. None of Forrest's family believed he would pass the initiation because they were all *floaters*. Surprising them had been the single, greatest day of his life.

Once the portal closed, Forrest shook off the nerves and stared across the snowy shore to the lake. Bioluminescent aquatic life glinted under the starry sky. He tossed the spent portal stone. It skipped across the water and displaced rising steam before finally submerging. Glowing algae eddied and swirled as it sank.

He sensed wildlife in the woods behind the lake. Owls. Prowling wolves. Smaller creatures scurried in the dark. Larger ones waited for prey to walk into their trap. This sense of connectedness would fade when Forrest stepped beyond the Crystal City walls. He'd been preparing for it, but he didn't like it.

He started toward Rush's cabin on the lakeside. Smoke curled from the chimney. A plant on the inside grew out of the window and through gaps in the thatched roof. Moving shadows displaced the soft light from the window—a *lot* of shadows.

How many were in there?

He had half a mind to turn back and make some excuse, but Rush, the burly silver-haired wolf shifter burst from the door with a scowl. With his long hair half tied, the sight of his fur-tipped fae ears flattening was clear. It was either a sign of accession or—

"You're late," he snapped.

—anger.

Forrest opened his mouth to explain but honestly didn't know where to start. With the illegal party, his spiraling half-brother, Cloud's weird request, or the Sluagh's message in his mind? Instead, he rubbed his fist in a circle over his chest in the fae hand sign for an apology.

Rush's brow lifted, his nostrils flared, and he waved Forrest onward to come inside. Clarke waited at the door. Her long red hair draped in tangles down her shoulders. Like Rush, she had dark circles under her eyes. Being a powerful Seer, she'd never slept well at the best of times, but these smudges were the toll of losing her only daughter.

Guilt flashed through Forrest. He shouldn't have dawdled coming here.

He glanced around the cabin as he stood at the threshold and kicked the snow off his boots. Shade and Silver were there. He was a vampire in the Twelve, and Silver was his human mate, recently turned from her life in Crystal City.

Thorne—Rush's adult son—and his human mate Laurel sat on the bed. The humans were all thawed out from the old world.

So... he was surrounded by three Well-blessed and mated couples. Great.

Each had matching glimmering blue markings twining up one arm—it was a permanent symbol of the Well's approval of their union. The pairing also allowed them to share mana and emotions... and rumor had it, on rare occasions, thoughts. The humans who had thawed from the old time were abundant in personal mana stores, so the partnerships had been advantageous for the Guardians who fought to protect the Well.

Forrest took in the females, all powerhouses in their own right. Laurel had learned to fight. As a human assassin—a Reaper—Silver already had the skills. She'd bested Shade multiple times... as the story went. Shade had proudly told them all one night of how he'd seduced his murderous mate into being with him.

Forrest put his snow-dusted cape in Clarke's awaiting hands.

The cabin was one room. A bed in a corner, a modest kitchenette in another, and a fireplace occupied by a family of elemental sprites on the third wall. The plant Forrest had seen poking its leaves through the roof turned out to be an overgrown monstrosity, yet its leaves provided a comforting canopy over the bed that called to his nature-loving elvish blood.

Shade lounged on a chair by the fire. His casual clothing seemed wrong for the warrior. Forrest was used to him wearing Guardian leathers, but since Shade's mate's actions were directly linked to the kidnapping of Willow, Rush had refused to allow her to live at the Order, and Shade refused to leave Silver's side. She deeply regretted her part in the kidnapping but had spent the past few weeks relentlessly preparing Forrest for what he'd find beyond the Crystal City walls. She'd also set up a people-smuggling operation to ferry Well-sympathizing humans out of the city.

Shade's bronze hand idly wrapped around Silver's pale braid as she sat on the floor, watching the fire. Flames flickered against her caramel skin as the fire sprites danced on the wooden logs.

"Forrest," Shade greeted, his voice somehow both smooth yet sharp.

"Shade," Forrest returned, then added, "Silver."

She gave Forrest a tight smile. "It's good you came."

"Of course." Forrest turned his attention to Laurel and Thorne.

Thorne looked much like his father—silver hair, pale skin, fur-tipped pointed ears. Both shifted forms into a white wolf. Both had a warrior's physique. Except where Rush's hair was long, Thorne's had been shaved at the sides, and a leather cord pulled back the medium length on top.

"Aeron not coming?" Thorne inquired.

Forrest shook his head and left it at that. It wasn't as if anyone expected Aeron to join the mission with his deafness, but since learning he was Forrest's half-brother, most assumed he would be here for support. Forrest avoided seeing pity in their eyes and gave another room check before noting, "I thought Ada would be here."

Ada was the best healer they knew, and while she'd recently had a child with Jasper, the Seelie High King, she'd always done her best to help the Twelve. Jasper was still technically a Guardian—it was impossible to revoke that gift. Ada was also a close friend of Laurel and Clarke.

Laurel answered, "She's at the Summer Palace with Peaches and Haze. Peaches is about to give birth."

Forrest couldn't help the wash of disappointment. He supposed a baby trumped getting the elfin tips cut off his ears.

Clarke rushed to him, eagerly saying, "I've been practicing my healing, and I think I'll do a good job."

"You *think?*"

Her words sounded confident, but the silent treatment everyone gave didn't make him feel better. It was as though they'd all been discussing this before he'd arrived. She bit her lip.

"What aren't you telling me?" he asked, folding his arms.

"Nothing," Clarke said too quickly, but the look of warning on

Laurel's face changed Clarke's mind. "Okay... there is one thing. It's the taint they've discovered in the Well."

Forrest rubbed his stubbled jaw. "The one Leaf and the Prime are investigating? I've not noticed a problem when I draw mana." He looked around at the group. "Have any of you?"

Shade casually lifted his hand. "I tried to shadow walk the other day, and instead of landing where I wanted, I found myself miles away from the target."

"I feel something off with my gift," Silver added, hugging herself. "You know I pull from the inky side of the Well, and something just feels off."

Silver's gift was a black smoky substance that poured out of her chest. It poisoned and necrotized anything it touched. Shade had taught her to control it, even to reverse the effects, but if that control slipped... if anyone's control slipped. He frowned at Clarke.

"Are you saying something could go wrong when you heal me after cutting my ears?"

She took a deep breath and then answered. "Yes. This sporadic risk is why Ada hasn't been in a rush to come back and help Aeron beyond her initial attempt. She's concerned she might irrevocably damage his eardrums, and then he could be permanently deaf... or worse. Jasper won't let her leave Helianthus City now the Seelie have declared war with the Unseelie. She's still trying to convince him to call this war off—especially now that Maebh is appeased momentarily—but he's overprotective of his child. While Peaches and Haze are there, they'll be distracted with the pending birth." She sighed again. "I guess the point is, we're on our own for now."

The birth would be stressful for Haze. He was a big fae, and Peaches was small.

He raised his brows. "You think Jasper will just forget he's declared war while the birth is happening?"

"Maybe." She bit her lip. No one else looked confident as she added, "I haven't seen a war between the fae peoples in my dreams, and neither has Preceptress Dawn. We're hoping it's just a misunderstanding or a fluid future."

"What have you seen?" he asked, curious if the Sluagh were close to the truth. Or if they were messing with him. Caution sizzled over his skin. He wanted a little more information before he told them what he'd heard. There was no point in worrying Clarke when she was already out of sorts.

Clarke avoided his gaze. "I can't concentrate with Willow gone."

The aftermath of her words smothered the room. Rush looked tense. Forrest couldn't tell if it was because the Sluagh were right, and he knew it... No. That was genuine concern on Rush's face. He was as distraught over Willow's disappearance as her mother.

The Sluagh were probably trying to start trouble—Unseelie to the core.

"All right," Forrest said, cracking his knuckles. "Let's get this done, then."

Shade vacated his chair and gestured for Forrest to take it. Silver handed Forrest a leather strap.

"You'll probably need that," she said.

"I brought *manaweed* and other options for pain relief," Clarke offered, but Forrest shook his head as he put the strap between his teeth and sat facing the fire.

Taking a mind-altering substance not only affected his chances of survival but losing inhibitions never ended well. His kinship with the animal kingdom meant he had a habit of delving into his primal state. And while it was decades since his family beat the feral out of him, the fear always remained.

He knew not what he could become if he let that guard down.

"Need to stay sharp," he garbled his excuse.

Rush grunted approval before holding a knife to Forrest's ear.

"Wait—" Forrest removed the strap and frowned at the shifter. "You're not doing it, are you?"

"Why not?"

"I just think..."

Silver narrowed her eyes at the mana-fortified bone blade in Rush's hand, then said hesitantly, "A woman will do a cleaner job."

Rush growled, "I lived alone for over fifty years. I filleted fish and skinned game with this knife. I'm the best person to do this."

"He's not an animal, Rush," Shade snapped.

Forrest tensed at the words. They struck too close to home, and he knew he had no right to be wary of feeling like a beast when he sat amongst warriors who were part beast. But sometimes, a trauma in youth was so significant that it permanently festered in adulthood.

Clarke put a placating hand on Rush's shoulder. Reluctantly, he handed the knife to Laurel.

"Why are you giving it to me?" she asked, eyes wide.

"You can cauterize the wound with your gift as you cut," Rush explained.

"But Silver used to be a weapons engineer." She handed the blade to Silver, who also gaped.

"I don't think that gives me... you know what?" Silver stood and put her eyes on Forrest. "I *am* good at cutting—"

"I'll bet you are," Rush grumbled under his breath. Clarke jabbed him in the ribs, and he flinched.

"We need her," Clarke hissed. "Be nice."

They might not be friends, but even Forrest could see Silver wasn't a bad person. She had just been on the wrong side of the war, had been told the same lies as the other humans, and knew not the truth of it. Silver's reasoning for joining the human side was that she didn't want to give up her access to forbidden items and the technology humans had fought hard to improve because of them. But after her time in Elphyne, she'd learned not all was lost. Those deemed worthy of the Well—Guardians—were sanctioned to use metal and plastic. Silver was welcome to repurpose her knowledge through them for the good of all.

"I'm not squeamish," Silver continued talking to Forrest as if Shade wasn't standing behind her, ready to sink his fangs into the wolf shifter who'd insulted his mate. "I'll do it. If you permit me."

Forrest studied Silver. She had a stern look about her. She was a fighter, and the truth was that he was already putting his life in her hands. Everything he'd learned about the inner workings of the complicated human city was from her mouth. It was either go all in or go back to being invisible. He wanted to laugh at the bitter irony; to become seen, he was erasing his identity.

"Do it," he said, fitting the leather strap again between his teeth. He braced as the feather-light touch of a woman's fingers raked through his long hair. He didn't braid his hair as much as Aeron did. Braids were a sign of status and education.

As a bastard, Aeron had been refused the right to braid his hair in the Autumn Court. But he claimed that right for himself when he'd become a Guardian.

Try as he might, Forrest could never figure out the braiding thing. He just wasn't as refined as the other elves in his family—even in the state Aeron was in now, he'd still managed to stumble back to Forrest's bed. Given a chance, Forrest would have found himself in the woods, burrowed into the peat under a tree and loving it.

Silver tossed the long length of his hair to one side. She traced the pointed shell of his elfin ear. It took every ounce of restraint not to shiver in response. The last time a female touched him like this was his mother in childhood.

Pulling his gaze back to the fire, he watched the resident fire sprites toss embers to each other. Maybe he could get through the coming pain if he focused on that. Alternatively, he could remove his mind and put it inside an animal. But that would insult the purpose of his mission—Willow. A child who'd been kidnapped and could very well be suffering in worse ways right now.

He latched onto a memory of Willow.

She'd been maybe four. Forrest had returned from a mission, torn up and bloody, but the child hadn't blinked twice at his state.

"Uncle For-west," *she'd whispered loudly from her hiding spot beneath the staircase. She beckoned to him.*

Glancing around, he couldn't see anyone she was hiding from but knew she was a handful for her parents. She might be in trouble. Or this might be a game. He would never ignore a child, so he went up to her and crouched.

"What is it, Willow?"

"Yesterday we're going to the cabin, and I don't wanna," she whined.

As a psychic, she often mixed up her tomorrows and yesterdays.

"Why not? The cabin is fun. You can see Gray."

Gray was Rush's wolf companion. Willow complained more about missing her friends and a pair of shoes she loved.

"You'll be back," he said. "And you can bring your shoes with you."

She looked at him, stunned. Like she'd not thought of it. Then, before he could say another word, she ran away. He'd scratched his head and laughed to himself. For the life of him, he'd never understand kids.

Forrest focused on Willow's innocence. How it could be corrupted. And how she'd need help. *This*, he thought. *This is why I will cut my ears.*

Silver murmured something to Laurel, who came to stand by her side. Then she pulled his ear and sliced slowly. At first, he felt nothing. Then fire exploded through his head. He grunted and held his breath. His eyes watered, but he bit down until it felt like his teeth would crack. Pain radiated in waves as Clarke followed Silver's cut with her attempt at healing. Together with Laurel simultaneously cauterizing his wound, they worked on smoothing the shape of his ear so it appeared human. Cool healing sensations mixed with fire, and the contents of Forrest's stomach heaved.

The next hour passed in a blur of pain and nausea as everything that identified Forrest as an elf was stripped bare. The blue, glowing Guardian teardrop beneath his left eye was gouged out. They had to cut deep, leaving a scar they would use to strengthen his claims of being tortured by the fae. When done, he spat the leather strap into the fire and guzzled a glass of water before breathing deliberately until nausea ebbed.

"Here," Clarke said softly as she handed him something.

He squinted as the black object in his hand came into focus.

"What is this?" he asked.

"An eye patch," she explained. "In case the Guardian teardrop grows back unexpectedly."

Good idea. No Guardian in history had cut his mark out. Ever. They didn't know if it would grow back—or worse, if his ability to simultaneously hold metal and draw mana from the Well would work. He may very well have stopped being a Guardian.

Only one way to find out. He fitted the patch over his eye and everything went dark on one side. He shook out the last of his tremors, and then Forrest beckoned for Shade to hand over his metal dagger.

They all held their breath as Forrest's fingers closed around the forbidden object. He tried not to think about fear leeching warmth from his body. It was one thing to *look* human. It was another to *be* human. He could only stomach this mission if he knew he was returning as a Guardian.

But he felt no loss of connection to the Well with the metal blade in his hand. To prove it to the others, he called on the wind until a hurricane danced in the room, and the sprites spat their high-pitched curses at him for disturbing their fire. He handed the blade back to Shade with an exhale of relief.

"Let's go," he clipped.

"First, let's review the plan one last time," Silver said, arms folded. Forrest imagined she'd be a hard mate to live with, but for all her staunch and unbending will, she'd also be a formidably loyal partner. A spark of longing burst in Forrest's gut, irritating him further when he realized he was pining after someone to share his life with—even if they'd be hard to live with.

"I got it," he grumbled to Silver.

"But I want to hear it."

"I turn up at the gates, say I thawed from your time, and have spent the last few turns of the moon—"

"Months. Humans say months," Rush growled.

"I knew that."

Rush's brows lowered. "If you don't take this seriously, I'm going myself."

"You can't," Clarke exclaimed. "Stop saying that. You'll only make it worse. You know I've seen every possible outcome. This is the way we must do it."

Only make it worse.

That's what the Sluagh had said in Forrest's mind. He lifted his eye patch and rested it on his forehead. First the Sluagh, now Clarke saying a similar thing. His instincts went haywire.

"You saw every possible outcome," Forrest said deliberately. "Then why did one of the Sluagh warn me that if you try to rescue Willow, you'll only make it worse?"

Clarke's pale, freckled face stood out starkly beneath her red hair.

"What is he talking about?" Rush asked, his voice turning soft when directed at his mate.

"Clarke?" Thorne stepped forward. "What aren't you telling us?"

"It's nothing." She steeled her spine and lifted her chin. "She's my daughter, and I refuse to allow her to stay in that city a moment longer than she has to. She needs to be with us. To learn from *us*. That's all you need to know."

Crackling fire filled the silence. Even the sprites sat still as the flames consumed the air around them. Doubt prickled Forrest's skin, but it was too late to turn back. He'd changed his appearance.

As a Guardian, completing grueling exposure training was compulsory, so being cut from the Well wasn't debilitating. He'd studied human history enough to pass as one of them. With each passing day, his usefulness here was coming to an end. If he didn't move forward, he would be standing still with the dark thoughts and urges he'd spent a lifetime suppressing.

"Be careful," Silver said quietly, eyes staring off into the flames as she hugged herself. "There are pockets across the city where the Well is connected. I accidentally unleashed my gift a few times until Rory made me a silver vambrace to keep it blocked." Her eyes slid to his. "You don't know what will happen if you suddenly connect."

He gave a curt nod. Expect the unexpected.

"Pockets of connection," Rush mused. "If you find one, use your familial bond to Aeron to communicate through the water. I'll make sure someone is around him to see it."

Aeron might not give a shit, is what Rush's expression really said.

Forrest dressed in the threadbare attire Clarke had procured for his disguise. Once he was done, Shade took hold of his arm. "I'll take you to the dead woods outside Crystal City. From there, you can walk in, and your disconnection to the Well will be gradual and tolerable."

They hoped.

"Good luck," Clarke said, eyes glistening.

"I won't need it," he replied and held her stare, despite the uncertainty creeping into his soul. She didn't need to see that part of him. "I'll bring your daughter home."

CHAPTER
FIVE

Shade shadow-walked Forrest into the dead woods closest to the human settlement. From the moment Forrest's boots landed on the muddy ground, Shade's shadows receded. Forrest's mind latched onto creatures in his range, testing his environment.

It had taken Shade two attempts before they arrived. His first attempt had overshot his target and almost ended in the closest ocean. Shade blamed the taint on the Well for his inaccuracy.

Concerned, Forrest questioned Shade. "How often has that happened?"

"A few times." Shade's dark brows pinched in the middle. His leathery wings were shifted away so, like Forrest, he had no natural shelter from the rain. "And another reason I could travel with only one other besides myself. The more fae I try to shadow walk with at one time, the further from my target I am."

"That's not good news."

"Put it out of your head. All you need to worry about is returning Willow to her parents."

Forrest bristled but nodded. He glanced at the city in the distance, a fuzzy blob against the night. Security spotlights cut like swords through a haze, reminding him of the danger he'd find as he approached.

"Why would one of the Sluagh warn me about this if it was nothing?" he queried, still unable to let it go. He might get a candid response if he brought it up without Clarke or Rush there.

Shade paused as he considered Forrest's words. "Varen?"

Varen was the Six's Seer.

"I honestly have no idea who spoke. Didn't see him properly. I only heard his voice in my head. Whoever it was fed." Forrest shuddered at the memory.

"I'll keep an eye on them," Shade offered. "And Aeron."

Communication might not even be possible if Forrest couldn't connect to the Well inside the building. Or get outside for a short period and be let back in. At the very least, they figured, if Forrest could get into the dead woods here with Rory and Willow, he could find a puddle of water and open a connection to Aeron to request immediate transport home.

Rush had said if he didn't hear back from Forrest in a few weeks, he and Thorne would camp in the woods until he did.

"You ready?" Shade asked.

Forrest nodded.

"Where do you want it?" Shade cracked his knuckles.

"I guess any—"

Shade punched Forrest in the jaw. Pain watered his eyes, and he doubled over to spit out blood. That hit over an old scar. The vampire didn't wait for Forrest to recover. He continued his assault. He punched in the gut, stomped on a knee, and then used his talons to scratch Forrest on the neck. Forrest took it without complaint, but when Shade went for his face a second time, Forrest caught the vampire's fist midair and snarled. He summoned any creature within range. Screeches answered his mental call, letting them know they were ready to fight. Birds would peck Shade's eyes out. Scorpions would poison him. Waradas would eat him.

"You're enjoying this too much," Forrest grumbled, then shoved the vampire away.

A smirk twitched on Shade's lips as he ran a hand through his medium-length hair. "Can't blame a vampire for having a little fun."

"You're sounding more like a crow."

"Take that back." He pointed at Forrest, deadly serious.

Shade was right. A crow would have stabbed perilously close to a vital organ and then steal the organ to sell in Cornucopia. He tested his weight on the newly injured leg. Pain lashed his knee, and he limped, which was precisely what was supposed to happen. He had to appear as a tortured human escaping the mad fae's clutches.

Time to get going. The longer he spent on this Well-linked ground, the faster his healing, and his injuries had to be noticeable when he arrived at the city gates. Forrest touched his fingers to his lips and pushed his hand down and out toward Shade in the fae hand sign of gratitude.

The twinkle in Shade's eyes disappeared.

"No, Forrest," he said, tone somber. "It is Silver and I who thank you. In doing this, you're helping my mate make amends for her part in this disaster. One day you might need a favor from a vampire and his Well-blessed mate. We will be ready."

To bind the favor, Shade slapped his palm on Forrest's forearm and snapped the bargain into place using his mana. When the time came to collect, Shade would have no choice but to honor it.

"I'd best be going before I heal," Forrest said, clearing his throat.

"Silver gave one last piece of advice." Shade gathered his shadows around him for the journey home. "When uncertain, be vague. Their old world was enormous and full of lies. It was easy to get lost in a crowd."

Darkness swallowed the vampire, and then he was gone. Left alone, Forrest stared again through the rain at the city in the distance and started walking. The journey across the barren plane was a few miles.

He checked his attire one last time. The eye patch fit snugly over his scarred eye. He traced his fingers over his ears. *Smooth*. Clarke had done an excellent job, as did Silver and Laurel for their part. He flattened his hand down the threadbare clothing—breeches and a shirt with holes. No cape, despite the frigid weather. Of all the fae courts the humans knew about, they knew least about the Autumn and Spring Court. This suited Forrest fine.

Like the notorious Winter Court, the Autumn Court also flaunted the humiliation of humans in a public forum. From musicians forced to play until their fingers bled to raiders being taught lessons. Unlike Maebh, the Autumn Court King never allowed a human to escape to tell the tale.

The hope was that the human leader Nero would be so intrigued with Forrest's story that he would invite him straight to the tower where Silver predicted Willow had been taken. It was where Nero and his daughter Rory lived. It was a reasonable assumption.

Go straight to the viper's den.

As he limped, he rubbed mud over his clothes and face before refitting the eye patch. He noticed his wounds had stopped bleeding. *Healing too fast.* He started jogging, wincing at pain jolting through his body. Within half a mile of leaving the dead woods, his connection to the Well faded, and the pain he felt amplified tenfold. Life around him was already dark, but it suddenly became dull as the agony at the loss of connection expanded from a thud to a hammering in his head.

It was as though a thousand carrion birds picked at his brain, screeching and feasting until he felt sick, bereft, and insane all at the same time.

By the time he was within earshot of the opaque crystal walls and iron gate, he didn't have to fake his exhaustion and injuries. He stumbled. He trembled and sweated. His limbs were heavy. His lungs burned. His self was torn out; the final piece of his identity was removed.

He'd prepared for this, but there was no comparison between training and the real thing. There were ways to trap mana within his body, so the loss of connection didn't hurt, but it involved dipping into the inky side of the Well, which had grave consequences. When Rush had been cursed, he almost lost his life. The power-enhancing tattoos the crow shifters and Haze had could very well come back to bite them. Forrest didn't want to risk it. At least this way, he was more human than fae.

How anyone in their right mind would voluntarily live like this was beyond him. Floodlights blinded Forrest as the guards discovered him.

Time for the show to start.

"Help," he croaked as he stumbled closer, making sure to almost trip.

Mud and blood from his wounds streaked down his body. He collapsed onto the wet ground and concentrated on catching his breath until a metal hatch in the gate slid open, and eyes peered out, assessing.

"Please," Forrest begged. "I'm one of you. Let me in."

Then he babbled an almost incoherent explanation about being held captive by the fae and waking up from another time. With his connection to the Well completely severed, it wasn't hard to fake his condition. He dropped to a knee and waited with his head bowed. The hatch closed, and the gate opened with a loud creak. Heavy steps sloshed closer until they stopped before him.

Forrest looked up and blinked through the rain.

A soldier in all black carried a mechanical gun the size of his forearm. He had the physique to carry the heavy weapon, too. Staunch, solid, perhaps equal height to Forrest. Unaffected by the downpour, he looked down with a stern expression.

"What's your name?" he barked.

"Forrest Smith," he replied. Forrest was a name back in the old time too. It was better to use the same name to avoid slip-ups. It wasn't as if anyone inside apart from Willow would recognize him.

"What are you doing outside the gates, Mr. Forrest Smith?"

"I just told you," he gasped, exasperated.

"I want to hear it again."

"I've never been inside the gates. I..." He repeated his blubbering explanation similar to that of Laurel's awakening. He said he woke in a dark cave with his clothes disintegrating around him. He'd vomited black sludge—a side effect of being frozen for so long.

The guard moved Forrest's stringy wet hair to inspect his ears. When he checked, presumably for weapons, Forrest made sure to wince and hiss at the appropriate times his injuries were touched.

"You're wearing fae clothes," the guard noted. "Why?"

For Crimson's sake.

"Their soldiers captured me. I was a prisoner for months. They forced me to do their bidding, laughed at me, ridiculed me." It wasn't even a lie. He licked his lips. "They did worse things. It took me this long to escape."

"Where?"

He narrowed his eyes. He knew they tried to trip him up by asking the same questions, but he was ready to pound his fist into the man's eye.

"The Autumn Court," he replied.

The guard studied Forrest for a moment before lifting his gun and pointing it at Forrest's head.

"Who was the final president of the United States back in your time?"

Fuck. What was that Well-damned name Silver and Clarke had said? So many of them were in his head. Eventually, it came to him. He said it, and the guard lowered his weapon, but he didn't let up.

"Who was your favorite baseball team?"

Fucking games. "Cubs."

"Television show."

Forrest's mind blanked. Television. That thing where humans watched people dressing up and pretending. He swallowed a hard lump. *Be vague. Lie.* "I worked on a farm. Too busy to have a favorite."

The guard's eyes narrowed harshly. Forrest sensed the next one would be tough.

"Fast food?"

"Cheeseburger."

The guard grunted, raised his brows, and said, "Welcome home. You're safe now."

Breathing a sigh of relief, Forrest hung his head in gratitude. He didn't believe that that was the last test, but he hid his wariness. Another two soldiers emerged from the gate and helped Forrest stand—or made sure he couldn't run. Tension still thickened the air. Feeling the cold more than when he'd been connected to the Well, Forrest shivered and rubbed his arms before limping through the gate.

It wasn't just the cold. Every injury Shade had inflicted felt worse. *Breathing* felt worse.

"Wait here," the first guard said as the big metal doors closed behind him with a thunderous finality.

Forrest surveyed his surroundings and tried not to look stunned. Grey buildings covered in black soot and grease spilled outward from him. A chemical stench seared his nose. Flickering lights that buzzed like manabeeze but weren't lined the wet streets. There was nothing magical about those lights. They were artificial and cold. Mist wafted from circular drains in the ground. Probably from an underground sewage system.

A barbed wire net hung between the crystal boundary and the enormous central tower at the city's center, a few miles away. The tower had to be at least two hundred levels high and was the city's only building of its kind. The rest were short, squat, and dull. The tower stood tall and proud, like an obelisk.

He looked up. Clouds. Mists. Fog. Rain. Even if the stars and moon became visible, Forrest wasn't sure he'd ever find them through the chaotic web of barbed wire rusted with blood stains and clumped with feathers. Some of those would have been from fae. Some were probably just curious, innocent creatures.

That's what Forrest missed the most—his connection to the animals. More than the sense of belonging the Well gave, it was the knowledge he wasn't alone. The animals had always seen him. They'd existed in harmony without pretense. They were honest.

Forrest narrowed his eyes at a group of humans walking away under the cover of a handheld shelter. They didn't notice him, so he took his time inspecting them. Drab grey clothing, just like the guards. Forrest had seen how silks and fabrics were dyed at the Autumn Court. They'd used plants, and creatures found plentiful in nature. If these humans had no access to that supply, he supposed they'd not waste precious resources on something so benign as clothing.

While waiting, he shivered in his wet clothes for what seemed like a good turn of the hourglass, maybe two. During that time, at least another three groups of humans walked by. They cast a curious glance his way but continued, eager to get out of the rain.

"President Nero wants to speak with you directly," the guard announced, then glanced at Forrest's split lip and bruised face. "You can rest assure that he's going to teach those Tainted fuckers a lesson in retribution."

Forrest suitably echoed the guard's angry face, hoping it gave him a show of camaraderie. He gestured for Forrest to follow him into the gatehouse where more soldiers gathered in a stark room, staring at diesel-fueled machinery with flashing lights. One gave Forrest a pile of folded, dry clothes.

"They might not fit," the guard said, "but they'll do for now."

Forrest almost touched his fingers to his lips before he remembered humans had no problem saying thank you or apologizing to each other. They must hand out debts like coin. Still unable to bring himself to say the words, he smiled tightly instead.

He sniffed and, thinking his nose bled, checked. But it was watery. He stared at it, alarmed. Was this... was he sick?

"Do you need a physician?" the first guard asked.

Physician... physician... Forrest wracked his brain for the definition, but when the guard pointed at Forrest's nose and then his grazed face, it came to him. *Healer.*

"I'm fine," he replied. "Had worse at the Autumn Court."

"I'll bet you did, son. Come on. I'll take you somewhere you can clean up, get warm, and then I'll take you to see the president."

"Then what?" Forrest asked, pleased that if he'd convinced this soldier he was human, perhaps he could convince more.

"Then that's up to him."

"Thank you," Forrest forced himself to say. His mind revolted at the word, but he kept the image of Willow as a reminder of his goal. Silver hair, little fierce snarl, tiny hands. Innocent.

He shouldn't be complacent about being accepted. He had the sense the test questions were only beginning.

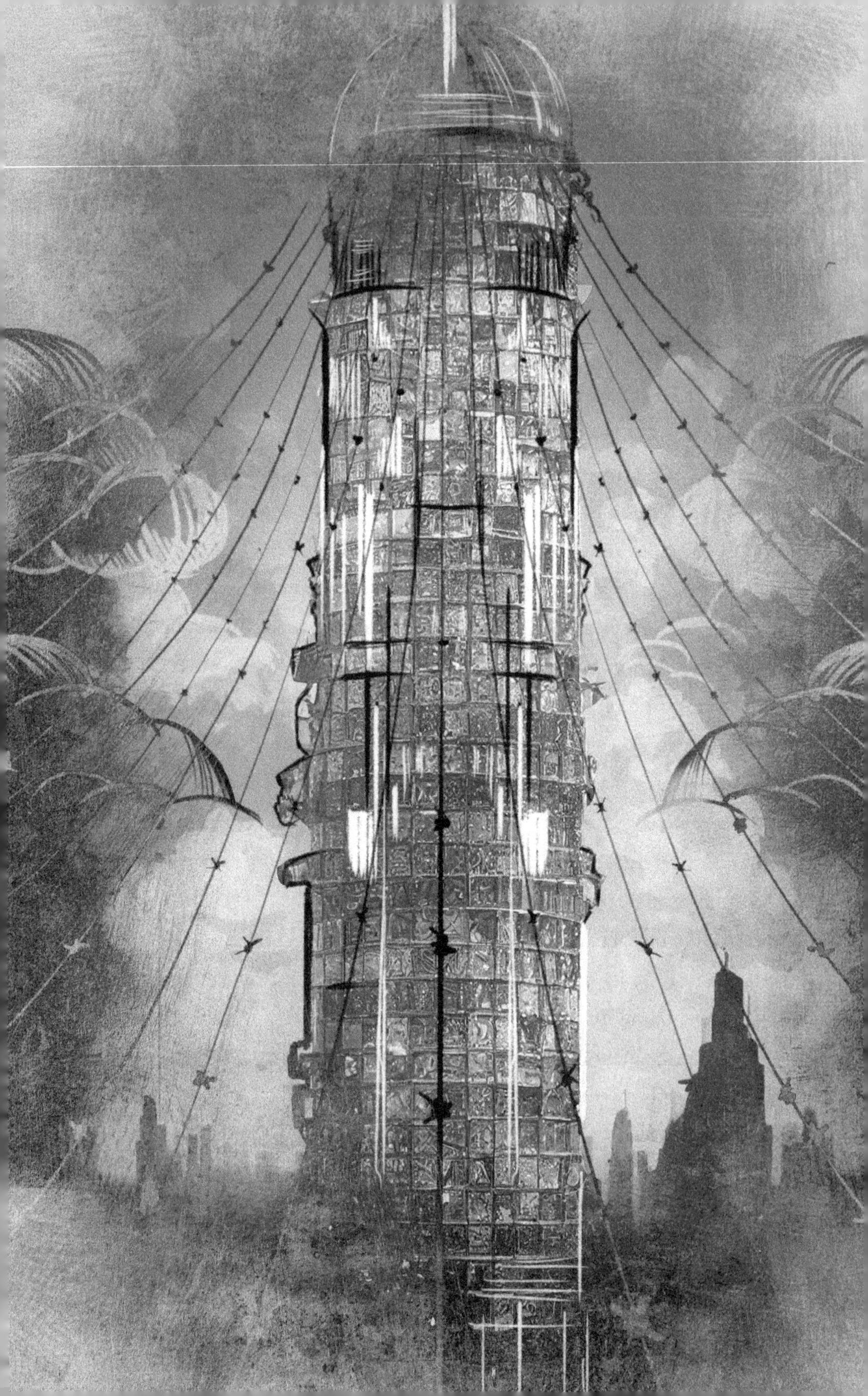

CHAPTER SIX

Applause filled the long dining hall as Melody stepped out from her piano to take a bow. She halted a quarter way down. One more inch, and those bountiful puppies would tumble from her indecently tight dress. She hated it. Since she'd arrived in this time and put on the weight Nero demanded, her body didn't feel like her own. But she kept it all in and smiled graciously at the audience.

She always did.

Her band joined her, and they held hands in a line. Melody's smiling expression was stone as she lowered her face to the ground again. This time, her gaze caught on her peep toe shoes and the red nail polish so garish under the bright spotlights.

The applause died, and Melody's companions pulled her up as they straightened. Thrown off guard by her nail polish, she did something she knew not to do. Her gaze shifted to the first member of the audience in her line of sight. Military leaders and their families occupied the closest dining table to the stage. The Captain's dark slash of a mustache stood out starkly against his pasty skin. He made eye contact, and she petrified like a deer in the headlights. *Trucker.* It only now registered he reminded her of him.

A slow, proprietary smile spread across his thin lips as though he thought she'd looked at him on purpose. He joined his fellow diners in clapping his hands.

The spotlight shut off, casting the stage into cool, private relief. For a few minutes, she could breathe again. Safe. But not for long. Soon she would be back on stage for the second act of the night's performance. At least for the next act, she was allowed to play a song of her choosing, which was always something from her time. Something to remind these people that they had a past. That they had existed. That world *did* exist.

Her fingers twitched at her side. The beat to *Iko Iko* echoed in her head, and she smiled. The impromptu renditions of that song were the first of many. Melody hadn't known that summer in Arizona that her mother's new job was a Vegas janitor. It was the start of Melody's obsession with the stage. Her mother gave up everything for Melody's career.

It paid off in the end.

But only for a short while, and then the nuclear fallout came, wiping out everything.

Melody focused on warm memories of her mother and ignored the Captain. Forcing herself to channel her showman's training, she gracefully coasted down the stage steps. While her cohorts mingled, she went to the dais overlooking the entire dining hall from the far end.

Half-time intermission meant a visit to the president for an update and sometimes a change in the playlist.

Nero watched her approach. The stormy night sky through arched windows behind him reminded her that it was worse out there than here. Her cream dress, pale skin, and platinum hair made her look like a ghost. The Tower guards standing before his table barely glanced at her as she walked past them.

Nero was a tall, dark-haired man in his late forties. He wore a tailored suit with gold embellishment on the epaulets, collar, and breast pocket where a perfect blood red rose was caught halfway between budding and bloom. He seemed a little young to have a full-grown daughter, but the history around his family's rise to leadership was as murky as the sky behind him. Once, not long after she'd awoken in this time, Melody had asked around. No one gave her a straight answer. They either stared blankly or changed the subject. And since Melody's acquaintance with the president's daughter, Rory, was just that—an acquaintance—Melody never felt comfortable asking her. Rory was busy running the Reapers, and now, by the looks of it, she schooled a small child to eat her food correctly.

Melody hadn't recalled seeing the silver-haired little girl before, but the population of the Tower was almost eight thousand people. She was probably babysitting. As soon as the thought hit, Melody dismissed it. Babysitting and Rory weren't two words synonymous with each other.

"Your performances are becoming dull, Melody." Nero dabbed the corners of his lips.

And just like that, Melody's post-performance high crashed to earth.

He dabbed his mouth two more times, despite no food stains being there. She waited patiently beside him, not sitting in the singular vacant seat. He'd have invited her immediately if he wanted her to sit.

His strange quirks were deepening. Melody wondered if his mental state was healthy and then immediately shut that train of thought down. She didn't want to know. *Stay out of it, Mel. None of your God-lovin' business.*

"I'm afraid new source material has been scarce," she replied.

"Did I not send you a new source?"

"Yes, Mr. President, you did." She hesitated before continuing. She'd only had a few sessions with Sid, but they were the same stories. What else could she do, make up content?

Nero didn't like her pause, and his jaw hardened. "Do you have something to say?"

Summoning courage, she answered, "I don't believe the Reaper you sent has more to tell me that I don't already know."

A low grumble of displeasure came out of him. Was it because she voiced an opinion, or because the said opinion was not something he wanted to hear?

She also may have invertedly thrown Sid under the bus. Hand-breaking vampires weren't exactly high on the propaganda fearsome scale. There had been another story Sid told of his team having their minds taken over by the vampire, but the worst they'd been forced to do was twiddle their thumbs.

She opened her mouth to steer the conversation away from laying blame on another. Nero slammed his hand on the table, rattling cutlery and crockery. No one in the room dared to look their way.

He crooked his finger and leaned toward her. She bowed to meet him. A lock of her styled hair escaped. She couldn't bring herself to pin it back in case he saw her trembling fingers. Instead, her fist clenched tighter.

"I want fear, Ms. Melody," he whispered harshly. "I want these citizens quaking in their boots at the very mention of the Tainted. If you need reminding of what it means to feel fear, perhaps a trip down to the Histories Hall will give you some ideas. There are plenty of books down there to draw material from."

"You want me to lie?" she whispered.

"Fear," he growled, "Is not steeped in the truth. It is the dark possibilities in the shadows. It is the what ifs and what might be. It is the mind playing tricks on us." He sat back, studying her. "Why do you think our minds do that, Ms. Melody? Why do we overthink and obsess over fear?"

She had no clue.

"It is because," he answered, "our subconscious warns us from genuine danger, and sometimes reality is incomprehensible. No one is afraid of gibberish, are they?"

"No, Mr. President."

"Your latest songs have been nonsense and gibberish. You're better than that."

"I think—"

"You *think*?"

She bit her lip, holding back her sentence. She was going to say she needed more time to come up with quality content. Multiple new songs a week was hard. She used to take months sometimes to get a tune and lyrics right.

"They need a target to fear." He stared at her some more. "If you've forgotten what it feels like to be afraid, I'd be more than happy to arrange a demonstration."

Sweat prickled the back of her neck. "That won't be necessary, Mr. President. I'll do better."

His expression softened as he took Melody's hand. She forced her fist to relax. His fingers were cold, despite the warmth in the room. His thumb rubbed the back of her hand, and his eyes lost focus as he stared at her pale skin. Her back ached from leaning.

"You people from the old world must serve as a reminder to those of us today that the world was once, not only habitable for us humans, but that it flourished as our domain. You're not eating enough. You are too thin. Do you understand?"

Too thin?

He lifted dark eyes to her, and Melody wanted to say she could read them, but the truth was she saw nothing. They were empty, soulless... like a void. He was a sick man; she only now understood how deep his depravity went. He was too clever for her. Too influential. She meant nothing to him but another cog in his machine.

His grip on her hand tightened until pain stabbed her bones. Melody bit back a whimper and schooled her face into a serene expression. No one must know what they discussed. As far as the public understood, Melody was an entertainer Nero showered with favor because of her history and talent. But the fiery eyes of a spotlight could burn just as they could warm. Sometimes it was better to live in the dark.

"If the Tainted have their way, humanity will be extinguished. *You* will be extinguished. We don't want that, do we?"

"No, Mr. President."

"Good girl." He held onto Melody's hand but loosened his grip.

For a moment, he lingered with his thumb brushing her skin, his eyes on her—but it wasn't sexual. Never with him. It was calculating, machinating, and cold. Sometimes he stared so hard that she wondered if he tried to read her mind. She braced for a continued lecture, more pain, but then a Tower guard rushed up to the table and kneeled before Nero.

"Mr. President, I'm sorry to interrupt."

Nero pursed his lips. His nostrils flared. Melody could have sworn everyone in the hall held their breath. Rory and the child, who weren't in earshot, looked over from their table about twenty feet away.

"What is it?" Nero asked the guard, his grip tightening around her hand once more.

The guard stood with his feet shoulder-width apart. His uniform was different from the others. Where most wore simple attire, this guard had metal embellishments on the sleeve. He licked his lips and answered, "A man has arrived at the gates claiming to be from the old world. Would you like me to take him to the garden as per your usual interview process?"

Nero stilled. He glanced at Melody and tapped his chin, deep in thought as he turned her hand over.

"Did you ask the preliminary questions?"

He stuttered when he spoke. "O-of c-course, Mr. President. I wouldn't d-dream of interrupting your dinner if I hadn't. He's passed them all."

"I don't like your tone."

"Apologies." He bowed and stayed staring at his feet as he hastily added, "Mr. President."

"How long has he been awake?"

"He claims close to a year."

"And he's survived living with the Tainted this whole time?"

The guard's eyes darted to Nero; Melody presumed to check if it was a trick question. Of course, someone who'd just arrived at their gates claiming sanctuary would have been living outside the walls. But the guard responded politely, "Yes, Mr. President. He's scarred. It appears to have been an ordeal for him."

At the mention of scars, Nero perked up. His shark-like gaze bounced again between Melody and the guard as he considered his following words. He turned to the military leaders and oligarchs pretending not to watch from their distance at the table, but it was clear they paid attention. Melody fidgeted. This was getting awkward. Why was he allowing her to hear this conversation?

Thoughts whirled in her head. Was it really as he'd said, his use for her was wearing thin? Was this the sort of thing they did before they killed someone—let them in on State secrets?

Other musicians had gone missing in the past. Some said the fae stole them, then forced them to play in an endless loop for their sick pleasure until their fingers bled. The story didn't quite add up before. Melody had always thought with security so tight and the barbed net, no fae entered the Crystal City gates... but maybe that was a lie. A cover. Perhaps they came in all the time.

"Why did he not come for sanctuary from the moment he thawed?" Nero asked.

"He said he was a prisoner. Forced by magic to do their bidding."

Nero let go of Melody's sweaty hand, and she fanned her face. *Oh, God.* Maybe Nero was right. Maybe they *should* fear the Fae.

"It's your lucky day Ms. Melody," he said. "You will have another new source of material. Use him well."

A bell rang, signaling intermission was over.

"Play something by Beethoven. Show me why you're here. Dismissed." Nero gestured for Melody to leave.

As she walked back through the dining hall toward the stage, proud of her steady gait, she held her aching hand against her stomach, hating how sucking it in made her nauseous. The urge to keep walking up the steps and off the back of the stage was overwhelming. But this newcomer was the reminder of her safety. He'd lived for one year in the hands of the enemy, forced by magic to do their bidding. The stories he told her would be horrific.

He might also value a familiar face. There had been no one Melody could talk to when she woke up in this world. Apparently, she'd been found completely frozen by Nero's men, still clutching remnants of the blouse she'd been shopping for in Vegas. Shonda wasn't with her, and the Tinker was the only other human from Melody's world. But she kept to herself.

As she walked, Melody glanced around the dining hall. Most of the stragglers wandering between tables were now returning to their own. If there was one thing Melody could applaud Nero for, it was how he commanded respect for the performance. Anyone talking or moving during her act was swiftly ejected from the room, and their spot at the coveted elite dining experience was given to the next on the waitlist. And he never interrupted.

He requested Beethoven, but he said nothing about which rendition, she thought, unable to hold back the small rebellious part of her old self. Something about tonight made her feel brave. Maybe she would shake things up and do the epic version.

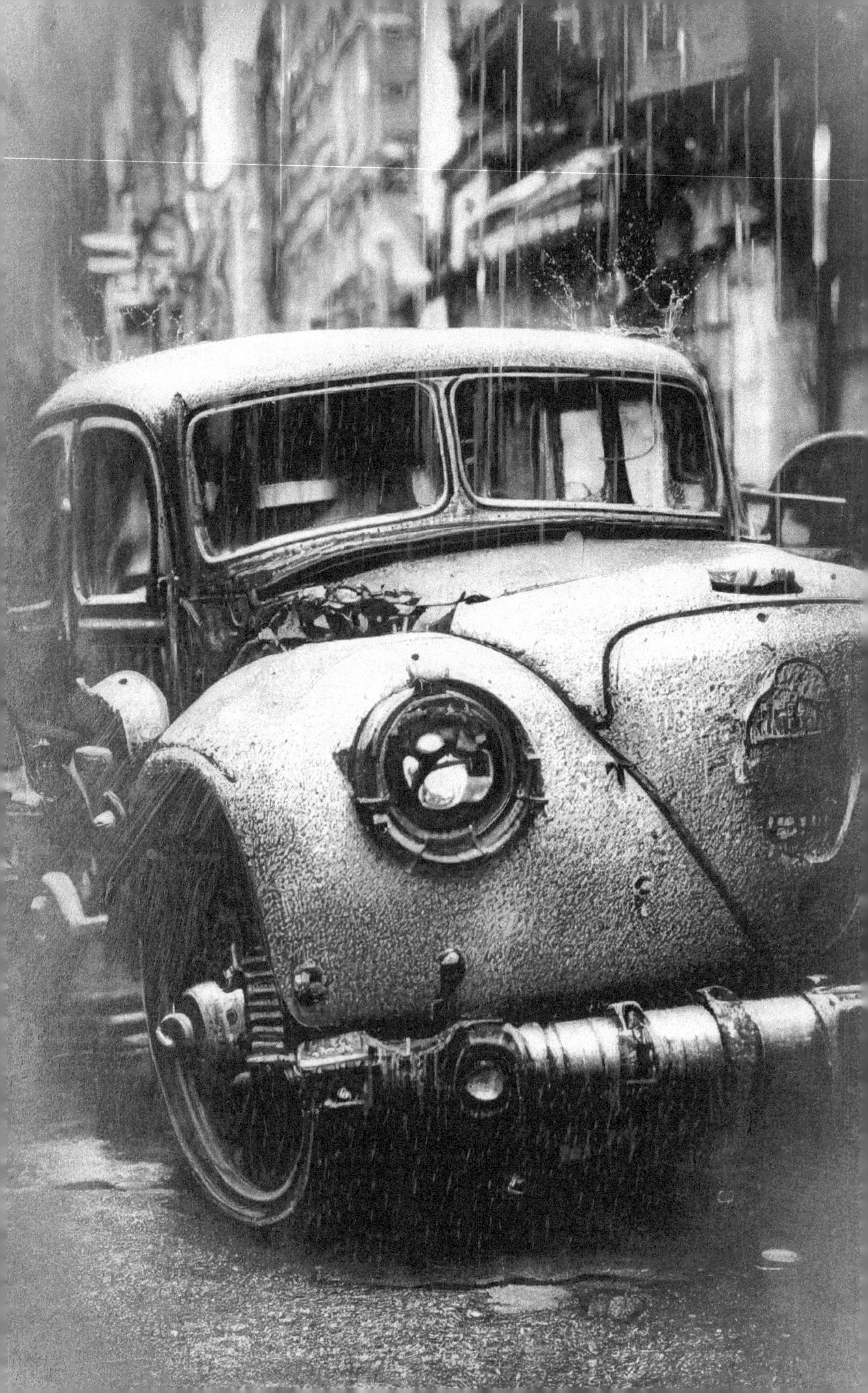

CHAPTER
SEVEN

With a guard at his rear, and one leading the way, Forrest limped down a long, dark corridor in a building near the city gate. If he'd been in Elphyne, his knee would have halfway healed by now. The weakness irked him more than he thought it would. When he'd dressed into the stiff pants and shirt they'd supplied, it hurt to lift his arm and bend his knee. He hated it. Everything in this city, from how he felt to what he saw and could safely say, would take getting used to.

He'd kept on his wet boots, and his hair was still damp, but apparently, he looked presentable enough to meet the president.

Forrest was a little surprised to have been accepted so quickly. When Silver had turned up at the Crystal City gates years ago, she'd been housed in a holding cell for days before being invited to enter their society—and the humans had a psychic who'd predicted Silver's arrival. They *knew* she was coming, yet they were still wary after she'd spent time in Elphyne.

And here they were, letting Forrest walk straight in. Something else must be at play.

Their leader killed the humans' old psychic because he knew Clarke—a more powerful psychic—had thawed. He'd attempted to kidnap Clarke, failed, but now had Willow—her psychic daughter. Had Willow unwittingly given up Forrest before he'd arrived? She was only six. Perhaps she didn't know what she'd done. Children often say things without realizing it.

Using the cover of the handheld shelter Forrest had learned was an *umbrella*, they took him through the wet, dismal city streets.

Guards keeping watch stood on top of the opaque, outer crystal walls, eyes focused on the wasteland surrounding their city. But no guards at the end of the short street heading into the city. The barracks and military housing made way for industry and domesticity.

Forrest was prepared to walk the few miles to the tower, but the guard stopped him and gestured to a strange metal box on rubber wheels. Forrest's confusion must have been evident because the guard smirked and said, "Been a while since you seen one of these, eh?"

Forrest had no idea what *it* was. "Definitely."

"Get in." The guard opened the box door. "I heard about your time from a few others like you. They said you had plenty more of these on your streets, didn't you?"

"Plenty," Forrest agreed. He still had no idea what it was as he lowered himself and entered through the door, realizing what it was from the moment he entered. *Ah. So this is what a car looks like.* He'd had trouble imagining it when Silver had told him.

"Heard they were faster and easier to drive, too," the guard rambled. "This model must look pretty strange to you, what with all its turn cranks and buttons."

Two rows of bench seats were inside the car. Windows gave them a view of the outside. Forrest slid into the front and was about to keep sliding to the side where a wheel poked out of a dashboard, but the guard stopped him.

"No, you don't," he clipped. "Only guards allowed to drive."

"Right."

Forrest settled on the passenger side and waited for the guard to move to the front of the car, bend and turn a crank. Within seconds, the vehicle shuddered to life, snarling like a vicious Well Hound. The guard opened the driver's door and slid onto the bench seat before the wheel. He moved a stick stuck in the wheel and planted his foot on the floor. The car jerked, and they rolled forward.

Incredible.

The car fed on diesel. Forrest wrinkled his nose at the polluted smell.

During the bumpy journey, he kept his gaze steadily ahead and tried not to let his unease show as they moved through the streets. Tension rode his body, causing muscles to leap beneath his skin.

The city whizzed by at an alarming speed. As fast as flying on a kuturi... but protected from the elements and, he supposed, effortless. He could see the appeal in making this machine but could also see why walking, riding, or portaling would have been just as easy. And less smelly.

Gray-clothed people walked about, but for most of the journey, they seemed to be headed indoors or swiftly traveling between buildings to escape the weather.

They'd all said elves were the closest fae race to humans, but there was no majestical architecture here, just gray bricks and block-shaped buildings. No affinity with nature. It was all concrete and mud. No farming. Perhaps there must be somewhere, but he'd only see it in daylight.

He glared at banners hanging from rooftops with a familiar man's face—Nero—and the words "Humanity First."

Apart from the obvious differences, the humans seemed quite normal. Males walked with families. Children who were supposed to be in bed were causing mischief. Revelers caroused in a tavern. As they passed, one of the unruly was kicked outside and settled morosely in the wet street, where he promptly vomited.

Another couple caught his eye. Two lovers kissed under the false light of a street lamp, oblivious to the rain. She smiled up at him. He brushed her cheek. River's taunt came to mind. Forrest had to admit that a part of him yearned for connection. To be *seen* by another. To be loved. But as soon as the urge found him, he pushed it away.

He was here to save a child. Even if he did come out of it unscathed, there was too much happening at the Order. Aeron needed help. The Well had a taint on it. This war between the humans and fae was heating up. His animalistic inner urges had no place in a civilized relationship. His feelings had never been a factor in his fate.

With every bump the vehicle made, memories jostled out of Forrest's mind.

You're nothing, his brother Luthian sneered, shoving him against the wall. *You're not worth my voice. You will be dead soon.*

I won't be dead. I'll be sacrificed to the Well, his stubborn, childish voice had declared. *And I'm going to come out a Guardian. Just you wait.*

Mocking laughter followed Forrest as he ran away, escaping the cruel taunts from his sibling. At the time, Forrest had been grateful for any attention. The other siblings would pretend he wasn't there.

"What's that sound? Did you hear something?" Arwyn asked.

"Must be the wind."

The car jerked to a stop.

"We're here." The guard pressed a button near the wheel, and the rumbling shut down. Forrest took his lead from the guard and exited the car, carefully checking his surroundings.

They were at Sky Tower, the central eyesore of the city. Made of tarnished, rain-soaked glass that, at night, looked like the dark end of the ocean—thick and ominous, hiding horrors in the deep. Every so often, a light within flickered on; a small square came to life. Shadows moved in the murk as inhabitants went about their business.

If the entire building was populated, there would be at least a few thousand inside... maybe as high as ten.

The cool wind gusted down the narrow street, bringing the bite of rain.

"Quickly," the guard shouted and jogged to the grand glass doors at the tower's base, holding an umbrella to shelter himself.

Unaffected by the elements, Forrest strolled after him. Up close, he realized the building wasn't made of tarnished glass but some kind of crystal that had been dug out of the earth. He'd never seen such a structure anywhere in Elphyne. Even the palaces were only a few levels high.

So this was humanity's monument to their dominance over nature.

Surrounding the building, at five-foot intervals, guards dressed differently from those posted near the gate. These uniforms had colors ranging from navy to red.

Forrest lost count of how many guards manned the Tower perimeter. He surmised more than at the boundary walls, which led him to conclude that what was in this tall building was more valuable than what was in the greater city.

Nero.

Interspersed between guards were groups of people huddled on the ground. Were they additional security? Two guards collected Forrest. They flanked him as they walked across the street and to the building. The closer Forrest went, the more he noticed strange oddities—like the huddled people were sickly looking. Sores on their mouths. Tired eyes. Skin and bones.

So not security but perhaps homeless people from the city trying to get close to the enormous Sky Tower overshadowing everyone.

Inside the building, the acrid stench Forrest had associated with the car's engine dissipated. The floors were polished to a mirror. More banners of Nero's face. Cleanliness, exotic materials, and surprisingly, the first sign of organic nature Forrest had seen since arrival. Flowers in vases brought pleasantness to the drab room. It was like walking straight from the wasteland into one of the palace ballrooms back in Elphyne. The exorbitant, colorful luxury inside didn't match the outside.

The guards took him to a gate made of tarnished brass. Beyond the entrance was a small cavity that probably fit six or eight people.

A long wire dangled from up high, and mechanical whirring and clanging came from within when they pressed a button on the wall. Was this another vehicle?

Eventually, a cage descended. It reminded Forrest so much of the cages fae used as punishment. The suffering came from being raised so far off land that the connection to the Well was severed. It was agony for fae who'd never felt such a soul-rending sensation.

But he was already disconnected. This would not hurt him.

The Tower guard opened the cage door, folding it into itself, and then nudged Forrest forward. "Get in."

Forrest's fists clenched at his side. He cast a narrowed glare at the guard, set his teeth, and entered the small space. Once inside, he faced the brass door as it closed and forced his fists to flex and relax at his side.

Willow.

He was here for the child. His memories of being shoved by guards into small boxes as a child had nothing to do with it. Willow *was* that small child. He hadn't been for a long time.

The guard hit a single button amongst many on a panel, and the entire room shuddered. Mechanical whirring sounded again. Forrest's stomach dropped as they moved upward. His gaze darted about, curiously searching through the glass cab walls for clues of his surroundings, but he found another group of identical men standing in a cab beside them—also rising at the same time.

One of the men had an eye patch.

Forrest froze when he realized what he was looking at. His reflection was so crisp and sharp that he'd assumed he was looking through a window. Never before had he seen himself so clearly. He wanted to reach out and confirm it was just his reflection and not one of the Sluagh's host of the unforgiven dead. But there was the leather eye patch hiding his scar. There was his single brown eye, looking back at him. He'd never noticed the freckles across his bronzed nose in the handblown black glass mirrors in Elphyne. Never seen the pores on his skin nor the old scar running down his jaw. The new scars were vivid and purple.

He certainly wasn't in the same league as a queen's ex-concubine like Shade.

Forrest's stomach dropped. The tiny, mirrored cab stopped shuddering. The doors opened, and the guards walked out. The window facing them was not the same one he'd left before entering. Then, the view had been to the gray pathway outside and the guards on duty. Now, it was a blanket of darkness and clouds. He walked to the window and glanced down.

White clouds surrounded the tower, and further out, the shadowed shapes of buildings sprawled amongst the mist. They had to be at least one hundred stories high. Halfway up the Tower, perhaps. He would see better tomorrow.

"Quite the view, eh?" said the first guard. "Get used to it. As a permanent Tower resident, it's the only view you'll see."

Forrest's brow arched. "I'm not allowed to leave?"

That would be problematic if Willow wasn't housed here.

"For the safety of our elite, we don't allow commoners to mingle."

"Elite?"

"Your job has been assigned. We're taking you to your quarters where you can get cleaned up, and then you will have your meeting with the president."

"But they don't know anything about me. How could they assign me a job according to my usefulness?"

No answer.

He'd not even told them of his skills with animals. After Silver had explained they'd allocate him according to usefulness, he'd assumed it would be in stables or an abattoir. But now, seeing this cold, concrete prison, he couldn't imagine it housed animals.

The guard guided Forrest into the foyer area and down another narrow hallway. The conversation grew louder, spilling out like a wave with the smell of salty, mouth-watering food. It wasn't long before they entered a large hall with high ceilings. Curtains draped every wall, blocking the view from outside.

Circular dining tables of different sizes were scattered about the room. There were between one and two hundred people, ages ranging from newborn to elderly.

Forrest gawked at the old white-haired and wrinkled humans. They were wrinkly like brownies. But bigger. The people in this room didn't dress in the gray scraps he'd seen the commoners wear outside. No, they had thick silks and fluffy extravagance.

At one end of the vast room, a high stage sat in the dark with a vacant piano and strange drums to keep it company. To the back end of the room, on a raised dais that lorded over the gathering, sat an important solitary man. Short dark hair. A dark suit with gold trim on the shoulders and buttons. Rose at the pocket. Impeccably groomed, he seemed almost unreal. Like a doll. Or the epitome of the cartoon picture on the banners.

But Forrest knew where the man received his porcelain complexion—stolen mana pulled straight from the heart of a fae. It was the type of mana that reduced a fae's lifespan. Potent. Powerful.

Madness-inducing when ingested by someone other than the original occupant.

They'd assumed his habit would have made him crazy. But watching him calmly sit at his table, alone and nibbling on his food, Forrest wondered why he wasn't more disheveled. Perhaps ingesting mana didn't affect him the same way it did others. Or... worse, maybe he was already insane.

With caution nipping at his heels, Forrest glanced about the room as he followed the Tower guard toward Nero. He passed dining tables overflowing with food and drink. Rosy-cheeked diners were dressed in bright colors and opulent silks, their hair and face lacquered into various styles. These elite weren't so different looking to the royals and gentry of the fae courts. But these weren't allowed to mix with commoners. They were essentially manacled with gold, jewels, and silk.

Interesting.

Almost at Nero's table, Forrest swept the room with his staunch gaze, searching for that elusive shock of silver hair. Small. Pale. Exotic looking. The child should jump out at him in this opulent mess. His heart leaped into his throat when he found Willow. She sat at a table not far from the dais and was being instructed by a woman with a stiff spine. Her tailored uniform was similar to the Tower guards—but trimmed in shiny copper. A portion of afro hair over one ear was shaved, but the other half was fashioned into neat dreadlocks clamped by copper beads. She had a fierce beauty and seemed to be in charge of Willow's guardianship.

That must be Aurora, or Rory, as Cloud had called her. She was the Unseelie High Queen's lost half-ling heir. Although Maebh was darker skinned, Forrest could see the genetic similarities in her facial features. Rory had no idea of her direct relation to one of the most influential people in Elphyne.

She'd kidnapped a fae child. She'd lead the team that decimated the Order with metal weapons. She'd murdered his kind. And now, she sat smiling tightly as Willow attempted to choose the correct cutlery for her meal.

Getting out of here with a child would be hard enough, but it would be impossible to bring Rory too. If she got in his way, if he had to choose... he would choose the child.

Forrest let his assessing gaze travel over Willow and breathed a sigh of relief. She was alive and safe—

"Oof!"

Forrest bowled headlong into someone.

Smells like jasmine and... Female.

She squeaked and latched onto his arms as he, in return, stopped her from falling. The sight and smell of her feminine perfume sent him into a complete social shutdown. *Captivated.* Blond, perfectly styled hair. A figure with curves, both soft and hard and indomitably feminine. When their gazes clashed, he forgot to breathe. *Beautiful.*

Her eyes were two soulful hands reaching inside his chest to squeeze. A flush of attraction scored through his body, waking up needs he'd spent so long repressing. He had to growl, low and deep, to stop himself from moving closer, from running his nose along her neck and marking her scent for later.

So he could hunt her down.

His intense reaction startled him. She pouted as her shock turned to something he couldn't decipher... irritation, curiosity, maybe embarrassment?

"So sorry," she mumbled, eyes skating away. "I wasn't looking where I was going."

He'd caused her discomfort. He scowled and stepped back, disengaging but still feeling the ghost of her plushness against his body like a lingering embrace. She still held onto his arms.

"It was entirely my fault," he admitted. His fingers twitched as he wanted to hand sign his apology.

She stared wide-eyed at her hands on his biceps, then gave a quick squeeze before letting go like he was on fire. Blushing, she mumbled something under her breath about a Viking, but he didn't know what that meant.

"Sorry," she blurted, blinking rapidly. "I didn't mean to do that." Her eyes darted to his biceps again. "Squeeze your muscles. I mean. Yeah. It's just um… okay." Her brows lifted. "I don't mean they're oh-*kay* muscles. I meant …" She shook her head, cheeks turning an even brighter red. "I should go."

"I am truly sorry for any discomfort I caused."

Her eyes roved over his figure and then up to the eye patch before smirking and saying, "Honey, discomfort is *not* the word I'd use."

He opened his mouth to reply, but the Tower guard blocked Forrest's view of her and cleared his throat before gesturing to continue walking toward Nero—the same direction the blond had come from. When Forrest glanced back at her, she'd already moved toward the stage at the front of the dining room. Her hips swayed as she walked, and in that tight dress, his eyes went straight to the outline of her round buttocks as they clenched and released with every step. Everything about her had cast a spell on him. Too late did he realize he stared inappropriately.

The waiting guard raised his brows.

Forrest tugged at his collar, cleared his throat, and then allowed himself to be led to Nero's table. So thrown off, he lost all sense of purpose until Nero looked up and settled his gaze on Forrest.

His purpose slammed back. Willow was only feet away. He wanted to reach out to the child, to let her know he was there to help, but it wasn't the time. She straddled the age where she might accidentally reveal his identity in her excitement seeing him. He kept his face tilted away from Willow's direction.

Play the part. Wait. Then, when the time is right, find Silver's smuggler contacts and escape with Willow. But "when the time was right" was up for debate. He had to convince Rory to join him or find a way to haul her drugged or knocked-out body with a child in tow.

"So," Nero said, his voice as unnatural as he looked. "They tell me you're a special person, Mr. Smith." He let his shrewd gaze take in Forrest's injuries and then motioned to the vacant seat at his table for two. "Sit."

Forrest stepped onto the dais and slid out the chair opposite Nero. When he settled, he had a view of the stage. The blond was up there with others, preparing for a performance. Every cell in his body wanted to watch her, but he forced his gaze back to Nero. This next part was probably another test. Silver had mentioned something about a meeting with the president.

"This must all seem rather strange to you," Nero said. "But you're not the first of your kind to seek asylum at our gates. You're among friends now. You can rest easy; there is a way forward."

The words sounded rehearsed. Forrest nodded. He imagined that Nero's words would be very appealing if he were a stranger at this time.

Nero took a sip of the wine from his glass and didn't speak again until he put it down. "They tell me you were trapped in the Summer Court."

"Autumn Court," Forrest corrected.

Nero smoothly apologized for his mistake, but Forrest sensed he'd blundered on purpose. A man like Nero didn't make mistakes.

"How did that happen?" Nero flicked a casual finger toward Forrest's eye patch.

Forrest lifted it and revealed the jagged scar over his brow, closed eyelid, and down his cheekbone. He figured if he controlled the reveal, Nero was less likely to run his own inspection. If Nero forced Forrest to open his eyelid, he would see the iris below intact.

"They used magic to compel me to do their bidding," he mumbled, dropping the patch. "The king said I looked at him funny, so blinded me as punishment."

Without mana binding his words, forcing himself to tell the truth, Forrest was free to lie as well as any human. It felt odd. He didn't have to reach too far into the make-believe to tell this tale. He'd lived through it.

Nero spoke thoughtfully. "I have heard many monstrous tales about the queen in the north and the king in the south but have not spoken to someone who's seen the inside of the Autumn Court. You will be a valuable source of information, Mr. Smith." He turned his gaze to the stage as the lights dimmed. "In exchange for safe harbor, shelter, and food, I want you to tell your tale."

"To you?"

"To her."

He nodded to the stage as the blond, curvy woman Forrest had bumped into took a seat at a grand piano.

"I don't understand."

"Give me your hand."

Nero's fingers unfurled to reveal a pale, soft palm. Forrest had no choice but to give Nero his hand. Shock hit Forrest like a bolt of lightning as a sliver of mana oozed through their connection.

"I do this with all our newcomers," Nero explained. "Especially those who will spend time with Melody. No need to be afraid."

"Sorry," Forrest mumbled, hoping his surprise would appear nervous. "I'm a bit jumpy after what they did to me."

"Understandable." Nero put his thumb on Forrest's inner wrist. "I'm going to ask you a series of questions and determine through your pulse fluctuations whether you are lying or not."

Except, it wasn't through Forrest's pulse. Somehow Nero was connected to the Well. That little jolt of mana traveling through Forrest's body was now hunting for an echo of itself.

RORY

CHAPTER EIGHT

The Order had known for a while that Nero ingested stolen mana to keep himself young, but now Forrest knew Nero could manipulate it too.

How was this possible for one so opposed to the ways of the Well?

How was it possible here, in a place completely disconnected from it?

The Well only flowed for those who respected it. His entire career as a Guardian was based around protecting this harmony. The old humans destroyed the world. Only through obeying these new rules did they hope to avoid doing the same. Yet, here was a man who perverted mana and still found himself in a situation of power.

It sickened Forrest. It confused him. It drove him to urges so violent he had to swallow them down. The atmosphere thrummed with danger. The conversation around Forrest suddenly held a bite.

He was deep in enemy territory and without any advantage apart from the physical skills he'd honed as a warrior.

"What is your name?" Nero asked casually as his mana hurtled through Forrest's veins, hunting for lies and betrayal.

"Forrest," he replied, suddenly grateful he'd used his name for this mission. He could see the value in Clarke's advice to stick close to the truth.

"Are you fae?"

"Why would you ask that?"

"Answer the question. Yes or no."

"No."

The lie punctured Forrest's heart, but he held steady as Nero continued to ask invasive questions. He pulled no punches, but Forrest had prepared. As long as he stuck to his story, he should be fine. If he wasn't fine, a serrated dinner knife was within reach. If he went down, he would take the megalomaniac with him.

But while they spoke, Nero's mana zipped up Forrest's veins, hit his neck, then trailed along his jawline to where his Guardian teardrop had been cut out. The mana burst lingered, tickling beneath Forrest's eye like a hound hunting for an old scent. He held his breath, waiting for his identity to be blown, but the mana zipped away.

Nero let go of Forrest's hand, once again adopting the calm looseness in his posture.

"Well," Nero drawled, turning his gaze back to the stage. "You are one of the lucky few. Some from your time have not escaped the Tainted. Too many have become brainwashed or corrupted or worse, six feet under. But, as I mentioned, there is something you can do to help our cause."

The lights dimmed, and an atmospheric thunder rolled over the room. Conversation hushed. Attention turned to the stage.

"We'll finish this conversation after the show," Nero clipped.

He stared at the stage so hard that Forrest had the sense if anyone interrupted him, they would lose more than an eye. Nero wasn't the only one engaged with the stage. The entire audience was enraptured, and all that sounded were soft drums.

Shivers ran down Forrest's spine as the drumming increased in intensity. He forgot about the deadly man next to him, the child he needed to rescue only tables away, and the room full of his enemy.

Immaculate and poised at the piano, Melody laid the base to the backdrop of her brooding drums—three singular notes repeated. Slowly, she added more notes as two tall, slim men carrying string instruments stepped forward into the light.

They were as oddly dressed as the men in the crowd. Heavy finger rings glinted under the spotlights as they moved into position—bows over violins.

Despite playing the soft singular notes, Melody stood. Another female took her place, seamlessly taking over her repetitive base notes on the piano keys. Melody moved behind one of the men and placed her hand over his as he fitted the instrument under his chin. She pressed her cheek to his shoulder and guided his movement as he stroked his bow across the strings, teaching him how she liked it.

There was something intimate... something sensual about their union that had Forrest shifting in his seat and wishing he was that man, despite not having a musical bone in his body. Melody didn't stop there. She moved to the next male and guided him too, teaching him a captivating tune to play with light and steady fingers before sliding behind a set of drums under the spotlight.

When she straddled the seat, a split in her dress made itself known and exposed a creamy thigh. Beside her on each side was a machine in the shape of a conch he'd once seen on the sand of Helianthus City. Focusing on that conch, he realized music came out of it. He cocked his head. *Fascinating.* Perhaps it had been trapped there like one could trap music inside specific mana stones.

Melody picked up sticks and started beating the drums, blending her new sound into the foundation she'd laid with her band—all with the original class and aplomb she'd begun with.

But then the beat suddenly shifted.

It became deeper. Raw. Harder. Primal. Her slick blond hair came undone. A sheen appeared on her upper lip. A reckless flush to her complexion. A brightness to her eyes. She hammered the drums without a care in the world for her appearance. It was vibrant, enticing. And arousing.

Forrest lost himself. He became her slave. The violins, the piano, and the drums thrummed toward a climax so loud and terrifying that he existed amid a storm. Thunder. Gale force wind. Rain. Bone-numbing awe. The music pulsed and pushed against his skin, against every person in the room with their jaws open.

They soaked up her performance. The music. The way she shattered expectations. The way she oozed primal femininity, tossing her head back in abandon, eyes clenched, and brows knitted as though the music possessed her.

Mesmerized, the audience would be lambs to the slaughter if the Cadre of Twelve entered right now. But Forrest imagined they would die smiling, basking in Melody's glory like the merfolk on the Helianthus warm sea-side rocks.

The music stopped.

Her breasts almost spilled from her tight dress in the stunning aftermath. A breath. Two. And then the possession was over. She was at the piano again, nudging her companion aside to repeat the slow melancholy refrain from the start, bringing them all down from the high she'd created, holding their hands, walking with them until the end.

Nero's voice barely registered beside Forrest. "Have you ever come across a person so remarkable you hardly believe they exist?"

Forrest clicked his jaw shut and glanced around. It was as though she'd cast a net of mana and ensnared the room.

"You see, Mr. Smith," Nero continued. "She is the living reminder of what your old world used to be. She is better than any film or picture book. Here you can touch her, hear her, fall in love with her."

"Fall in love?"

Nero smirked quietly. "Of course, I don't mean you specifically. She is a marvel to be shared. She will never belong to one person but all. Do you agree?"

"I..."

The lonely piano refrain died, ending the performance and saving him from answering. The lights came on, and Forrest felt he could breathe again. Women fanned themselves. Men adjusted their belts. Children started being children again.

"Melody is our harbinger and our entertainer," Nero explained. "I want you to tell her all the horrible and nasty things the Tainted did to you. Spare no detail, no matter how humiliating. She will package it in a way the folks here understand." A pause. "Mr. Smith, are you listening?"

Forrest tore his gaze from where Melody tidied her hair as she prepared for another song. He met the man's eyes. "I'm listening."

"Hearing Beethoven again must be unsettling. Hearing Melody perform it in her unique way is another experience altogether." Nero scrutinized Forrest for a moment. "Don't you recognize her?"

A squeeze inside Forrest's chest told him he should... rather, someone with a history like him should. He gave a tight smile.

"I lived on a farm far from the city."

Crimson, his excuse sounded worse every time he used it. Living on a farm would explain his physique, affinity with animals, and lack of understanding of popular culture so long as he claimed he wasn't connected to their spiderweb technology. That last one was a stretch, but Silver, Clarke, *and* Laurel insisted it was believable.

"Right." Nero adjusted the cuffs of his shirt and sat back to give his full attention to the stage. He said nothing as another female, not part of the band, fussed with Melody's appearance. Melody waved her off, and the band started playing again.

"She has one more song to perform," Nero said quietly. "After which I will write a letter for you to hand her. But first, the guards will show you your new quarters. After tonight, you will meet with her daily to impart your knowledge. Am I understood?"

Forrest opened his mouth to decline the offer. He needed more freedom to find a way to get to Willow. He couldn't be tied up daily, watched, and accounted for.

"You'll soon learn there is a way of doing things here," Nero said at Forrest's pause. "As I'm sure a man with your experience appreciates, it is disorder and chaos out there. So we must have order and structure here for the safety and survival of our pure race, the rightful occupants of this earth. Humanity first." Dark eyes slid to Forrest's just as the music started once more. "Don't you agree?"

Humanity first. Now Forrest understood. It wasn't only about putting humans above the fae but that humans had a right to the land first.

"Of course." He nodded, a bitter taste in his mouth. It wasn't as if the Well had sprung into being after the nuclear fallout. It had been there before life existed. It had been there until humanity stifled it and almost destroyed it with their greed. Humanity first, indeed.

"Good. I'll have you removed if you speak further during the performance."

Forrest blinked, wanting to point out that Nero had been the one to speak first but knew it wasn't worth it. He cast his glance over the crowd before the lights completely dimmed. Willow and Rory were gone. With a knot tightening his stomach, he sank into his seat and turned his face toward the stage. As Melody opened her red lips to sing, Forrest thought that perhaps meeting with her wouldn't be such a bad idea. She played here nightly. This room may fit a few hundred people, but Melody had spoken with Nero, and he seemed to value her. She might run in the same circles as Rory. If Forrest was careful, he could wring Melody for information while feeding her lies. He could use her to get what he wanted.

CHAPTER NINE

With sweat still dampening her skin, guards escorted Melody and her band back to their quarters. After fans had accosted her in the hallway a few weeks ago, some even groping her inappropriately, the guards became a necessary part of her pre and post-show routine. It was only a matter of time before they followed her in every aspect of life.

When Nero had heard about the incident, he decided not to take chances on another. She wished she could say it was out of concern for her welfare, but he wanted his prized harbinger to be at full capacity every night of the week. Melody hadn't been this exhausted since she'd done her first and only stint on Broadway in her early twenties. Granted, it had been a steppingstone into stardom for her, but there was a reason she moved to a solo career. She wanted to play her instruments as much as she wanted to sing.

"That was incredible," Caroline gushed. "You're so talented. I can't believe you teach us so much."

"I can't take all the credit," she replied. "That new gramophone recorder the Tinker invented did half the work." She sighed, running her palm beneath her damp nape. "What I wouldn't give for a good sampler or effects pad. Any electrical equipment, really."

Timothy scoffed. "I think it will be a while before we can reclaim DJ technology."

"So sad so much was lost after the fallout," Andrew sighed, agreeing morosely. He shared a look with his lover. "I think I would have liked to live in those times."

"We're so lucky you're teaching us, Mel." Caroline gave Melody a quick hug, and then they fell into companionable silence as they walked.

Melody loved sharing her knowledge, but as she glanced over at the guards shadowing them, she sometimes wondered if it was worth the cost of her freedom. The fae might be fearsome... but so was Nero.

They arrived at Timothy's quarters and did what they always did. They group hugged so the men could get one last embrace without their affection looking obvious. When they disengaged and said their goodbyes, Melody continued with Andrew and Caroline.

She'd walked this passage nightly with them for months, yet something about this night kept her thoughts returning to the quality of life here. Perhaps it was the sudden appearance of the stranger she'd collided with. He certainly wasn't from around here. His skin was too sun-kissed, and he was too hard—both his physique and his demeanor. And that eye patch. Was she dumb for being attracted to the mystery of it?

It was more than attraction. It was the tiny kernel that he'd lived a life somewhere not here. And there he was, flesh and bone, healthy and virile. Not in pieces. Not carved up as some fae meal. He brought with him the possibility that perhaps Melody had been drinking her own Kool-Aid.

Maybe life out there, as dangerous as it seemed, wasn't a dead end for them?

Andrew was the next to go. Caroline was only a few doors away. To Melody, this building felt like a giant hotel resort complex. Sometimes she wondered if she was still in Vegas and if this was a weird, whacked-out dream. The building boasted living quarters, dining, and hydroponic rooms. Floors with pets and animals, historical museums, and a business floor where the oligarchs plotted their world domination. There were plenty more levels Melody hadn't explored yet, but she wasn't particularly inclined to.

She felt an iota of peace only on the stage and in the president's garden outside.

Resisting rubbing her tired eyes in case she ruined her makeup, she said goodnight to Caroline and strolled in a daze toward her suite. As the star of Nero's show, her living arrangements were more luxurious than most, and with perfect sky views. She wasn't sure how long it would stay that way.

Last night, during their private intermission chat, he'd also revealed his intentions to pair her with one of his trusted elite at this year's Phoenix Ball.

"*A woman of your youth and talent must be bound by a man's belt, Melody,*" he'd declared. "*I've allowed you long enough to come to terms with the ways of this world. It's time you adhere to them like everyone else.*"

She groaned inwardly at the reminder.

"*It is for your protection and prosperity.*"

The first she'd learned of the betrothal ceremony after waking in this world, she'd wanted to stick her finger down her throat and puke. And then, when she'd learned that as part of this ceremony, the men gifted their intended a belt—she'd freaked. Gone were the classic wedding bands. In were *belts*. Some were decorative, and some were plain. A woman's belt reflected her status, or rather, the status of her husband.

There were customs surrounding the exchange of belts, most of which Melody had studiously ignored by shoving them into a bottomless pit where she refused to acknowledge arranged marriages.

She'd tried to laugh it off when Nero had first told her about it, but then he'd explained the betrothal tradition was steeped in their survivalist history. It dated back to the dark days after the nuclear fallout when the last remaining humans had been quarantined and locked in bunkers for decades while the world above recovered from the nuclear winter.

There had been so few humans left in those dark centuries that pairings and lineage were carefully constructed so the DNA of the human race would thrive. It sounded like a bunch of archaic, purist bullshit to Melody. But what did she know about this world?

It was her job to sing and then shut up.

It's not your job to think.

Melody wasn't sure what the excuse was for continuing the custom now, except that it kept women under control. And she knew exactly who'd been in Nero's ear about matching with her. She shuddered, suddenly feeling nauseous.

The Captain had leered at her from the front row table the entire night. Sometimes, she would take a turn of the room with her band, but tonight, somehow, she'd wanted to get out of there as quickly as possible. Which was a shame considering the stranger she'd bumped into.

Conjuring his face *again*—knowing full well she couldn't stop thinking of him—the same thrum of awareness zipped through her as it had when she'd crashed into him... when she'd grasped his powerful biceps to stop herself from falling, and when she'd locked eyes with him. Well, one glorious brown eye. The other had been curiously covered with a scrappy leather patch, a purple scar above and below it.

There had been a rugged, untamed handsomeness about him.

The patch, scar, auburn hair, pine smell, and male sweat. The muscles—dear Lord, the muscles. *Hard. Big.* She fanned her face. It all added to his overall wildness. He had an athletic body, lithe and liquid, but with a coiled strength she didn't often see inside Sky Tower. Only that new guard, Sid, had come close to this man's presence.

Maybe the new man was another Reaper.

She didn't see too many of those. Sid had been relocated because of his injury. Maybe that eye patch meant the newcomer was in the same boat. Reapers usually stayed outside with the everyday city folk.

And she'd squeezed his biceps! Of all the stupid, blushing, and bumbling things to do. She'd been so—Melody's steps faltered when she realized the hallway was eerily quiet. No footsteps from guards shadowed her. The hairs on the back of her neck lifted, and she turned.

The guards were gone, but the Captain walked up, his strides decisive and sure. Searching the hallway for her chaperones, she found none.

Melody's heart jumped into her throat. She weighed the distance to her suite. Twenty feet away. There was no way she could get there before the Captain arrived. Even if she ran, she'd only look like she was fleeing. It was too late to pretend she'd not seen him. She swallowed and then stretched her lips into a smile.

And immediately wished she hadn't.

The determined look in his eyes turned lecherous.

"Ms. Melody," he said as he arrived toe-to-toe with her.

She'd always believed the world was made up of vibrations. Some sounds were emitted at a frequency on the same level as her heart. Others were not. The Captain's voice was in another symphony altogether. Another orchestra. Another world.

He put his hands behind his back and looked down his arched nose at her. His jacket opened to reveal a soft, narrow chest. His tucked shirt held back a small pot belly. A skinny belt patterned with glittering Phoenixes caught her attention. She tried to keep her eyes on his face, despite knowing why he displayed his belt so proudly.

The belt so candidly represented his intention toward her.

"Captain," she greeted, conjuring that false grace she often used on the stage.

"I hoped to catch you after your show, but you left quickly."

"Bless your heart for thinking of me, but I wasn't up to mingling tonight."

His eyes narrowed. "I heard you were to receive a gentlemen caller."

Her brows lifted. Had Nero already announced her availability to other eligible men? And by eligible, she meant the ones carefully selected by his proxy so that whoever she coupled with would make a strong match, both in DNA and politics. The ruse she could choose was a straw man distraction to make women believe they had agency in a world that smothered it.

"Again, I must apologize. I'm going to sleep. No callers." But as the words fell out of her lips, she couldn't hide the tremble, despite her years of practice. Sooner or later, she'd have to accept her fate.

He rocked back on his heels and considered her words. Clearly, he'd hoped for an invitation into her apartment. When he didn't get it, and she was about to take her leave, he grabbed her upper arm. Pain pierced her flesh. He seemed to relish her whimper. His pupils dilated. His nostrils flared.

"You know my intentions," he ground out. "Why must you keep dancing around them? I am losing my patience."

"I'm not sure what you mean." She tried to pull her arm back, but it bruised more.

"I am on your approved shortlist. If you accept my belt now, it will make the ceremony run smoother."

Approved shortlist?

Melody searched her brain for more information. Some betrothals were arranged as early as childhood. She didn't realize there was a publicly accessible list. Or maybe it wasn't public.

If she agreed to wear his belt like a damned medieval girdle, she showed the entire Tower she was his. Others on the list would pull out of the running before the ceremony, and the matchmaker would have no choice but to pair them together on the day. She forced her lips to stretch into a smile. "Until the Phoenix Ball, I don't have to accept anything."

He slammed his palm on the wall beside Melody's head. She flinched away as the sour whiskey on his breath wafted into her face.

"You are *mine*, Ms. Melody."

His eyes dipped to her lips. He clamped her jaw with his forefinger and thumb. Barely restrained anger simmered in his gaze as he tightened until she tasted blood.

"Who else are you waiting for? Nobody wants you," he snarled quietly. "You talk with a strange accent. You're opinionated. Apart from your talent, you're nothing but a sack of swollen potatoes. The sooner you come to terms with my offer, the easier it will be for you."

She refused to let him see the humiliation on her face. Her head swam. Her vision blurred. *Sack of swollen potatoes?* Her heart galloped a million miles an hour. The weight wasn't her fault. She… oh, God. She…

But there was no use fighting him. He was right. She'd put off the betrothal for as long as she could. Her friends had to do it. Andrew and Timothy had to do it—despite their love for each other, they were being separated. *Everyone* had to do it.

At some point, she had to pick one of the suiters. She was lucky she even got to choose. Some, like Andrew, didn't get to decide. He was placed with an available bloodline. Sometimes there was only one.

And she needed protection, as Nero had put it, so why wouldn't he pair her with a leader in his army? He might have set this up for all she knew.

Sometimes Melody wished she didn't like the things she did. Sometimes she wished that the soul-shattering rightness of music didn't affect her so. If she'd been a simple girl without dreams and talents, she'd have been looked over. She'd have faded into nothing. It might have been a simple life with her mother, but she would have been happy. Whatever divine intervention had brought her to this time would have overlooked her.

Heavy footsteps caused the Captain to ease off her. It wouldn't do to be seen touching his bride before the ceremony. He wanted Melody to fall at his feet, gushing his praises. The footsteps turned hard, resolute.

Melody braved a glance up, caught a single furious brown eye, a flash of auburn hair, and then the brawny stranger from the dining hall yanked the Captain's arm back at a painful angle and shoved him to his knees—right before Melody. It all happened so fast that her mind couldn't catch up. With a single, broad hand, the newcomer forced the Captain's face to Melody's toes.

"Apologize to the lady." The newcomer's voice was deep and gravelly like a beast as he bent over his prey. It was as though he was born to dominate. "Beg her forgiveness."

The Captain struggled but only succeeded in wrenching his arm tighter.

"You don't know who you're messing with," he snarled.

"I know enough," the man clipped, holding the position, barely breaking a sweat. He pushed the Captain's cheek flat against Melody's toes. "You're not fit to touch her. Lick her feet and show her you're sorry."

Melody's jaw dropped.

The Captain refused and was rewarded with a knee in the back. He squealed like a pig and licked Melody's feet, tears leaking from his eyes as he gasped and hiccupped in pain. Snot dripped down to his mustache and drooled over her feet.

Satisfied, the newcomer let go, still without a drop of sweat on his brow.

The Captain's palms slapped on the ground. He pushed himself up, face red, veins protruding in his forehead.

Her protector folded his arms and stepped between her and the Captain, who wiped his snot and glared at Melody. The Captain's calm stare chilled her to the bone, and she knew, without a doubt, that bruises would be the least of her worries the next time she was alone with him.

Panic pulsed beneath her skin. She was Nero's favored musician but not a general in his army. She knew what would happen next. Nero would appease the Captain by handing her over to him. Then he would use his belt to bring Melody into line. Everyone would be happy.

Except her.

"Oh, you really shouldn't have done that." The Captain buttoned his jacket to hide his belt. That simple action turned Melody cold. Custom said the belt was only for the betrothed's eyes. Melody was anything but safe. He shifted his dark gaze to Melody. "And you'll be sorry you let him."

THE
CAPTAIN

CHAPTER TEN

Forrest barely restrained himself. He didn't know what had come over him, but instinct roared to the surface from the moment he'd seen the much larger, more powerful man using his brute force to push Melody against the wall. He saw red. He smelled blood. Still, even now, staring at the Captain as he walked away, whining like a scorned *wolpertinger* in mating season, the image of the assault burned into Forrest's mind.

His muscles still twitched with adrenaline.

Prey. Kill. Remove the threat.

He forced himself to breathe and flexed his fingers. He'd let himself do just that on too many occasions—hunt the prey. Kill it. His instincts were what elevated him to the Twelve's level. When Forrest had his victim in sight, he didn't stop until only one of them was left. But this only happened when he let it. When he knew it was time for battle.

Shame and self-loathing washed over him. How could he lose control so viscerally? For a stranger, no less. The enemy.

"He's right, you know," she mumbled, bringing his attention back to her arresting eyes. "You shouldn't have interfered."

A million responses churned in his mind, the least of which was that he would do it again. *This wasn't him.* He'd possibly ruined his mission in a few hot-headed seconds. He stood there mute under the impact of her beauty while his mind scrambled to catch up, to come up with a solution that would make this next part count. He might not have another chance.

"I need to talk with you," he said abruptly. At Melody's bewildered blink, he held out the letter Nero had given him. "Your president wants me to impart stories from my time in Elphyne. That starts tonight."

"I..." Her lips opened and closed. "I usually sit with the storytellers during the day."

"Tonight." His tone came out more gruff than intended.

For Crimson's sake. He was acting like a floater, making demands soon after a man had accosted her. What was wrong with him? He relaxed his posture and stepped back, so he didn't seem threatening.

She opened the letter.

"Forrest," she murmured as she read his name.

A thrill entered his body at hearing his name on her lips. Then he mentally kicked himself for not introducing himself properly.

"Says here you arrived at the city today. You're from my time, but after you woke, you were captured by the Autumn Court, where you've been tortured and humiliated for months."

He gestured awkwardly at his scar and bruises. She fidgeted as she considered his words.

"I can find the guard to explain if that helps," he offered.

He searched down the hall, but the coward who'd brought him here was nowhere in sight.

The young, nameless Sky Tower guard had taken Forrest from the dining hall on Nero's behest and shown Forrest his new simple living quarters a few levels down—a single room with a bathroom, some clothes, and basic hygiene supplies.

Free meals were served in the dining hall daily. A free market was on another level. Education and other services were also free. It sounded too good to be true.

The only payoff was that he could never leave the building and had to accept any job handed to him. It didn't bother him. He would be out of here in a few weeks. Maybe less.

Melody hesitated. Despair flashed deep within her eyes. His cheeks heated because he was the one who'd made her feel that way.

"I have made matters worse for you, haven't I?" he asked quietly.

"Probably shouldn't have made him lick my feet." Her lips twitched into the shadow of a smile. "But I guess if you've been living in the wild, tainted lands, then you haven't had a good example of a society in a while."

It took him a delayed moment to perceive the insult to his people, but he couldn't blame her. She didn't know otherwise. He scrubbed his face.

He had to find Willow, convince Rory to come to Elphyne, get a message out to Silver's smugglers who would help them get out, and somehow stay incognito until it was time to go.

His fingers curled into fists, and he tapped his brow, frustrated at himself.

"I think we both need a stiff drink," she said, pity in her voice. "Come on, honey. I've got something in my suite you might appreciate. We can figure out what to do next together."

Forrest exhaled as she walked toward a door at the end of the hallway. But, as he watched her slot a brass key into her door lock with trembling fingers, he knew she was far from relieved.

"I won't hurt you," he said. "If you feel safer with a guard here, I will find one."

She gave a nervous laugh. "It's not you I'm afraid of."

The door clicked open to reveal a suite decidedly more luxurious than his newly appointed quarters. Views at the window were vast, from east to west, showing sky and city. Like his room, this was one space divided by floor-to-ceiling tapestries and curtains. No inner walls, just clever ways of making it feel like multiple rooms. The first living space they entered looked for entertaining. It had sofas and upholstered chairs. Food platters lush with pastries and sweets spilled from a tray sitting on a table between the seats.

Off to the side, an arrangement of musical instruments scattered haphazardly. A piano and string instruments. A set of complicated drums like the ones she'd played on stage were squashed against a wall. A gold harp was in the living room next to a sofa, on an angle as though it had been played recently and left in a rush.

A small kitchen near the long windows also had fresh food on platters. Behind the kitchen, gauzy curtains with golden tassels separated the lamp-lit bedroom. He glimpsed shadows and shapes beyond the curtains and reflections in the long windows.

"Please," she said, indicating the sofas near the entrance. "Take a seat."

She went to a side table against the wall where a decanter of golden liquid sat on a tray. She poured two glasses before bringing them over.

She nodded to his drink as she handed it to him. "Whiskey. Usher's. And not the singer—although I've seen his whiskey collection, and it wasn't half bad—no, this was an honored gift from Nero's private collection. Thousands of years aged."

Forrest sat down and eyed the food. His stomach grumbled.

"Please, help yourself," she said. "Lord knows I don't need it."

Forrest didn't need to be told twice. He extricated a sweet pastry and devoured it quickly before moving on to another.

"He only brings fancy gifts with news that's hard to swallow."

He raised his brows as he chewed, silently waiting for her to elaborate, but she only kicked off her shoes and sat with her feet tucked beneath her bottom. Her dress pulled tight across her body. She scowled and tried to rearrange herself but ended up covering her stomach with a pillow.

Her long lashes fluttered closed as she took a sip, relaxed into her seat further, and then moaned as she licked her lips.

"Are you okay?" he asked, his eyes traveling over her. "He didn't hurt you, did he?"

Her gaze clashed with his and then skated away. "I'm used to it."

"You're used to men pawing at you like you're a piece of meat?"

She made a dismissive face, and his anger woke up, heating his insides, blurring his vision red. He put the pastry down, ready to say something, but she spoke first.

"It comes with the territory. Back home, my security detail wouldn't leave my side until I was safely locked in my house. Especially after a show. That's when the most... enthusiastic fans came out." At his frown, she added incredulously, "You don't recognize me? From before?"

Nero had been surprised as well.

Her brows winged up at his silence. He caught a flash of that confidence again, and then it was swiftly stamped out as she tried to tug the split of her dress over her thigh and then shrank a little into herself.

"I suppose I look different now." She clutched the pillow at her stomach.

He cocked his head. She looked ashamed. He didn't like it.

"I worked on a farm," he explained. "Off the grid."

"Oh. Really? But you've still never heard of me?"

He shook his head.

"What about this?" She belted out a catchy tune, her voice elegantly filling the room in a way that sank down his spine. At his blank face, she stopped and shot down the last of her whiskey before pulling out a tin box from somewhere on the sofa. She opened it, retrieved a white stick, and placed it between her lips. It looked like a roll of manaweed... but obviously not. She clicked a copper gadget near the blunt. To his surprise, a flame zipped out of the device, scorching the stick as she sucked in a breath. She gave him a sideways glance. "You don't mind if I smoke, do you? I figure I survived the apocalypse, so why stop now? You know?"

"Why would you stop?" he asked absently, mesmerized by how her pink tongue touched her teeth as she cleaned something off it.

Her sudden laughter made him sit up, snapping out of his daze. What had he said?

"Oh, you know, sugar." She waved the smoking white blunt before tapping it on a tray to rid the ash. Then, on a sudden fierce frown, she squashed it. "Tried to quit for years. Mom never smoked a day in her life, but the big C still got her."

"Big C."

Another confused look shot his way, and he almost bit his tongue as a reminder to stop commenting on things he didn't understand. He was going to blow his cover—time to get this conversation back on track.

"What did the Captain want?" he asked.

"I have a better question," she answered as she settled back on the sofa, grabbed her pillow to cuddle, and then tucked her feet again. "If you're a farm boy, how did you get one over a military man?"

"Luck."

"That wasn't luck. That was skill." She gave his physique an obvious once over. "You have the body for it. You're covered in scars as though you fight. You escaped the worst of the Tainted and are here, alive, to tell the tale. So, tell me. What kind of military did you serve in? Seals, Rangers, Special Ops?"

"I thought I only had to tell you about my time in Elphyne."

Her face shut down. He'd been too abrupt.

"Right. Of course." She reached between more cushions, fished around for a bit, and then pulled out a small notebook and pencil. "Go ahead. I'm ready."

A tug of guilt hit him squarely in the chest.

The mission, Forrest. Willow. Rory.

He wracked his brain to find a way to bring up the girl without sounding suspicious, but all he ended up giving was a pain to his temple. He launched into a rehearsed retelling of his cover story.

"I woke up in a cave. I had no idea where I was. Some fae found me and realized I was human." He waved at his ears. "They took me as a slave and forced me to work for them." He shook his head as though pondering in horror. "Their magic made it so I had no choice. I couldn't speak when they told me to shut up. If I displeased them, I was tossed in a dungeon until they remembered me." His mind traveled back to his childhood and those long cold nights when everyone but the animals forgot about him. "Sometimes, it was better in the dungeon. Sometimes I was so alone and empty of physical contact that I was ready to perform like a monkey to get their attention."

He cleared his throat, feeling too raw. Those memories had been hidden for so long that he'd forgotten how awful they made him feel.

Melody listened patiently, but when he was done, she put the notebook down and said gently.

"That sounds terrible, and I'm so sorry you had to go through that. I can't imagine being in your position. But..." She bit her lip. "I've been told I must provide new material, and unfortunately, your story is similar to something I've heard before. An escaped human from the evil queen's clutches told us all about being forced to do her bidding, no matter how humiliating. This might sound insensitive, but I need details no one knows."

Forrest tapped his foot, irritated.

"The president seems to think you'll have plenty of insight since you lived there."

Tap tap tap. He ground his teeth. "How am I supposed to know what you've never heard before?"

"I guess we just keep hashing it out."

This was going to be a long night.

"While you're thinking," she sighed tiredly, tugging on her dress. "I might get into something more comfortable."

⚖

Forrest was supposed to come up with more stories, but from the moment she walked into her room, he was distracted. She frequently passed the opening between gauze curtains as she hunted for clothes. And the way the room dividers were set up, her lamp-lit silhouette reflected in the windows beyond the kitchen.

He wrenched his gaze away with a frown. An unavoidable heat crept up his neck to burn his ears. Watching a woman dress had never been something he'd cared to watch, but the inexplicable pull to turn his head back was a battle more challenging than against any djinn.

Attempting to shift his thoughts, he latched onto his mistake in the hallway. He'd messed up and couldn't understand.

Why had he snapped?

Was it seeing Melody treated that way? He'd ignored worse in his job. Guardians policed the abuse of the Well, not get involved with general politics. That was a clear and distinct rule the Prime gave upon their acceptance to the ranks. Their resources simply did not stretch that far.

Maybe he made a mistake because of the comedown of being cut from the Well. His nerves were all raw and twitchy.

Then it hit him.

His father used to treat his mother like that. Forrest remembered seeing the same thing—chin gripped between forefinger and thumb, her against the wall. He frowned as the memory sharpened. Like the rest of his siblings, his mother had never cared much for Forrest. He was the seventh, the invisible child. He was treated like a wyrm, so why had this triggered him?

Thinking back to how Melody's beautiful eyes had been fraught with fear, he knew why. That look had been in his mother's eyes as she'd looked at Forrest, not his father, while he assaulted her.

He was shocked at the revelation. More shadows peeled away from the dusty corners of the memory. His father had been upset with his mother because she'd been consoling Forrest for a bruised thumb, her fingers tickling his hair—*oh, that feeling*—he scratched his head to conjure more of it.

He'd forgotten how mother had affectionately tickled his hair whenever he'd walk by. Being so little, she'd hardly have to reach. That lingering touch, that secret sweep of hair behind his ears, had given him something warm to hold onto in the lonely hours.

Like dominos falling, more memory blocks fell. His mother had trembled, just as Melody had. She'd flinched from Forrest's father on too many occasions. He'd probably beaten her compassion out until she was a ghost of her former self. Forrest could see that now. His mother had become like the rest—a woman who cared for no one... not even herself.

Forrest had spent most of his life hating his family, but perhaps some of them had been victims, just as he was.

Hearing a sweet tune hummed from Melody's room, he glanced over and caught his breath. Her reflection in the window was clear as day against the night outside.

Look away.

He couldn't. With each glimpse of her creamy flesh, everything turned tight inside him. In a trance from her expressive voice and feminine grace, he drank in her every movement like he was starving. He imagined he could scent her across the void, and the delectable sweetness made his mouth water.

Never before had he wanted to taste a female like her. Never had he been violently drawn toward another. He wanted to consume her with a hunger bordering on irrational.

As his breath became jagged in his chest, he focused on the food before him. The skin beneath the eye patch itched, and he rubbed it vigorously. Her humming stopped as she padded back into the room on bare feet.

"That feels better," she sighed and sank back onto her seat.

He couldn't look at her.

He had to keep his eyes on the food. If he looked up, he'd not see the new clothes she wore but the irresistible taste of skin beneath. If he looked up, she'd see his arousal all over his face. He didn't know what to do.

"Did you think of something?" she asked.

He cleared his throat and stared at his fingers. "I... ah."

"You look a little flushed. Oh, for Heaven's sake. Where are my manners?" She hurried to the kitchen. "I forgot to get you a glass of water."

While she filled up a glass at the faucet, she continued to talk. "I was thinking on it while I dressed and have decided there's no need to worry about Captain Jackass. I'll say something to the president. I'm sure he'll understand. Best we keep on his good side, first, and get some new material for the next show." She returned and stood before him, waiting. "Hun, are you sure you're okay?"

Her feather-light touch rested on his neck where Shade had scratched. He forced himself to look at her and found concern radiating back at him. It was a balm to his turmoil, and he wanted to bask in her attention.

Which was why he knew he had to leave. She shouldn't have to make some kind of deal or apology to Nero for his actions. It was his responsibility. He stood up suddenly and bumped into her, spilling the water down his shirt and lap.

"*Well-dammit*," he cursed, then bit his lip, realizing it was an utterly fae thing to say, and then he was furious at himself all over again.

"Oh no," she gasped.

She dashed back to the kitchen and found a towel before returning to dab it down his front.

"I'm so sorry," she said, frantically wiping him.

"Not your fault."

"No, but I was standing so close. I keep forgetting how big and clumsy I've become. I'm so stupid." Her voice tightened with self-deprecation. "I'm just not... God, I'm so..."

He trapped her hand flat against his ribs. Their gazes clashed. A thousand reasons why it wasn't her fault stuck on the tip of his tongue. He wanted to tell her she was beautiful and that her size had nothing to do with him knocking into her. He wanted to lick every creamy surface on her body... and then the pink places too.

But the longer he stayed, the further he was from his goal.

He needed time to collect his thoughts.

"I should go." Yet, he couldn't let go of her hand. Just a moment longer with her palm pressed against his front... so close to his heart beating wildly.

"But the—" She glanced at her open notebook on the sofa.

"I'll speak with Nero first thing in the morning," he promised. "Then I can call on you afterward, and we can continue."

Before she could utter another word, he left.

CHAPTER
ELEVEN

Forrest couldn't sleep.

After Melody's, he returned to his room and went to bed. He ached from his wounds and couldn't stop thinking about his actions. He was supposed to be as anonymous as possible. But expecting to make no waves on this mission was a silly notion.

Willow was in the care of the city's deadliest female—the same female Forrest had to convince to leave with him. This building was in lockdown and carefully patrolled. Finding a way to get close to Rory would take time. He hoped Clarke and Rush understood that. Even if he decided to forget Rory, get to Willow and steal her away, escaping unnoticed would be near impossible without help.

So, Rory had to be involved.

Forrest was at a loss for what to do next. He tried to imagine what Aeron would say... rather, what he would have said before his injury. Despite Forrest being older than his half-brother, it was always Aeron who knew what to do. He had a quiet fire about him that kindled and sparked at the right times. He had never been in denial of what he wanted.

Aeron was fascinated with knowledge. He hated mystery. If he didn't understand something, he would do everything in his power to turn it inside out and study it from all angles until he did. This innate gift for solving problems was probably why Aeron struggled so much with his injury. He wasn't a healer—this wasn't something he could learn. The Well either gave the gift of healing, or it didn't.

Forrest hoped Aeron would soon realize he could turn his problem-solving skills to learning ways around his new handicap. If he didn't, Forrest would help him as soon as he returned.

So... Forrest stared at the dark ceiling, pondering. So, if Aeron was here—the old Aeron—he would quietly spend time studying and learning about the hostile environment before he made his move. Aeron would use what he already knew to come up with a contingency. That's what Forrest should be doing.

No more waves.

He must have fallen asleep but awoke when the first hues of dawn colored the sky. He dropped to the floor with renewed purpose and completed a circuit of Guardian training exercises. Push-ups, crunches, squats, and anything else he could think of. Growing weak was not an option, especially if he was basically human here. No gifts to help him in battle. He showered, dressed, and left to find breakfast.

He found it in the dining hall. The breakfast crowd was a slightly different mix of people to those at the evening concert. These were still dressed in luxurious clothing compared to what he'd seen outside, but they were slightly subdued. Fewer frills and ribbons. Less volume in the dresses.

A buffet with steaming, aromatic food sat before the empty stage, now closed over with curtains. Servers standing behind the buffet distributed food onto plates, almost like rations. He took a plate and smiled at a female server with wrinkles around her watery eyes.

Her kind face reminded him of the brownies who raised him. Maybe that was what prompted him to start his fact uncovering mission here.

"I'm new here," he said with a hesitant smile. "You wouldn't happen to know how I could speak with the president privately?"

Maybe he could get ahead of last night's situation with the Captain. He worried all night that he'd caused trouble for Melody. It sat like an unwanted visitor on the fence of his mind.

The server raised her brows at him, looked at his eyepatch, and then shrugged as she spoke.

"Top floors are out of bounds. You'll have to put in a request with the registrar and wait your turn like everyone else."

Annoyed but not surprised, he pointed at the food items he wanted on his plate.

"And when does he have breakfast?"

"He only eats down here in the evenings."

So, the only place Forrest could speak to him would be tonight. That wasn't good enough. He had to get to him before the Captain did.

"Who would I speak to if I had an urgent message?"

She pointed at a guard sitting at a round table, two back from the stage. Metal trimmings on the shoulders signified he was of rank. Forrest tried to remember the type of metal the Captain had and wondered if this trim outranked him. If Forrest said something to him in confidence, would he ignore Forrest's claim or twist the message until it made Forrest look like he was at fault?

"Can I trust him?" he asked the server. When she looked at him oddly, he added, "Is he a decent man... toward women?"

Would the guard be sympathetic?

The server blinked at him. Something like curiosity flashed in her eyes. She glanced around to see if anyone was in earshot and leaned closer. "If you have sensitive information, then the best person is the president's daughter. She's good to women. Gives us the same opportunities as men. You'll find her sitting at the table at the back. Look for the copper."

Forrest had assumed Rory was as bad as acidic blood in a Well Hound. She'd spearheaded Willow's kidnapping. Cloud held a grudge against her. But maybe, like others, there was more to her than they knew. He glanced over to her table. *She's alone.* Perfect.

"Thank you," he said to the server. "I owe you one."

The woman blushed and looked down. He walked away with his plate, loving how easily the lies were coming now. It felt oddly liberating to have no restrictions on his tongue.

Forrest wended through the room and placed his tray on the table opposite Rory. Dressed in her Reaper uniform, she looked formidable as she scowled at her food. Copper beads tinkled in her hair as she turned the full force of that scowl on him as he sat.

"Did I say you could sit?" she growled.

"I'll only take a moment of your time," he promised. "I'm new. Arrived yesterday. Was one of the—"

"I know who you are, Forrest Smith."

His heart stopped beating. Did she recognize him from the battle at the Order? But he'd been too far away. It had been chaotic. She'd been busy nabbing Willow.

"I have information about one of your military leaders," he offered.

Her brows winged up, and she sat back with arms folded.

"What makes you think I give a shit?" she said.

But she didn't tell him to leave, so he continued.

"Last night, your father instructed me to tell Melody my story. When I arrived, I found one of your military leaders assaulting her against the wall. I intervened. He wasn't happy. I thought the president would like to know his harbinger is being treated poorly by someone he, no doubt, trusts."

"My father trusts no one."

They locked eyes for a long moment, and Forrest wondered if he was about to be booted out, but Rory picked up her fork and pushed potatoes idly on her plate. Her next words had lost their enthusiasm. "Mel would have told me."

His eyes narrowed. "You're friends with her?"

"I don't have friends." That gusto came back. Her fork hovered over a potato chunk before stabbing. "But she would have told me."

"She's in danger," he stated.

Rory put the bite into her mouth and chewed as she stared at him. He could virtually see the thoughts collide behind her eyes: Why did Forrest care? Was he telling the truth? Was this news worth sharing with her father?

It irritated Forrest, and his animal side triggered instead of retreating.

"Perhaps I overestimated you." He snatched his tray.

Rory used her fork to slam his tray down. Her nostrils flared as she lifted her gaze to him.

"You come to my table uninvited, make demands, and now you insult me." He expected more sharp words, but she backed off. "Why do you care about Mel? What's it to you?"

"She was hurt. You'll see the bruises on her arm match his hand. After what I've been through with those tainted-fuckers, I didn't expect to see the same treatment to my own kind here. That's all."

Something shifted in her eyes. A softening. Barely.

"I'll sort it out." She waved him off and went back to her food.

"She needs better security detail," he pressed. "The guards assigned to her were nowhere in sight."

Rory narrowed her eyes and ground her teeth, clearly done with this conversation. "I said, I'll sort it out."

He searched her face for signs of falsity but found none. Perhaps he could use this to his advantage. Increase his standing here. Get access to more levels.

Get close to Melody.

"I'd like you to consider me to be her guard," he said, completely serious. "I have to work with her, anyway. I've spent time with the worst evil out there and survived. I can keep her safe."

Rory laughed. "I can't decide whether you're developing an unhealthy attachment to our special lady or you're a regular knight in shining armor."

"Ask Melody what she wants."

"There you go again, assuming you have the right to tell me what to do." Her expression scrunched with irritation before deadpanning. "But you're new here, so I'll let you off. Speak out of line again, and I won't be so forgiving. Like I said, I'll sort out the fucking cunt who hurt her. Now leave me to eat in peace. It's the only time I have to myself these days."

"Thank you," he said, exhaling. He knew he shouldn't care what happened to any of these people, including Melody, but if there was anything he'd learned from spending time with the six humans mated to his fellow cadre members, it was that there were good and evil in both sides of the war.

Melody was no criminal.

And now, after seeing the resolution in Rory's eyes as she nodded back to him, doubt wrapped its barbed coils around his mind. What if Rory was in the gray zone too?

So much for not making waves.

CHAPTER
TWELVE

Melody woke with an ache in her arm and jaw from where the Captain had bruised her. But her mind was on the enigmatic man who'd been in her room late at night. Who knew what the Captain would have done if he hadn't been interrupted? She lay there thinking about how terrified she'd felt, how her body couldn't stop trembling after the Captain's touch. Then how it had warmed and relaxed when Forrest held her palm against his water-drenched stomach.

Hard abs. Strong. She'd felt so safe… and a little, dare she think, attracted to the strength in him.

He'd brought a mighty man to his knees, to tears, to licking her feet.

Oh my God.

She sat up suddenly. Blood rushed to her head, and she held it. Then she remembered Forrest's state as he left her place. With spilled water down his front. She'd tried to mop it up by putting her hands all over him and then *blabbering* about God knows what.

She tossed off her covers and, still scowling, took a shower before putting on a casual dress that gave a much-needed cinch at the waist and flared at the ankles. This was one of her favorite dresses. It made her feel like her old curvy self, not the bloated one the Captain had called a sack of potatoes.

She quickly put the words out of her head before they haunted her all day.

She couldn't help wishing for a good pair of sweats and the comfort of an oversized hoodie. But she was kind of glad not to have those slouch clothes around. At least this dress accentuated her good parts. She'd hate for Forrest to see her—

God, stop it, Mel.

He is not part of your future. *This* is your reality—making music for a megalomaniac and finding a way to avoid betrothal to another one. Melody smeared fog from the mirror and stared at her reflection. Flushed, plump cheeks. She hardly recognized herself.

Some parts she liked. Some she didn't. But that was the package deal when in the spotlight. She would never be happy with her appearance. She was constantly judged for it and would always find something to dislike, even though logic said she should do otherwise.

There were times on tour when smoking a packet a day and not eating made her gaunt and sick. The media had a field day with those times. *Is Melody sick? Is Melody pregnant? Is Melody addicted to drugs while pregnant?*

Her mother would genuinely be sad about her picking up the habit again. She had to stop.

"No need to feed the beast unless it's your own, sugarplum."

As Melody slathered cream on her face, she thought about how weird it was that Forrest didn't know who she was. Not to toot her own horn, but in her time, she'd not met a single person that didn't recognize her. It was just fact. But maybe she was being conceited. Perhaps she missed the attention. Maybe it was also weird that he didn't know the Big C.

Was it?

No.

But was it?

Come to think of it; there was much about that man that didn't seem quite right. He sounded formal sometimes, yet at others, he had a wild look like a lion caught in the hunter's headlights.

Well-dammit, he'd cursed. It was a weird way to say dammit. Perhaps that's how the fae said it, and he'd spent too much time on the other side. That's what it must be.

She wrangled her unruly platinum hair into a bun and immediately thought of his messy hairstyle. Some musicians rocked that look. Their rugged, tortured vibe made her legs go weak, and her panties drop. Many of her lovers had been exactly that, tortured artists. But those lovers were few and far between when she was famous. Trust was hard to come by. She'd been lied about in the tabloids far too often to persist with an open relationship.

In the end, at a ripe old age of thirty-one, she was lonely while beloved by millions. And when her mom died, her life had gone to hell in a handbasket.

With a sigh, she tugged out the bun and brushed her hair into the usual feminine waves common in Tower fashion. She looked her reflection squarely in the eyes.

"One day, we'll have everything we want," she promised.

The problem was that Melody wasn't sure that goal was attainable. Maybe it never had been. Mainly because she didn't know what she wanted, only that there was an emptiness inside her soul, craving to be filled. She used to think music was the answer, but it was only the band-aid. It was her therapy, not the answer.

"Get a grip, Melody. You need new material for tonight's performance. Focus on that. The last thing you want is to be one of the missing musicians Caroline talks about."

Melody shuddered. She should be fine if she stayed on the president's good side.

Not having a song for tonight was making her sweat. And that ruined her makeup application. She dusted powder over her skin, careful to cover the new bruise. Then she drew smooth lines over her eyelids with black liner. She lathered gloss over her lips until they glistened like dew.

Feeling more like herself, she smoothed the simple dress and slipped on a tailored jacket. Catching a rare glimpse of sunshine outside gave her the idea to forgo breakfast and head down to the president's garden for a morning session before others arrived. That place always made her feel better. Inspired even.

Afterward, if Forrest didn't turn up as promised, she would track him down and insist he give her something to sing about, or she would have to make shit up. Either way, she would have a new song to teach her band by the afternoon.

The president's voice rang clear in her mind. *If you've forgotten what fear feels like, I'd be happy to arrange a demonstration.*

Gathering her notebook, she walked to the door and opened it

—Forrest waited, freshly washed and in new clothes. He looked more delicious than yesterday. That auburn hair was brushed and pulled back into her favorite style—haphazardly knotted at his nape. He'd shaved, but the shadow of his beard still accentuated his sharp jaw. It was as though he was too manly for the razor to work.

She almost giggled at the thought of a razorblade fearing his scruff.

His olive-green shirt looked perfect on him, bringing out the hazel in his brown eye—such a shame the other eye was injured. But the leather patch only gave him a sense of mystery she wanted to explore. Not an ounce of fat on that toned, muscular body.

Spending time with this specimen of a Viking wasn't going to be easy. Once her mind went *there*, it was hard to take back. Might have to let it all out in her songbook. Her fingers twitched on the cover as she started to hear a tune... then lyrics. She hadn't written her own music for years.

And she was staring at him.

For a long time.

"Hi," he eventually said.

"Um. Hi."

"You look..." His gaze dragged down her body, and she wanted to reach for a pillow to hide from scrutiny. She sucked in her gut instead. "You look radiant."

"Oh." She blushed. "I didn't think you'd be here this early. I wasn't expecting you."

"I didn't mean to imply—" He scratched his head. "Let's start again. Hi. I'm early because I couldn't sleep."

"Me neither."

"I already went looking for Nero."

Melody's fingers tightened around her notebook. "Oh?"

"Couldn't find him." His frown deepened. "But I spoke with his daughter and explained what happened. I'll stay with you until your performance and then walk you home. If the Captain comes looking for you, he'll also find me."

"Honey," she said as gently as she could. "While I appreciate the benefits of a well-mannered and protective gentleman, I don't need a round-the-clock chaperone."

Then why did her stomach do a little flip at his words?

"It's the least I can do for the trouble I've caused," he said.

"Let's not get ahead of ourselves. We don't know there's trouble yet." She stepped out of the apartment and shut the door behind her. Remove the fact that she'd enjoyed his company, the day she accepted a bodyguard was when she lost all freedom here. "Look. You're more than welcome to accompany me to the garden. But no chaperoning. We're just two people gettin' some work done in the great outdoors."

"Understood." He followed her as she walked, carefully eyeing anyone who walked in their vicinity.

Humor stole into her, and she couldn't help smirking.

"Farmer, huh?" she teased.

He gave her a sideways glance but made no comment, which broadened her grin. There was something about this man. He had a calming way about him, which didn't make sense. She shouldn't feel so relaxed with a virtual stranger.

Maybe it was that he'd gone out on a limb to keep her safe, despite never having met her before. Anyone who did that must be a good person. And out of anyone he could have spoken with, Rory would have been her best bet too.

Feeling much better about the situation, she took him to the ground level. Tower guards glanced warily at them, but they allowed them through when she requested to visit the garden. She was one of the few on the approved list. So far, in her months visiting the garden, she'd only ever bumped into Rory, Nero, and another from her time called the Tinker. She was a petite, curly and black-haired woman with an incredible mind. She wasn't much of a conversationalist, but the MIT genius had recreated a gramophone from memory so Melody could record a beat to layer over her performance.

At the rear of the lobby was a nondescript door leading to a long-walled path. After a quarter-mile of walking, they arrived at a wrought iron gate. The smell of fresh cut lawn, gardenias, and sunshine warmed her soul.

The gate creaked open on rusty hinges.

Inside was like another world. Greenery. Birds twittered. Water flowed from a fountain. Hedges were in a maze formation. There were facsimiles of great marble statues she recognized from history. They couldn't be the real thing. Too much time had passed, and the stone would have crumbled... unless they'd been frozen too? Was that even possible?

When her feet touched the lawn, invigorating energy rushed into her, and she smiled, tilting her face to a sun that suddenly felt warmer. "God, I love it here."

Forrest's breath hitched behind her.

"I know," she sympathized. "It's a lot to take in. I always come here when I'm feeling blocked. Just a second in this garden makes me feel so inspired. I can't believe he keeps it all to himself. There should be a law against it, but, you know... he *is* the law."

At Forrest's silence, she turned to check on him. He braced himself on the hedge, eye closed, frowning, and swaying on his feet.

"Forrest." Her brows knitted in the middle. "Are you well?"

He nodded.

"Are you sure?" She stepped toward him, but he straightened before she could offer a hand.

"Just a little dizzy. I'm fine." He gestured for her to keep walking.

She wasn't convinced. Maybe those injuries were worse than he let on. Her gaze skated to the wound on his neck only to find it was almost gone. She could have sworn it was worse the night before. He gestured forward again. "After you."

"Right," she said, shaking off the weirdness. "On we go. I like to work from the center of the maze. There's a stone bench near a fountain, and despite it being a little gruesome, the space is just so divine to work from."

He scrutinized the area. "You think anyone else is here?"

"Probably not. It's early, and only a select few are allowed."

"I'll bet," he mumbled.

"What?"

"Nothing. Lead the way."

A little confused, she frowned at him before turning and heading into the short maze. After a few minutes of walking, they emerged at the center of the manicured garden. The roar of a large fountain seemed like it came from the minotaur statue, not the water itself. That statue was the only thing she didn't like about this place. It had a collar connected to manacles on thick wrists and ankles. But the weirdest thing was the shiny tar coating its body and the black feathers stuck to it.

It reminded Melody of the old stories about sinners being covered in tar and doused with feathers before being forced to walk the streets in shame.

This was meant as a reminder to whomever Nero invited so that they remembered the truly abhorrent nature of their enemy. For was there anything more beastly than a half-man half-bull covered in sin?

Melody felt shame when she looked at it.

Fine mist tickled her face, and she forced herself to take in the rest of the garden with a big sigh. Determined to keep her positive outlook, she sat on a stone bench against a rose hedge. The fragrance was both heady and intoxicating. Somehow, the roses were always in bloom. The gardener must be a miracle worker.

Melody opened her notebook and waited for Forrest. "I'm ready."

His gaze was glued to a small robin twittering on the fountain's basin. Although she often heard birds here, they were rare and shy, preferring to stick to the shelter of the trees on the garden outskirts. They rarely flew. Probably terrified any sky would razor them like the net high above them.

Forrest slowly walked toward it, then paused. "The birds are trapped here."

She nodded. "The netting that keeps the Tainted out also traps birds in. I suppose it's a necessary evil for our safety."

That's what Nero said, anyway.

Forrest's expression quickly morphed into a glower. The bird and he stared at each other. Then it twittered and flapped its wings before disappearing. Still tense and gruff, he joined Melody on the bench and rubbed his palms down his thick thighs, clearly ruminating over something. When he didn't speak, she assumed it was because of the story he was about to tell. He'd tried to keep it basic last night, but she had to gently encourage him to go deep into the darkest part of his soul.

She wished it wasn't so, but there was no other choice.

"So," she said. "If you start with anything about your experience with the Tainted, I can let you know if I've heard it or not, and then we can go from there."

"Fae are not tainted. I don't know where that load of kuturi-shit comes from." His jaw clenched as he glared at the minotaur.

"But hasn't their blood been contaminated by whatever toxin left them with mutations? Or radiation?" That's what they'd told her, anyway. "Can't we all somehow catch it?"

His brows lifted. "You think being fae is some kind of disease?"

Suddenly the words that had left her mouth sounded so stupid. Multiple humans had returned to Crystal City from those lands. None of them had sprouted horns or mutated. Reapers visited frequently. They spilled fae blood, so if the claim was valid... Melody suddenly felt sick. How could she not have seen this truth before?

"I guess it's easy to believe something everyone says," she mumbled. "I suppose it doesn't matter whether we get infected. There's still danger out there. I still have tales to tell. We've all heard about the monsters like the minotaur there. We've heard about the evil queen and her humiliating degradation of humans. We know about vampires. About a lot, I suppose. I guess I need something we haven't heard of before."

How did he know what she didn't know unless she told him everything? Flustered, she smoothed her hair.

Forrest braced his elbows on his knees and stared at the minotaur. "You know about the Sluagh?"

"Of course. They're the worst. They stole human souls all those years ago during the war."

"About the Ring at Cornucopia?"

She flicked open her notebook and turned to a page of notes. "That's the gladiator-style arena criminals are sent, right?"

"I don't know what else to tell you."

"There has to be something... anything. What about your personal experience? It might be hard to talk about your time in the Autumn Court, but if we start there, I might find something to use."

"You want to glorify my trauma."

"Not glorify. Use it to warn others. To save them. I need something that will tug at their heartstrings. Something emotional."

"You want to humiliate me all over again," he pointed out. "I ask you, who is the biggest monster—the fae or you?"

Her lips clamped shut as shame washed over her. "You're right. I know," she said in a small voice. "It's deplorable that I'm asking you to relive your nightmares. But if I don't give the president something new, he's..."

She didn't even want to think of it. No use talking about it. But Forrest's head snapped her way nevertheless.

"He *threatened* you?" Forrest's voice was a snarling, deliberate, lethal promise. "*That* is the man you follow?"

"It's not like I have a choice. It's either him or the Tainted." She flung her hand toward the wall. "You of all people know how bad it is out there."

He stared at his feet, a permanent scowl on his face. "Fine. I'll tell you a story."

Thank God. She hated the way this made her feel and just wanted it done.

She opened her notebook again and waited.

"There was a boy," he said, short and clipped. "Who shared the dungeon with me."

"A boy," she repeated as she wrote.

"He was a prince—"

"A prince." She wrote enthusiastically.

"—locked up by his family for days with no visitors. He was the seventh legitimate heir of the long-lived reign. His sole purpose was to be the family's sacrifice to the Well."

"The Well demands a sacrifice?"

He shook his head. "The Order of the Well needs Guardians, but the only way to receive the ability to hold forbidden items like metal and plastic is to be judged and deemed worthy by the Well. Can you imagine giving this advantage to evildoers?"

"No, I suppose not."

"This initiation involves diving into a specific lake where, let's just say, more die than survive. The royal family thought that sacrificing one of their own would endear their subjects to them. One royal equaled thousands of commoners. When the Order came once a year to demand tributes, they could let everyone else pay without a guilty conscience because they had also promised to do so."

"That's horrible."

"That's the Unseelie for you. What should be voluntary was not." He scrubbed his face. "But I suppose the Seelie behaved similarly until the new king changed things."

"New king?"

"He was a Guardian before he took the throne, and his mate is a —" He studied her for a minute before continuing. "He's married to a human like you—like us."

"I don't understand."

"Queen Ada is a powerful healer, but she's also a human who's thawed from your time."

Melody's eyes widened. "She's magic too?"

"There are more humans who come from our time that have access to the Well."

"Did you?" she asked.

He went quiet as he considered her question, and then he shrugged.

She scoffed. "Well, I'm not. That's for certain."

"Until you're connected to the Well, you might not know if you have the potential."

She tapped her pencil on her chin. "I wonder how many of us are out there? And if all of us have potential."

"Only a handful out there, just like in here." He cleared his throat. "Or so I heard."

"I didn't know that. I'd heard through the grapevine that some humans from our time went out there, but I was told they'd all died."

Her thoughts tripped on things that weren't quite adding up. Was Forrest lying to her? Or was someone like her truly living her best life as a queen? Why did Forrest come here seeking refuge if it was so good out there? Surely a man would be able to protect himself more than a woman—but Ada had become a queen.

"Is she coerced?" Melody asked, thinking of how the Captain

had treated her. Some partnerships weren't consensual. Forrest himself had been forced to do the bidding of fae.

He looked at Melody as if she'd sprouted fur. "Of course, she's not. They're mated. *Well-blessed* mated. Everyone knows that."

"I don't know what *that* means."

"It means the Well has approved of their partnership. It's seen into their souls and has declared them a perfect match. As a reward, it allows them to share each other's emotions and mana. Sometimes they can speak mind-to-mind." He turned to the fountain. "Although that last one is rare and only spoken about in history books."

"Soulmates," she whispered. "That doesn't sound too bad. Kind of romantic."

Realizing they were getting off course, she put her pencil to paper. "You were saying about the prince?"

Forrest stretched his long legs out and gave a resigned sigh. "The forgotten prince of autumn elves was the youngest in his family. From the moment he was born, the royal family ignored him. Even his mother left his care to the wet nurses and brownies. There was a time he tried everything in his power to get their attention, from begging to gifting to performing. They ignored him. What was the point of loving something fated to die?" He cleared his throat. "By the time I met the child, he was locked in a cell because he'd snapped. He lost his mind trying to get their attention, even if it was to infuriate them."

Melody's heart ached for the boy. "How could they be so cruel?"

"The potential for cruelty is in everyone," he countered, and when she didn't comment, he continued. "Locked up for days on end, ignored by all, the boy's only friends were the animals he could speak to with his mind."

"Only friend until you came along."

He turned to her, and something shrewd passed over his expression. "Right."

"Sorry," she said. "I keep interrupting. Continue."

He shrugged. "It's fine. Do you need more?"

"I guess." She flipped through her notes. "Whatever you can give me."

Another big exhale from him before he spoke. "While he was locked away, the elf spent a lot of time living in the minds of animals until there were times he wasn't sure which species he belonged to. The worst part was that no one came for him. No one cared. He was just a shell living on straw in the dungeon. No one cared that he didn't speak or wash or eat. They only brought him out, cleaned him, and kept him alive for official occasions. For appearances." The word came out through a sneer, but then something sparkled in his eye. "Then someone turned up who was treated worse than him. A three-year-old boy—a bastard half-brother. Suddenly he wasn't alone anymore. He had someone to play with. Someone to care for. Someone who cared back."

Melody shut her book. "I feel so bad for them."

"Don't feel bad. They escaped."

"What happened to them?"

"The prince met his fate. He was tossed in the ceremonial lake but didn't die as the royal family assumed. He survived and came out stronger than all of them."

"And the half-brother?"

"He jumped into the lake after him. He also survived. The Well rewards those pure of heart and punishes those who aren't."

"And what happened to the rest of the Autumn Court?"

"They're still there." He stared hard at the fountain. "Still wreaking Unseelie havoc."

The story wasn't fearsome enough to satisfy Nero's blood thirst, but she couldn't bring herself to ask for more. That he'd shared was poignant, and she sensed it meant more than she could understand. She'd asked for a horrifying story, and he gave her that. From how he stared at the fountain, she knew it was a lot to dredge up. Seeing children treated so poorly must have been horrible. But if that was the most palatable thing he could recall to tell, then she couldn't bring herself to ask for more. It wasn't right.

She couldn't do this anymore.

It all seemed too personal.

"Thank you," she said softly. "For sharing. I'll do my best to honor the story. Did the boy have a name?"

"Nobody gave him a name until he joined the Order. If they had to call him, it was by his purpose—Sacrifice."

She nodded. "Okay. I think I have something to work with. At least a start. I just need a few moments by myself to sort through things and put the story to a beat."

"You want to be left alone?"

"If you don't mind."

He stood up. "I'll go for a walk. But I'll be in the garden. Shout if you need me."

Dopamine washed through her. She swallowed to stop herself from launching into his arms. There was something so tragically attractive about him. The passion in his voice, the determination on his expression, the scars, and the missing eye. The torture he'd no doubt suffered.

It all fed into the notion that this man was loyal to a fault, and he hated to see *anyone* suffer. She had the sense that his respect would be hard won, but once he gave it, he would never take it back. Looking at his strong hands, the same hands that had pushed the Captain down to his knees for her, she realized that she might be one of the lucky few.

She opened the notebook and hoped she wouldn't blow it.

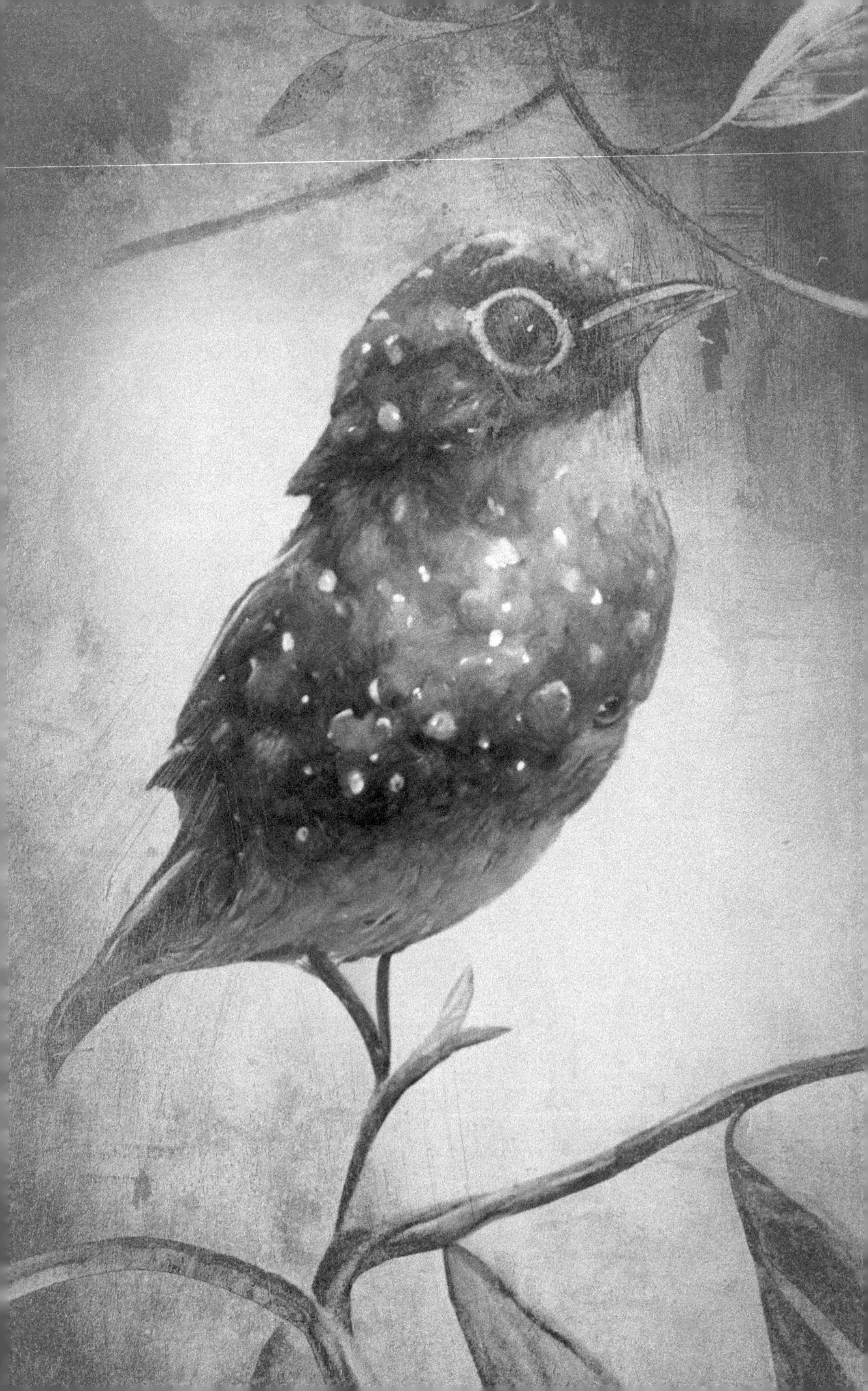

CHAPTER
THIRTEEN

Forrest hadn't meant to tell Melody his story, but it tumbled out when she asked about the worst thing that had happened to him. Having someone listen avidly to him was a foreign experience. But she sat there with her beautiful eyes never leaving his face.

To be seen in such a way rocked him to the core, and he wanted more. Craved it. He wanted to tear open his soul and let it all pour out. He wanted her to make music from his heartache just so she would look at him in that intense, beautiful way.

In Elphyne, they said human artists saw the world as no one else did. They appreciated every grain of sand, every ray of sunshine, and every iota of life—from the dark to the good. There weren't many fae musicians—not like Melody. Forrest assumed it was because the fae lifespan was so long that they became dull to the simple joys and details. In comparison, the human lifespan was fleeting but saturated. Probably why fae kidnapped human artists.

Melody would be a treasure in Elphyne just as she was here.

Walking through the garden now, feeling the Well trickle into him like an old friend, he should have been ecstatic. But he felt bereft, as though the life-giving magic was nowhere in sight. And it was all because he wanted to be back there with her, basking under her attention like a mermaid on sunny rocks.

Forrest forced himself to focus on the robin chipping its way from hedge to hedge before him. Never fully flying, just coasting. He hated how creatures born to fly had their wings clipped because of fear.

Follow me... the little robin chirped in Forrest's mind. He followed it through the hedged garden path. Forrest touched leaves on plants and inspected the damp soil as he walked closer to the high garden boundary wall—mana still flowed, but it weakened the further he went from the center of the maze.

The rest of Crystal City was desecrated land. The Well refused to flow under so much metal and plastic. But here... here it was alive. Perhaps Nero orchestrated this haven on purpose. He knew access to the Well was beneficial to him. It would give him power over humanity if he had a secret supply. And if what Melody said was true—access to this garden was only given to his daughter, Willow, Melody, and another human from her time called the Tinker.

He would stake his bow and arrow on this restriction so Nero could remain young. He truly wanted the best of both worlds. He'd somehow figured out how to hold a supply of mana within his body despite no connection to the Well. But how much and for how long was another question.

Hurry up.

Forrest rolled his eyes. Robins had short tempers to match their little minds. He'd been surprised to see it when he'd walked into the garden. The robin was timid at first. The birds trapped in Crystal City were traumatized. They feared humans.

But he wasn't human.

Cresting the corner of a long hedge, Forrest came to the high stone wall blocking them from the rest of the city. He ran his hand over the uneven surface and then turned back to the angry bird chirping at him from another hedge.

This way, dumb-dumb.

He narrowed his eyes at it. "Call me dumb-dumb again, and I won't help you escape."

It stopped chirping and puffed its chest feathers out. They stared at each other. Then it tweeted and skipped to a fallen log pushed up against the wall.

Here. It hopped around a hollow part of the log. A small pool of water gathered there from the recent rain. It was big enough for Forrest to see his reflection. It would work for the communication spell he needed to cast. Mana flow was weaker here but not completely cut off.

"Thank you," he murmured, and then he told the bird that to get through the barbed wire nets blanketing the city, he would have to take over their minds and pilot their bodies to safety.

Sky cuts, it protested.

"Yes, but not when I do it," he explained. "I can get you through."

But the robin flapped its wings and hopped away.

Forrest understood fear. Maybe it would come back, maybe not. Right now, he had more important things to do. He swept his surroundings with both his sight and his advanced hearing. Melody was still near the water fountain, a few hundred feet away. Her pencil scribbled softly. She hummed under her breath and tapped her foot.

Before he became entranced in her new song, he used his mana to cast privacy wards around him so no one heard his following conversation. Connecting through mana long distances only worked in water and with a blooded relative. Aeron and Forrest shared the same father. The Well recognized their familial link.

He crouched and scratched his palm on the log. The moment his blood hit the small puddle, an unnatural blue light glimmered on the surface. He hoped someone around Aeron would notice the light because if he was still... what—he scowled at his callous train of thought—*still mourning the loss of his hearing?* Perhaps even the loss of the only home he'd ever been welcome in, because if Aeron couldn't be a Guardian... he might not be allowed to stay at the Order.

Of course Aeron would be upset.

He had the right to his feelings over the matter. Forrest should be there with him, guiding him as he did when Aeron was young—protecting him as they grew up in a cruel court. It wasn't until they were both Guardians and well into adulthood that their roles switched. Aeron had become the wiser, more academic of the two, while Forrest was content to be with his animals and forget about the world turning.

A likeness of Aeron's scowling face formed in the puddle. He looked down at the body of water closest to him when the connection had solidified. From the stone walls and cupboards behind his head, and the soapy suds on his hands as he beckoned someone over, he was in the kitchen washing dishes.

Forrest wanted to laugh. The brownies would have been mighty pissed off about the party. It was an honor to have them work at the house of the Twelve, but every cadre member knew that if you abused that honor, you'd have to do the cleaning yourselves.

Leaf came into view. The tall, blond elf had his hair neatly brushed and long around his shoulders. It didn't look like he was washing dishes. He'd be the one barking orders and setting the punishment.

"How goes the mission?" Leaf asked, his deep voice slightly warbled through the water.

"She's here," he replied. "She's unharmed."

"Clarke and Rush will be happy to hear." Leaf's brows drew together, suddenly holding up his finger to indicate Forrest should wait, then pointed at someone out of view. "Did I say you could stop?"

Curses could be heard in the distance. It wasn't Aeron. It must have been one of the crows. This time, Forrest couldn't hold the smile.

That reminded him.

"One of the Sluagh fed on a partygoer the night I left," Forrest said when Leaf turned back to him. "I saw it as I stepped through the portal."

"We know. I found the body." He shook his head, disgusted. "The Order is falling into a state of disrepute."

"The Sluagh told me to pass a message onto Clarke that she should stop trying to rescue Willow, or she'll only make it worse. Whatever that meant."

The tendons in Leaf's jaw flexed. "What?"

"Rush or Shade didn't tell you?"

"No."

Shade was not a fan of Leaf, so that might explain why he'd avoided speaking to him. But none of the others had mentioned it. Something was off. "Clarke said not to worry about it, but I don't know. You should speak with the Six and find out what they meant."

Leaf's nostrils flared. For all his aplomb and confidence, even he hated speaking with the Six. Simply walking up to their doorstep was inviting trouble.

"Maybe ask Violet," Forrest suggested. "The Sluagh seem intrigued with the new Well-blessed women."

"Indigo won't let her near them after the voyeuristic act they pulled. None of the vamps want their mates near them—especially Shade. I'll go. They'll speak to me, or I'll make them."

He would *make* the Sluagh speak to him? No one had that power except maybe Jasper, who was busy being High King of the Seelie. It was offhand comments like this that made Forrest think Leaf wasn't who he said he was.

"Tell me about Willow," Leaf demanded. "And Aurora."

"I haven't had a conversation with Willow yet. She's kept somewhere by Aurora—Rory. I have to gain their trust. The people here believe my cover. For now. But I've..." He decided to keep his slip up with the Captain to himself. That irrational behavior wouldn't happen again. "I've got something in the works. This might take longer than we planned, but now I know there's a place I can access the Well. I can update you."

Leaf's blue eyes seemed bluer in the water as they narrowed. "I was about to ask about that. How did you gain access while in a desecrated place? Rush never mentioned it."

"Nero has a very private walled garden. I don't think it's visible from the outside. Whatever he's doing here to keep access to the Well, it's working. He's also got some kind of gift he used to test if I was fae or human."

Leaf paused, considering. "Are you sure you passed the test?"

"I was completely cut from the Well. Even my Guardian mark was missing. It fucking hurt to lose that access, so yeah, I'm pretty sure I was as human looking as you can get. I don't know what Nero hoped to achieve searching for the connection while I was nowhere near access, but maybe he doesn't know as much as we think he does about how mana flows."

Leaf's gaze turned distant. "Do you know whether Nero's gift is innate, like the females, or is it stolen?"

"I don't know."

"Find out."

Forrest nodded.

"What's next, then?" Leaf asked.

"I keep earning their trust. I find a way to get close to Willow without her blowing my cover, and then I get out of here."

"And with Rory."

"She's going to be the hardest to convince."

"She's part fae. We made a deal with Maebh to bring her back."

"But—"

"Forrest," he warned. "The only reason Maebh called her monstrous pet back to heel was because of this deal enforced by mana. Find a way to make it work. The next time you connect this way, you might not get through. The taint on the Well is thickening. We need to wrap this mission up so everyone is back safe, and we can focus on—" He bit off his words, but Forrest knew what he was going to say. *So we can focus on more important things.* Leaf could be a cold son-of-a-witch, but he was a good team leader.

Fuck. "Fine."

"Good. Do what you can to expedite things and then get back. If you can't convince her, bribe her. If you can't bribe her, drug her. If you can't drug her, knock her out."

"Yeah, I get it. Use every tool in my kit."

With that last word, Leaf called Aeron back to cut the connection. Forrest didn't even have a chance to ask if he was okay before the puddle went dark. He straightened and kicked the log, splashing water everywhere, which in turn made him more frustrated. But he swallowed it and dropped the privacy wards.

As soon as sound filtered back, he knew something was wrong. Melody's quiet humming and tapping had stopped.

They weren't alone in the garden.

CHAPTER
FOURTEEN

Cornelius Rutherford was the general of the Crystal City army. He was called the Captain not because of his station but because of his ability to captain a ship. The seas and rivers had been a friend to humanity over the past few hundred years, but now that the feral Tainted were close to figuring out humans traveled by boat to conduct raids, these avenues were drying up.

It wasn't only by boat. Using a particular invention allowed them to portal an entire ship to another location. But the special instilled fuel that ran this invention was also drying up and getting harder to obtain.

Wind buffeted his face as he stood on the city docks and gave the new airships a last look. They were almost complete. The weapons were done. All they needed were a few final critical ingredients before they could launch their fleet into the sky and start reclaiming the land of their ancestors.

"Cornelius," President Nero said, coming up behind him.

"Mr. President."

"Thank you for meeting me out here on this windy day. This conversation is best had outside."

Away from prying eyes and ears, he meant. Cornelius raised his brows and rocked on his feet. Must be classified. Perfect timing. This allowed him to fish for information regarding the upcoming Phoenix Ball. He was done waiting for that ungrateful woman, but he refused to let her win. He would see to it that she was his, and then he would have a partner befitting his station. She knew how to perform. She knew how to bend the will of the people with her words. Nero knew it, so he kept a close eye on her.

But she had to be married, and the president had remained opposed to the idea for—Cornelius's mind clouded when he tried to recall how long that had been. No matter. Ms. Melody's bad attitude would soon be trained out of her, and before the following year's ball, he would have a picture-perfect wife just as he had always planned.

"What is it you wish to discuss?" he asked, hating how he let the president go first. Always first.

"I have received a formal complaint that you assaulted Ms. Melody in the hallway and paid off Tower Guards for the privilege."

"What?" he spat. "*Assaulted* her? It is not I who should have the complaint against me but that one-eyed newcomer. He—"

"I don't care," he clipped.

"But—"

"It doesn't matter." Nero's dark, soulless eyes scoured the tumultuous sea. "I need you to hunt for more fuel sources. Bring them back, and you will have your wife. I will personally see to it."

Cornelius clamped his lips shut. *Interesting.* "Do you have a location, or do I need to repeat what we did last time?"

Nero handed him a piece of paper. Cornelius unfolded it and read. He let the information soak in and then pulled out his flint lighter and set the paper on fire. A gust of wind caught the smoldering letter and took it out to sea, but it was ash before it hit the water.

"This could take longer than two weeks," Cornelius said.

"And?"

"The Phoenix Ball is before that."

Nero did not comment.

"And?" Cornelius prompted.

"And what?"

Cornelius blinked at his leader and wanted to slap him across the face. Clearly, he had no concern over Cornelius making it back for the ball in time to claim his bride.

When Nero perceived the insult on Cornelius's face, he raised a challenging brow and said, "Then we need to be back with what I want before then."

"Is this punishment?"

"This is something that needs to be done."

It was punishment as plain as day. Cornelius opened his mouth to say so, but Nero's mood swiftly changed from agreeable to murderous in the blink of an eye. And then he realized that Nero had said "we."

"You're coming with me?" Cornelius asked.

"Is there a problem?"

There were no words to describe the chill that ran through Cornelius's body, and he felt compelled to say, "No, Mr. President."

"Good. We leave after this evening's performance."

As Nero walked away, his footsteps thudded on the wooden dock, and hate grew like an infestation of vines around Cornelius's chest. All that man needed to do was look Cornelius's way, and he forgot his wits. The notion made him cringe and simmer with barely restrained retaliation.

Shaking it off, he brooded over the new mission, turning possibilities and scenarios in his mind. It was doable. As long as there were no surprises, he would be back in time, and the president would follow through with his promise. He was a megalomaniac, but he wasn't a fool. He knew there would be trouble if he got Cornelius on his wrong side.

Cornelius owned half the docks. He controlled the seas. He brought in illegal fae goods and raided for rare materials. Without him, Nero didn't stand a chance of winning the coming war. He certainly wouldn't have the fuel that powered his secret portal.

He would do what Nero asked, but not before he visited a certain complaining musician. If he wanted the harbinger under his control, he needed to start teaching her lessons on loyalty now.

The president didn't give a shit about the one-eyed man, so if he got in Cornelius's way again, he would suffer for it.

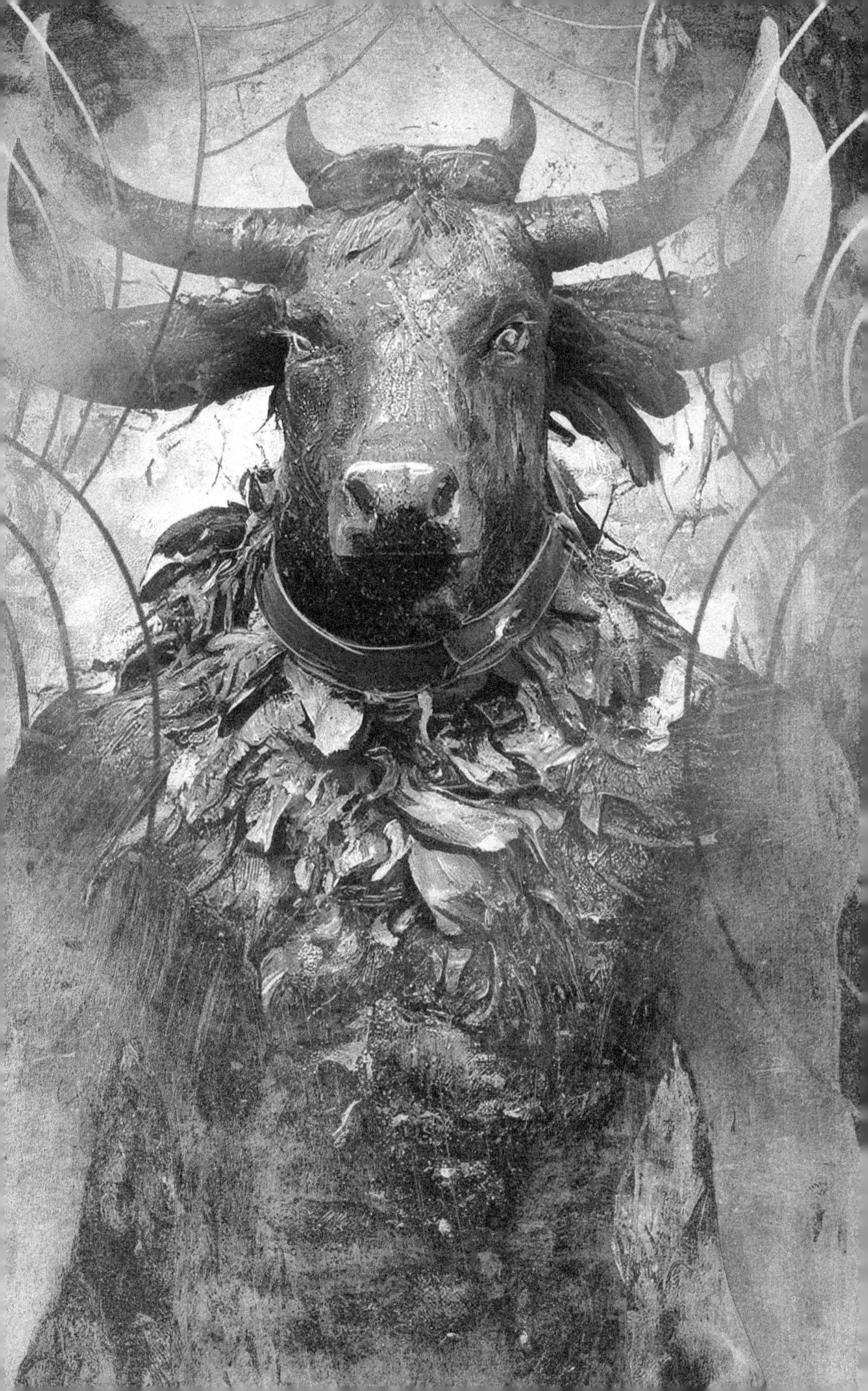

CHAPTER
FIFTEEN

Melody found herself halfway to a good song when she stopped, put her pencil down, and closed her notebook. If she continued, the song would be good enough for tonight's performance, but try as she might, she couldn't squash the feeling of wrongness in her gut.

Singing about the humiliation of a child was not something she wanted to do, in any sense, in any time. Especially for propaganda. She didn't care if it fed into the narrative Nero wanted. It was too real. Too raw. There had to be a line, and even though he might not have intended it, Forrest had just taught Melody that the enemy had a human face too.

"I've been looking for you."

Ice slid down Melody's spine. She twisted to see the Captain stride into the clearing with a determined look. His cheeks were windburned. His short hair and mustache stood on end. The metal embellishments on his uniform epaulets jingled as he walked. In his official uniform. He must have been outside the Tower and had come straight here.

Unable to hide her true feelings, she shuffled back on the stone bench and swallowed audibly before forcing a smile and greeting him.

"I wasn't aware you frequented these gardens."

How did he gain access? Melody was so sure he wasn't on the approved list.

"There is no place I can't gain access to in this world, Melody. There is no use hiding from me." He stopped before her, looked down his nose, and rocked on his feet like he did when he pondered something she wouldn't like. And when he flicked open his jacket and put his hands on his thin belt, she felt sick.

Again?

Why wouldn't he just leave it be? How could men be so clueless in reading the room? Melody wanted to believe it was a flaw existing only this time, but the truth was, she'd always had this sort of interaction. She was a magnet for losers and deadbeats. She used to think it just came with the territory of her career, but maybe it was more than that. Thinking back to that disgusting man who had propositioned her mother, she thought perhaps it was inherited.

And then she saw the revolver holstered under the Captain's arm. With his jacket open and wide, the copper-trimmed grip glinted. It wasn't a typical revolver. Cogs and wires made her think it had been modified. But for what purpose? All hope fled her soul, and she shrank. What was the point in fighting when the cycle would repeat?

"You know," he said, peering at her with his head cocked. "I walked here thinking you needed a lesson in humiliation. To learn what it feels like to be forced to your knees. But seeing you here, alone, perhaps you'll make the right choice, and I will forgive all. Take my belt. I had it made especially to fit your size. Wear it while I'm gone, and we will resume the inevitable path to our future when I return." The belt slid out from his trousers like a slithering snake. "Wear it, or *feel* it."

Melody gaped. She didn't know which part of that to be more furious about. He had it made *specially* to fit her size? Wear it or *feel* it? Know what it feels like to be on her knees?

She wanted to slap him across the smug face with her notebook. She wanted to make *him* feel something. So much was wrong with this new world, and it made her so sad. With trembling limbs, she rose from the bench and stood before him.

There were so many words on the tip of her tongue, but then he subtly shifted his posture to emphasize the revolver. Self-preservation stopped her words from blustering out.

He held out the belt, and she froze as her old insecurities crept in.

This wasn't her world.

It hadn't been for two thousand years. She should stop trying to force a square shape into a round hole.

"You have friends here, right?" he asked. "That band of yours. Those two men, their not-so-secret love, and that tiny woman with a big voice. What was her name… Caroline?"

Melody's blood turned to ice. "Leave them out of this."

"I can do more than that," he said, stepping into her breathing space and lowering his voice. "I can protect them. The president knows this and has agreed to my betrothal request. It's only a matter of time. Take my belt and save some trouble—*gah!*"

He looked down and shook his leg. *What the hell?* Melody frowned and stepped back, but the Captain continued to shake and then swat himself.

Oh, God. She covered her mouth. Little black cockroaches scuttled up his legs in droves.

He dropped his belt and stomped his feet, cursing profusely as they fell and scattered or burst beneath his boot. Melody hopped onto the stone bench just as she glimpsed a familiar shade of auburn in her periphery. Forrest casually walked into the clearing, his hands in his pockets, his attention squarely on the Captain.

"You," the Captain growled at Forrest. He swatted the infestation. "*You* did this."

Forrest's lips curved, and it was the first time Melody had seen devious intent in his expression. When he'd protected her that first time, his face had been full of determination and pure anger. This wasn't even the kind of uncorked rage the Captain had. It was the kind that said Forrest would wait for centuries for the right time to inflict the worst pain. And he would enjoy it.

Forrest stared at the bugs, then lifted his gaze to the Captain. "What's that old saying... like calls to like?"

"No," the Captain declared, stomping and kicking. "You did this."

The metallic click of a revolver being cocked bounced around Melody's skull, sending her into a panic. But Forrest was already moving. He scratched something into his palm, and within seconds, shimmering air around his hand became a long, ornately carved bow—arrow already knocked and sighted at the Captain.

Tainted.

Fae.

Melody *screamed*.

The high-pitched wail was so intense that the hedge leaves shook. Birds screeched. The Captain winced, but Forrest fired his bow. His arrow struck like lightning to hit the Captain's gun. It fired as it landed. Melody ducked. Was she hit? Was anyone hit?

Stunned, she could do nothing but freeze while the Captain turned his rage-infested face toward Forrest.

"*Stop, stop,*" she whispered under her breath. "*No, no.*"

Unconcerned, Forrest stalked toward the Captain. The bow in his hand winked out of existence.

They would fight—to the death—and Melody didn't know what to do. Whose side was she on? Forrest was one of *them*, but he'd never caused her harm. The Captain was one of her own, but he'd hurt her multiple times. Panicked, she jumped off the bench and stumbled toward the Captain. Maybe she could convince him to leave. Maybe he would—

"Go," she begged, taking hold of his shoulders. "Please, Cornelius. Just turn around and leave and forget you saw us."

His eyes lowered to hers and held. Something shifted in the atmosphere. It felt like power, and it came from *within* her. The hairs on her arms and face rippled from a wind that was not there. The Captain's dark eyes glazed over, then he nodded before turning calmly and walking out like a zombie.

Melody stood for a good two minutes watching the space he'd vacated, waiting for him to return, hardly believing what had just happened.

"I just..." she muttered. "And he just..."

"You used mana." Forrest's deep voice sounded too close behind her.

She whirled and stepped back.

He was the same man, but that ever-present wild look in his eye was alight with energy. He flexed his hands as though adrenaline still coursed through his veins, and he didn't know what to do with it.

"You lied to me," she accused.

"Yes."

"Fae can't lie."

"They normally can't." He calmly lifted his eye patch to reveal what was beneath—a perfectly functional eye to match the other. Seeing one had been arresting, but seeing both was breathtaking, just as she'd imagined. Was this the fae glamor they warned humans about? Too handsome to be real, yet too rough and sculpted from rock. It didn't make sense.

He looked at her like one does an injured animal. He spoke in calm and soothing tones. "Outside this garden, there is no connection to the Well holding me to that fae geas. I can lie like any human. Inside these garden walls, the Well flows. Ask me anything now, and I will be forced to speak the truth."

His wildness called to her. He was everything this city was not. He was the sun shining through leaves and the shadows dancing beneath. He was the chase of the predator and the teeth of the bear. Melody had never felt so... so...

"I mean you no harm," he promised. "I'm in this city to rescue a kidnapped fae child."

Melody's mind clicked into action. Child. There had been a new child that stood out from the rest. There had been something ethereal about her face and the way she had bared her teeth like a jungle cat every time she didn't want to do something Rory asked.

"The silver-haired little girl Rory has been dining with."

"Yes," he said. "She's the offspring of a Well-blessed union."

"What does that mean?" Her eyes narrowed, trying to recall what he told her that first night in her room.

"The Well approves a Well-blessed union. It cannot be bought or stolen. It just happens. It allows the mated couple to share mana and emotions. Their child is a powerful psychic. Her father is a wolf shifter—a Guardian. Her mother is like you—someone born in the old world and frozen for millennia. She has a tremendous capacity to hold mana."

Melody shook her head. This went against everything she knew to be true. The fae were animals. Horrible, terrible, twisted creatures who treated humans like dirt. But if that was so, why would a woman have had a child with one of them? Or become a queen, for that matter?

"No." She waved her finger between them. "She must have been forced."

"You don't believe that, do you?" Forrest stepped forward, and she stepped back. "Melody. Look at me. I've done nothing but protect you since I met you. Do you think I'm so terrible?"

Her breath came in fast as her mind whirled over recent events. "The bugs. The cockroaches. The bird... you somehow controlled them. Right?"

He shrugged. "Each fae has unique gifts. Most of mine are linked to animals."

"What the hell are you?"

His brows raised. "That's offensive."

"You know what I mean."

"I'm an elf."

"Where are your pointed ears? Are you glamoured?"

His face became stone. "I cut the tips off to appear human."

"The scars... the eye?"

"All a ruse so I can get in here and bring Willow home to her parents."

"Why couldn't they come themselves?"

"Believe me; they wanted to." His eyes lifted to the sky. "Still might do it if I don't come home soon, but they have a blue, glowing mating mark over their arms that is hard to remove. They wouldn't be able to hide the glow." He touched a fresh scar beneath his left eye. "My Guardian mark was cut out. It might grow back. Once the Well approves of you, it's never changed its mind. You'll understand soon enough."

"Me?"

"Your gift, I'll wager, involves your voice."

Her gift?

"I felt your scream down to my bones. It instilled terror into my very blood, and if you continued, I imagine we would have all been on our knees begging for mercy." He lowered the patch over his eye, once again reclaiming the identity of a simple human. "And let's not forget you just sent the Captain on his merry way without so much of a whisper of complaint from him."

The realization of what he said dawned on her. She could control people with her voice. *Her voice.* It was the only explanation for the Captain's sudden turnaround. He'd been in a rage, about to murder Forrest, who in turn wanted to murder him.

"I'm so confused," she said, holding her head in her hand. Forrest—a fae—was nothing like she'd been taught. He was... normal—sort of.

"Let me explain where we have more privacy. Please," he said. "The life of a child is at stake."

Her gaze snapped up. Met his. "How can I believe a single word you say?"

"Ask me anything," he replied. "While I'm connected to the Well, my answer will be true."

"I still won't know it's a lie."

"I could kill you and be done with it, but I won't." He collected her fallen notebook and handed it to her. "You know this."

She licked her lips. The notebook. The song.

"The boy in your story," she said. "Was it you?"

"Yes," he answered, and her heart broke.

"Oh, Forrest."

"I don't want your pity."

"You just want to rescue a child."

"Yes. And..." He seemed to turn something over in his mind.

"You said you wouldn't lie."

"I have to return to Elphyne with Willow *and* Rory."

"You're kidnapping her?"

"More like returning her to her family. She is the granddaughter of the Unseelie High Queen. She is half fae."

"Her father had an affair with one of the Taint—the fae?"

"Yes. And I don't think it was consensual. It's a long story. I'll tell you whatever you want later. Someone is coming."

"He's back?" Fear rippled through her.

"No, it's... Willow and Rory." His eye widened. "Don't say anything about this. Rory knows nothing about her heritage."

And Rory was as hateful toward the fae as her father was. "I understand, but I want in."

"What?"

"I'll help you on one condition. You take my band and me with you."

Horror crossed over his expression. "That's impossible."

"Say yes now while you can't lie, or I'm—"

"Yes," he clipped the instant Willow tore into the clearing, her silver hair flying behind her.

Hot on her heels, Rory arrived but stopped short. Her shrewd gaze landed on Melody before settling on Willow. The child had frozen like a statue. She stared at the spot Forrest had vacated—but he was nowhere in sight.

Gone.

Like a ghost.

Melody wondered if she'd imagined it all, but Willow seemed to sense he'd been there. If she said something, she would blow his cover. It was too early to reveal his identity. Rory would find a way to kill him.

"You must be Willow," Melody exclaimed and ran to the girl, cutting her off before getting to Forrest.

She blinked at Melody. "Aunty?"

Aunty?

"Sorry," Rory said through gritted teeth. "I think she calls everyone that. Wait. How did you know her name?"

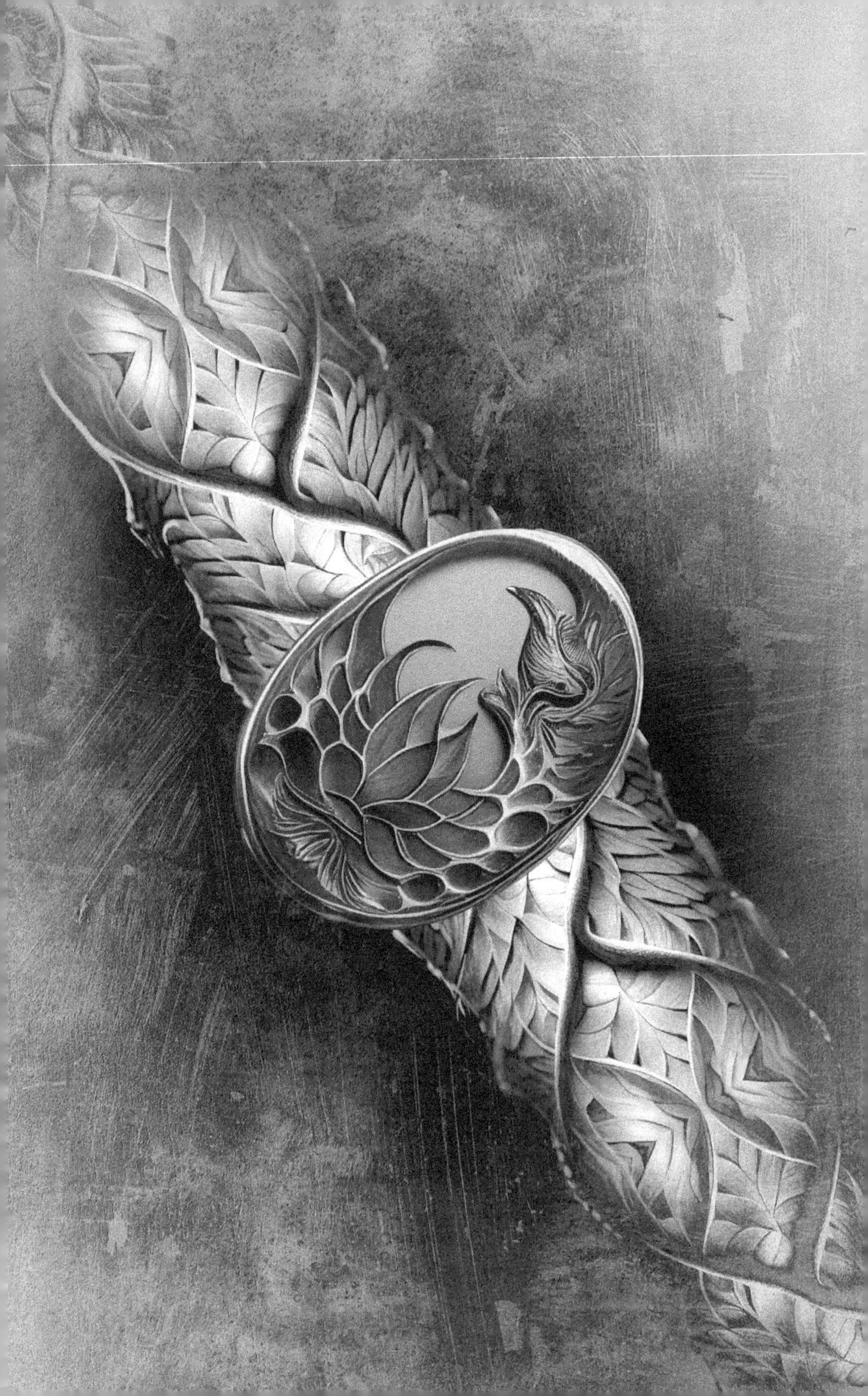

CHAPTER
SIXTEEN

Forrest listened to Melody converse with Rory and Willow from a distance. His mind whirled with everything that had just happened. He wasn't ready to reveal his presence. Leaf had been clear—they needed Rory back in Elphyne.

Silver had said Rory was the deadliest person she knew. Not woman. *Person.* Which meant she eclipsed every single soldier in this place. Apparently, Rory had studied anatomy like a healer, but for the opposite effect. To know how to end lives, not prolong them. Even in this garden, with access to his mana, he would have a bloody battle on his hands. And if Melody could connect to the Well here, then it was entirely possible Rory could too.

Her fae name was Aurora.

If she was indeed the offspring of a union between an old-world human and one of the most powerful fae in Elphyne... then it was fair to say Rory would be powerful too. Just like Willow was.

Nero knew.

He must. It was why this garden was built—to keep his access to the Well. To foster it. To allow his daughter—his secret weapon—to remain under his thumb. Forrest had always assumed Nero stole the mana he used to keep himself young, but perhaps there was more to it. Perhaps he stole it from his daughter.

Forrest zeroed in on the conversation.

"How did you know her name?" Rory asked, the tone of her voice turning hard.

"I must have heard you say it during dinner the other day," Melody replied. "I wasn't far away."

To her credit, Melody didn't balk. Although the rules of Elphyne bound Forrest's tongue, Melody's was not.

"Hey, sugarplum," she said to Willow. "You called me aunty. Does that mean we're going to be friends?"

"Of course, dumb-dumb. But..." Willow's voice trembled. "I miss my mommy. And my other aunties. Can you sing Bish Boys like Silver did?"

"Bish Boys? Do you mean Beach Boys?" Melody's brows puckered. "How do you know about them?"

"That's enough, Willow," Rory snapped. "Go to the other side of the fountain and work on your fighting stances like I showed you last week."

"But—"

"Willow," she warned.

"Can I talk to my friends?"

"As long as you're practicing, I don't care how many imaginary friends you talk to."

"Yesss." The little girl pumped her fist in the air.

"Now."

While Melody and Rory continued to converse politely, Forrest crept closer to the opposite side of the hedge Willow had settled. He located the closest robin, closed his eyes, and entered its consciousness. Then he piloted the feathered body to where Willow practiced fighting stances like a Guardian in training.

Except these weren't Guardian battle moves. Forrest had seen Silver doing the same movements in the past. They were training Willow to be a Reaper—an assassin of fae. He lost control of his anger, and the bird chirped, drawing Willow's attention. She gasped in excitement and locked eyes with the bird.

"I see you, Uncle Forrest," she whispered cheekily. "You need a better hiding place."

Hiding place—his mind went back to when he'd found her under the stairs, and his heart clenched. It took him a moment to realize Willow's words were in his head, not whispered aloud. He straightened and placed his palm on the hedge to ground himself. Then he gave himself over entirely to the bird.

"Willow, can you hear me?"

"Yes, you're pretending to be a bird."

"I'm here to take you home."

"I miss mommy and daddy."

"I know. Be brave for a little longer while I find the safest way to get you out of here."

She didn't answer.

"Have they hurt you, Willow?"

"Aunty Rory keeps me safe, but only if I'm quiet like a mouse and practice being a warrior. I showed her my angry face. But it doesn't work inside." She gasped with excitement and faced the bird. "It works here. You wanna see?"

Her face morphed from human to fae. Blunt teeth became fangs. Round ears pointed. Claws sprung out of her fingertips as she snarled. The robin Forrest puppeteered chirped, frightened. Forrest's loss of control over the bird wasn't normal. He flinched. Maybe the taint on the Well affected his complete domination of the bird's mind.

"Willow!" Rory shouted. "Leave the bird alone."

"Whoops." Willow shifted back to human.

"Don't say anything about me being here. Okay?"

When no answer came, he almost went over the hedge so he could speak with her face to face. The taint could be doing anything to him or the bird.

Black ink swam around his magical reach, knocking on the edges like an unwanted visitor. It might trap his mind inside the bird or shove him into another's consciousness. Cautious, he withdrew from the bird's mind as Willow whispered, "I can't leave. Aunty Rory needs me."

"Is that what she told you?" he sent from his mind.

No answer.

"Willow, don't listen to a word they say. They want to use your gift to tell the future, and then they want to use what you tell them to hurt the fae."

Still no answer.

"Willow," Rory barked. "Stop playing in the fountain."

Time was up. Rory and Melody were finished talking. At least Willow was safe. She wasn't hurt or abused. That Forrest knew of. But her growing loyalty toward her kidnapper was not good. The sooner they got out of there, the better. And to do that, Forrest had to find a way to get Rory on their side.

A HUGE PART of Forrest wanted to stay in the garden and escort Melody back to her rooms, but he wasn't ready to deal with Rory yet. There were too many pieces of the puzzle he needed to work over first, so he had to leave before he was discovered.

Loitering outside the garden in the foyer would only attract attention from the guards. He went ahead of Melody and broke into her rooms, hoping that whatever she'd done to the Captain would hold and that no one would sound the alarm and hunt him down. He also hoped that no matter what Melody had learned in the garden, *she* would keep her promise.

To help him get Willow and Rory out of there.

He sat on the sofa and helped himself to the fresh food on the table while he considered his options.

He'd promised to take Melody and her band into Elphyne—but none of them were warriors. How could they possibly help him during a battle? He turned over his conversation with her, wondering if there was a loophole he could use to get out of his promise. He'd only agreed after she added another sentence to her initial demand. She'd even asked him to say yes. That could mean that he didn't make a promise at all. He might not need to take Melody's band. Or even herself.

But if he could get Rory on his side, which was a big if, she would be an asset. She could turn the tide of the coming war. Rory would change everything.

And if he couldn't get Rory? If he had to leave her behind?

Melody had surprised him with a magnificent, powerful gift. She had *influence*. She was... his mind caught the memory of her eyes and how they'd watched him as he spoke. How her emotion bled through and how she felt for his story. How she saw him.

And then, once he thought about the eyes, he started thinking about the rest of her. That voice. Husky and throaty. Breasts that swelled every time she breathed, and how he wanted to bite them. Lips so plump he wanted to bite them, too. How he wanted to feel them wrapped around his co—

The front door opened, and he stood, cheeks aflame at being interrupted while fantasizing about the very woman who bustled in the door. She locked it behind her. Resting against the door, she stared at him.

The blond waves she'd carefully brushed in the morning were now windswept and wild. Her eyes were alight with mischievous energy he'd never seen in her before. Those lips... she bit the lower one, and he stifled a groan.

"I apologize," he said rather breathlessly. "I helped myself to the food."

"Eat it all, and then I don't have to."

"Are you well?" he asked, feeling waves of heat run through him. How did she have this effect on him? He could virtually feel her presence call to him, as though the enchantment still existed in her voice despite knowing it couldn't be. "I mean, you weren't accosted on the way back?"

"No, I wasn't." She sank onto the sofa and grabbed her favorite cushion to hug. "Actually, I've been feeling a little off since I left the garden. Kind of like I'm getting sick."

"I'll get you a drink." He went to the kitchen and searched the cupboards. "What you're feeling is probably losing connection to the Well. Aching, body shakes, bone tired."

"I never felt it before."

"You probably were never connected to the Well before."

He filled up a cup with water from the faucet and then handed it to her. He slipped his hands into his pockets and waited as she drank, searching for any signs of illness. Being disconnected could make one faint. It could do all sorts of things to a body.

"Thank you," she said after she was done and flopped back. Her blond hair spilled onto the back of the sofa, and the position of her reclined face drew attention to her exposed neck and décolletage. He had to force his gaze away.

"You're welcome," he replied and sat on the opposite sofa, facing her. "It will wear off soon."

"Fae, huh?" she said, watching him as he picked some more food.

He lifted his brows, felt the leather, and decided to dispense with the disguise. He removed the patch and tossed it on the sofa beside him. Rubbing around his eye, he cracked his neck.

"You're not afraid of me?" he asked warily. "I'm not going to leave this room and find a pack of guards waiting for me, am I?"

She looked him squarely in the eyes. "I meant what I said. I want out of here. It's been bothering me for a while, and knowing you... I don't know... I'm not afraid of what's out there anymore."

"There is plenty to be afraid of out there." He tried one last time to dissuade her. "Don't think it's all rainbows and dreams. Monsters are real."

"But that's what the Guardians are for, aren't they?" She cocked her head, too astute for his liking. "That's what you do, right?"

He gave a curt nod. "We do. We keep the worst away from the general population."

"And there are good people out there, right?"

He nodded again.

"And no one is telling anyone who they can or can't love?"

"I'm sure they try, just as they do here, but there are places in Elphyne—like Cornucopia—where no one gives a kuturi shit who you're with. Races mix. Seelie and Unseelie meld. There is a place for everyone."

"And me?"

"You would be asked to remain at the Order with the other Well-blessed humans until your gift is honed."

She relaxed further at his words. "I didn't want to be suddenly thrown into another world without support."

At the thought of other Guardians around her, Forrest tensed and frowned. She probably had a mate out there waiting for her.

"Oh, I almost forgot." She opened her notebook and pulled out a wax-sealed letter. It looked similar to the one Nero had given him on his first day, but the seal emblem was slightly different. Not an N, but a scythe.

"What's this?" He accepted the letter.

"She asked my opinion of you."

"Rory?" His brows lifted. "For what purpose?"

"You're to be my official bodyguard. Open it."

He cracked the seal, read it, and then paraphrased for Melody. "I'm to continue telling you my story, but since I'm in your company anyway, and I've demonstrated my skill at keeping you unharmed, I'm to report to the Tower Guard office as soon as possible to be fitted for a uniform. Then I must remain with you on every outing to and from your living quarters."

He folded the letter, put it down, and popped another small tomato into his mouth. "What did you tell her about me?"

"I said you were extremely hot, and I'd definitely do you if she didn't."

He choked and spluttered. "What?"

"Hear me out," she said, leaning forward. "We need her on our side. There's no way in hell she'll just suddenly decide to betray her father, but I know of one proven technique that has stood the test of time."

"No."

"Oh, yes," she said, completely serious. "You have to seduce her."

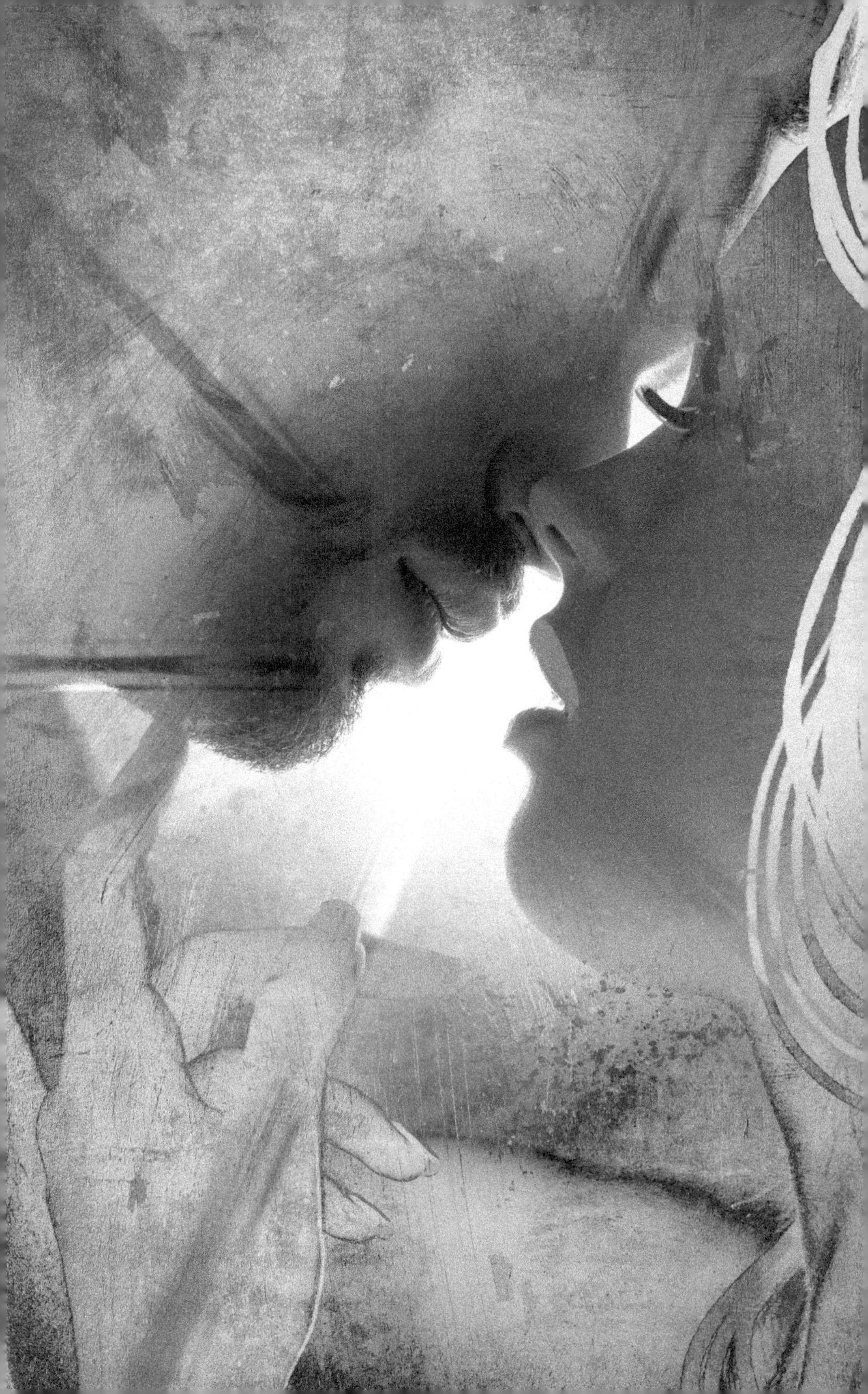

CHAPTER
SEVENTEEN

"No," Forrest repeated to Melody.

"You have to." She rushed over to him, sat down, and implored him with her eyes. "Apart from drugging and tossing Rory over your shoulder, this is the best way. She won't betray her father unless she's in love. It doesn't hurt her apart from a bruised ego. And I've already laid some groundwork."

"You want me to fuck her?"

She shrugged. "Would that be so bad?"

"And what, my dick is so magical that she'll give up everything she's loyal to because of it?"

"I don't know." She looked at his crotch and waggled her eyebrows. "Is it magical?"

"Melody, I can't," he gaped, seemingly horrified. "It's wrong on too many levels."

Melody had thought long and hard about this on the walk back to her room. The kernel of her plan began when Rory and Melody conversed while Willow played. Rory asked for Melody's opinion of Forrest, and immediately, despite everything that had happened, Melody blurted all the things she liked about him. He was strong, loyal, and a protector.

Sexy. Did she say strong?

He sacrificed everything for an innocent child, and the fact he thought this plan was wrong made him the good guy. Forrest wasn't the enemy. Melody saw him as her safety. Her salvation.

And Willow needed him too.

"Rory's attracted to strong men," Melody forced herself to say. She squeezed his arm, trying to impress the importance of her words. But again, like the first time she'd taken hold of him in the dining room, she was mesmerized by the solid handful of biceps beneath her touch. "Oh yes," she mumbled. "You're definitely her type. Good Lord, you're everyone's type."

"Melody." His tone softened.

"Forrest," she returned, still staring at his arm.

He took her hand and held onto it as he looked deeply into her eyes and said, "It won't work."

"Why not?"

Warm hands. Forrest has warm hands and kind eyes.

"It just won't." He let go and turned to the food, effectively dismissing her.

And that pissed her the hell off. "You better not be lying to me again, Forrest. We're in this together now, whatever happens. My life is as much at risk as yours. I get it, you might not be into her, or you might find the notion of seducing your enemy abhorrent. I would, too, so if that's the reason, just tell me. But I swear to God if you are still hiding things from me, if I can't trust you, then we're back to being—"

"Fine," he ground out, avoiding her eyes. "You want to know why it wouldn't work? I'll tell you."

He rested his elbows on his knees and glared at the sofa she used to be sitting on.

"I'm right here, Forrest," she said more softly. Maybe there was more to this. "If you can share, I'd like to help. I kept your secret. Whatever it is, you can trust me."

"Promise you won't laugh."

Okay... *color me intrigued.* She raised her hand and swore, "I promise on the sweet baby Jesus's bald head, I will not laugh."

"It's not because I'm opposed to the plan or using her that way. I'll do whatever I can to save Willow." He shot her a chagrinned look before shifting his gaze and saying, "I wouldn't know how to seduce her. I'm a virgin."

"Oh." She sat back. "But you're... *you.*" She gestured over his attractive body, face, and all that deliciousness around him. An elf. She could see him at home among the trees and animals. That russet hair set off like fire beneath the sun. Surely women in his world were attracted to that. And then it hit her. "Are you sexual at all?"

"Of course I am, but..." He scrubbed his face and then sighed. "You heard how I grew up."

"You were mistreated."

"I was *invisible.*" He said the word as though it gave him a sour taste. He rested an arm across the back of the sofa and met her eyes, unafraid of sharing his memories. "I was ignored for years. And then

I joined the Order, where Guardians are discouraged from having any long-term relationship because our life expectancy is short compared to other fae. We die in the line of duty. We go missing all the time. A rookie Guardian went missing in action last week. I might not come back from this very rescue mission. I stayed celibate because I didn't want to be like the others who used females and then tossed them away. Love doesn't exist in my world."

She blinked, letting his words sink in. A small part of her was troubled that perhaps, she'd made the wrong choice in siding with him. It wasn't that he was a virgin. No, it was because if there was no hope for love in that world, then what was she fighting for? But then something struck her. "What about Willow's parents? You said her father was a Guardian."

"They're Well-blessed. As I said before, those matings are rare. As the Order is an organization that honors the Well, they honor Well-blessed unions for Guardians."

"So it has nothing to do with love?"

"It has everything to do with love. They would die for each other. As would all the other Well-blessed mated pairs. This is just the path I chose for myself long ago."

She was confused. "You said love isn't in your world."

"I meant mine—me. Not Elphyne."

"So you're waiting for love."

"Yes. No. What?"

"You're a romantic."

"I'm pragmatic."

She sighed dreamily, not believing him. "I get it. A part of me will always hope, even through all the assholes I've dated and the assholes here, that I'll find someone who'll love me in the way Willow's parents love each other. I want the stuff of legends too."

She felt his eyes on her as he considered her words.

"We have to save her," she whispered. "She needs to be with her parents."

"Seducing Rory won't work. I wouldn't know where to start." His shoulders dropped. "Maybe if I was another fae."

"What if I taught you?" Yes. This could still work. The more she thought about it, the easier it sounded. "I know a thing or two about seduction. I've written songs about it. Lived it myself. I know Rory a little. You might think I'm not the kind of woman to have men eating out of my palm, but there was a time when I was at the top of my game."

He scowled. "You're exactly the kind of woman I think of."

She blushed and tried to hide the esteem his words brought. She blurted out more of her plan. "So then you know I'll teach you how to use your God-given talents, and soon you'll have her eating out of your palm."

"Toying with someone's emotions... I don't know."

"Rory is tough. She'll get over it, and if not... who knows... you might even fall in love. Maybe she's your soulmate."

He stood and paced back and forth alongside the sofa. He even tried to toss a few alternate ideas at her.

"What if we get her down to the garden, and you control her with your gift?"

"That could work," she agreed. "*If* I knew what I was doing."

"I'll train you." He stopped and shook his head. "But then there's a taint on the Well. It could end up ruining her mind. It could even backfire into your own. No. That won't work either."

"A taint?"

He sat again, but this time, *he* implored *her* with his eyes. "I'm laying all the cards on the table here, Melody. I don't know what it is about you, but I trust you. Our lives are in your hands when I say that our power source has been compromised, and we don't know why or how. It's getting worse. I must get Willow home, so then I can help my cadre find a solution."

"Forrest, I'm in. I won't give up your secret to anyone. You believe me, don't you?" His eyes searched hers, so she added, "I don't want to be forced to marry the Captain. I don't want to be locked in a tower singing untrue songs that incite a war. I don't want my friends to be trapped, either. I want us to be free. Tell me that's what will happen. Tell me I've been lying in my songs all this time about Elphyne."

"Elphyne is a dangerous place," he said. "But... like in the human world, there is good and evil. I can't promise that you'll find everything you ever wanted. But I can help you try."

Everything she ever wanted.

His words echoed her mother's old words. He held her hands in his and looked into her eyes so deeply and with such raw emotion that she had to believe this was the right choice. An evil person wouldn't give her a choice.

"Honey," she said, feeling herself melt toward him. "You say you have no idea how to seduce a woman, but from where I'm sitting, you're doing just fine."

His eyes widened, and he let go of her hands. She chuckled as he shuffled back.

"Lesson one," she said. "When a woman flirts with you, don't move the other way."

Her grin faded when she caught a haunted look in his eyes that verged on fear. She had to remind him softly, "Forrest. I need the full truth if we're going to work together. Did something happen to you? Is that why you're reluctant to do this? I can tell you're hiding something from me. And if I find out I've encouraged you to do something that offends or hurts you, I'll never forgive myself. Do you want to do this?"

He wanted to lie, she could feel it in the air, but he slowly and deliberately nodded.

She patted the seat between them. "Then let's talk. I won't bite. Unless you want."

She meant the last words as a joke, but something flashed in his eyes, and she could have sworn it was desire before he stamped it down and sat with wooden movements.

His eyes lifted to the ceiling. "I can't believe I'm agreeing to this."

"Lesson two," she said quickly in case he changed his mind. "Seduction starts slow, perhaps with a meeting of eyes across a room. You might let them know you notice, but give them space to think about it. Maybe you follow up with a conversation. Ask her questions about herself. Show that you're interested. Then a lingering touch. Done right, you'll have nothing to worry about."

"But what if it's me I'm worried about?"

"What do you mean?"

His grip tightened around her hand. This was really bothering him. She didn't know what else to do, so she shuffled closer and trailed her finger along his forehead to his ear, where she tucked his hair. His brows drew together and lifted. His eyes closed, and he shuddered.

"I'm pushing you too hard," she said softly. "I'm sorry. I can see there are things about this you're concerned with."

"Don't stop," he begged when she pulled her hand away, still with his eyes closed, looking almost like he was in pain and tense all over.

She returned her fingers to his hair, traced around his ear, and combed the auburn strands that had escaped his tie.

"It's about how I might react," he gritted out, his cheeks staining red. "What I might... do when I'm... you know... operating on instinct."

"You're worried you might embarrass yourself?"

He pressed into her touch. "Worried I might hurt you. Her. Whoever... I spend too much time in the minds of animals—too much time living as a primal being. I'm not a shifter. I've had no training to keep that side of me submissive. Do you understand?"

Instinct. Animals. Primal. "You think you'll lose control."

"Maybe." He shook his head. "This isn't going to work."

He was about to get up, but she pulled him down. "There's only one way to find out. Kiss me."

He shook his head.

"Wow," she mumbled. She understood now. "It's not the plan. It's the teacher."

"Melody," he growled. "That's not it. This just won't work. I know it."

"Yeah, you keep saying that." She found another pillow and hugged it, feeling suddenly very self-conscious. For a moment, with him, she'd forgotten all that had weighed her down. She'd felt like the old Melody, the Grammy award-winning superstar who could get any man she wanted. Now all she felt like was a sack of potatoes. "It's okay if you don't want to kiss me. Maybe I can find another teacher for you."

Caroline would probably go for it.

"Of course, I want to kiss you." With an angry snarl, he tore the pillow from her hands and moved into her personal space, so close that he trailed his nose along her jaw until he stopped at her ear —*flutters in her stomach*. The tone of his following words was so deep that it rattled her ribcage. "I've been craving a taste of you since I first bumped into you. Your sweet scent drives me insane with *want*. Why else do you think I almost murdered a stranger who had his cruel fingers on you?"

Melody's heart thundered. Did he... was he...?

Forrest tensed, muscles pumping, hardening, readying for battle. His breath shuddered angrily against her skin as though the memory of the Captain resurfaced, and he wanted to hit something. His body heat scorched the side of her face. All she had to do was turn, and their lips would clash.

She almost did it.

Her blood sang in his presence, begging her to turn. To tear off his clothes and... to feel him driving inside her. To feel him lick and love her. To *feel* like she had everything she ever wanted. Her gaze dipped to his fists on the sofa, to the scars across his knuckles, and a bolt of heat shot straight down to her core, igniting her desire further. Those were the same hands that had protected her. The idea he could keep her safe when she'd been feeling so lost was like a drug.

These lessons would ruin her.

CHAPTER EIGHTEEN

Forrest barely registered a knock at the door.

He was too consumed with Melody's scent. Sweet, feminine, and spiced with her arousal. It was a perfect concoction made just for him.

The Autumn Court Elves loved mixing apothecary elixirs that chased the pheromone high from their mates. They'd said it was the closest thing to the essence of the Well. Pure, carnal bliss in a bottle. They tried putting everything into their elixirs, and there had been a time when Forrest had been curious to try them. He'd wanted to prove that he didn't need to be mated, that he could *feel* something, that he could sate himself and move on. So, one day, when at the Order, when he was sure he was alone, he'd sampled one of them. All he'd ended up doing was torture himself with need when there was no female, no soft embrace for his cock. Nothing but his empty, calloused, punishing hand.

He vowed that day he'd wait until he found a mate or have no pleasure at all.

When he'd stepped in to protect Melody from the Captain, he'd told himself that his visceral reaction was just a fluke. There was nothing there. But there was no denying it now... his response was because of her. From the moment she bumped into him, something had unlocked inside him.

Desire.

Nothing had come close to this attraction. No female. No elixir. His mouth watered. His body tensed. His erection throbbed. Everything inside him wanted to be inside of her, and he was on a hair trigger waiting for permission. He didn't care about his inexperience. He didn't care they weren't mates. He didn't care that she wanted him to seduce the enemy. He would find a way to savor every part of her, and that was what frightened him most.

His need would only get in the way of the mission.

Someone knocked again, and he came to his senses. He pushed back from her.

"Someone's at the door," she mumbled. Then gasped. "*Someone is at the door.* It must be my band, but it could be wardrobe. Quick, put on your patch." She tossed the leather scrap to him. "We'll resume your lessons after the performance."

Lessons.

The word bounced around his head. While he'd thought she was too perfect to exist, she was thinking about how he would use his lips on another woman. He cleared his throat.

"Right." He fitted the patch over his head and retied his hair.

"Quickly." She smoothed the crinkles in her dress, ran her

fingers through her hair, and then opened the door with a broad smile.

Two men and a woman holding musical instruments blustered in. Her band. They all stopped short upon seeing him. Everyone raised their brows appraisingly and then looked at her for an explanation.

"Oh." She shut the door. "Everyone, this is Forrest. He's new."

"Hi Forrest," they all said before the smaller woman added a finger wave.

"Hello." He smiled tightly and then took his time assessing the newcomers, but deemed them no threat, so he said to Melody, "If you're not going anywhere else, I will be back in time to escort you to tonight's performance."

He wasn't too sure if she responded. The blood roaring in his ears drowned out any sound.

Exhaustion had hit him after he collected his new uniform from the Tower Guard office and received a short orientation for his new job. It was only midafternoon, but the day's events felt like a ton of shit had dropped on him.

He laid down on his uncomfortable bed in his cold, miserable room and realized, despite his growing feelings for Melody, none of it mattered. His feelings weren't a factor in this equation. They never had been. Decades after leaving his family home, he was still the sacrifice. He should suck it up, learn what he could from Melody, and then seduce the enemy.

⚖

Pain wrenched Forrest from sleep. His first thought had been that he was in the dungeon of his youth, beaten by the guards for dancing in his underwear during dinner to get attention. He soon learned attempts to be seen were not worth the pain and never did it again. But this wasn't that. This was a sharp and present danger. He came to his senses in the hazy gloom of his cold concrete room in the Tower. Two men in uniform were kicking the living shit out of him on the floor.

These soldiers were dressed like the ones who'd brought him in on the first day. Like the uniform the Captain wore. Military. Had the Captain remembered their altercation in the garden? Was Melody safe?

A boot to the gut had him gasping, and he almost struck out to take his enemy down with swift vengeance, but a voice slid through the gloom and made him pause.

"Not his face," the Captain said.

The two thugs punched and pummeled Forrest as he hunched into himself. He held back, bit his tongue, and took the beating. If the Captain didn't want Forrest's face bruised, he didn't want him dead. He just wanted to teach Forrest a lesson. This was one of those times he had to appear human. Weak. He had to let events correct themselves because if he came out on top again this time, and Melody couldn't wipe the Captain's memory, then Forrest was dead.

He felt like the hits went on for hours. He hated having to hold his punches and take the pain. But soon enough, they stopped. Footsteps receded. A heavy set drew close. The air shifted as the Captain leaned down and whispered in Forrest's ear, "That's payback for humiliating me in front of Ms. Melody. Now every time you wince in pain while I'm away, you'll remember she's mine, not yours. Don't even think about giving her your belt, or next time—" He nudged his boot into Forrest's crotch. "I'll make sure you won't need one."

When he was gone, Forrest attempted to roll onto his back. His injuries stabbed like knives. It took him until the sun set and the knowledge that he was late to pick up Melody for her performance before he forced himself off the floor. He stumbled to the bathroom, covered up the black and blue body, and then pissed blood into the latrine.

He decided right then and there that he would kill that man one day.

He would get all three females out of there—maybe the band—but then he would come back and stab the Captain between the eyes. Slowly.

CHAPTER NINETEEN

Melody had never been more excited about a performance than she had been that night. Feeling sexier and more confident than she had in a long time, she dressed in a particularly revealing dress that cinched her waist and hugged her hips. The satin fabric flared out at her ankles like a mermaid's tail. She channeled her inner Marylin Monroe with her makeup. Red lips. Retro eyeliner.

She would sing a new song she'd practiced with her band all afternoon. Call her crazy, but she felt bold and reckless after Forrest confessed to her on her sofa. He *was* attracted to her. She *was* attractive. And she had magic flowing in her veins... just not here in this godforsaken place. A place that felt worse now that she had a taste of the Well. It was like she'd moved from a symphony to a tone-deaf recital.

Was this what the fae felt like every time they stepped near the human settlement?

The band still couldn't know about her plan, but they were thrilled to skip the usual propaganda horror stories in favor of something lighter and upbeat. She'd decided she couldn't sing about the trauma of Forrest's youth. If Willow was in the audience, repeating bad things about her people would only damage a young person's brain.

Melody was almost sure she recognized the tune Willow had hummed under her breath when she'd been playing in the fountain. *Kokomo*. What else could Bish Boys mean? It was so random and odd that after spinning the words and tune over in her mind, she came to the only conclusion that it had to be that. It was further proof that everything Forrest had told Melody was the truth.

Only a child with a parent from Melody's time would know who The Beach Boys were, and singing it would bring a smile to the homesick child's face. Even now, waiting in the green room for the call, it brought an incorrigible grin, and she was virtually twitching on her toes.

The knock came.

"Quick. Assume the positions," Melody whispered to her band.

Caroline quickly plopped herself between the two men as they reluctantly drifted apart. A twinge in Melody's heart pulled. She desperately wanted to tell them she had a plan to get them all out of there. To get them to a happy place where they could be free. But it wasn't the time. *Soon*.

Melody opened the door expecting Forrest, but it was Sid, the guard from the previous night. Forrest had not picked her up from her rooms as he'd promised. She was told he was busy having his orientation for the role. She backed up to make room for the guard, a little concerned at Forrest's absence. Had she scared him off? Had something terrible happened?

"Let's go," Sid grunted.

"Where's—?"

Forrest walked in, and she exhaled in relief. He was whole. He was here. And call her disturbed, but she kind of fancied him in his new Tower uniform. The mandarin collar was unembellished and accentuated his sharp jaw. Now that she knew what he looked like without the eye patch, she wanted to see both his eyes. He met her gaze with a silent, intense study that made her think about what he'd said on her sofa.

I've been craving a taste of you since we first bumped into each other.

"You ready?" he asked, voice tight.

Something was wrong. She sensed it in his posture.

"Almost," she replied smoothly and then said to Sid, "Darling, if you go on ahead with the band, we won't be two shakes of a lamb's tail."

Sid, who didn't seem to have an opinion about anything, directed her band members out. As soon as the door closed, Melody stepped close to her new bodyguard. A thrill tripped in her stomach.

"Well, don't you look dashing in uniform," she teased under her breath, brushing his shoulder free of a stray strand of hair.

She wanted to do more than that, but at her touch, his lips pinched, and a small, pained grunt sounded deep in his chest.

"What happened?" she gasped. "Are you hurt?"

"The Captain and some of his men paid me a little visit." He walked stiffly back to the door, clearly not wanting to talk about it. "I'm already late. We have to go."

"Forrest," she said. "What happened?"

"Whatever you did to the Captain's memory still stands. This was in retaliation for that first time."

Guilt pierced her straight through the chest. "I shouldn't have sassed him. This is my fault."

He rounded on her. "Something like that is *never* a woman's fault. Understood?"

"But you're—"

"I'll be fine," he said through gritted teeth. "Let's go."

Without another word, he opened the door and ushered her out. As they walked the long corridor to the dining hall, she couldn't help noticing he moved stiffly. Her guilt deepened so much that she whispered to him, "I'm not singing about you."

They stopped just as they arrived at the dining hall. The conversation was thick beneath the sound of cutlery and crockery tinkering.

"Why?" he asked. "It's what Nero wants."

Her brows puckered. "It's wrong."

The anger still in his eyes tempered.

She left him staring at her and made her way to the stage. It had only been a day since the president gave her the directive to develop new material. So much had happened. She could stretch this a little longer if she played it right.

The nightly performance went well until it didn't. Her lack of sleep and daily routines were starting to catch up. She didn't notice a particular someone sitting at the front tables until it was too late. The Captain watched everything she did with the eyes of a shark. Last night, his stare had been unsettling. But now, it was disturbing. Melody reminded herself that he remembered nothing of their clash in the garden. Those eyes hid no memories beyond them.

Thinking back to the event, she recalled the feeling of the power leaving her body as it worked on him. The hairs on her arms had lifted. It was *real*.

She had to trust Forrest because the alternative was that she was on her own and going insane.

After she'd finished the first act, Nero didn't call her to his table. It threw her off a little. He usually wanted a chat because he left the dining hall before she finished for the night so he could avoid the crowd.

Melody prepared for the second act and had a moment of doubt. She knew he watched from his dais at the back, shrouded in shadow. The weight of his attention made the air thick. Perhaps she should sing one of her old songs to smooth things over, but as she glimpsed a shock of silver hair on a little head at a table not far from the dais, she knew she might not get another chance to sing to Willow.

Rory might keep the child locked away for days.

She glanced at her band nervously, but Timothy gave her the thumbs up. She forced her lips to the microphone to say, "This is a new song by an old, old favorite." She licked her lips. "The band who originally sang this song is called The Beach Boys."

And then she sat down at the piano and started playing. It was a fun, nostalgic song that Willow would enjoy. But it was the beginning of a rebellion for her and her band. They threw themselves into the out-of-time rendition of *Kokomo*. She was sure no one understood a single word of the lyrics, or how it conjured cocktails with Tom Cruise on the beach for Melody, but it made Willow happy. The band, too.

When the last notes died, not a sound was made in the audience. No applause. No murmurs. The spotlights on the stage shut down. Shadows bustled onto the wooden platform, and suddenly there was a hand at Melody's elbow directing her into the soft lights of the dining hall.

"Relax," Forrest whispered. "I've been asked to bring you to the president. I'm right here."

His voice calmed her nerves. He would be there. No matter what happened.

As they walked, intermission music started playing. Ridiculously dressed diners continued to eat and chat as though nothing had happened. Melody and Forrest passed the Captain's table.

"You sang beautifully," Forrest murmured again, the smooth tone of his voice low enough for just her ears. "Your voice is like watching stars fall. Bewildering and humbling all at once."

Tears stung Melody's eyes, but she relaxed further at his kind words. When they arrived at the president's table, Rory was also there. She stood behind her father's seat with her hands behind her back and her chin out. Not happy. *Shit.*

Nero wore the same suit he always did. Dark, tailored, trimmed in gold, and with a rose in the pocket. The gray slashed at his temples looked evil in the low light. His nostrils flared at Melody, then he glared at Forrest and back at Melody.

Melody expected a loss of temper, but not the cold, empty stare that caused shivers to skate down her bones.

"Explain why you haven't done as I asked."

Panic scorched her face.

"I wanted to take a break from the usual lineup," she said.

"By singing about tropical getaways?"

"I just thought with it being so cold here, maybe—"

"You *just thought?*" With each word, Nero's tone heightened from pissed to downright furious.

Her lips parted to speak, but he slammed his hand on the table. Melody startled. When those in earshot looked over, he smoothed his hair and suit before clenching his jaw. His next words were eerily calm. "It is not your job to think, Ms. Melody. It is your job to do as I tell you. *Look* how I tell you. *Sing* what I tell you. Marry or *fuck* who I tell you."

She recoiled as though slapped. Now, why would he say that unless he insinuated the betrothal ceremony?

"I am leaving for a short time," he stated. "My daughter is under strict instructions to keep you in line and make no mistake; if you step out, facing her wrath will be worse than mine. I will find another musician to take your place if I hear you fail your instructions again. And you—" He scowled at Forrest. "We do not have the luxury of being kind to your feelings if that is why she has deferred from telling your tale. We are fighting a war here. We need all the ammunition we can get our hands on. That means every bit of sickening, humiliating thing done to you. Or do you need a reminder of what we're facing?"

Forrest lifted the hem of his jacket displaying purple, bruised flesh.

"Your Captain has already taken care of that, Mr. President," Forrest said, his singular eye narrowing. "I will give Ms. Melody more material to use, but I will not apologize for keeping her safe."

Appeased and perhaps with a small note of respect, Nero sat back and studied him. "Good. Then we are on the same page. It pains me to remind Ms. Melody of her duty, but you know what we're up against. Desperate times call for desperate measures. We cannot let a minute go to waste."

Forrest nodded. "Those filthy Tainted bastards deserve everything they get."

Nero was quiet for some time. Melody and Forrest turned to leave, but with the first step taken, he said, "When you return to the stage, you will find one bandmate missing. If you wish to see her when I return, I expect you to do as you're told."

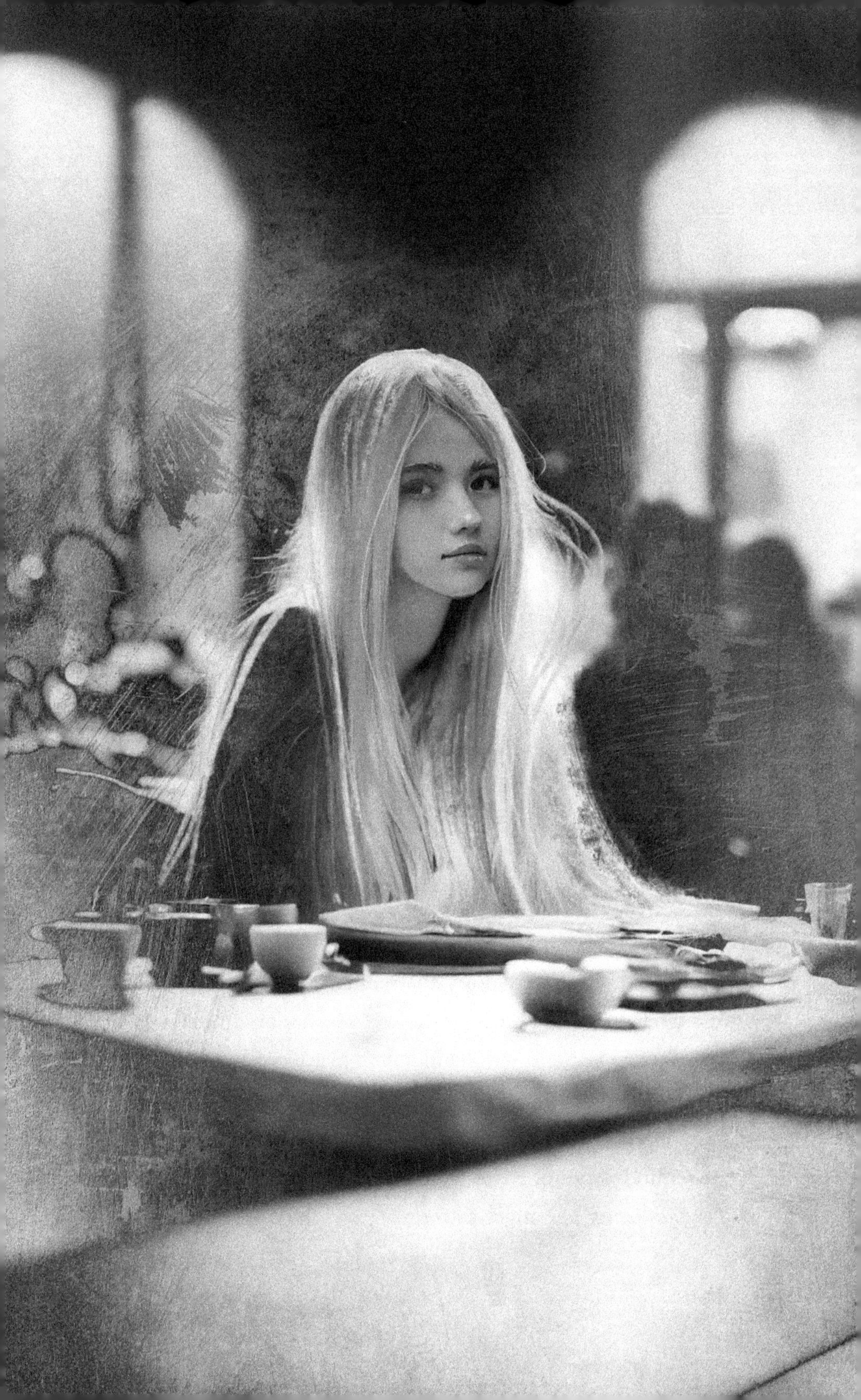

CHAPTER
TWENTY

Melody finished her performance like a robot. When it was done, she gulped down the bile rising in the back of her throat. She was so stupid to have taken a step out of line. She *knew* Nero had wanted a new song. Who did she think she was to play something so... *gah*. She wanted to scream, to let out her gift and shatter his eardrums. But here, in this cold empty prison filled with obscenely dressed people, she was as powerless as the rest.

It was a big puppet show, she realized. None of this was real. Suddenly, the painted faces in the crowd took on a new meaning. The richly dressed and fed people were just like her. How many of them had any real power?

Rats in a cage.

It reminded her of lyrics from an old Smashing Pumpkins song she loved during her angry grunge period. She'd worn nothing but band T-shirts, Doc Martins, and torn jeans. She raged against the world and felt every iota of angst. That song had been the epitome of how she and an entire generation had felt.

No power despite their rage.

And now Caroline was missing. Andrew and Timothy were beside themselves with worry. A guard had simply walked up like Forrest had done to Melody. He took Caroline away. They'd thought nothing of it. They'd thought she'd be back. And the Captain had sat through it all with a smug smile.

Nothing seemed to get him off more than seeing a woman oppressed.

The worst part was that Willow was also missing. Melody guessed the little girl would have mentioned the song's meaning to Rory. After all, Willow had been singing it under her breath in the garden.

Did this mean Rory was unreachable?

Had she figured out that little message for Willow to stay strong and cut it off before it could grow? How much of the song did Willow hear?

As Melody returned to her rooms with Forrest, she tried to recall Rory's expression. It had been unreadable stone. The only time she let any emotion slip was when Forrest lifted his jacket to reveal his bruises. There had been a glimmer of hate in her eyes. But what did that mean? By the time Melody said a teary goodbye to her friends and entered her cool, dark apartment, she was about to have a mental breakdown.

The usual spread of food over her table smelled sweet—rancid—despite being freshly put out probably moments before.

Sack of potatoes.

You're too thin.

It's not your job to think.

Melody screamed and shoved the trays of food to the floor.

"What if I ruined *everything* by playing one silly song?" she blurted. "Caroline could be dead. Willow could be—"

She choked up and covered her face. Losing it now wasn't going to help anyone.

"Melody," Forrest said softly as he lifted his eye patch. "It's not as bad as you think."

She shook her head. He slid warm, steady hands over her shoulders and rubbed her arms soothingly before tugging her against his chest. The moment her ear hit his sternum, he winced. She tried to pull away, but he held her head firm. After a moment, she settled by listening to the muffled thud of his steady heartbeat. He was her new song. He wasn't worried. He was calm. And he smelled so good.

Forrest held her tight.

Don't let go, she whispered in her mind. *I've missed this so much.*

All the pain and anguish she'd bottled up over her life threatened to burst out. The sadness over losing her mother. The agony over realizing she was alive, but no one else she knew was. The devastation of being locked in a tower with only the sky as her friend. And now this... this oppression and subjugation by a man who was supposed to be a savior to humanity.

"Think about it," Forrest said. "Now we know two of the most dangerous men in Crystal City are leaving for a few days. Caroline is alive. Nero said you'll see her again if you do as you're told. They plan on returning for the Phoenix Ball."

"That's more than a few days away," she sniffed.

"So, we have some time."

"But is Rory reachable?"

"I think she is," he said quietly. "She winced when I showed my bruises."

"She looked like she hated you."

"She hated what was done to me." She felt his chin rest on her head. "I don't think it was loyalty, or for me... but she seems to be the kind that doesn't like needless violence to your own people. When I spoke to her that first time, that was the angle I took. She made sure I was stationed as your personal guard."

"Nero said facing her wrath will be worse than his. What could he mean?"

Forrest was silent for a while as he considered her question. "I think when pushed to protect humanity, she does what is necessary. Or perhaps, like her grandmother, there is a vindictive side to her that we haven't seen."

Melody pulled back from Forrest. "I'm so sorry you were hurt. Is it bad?"

He didn't answer, which meant it was. *Christ.*

"Forrest, do you need to see a physician? Is there anything I can do?"

"If I can get to the garden, I can heal."

"Let's go now."

"Not tonight," he said. "We're being watched. I don't want a healer to look closely at me. We should carry on as normal until tomorrow. Follow your routine as much as possible."

"I usually eat breakfast and then work on new material in the mornings. I take a walk if I can. Then after lunch, I practice with the band and meet with wardrobe before dinner."

Concerned eyes landed on her. "Every day?"

"Yes. This is all I do."

His jaw worked. "They're using you. It's revolting."

"Rats in a cage," she mumbled.

"Get some rest. I'll be back in the morning."

THE NIGHT PASSED in a blur of anxiety for Melody. She tossed and turned and worried about Caroline's fate. Forrest seemed confident that all would be okay, but how could he be sure? Her tiny rebellion had catastrophic consequences. Nero wanted her to represent the bountiful past, but she couldn't be any further from the truth.

It pained her to admit, but back in her time, she had been on a one-way path to losing it all. After her mother had died, and Melody felt the hopelessness and unfairness of it all, she'd all but given up on writing new material. And when the world started freezing, she'd hardly had it in her to be afraid. Her friend had crystalized before her eyes, and Melody was numb already. That's when she realized she'd stopped *doing*. She'd already stopped moving. Stopped achieving. Long before the escalation of the nuclear crisis.

Melody's mother's voice rose from her memory. *"If you're not doing, you're waiting. Ain't that right, sugarplum?"*

When Melody opened the door to Forrest that morning, she was dressed and ready to go.

"I don't want him to win," she said, a determined set to her jaw.

Looking worse for wear, the fae had disheveled hair. Bruises discolored his neck above his mandarin collar. He checked over his shoulder to see if anyone heard her declaration. But these halls were usually empty and only for the residents to walk. She grasped his shirt and tugged him into her place.

He hissed at the movement and tensed.

"Oh, Forrest," she sighed, closing the door behind him. "What did he do to you?"

"Had worse."

"You said that before, but I don't care. It's not right. None of this is right." She was furious now that she'd had time to process it all. She might be a rat in a cage. She might be raging. But they *could* be saved. "He's a liar. He shouldn't be allowed to rule."

Forrest lifted his patch and settled his warm eyes on her. "This might be a good time to tell you that two Well-blessed humans—Clarke and Laurel—knew Nero once. Back in your time."

She stilled. Nero was like Melody? "How?"

"He had a man torture Laurel to force Clarke to reveal a code that unlocked weapons that destroyed your world."

Melody swooned. She downright swooned like an old silver screen star. She would have collapsed if it wasn't for Forrest's strong arms holding her up. It took her a long hard minute to gather her composure.

"You're telling me," she rasped, "that the man I've been helping is the one who destroyed *my world*?"

He nodded. "I'm sorry."

She searched his eyes. Nowhere in them did she sense a lie. What purpose would he have now? Nero had already proven he was despicable.

"I shouldn't be here," she whispered, on the verge of hyperventilating. "I should be out there, in Elphyne, with the others like me."

"Yes," he murmured, his gaze softening on her.

"We must do everything we can to bring Willow and Rory back. We have to help take those crystal walls down. Most of these people are just following orders. They don't make decisions."

The sun-gilt vibrancy Forrest seemed always to carry faded, and he stepped away.

"I've spent the night coming up with an alternative, and I think I've almost found another plan," he said.

"*Almost* might not be good enough. We have to prepare for the rehearsal dinner in less than a week."

But he wasn't listening. "I think I can befriend the Tower Guard who escorts you to your performances."

"Sid?"

"He used to work with Silver. I'm sure the vampire who hurt him was Shade."

Her eyes narrowed. "Your friend hurt him. I don't see how that will endear him to our cause. Rory is part fae. Sid is not. He has no mana, nothing to tie him to Elphyne." At Forrest's lost expression, she squeezed his arm. "We can do this. Come on." She pulled him out the door. "Time for your next lesson."

"Where are we going?"

"A brief turn in the garden will heal you, right?"

He nodded.

"We'll go there," she said. "And then I'm taking you to the Ancient History Museum. Remember I mentioned Rory is attracted to strong men? She'll probably dismiss you as beneath her if she believes you're a farmer. But if we can get enough information about you being Special Ops or some other military from my time, then she will be intrigued."

"Ancient History Museum."

"Yes," she said. "You could do with more understanding of the world you came from. Come on. Chop-chop. I need to be back here making music by lunchtime."

CHAPTER
TWENTY-ONE

Forrest felt mildly better after spending a short time in the garden. He still wasn't completely healed—not even half—and exiting the garden felt worse than before. But he kept that to himself. The only reason Melody was motivated was these lessons she insisted on giving.

And, reluctant as he was, it was their best bet. At the very least, it would get him close to Rory while she was vulnerable. He would have to devise an alternative if she didn't go for his story. Finding something to drug her with was next on his list of things to do, but he wasn't comfortable with that either. The way women were treated here in this toxic environment reminded him of his mother... how she'd been manipulated and forced to forget him, how Melody was being manipulated too.

Maybe if Rory knew the truth about her father and her lineage, she might think twice about her situation.

He decided against contacting Aeron. It hadn't been long. They wouldn't send out the search party for Willow yet. Forrest would let them know his timeline when he had something to tell.

He gave Melody a sideways glance as they traveled in the caged elevator to a lower floor. Unlike the sides of their cab, the front door was open as they descended. Levels whizzed by.

Brass gears, chains, cranks.

And the glimpse of life on other levels. The laundry on one floor smelled like soap. Food markets on another. School on a third. Melody explained it all to him.

He realized then that he couldn't leave her behind even if he wanted to. She would be dead by association after he left with Willow and Rory.

Once again, he wondered if life would be easier if he simply stabbed Nero through the heart at the next meal. But the bastard had survived an apocalypse he'd caused. He'd had the help of a psychic in the past, and who knew what else he had to work with? There would always be a card up his sleeve. He'd be more challenging to kill than the cockroaches Forrest had convinced to crawl up the Captain's legs.

Once Willow came of age and gave him information of worth, Nero would have a vast tactical advantage. He would be unstoppable.

"Here we are," Melody said as the elevator stopped in an underground basement.

Forrest pulled open the cage door, and they exited to an empty level full of ancient artifacts, paraphernalia, and pictures on walls. But no people. It was a veritable ghost town of ancient memories and lost lives.

"Where is everyone?" he asked.

She slid him a sardonic smile. "This stuff has been here for generations. It used to be the original bunker the humans quarantined themselves in. Now, the Sky Tower folk don't give a damn about it. I gather that it's just a kick in the guts to see all this wealth and history when they're trapped here. The commoners and workers outside don't even know this exists. But I like to come here when I'm homesick."

She took his hand and drew him further into the museum, through musty air, strange tapestries, and twists and turns. As they walked, lighting flickered on like it knew they were there. Forrest was hard to convince it wasn't magic, but Melody mumbled something about sensors and old technology.

They first passed through a hall with pictures and paintings of people on the wall. Melody didn't want to stop, so she pulled him through until they emerged at a large space filled with dead animals.

Taxidermy birds—or sculptures—hung from the ceiling. They also watched from alcoves decorated like natural habitats. He gasped at an enormous statue of the mythical El'fant with its floppy ears and tusks, almost like a muskox, coming from the side of a long snout dangling on the floor. So, this was where the tales came from. The creature was every bit as majestic as described.

They wandered through halls and corridors, and Forrest couldn't hold the marvel in. Animals of all sorts with inscriptions beneath set up in dioramas that must have been a likeness of their natural habitat. He touched fur. It felt so real. Probably was. How macabre of humans to stuff dead things.

"We have a few dedicated historians," Melody mentioned. "And a few…"

When she trailed off, he looked at her. She bit her lip. "A few what?"

"There's another museum. A fae one. It's a little ghastlier than this."

Fury inched up his neck in a hot wave. "You're telling me there are stuffed statues of fae in this building?"

The guilt in her eyes said it all. Before he could dwell on it, she dragged him along to another exhibit. Wax statues of people dressed in strange clothes were next. Artifacts with gold trim. Paintings on the walls of weird people in even more outlandish clothes.

"Over here," she said. "This is the military section."

As they crested a corner, a giant steel vehicle came into view. It had a ribbed metal belt for wheels and an enormous gun sticking out of the top.

"It's a tank," she explained. "For when heavy fire is expected. See that lid up the top? Soldiers would open that and climb inside. They would be protected with all the thick metal around them. Oh, look, here's what I wanted to show you."

She pointed at a series of pictures on a wall. The paintings were so lifelike.

"This artist must be incredibly talented," he muttered.

She chuckled. "It's a photograph taken by a camera." At his wide-eyed stare, she explained. "A camera is a machine that captures a mirror image of real life, and then you can print it on paper."

He nodded, pretending that he knew what that meant. More pictures showed great big war machines with giant guns—tanks and other vehicles. Ships. Metal birds in the air. Soldiers lined up looking menacing with their metal weapons.

"There was a lot of war in your time," he commented.

"Sadly, this is true." Melody continued explaining object names in pictures, but he stopped her at one where the men were dressed in sandy-colored clothes.

"Explain that?" he asked studiously.

"That's probably Afghanistan or somewhere in the Middle East. There was a lot of unrest in those areas. Since we're somewhere in America, most of the history here is from whatever was close by during the fallout. Those men were most likely American soldiers."

"It looks like another world. So much sand. Is it hot?"

"It's a desert. I suppose since the nuclear winter, you wouldn't know what one looks like. Yes, it's very hot. Not many plants grow there. Very little water."

"Desert." He straightened and hummed his agreement. "Seems like a place deserted by the Well."

"Maybe," she said, her voice pensive as she looked at it. "These are the sorts of soldiers you can say you worked with. They were elite and at the top of their game. Back then, war was more precise than broad. I guess what I mean is that there would be man-hunting missions. A single unit would be tasked with entering enemy territory and locating the bad leader. I suppose, kind of what you're doing here now."

No monsters. Only other humans they fought against. But it was most helpful to see the clothes and environments these men battled in. Forrest was sure he could use his warrior's knowledge to fill in the gaps. He was inspecting a collection of weapons in a glass cabinet when she said, "There's no easy way to ask this next question, so I'm just going to come right out and say it." He raised a brow as she continued. "How much about a woman's anatomy do you know?"

He'd always been comfortable with his lack of experience, putting it down to a deliberate choice, but when Melody asked the question, heat licked his face and ears. He had not been expecting that question.

He cleared his throat. "I... ah... I guess I know what I need to know."

She sidled up to him, completely unperturbed. "But do you know what our parts do for *us*?"

"You mean how you reproduce?"

"What I'm trying to say is, do you know how to get a woman off?" She took a deep breath. "Do you know how to bring a female to orgasm? I mean, if you want Rory eating out of the palm of your hand, you will have to show her a good time. Oh Lord, I assume female elves have the same anatomy as humans."

His eyes crinkled. "Yes, they do. Most High Fae are close in anatomy to humans, apart from a few basic different needs such as vampires drinking blood. Some males, though, like the pixies, their anatomy is a little different down there. And don't even ask about the Sluagh. Nobody knows about them."

"Okay, so I guess that's good. Body parts are similar enough that we can move this lesson to phase two. How to use them."

Talking about reproductive parts while Melody's plush body was so close made his cock harden and his breath quicken.

"We're doing this now." His voice was rough.

"We have to," she murmured as she lifted his patch onto his forehead and looked deeply into his eyes.

"I know, it's just..." He checked over his shoulder. Anyone could walk in. "I don't like putting you in this position."

"Honey, there are worst things than being pleasured by someone who looks like you."

His cock jerked. *Crimson.* Even if his mind was saying no, to protect her dignity, his body cried out for every dark and dirty thing he was too afraid to dream of.

Before he lost his nerve, he said, "Tell me what I have to do."

"Okay," she said with a small smile. "Firstly, don't make it sound like work."

His cheeks heated, and he nodded.

"This should be fun, so relax. Let's say you've charmed Rory enough over a few conversations. It's now the rehearsal dinner, and she's probably looking to blow off steam. Refill her drinks. Pay her attention. But don't treat her like a princess. Treat her like—"

"A warrior." His hands stole around Melody's waist and flexed against her lower back.

"If all goes well, and you get her alone, you should kiss her." She licked her lips. "With her permission, of course."

"A warrior doesn't ask for permission," he said gruffly. Needing to be closer, he tugged her hips against his. "A warrior takes."

"Then expect a fight," she breathed, lifting her lips to his but holding back from fully committing. "And if she says no, it means stop."

"Of course." With every syllable they spoke, their lips fluttered against each other. The tension was killing him. "This is a dangerous game we're playing, Melody."

"Is it?"

Her unique perfume switched his arousal from simmering to an inferno. The cheaply made trousers rubbed against his erection, and he felt it ricochet every time she trembled. Slowly, his sense ebbed away, and need pushed in until it was all he could think about.

"Show me how you like to be kissed," he said, voice low and barely there. *I'm ready.* "Show me so that I may learn to be your everything."

"Oh Lord, Forrest. When you say things like that, I wonder who is teaching who." She brushed her lips across his. She licked along the seam of his lips. "But it's good to start slow. Get a feel for each other."

He repeated her action. A quick slide across her lip, a quick swipe with his tongue, then he nibbled on the pillow of juicy flesh he wanted to bite. Holding it between his teeth, a low restrained growl rumbled at the base of his throat.

She moaned. "Now you're catching on."

He held her still by the jaw and then delved deeper, demanding entrance to her mouth so he could taste. He'd kissed before, but never like this. Never like it was worth savoring. She opened to him with a whimper. The meeting of their tongues was the single most erotic thing he'd ever experienced. It was more than the sensation, the salty-sweet taste, the heat. It was a direct line to his baser instincts, and he wanted more.

A low rumble started deep in his throat as he invoked urges he'd denied all his life. He pushed her against a glass cabinet, arching her back beneath his body. He swallowed her gasp and deepened their kiss, taking what he wanted from her, demanding more.

He was bursting with need and had no idea where to focus it. Stay on her lips. Kiss down her neck. Lick those pale, bountiful breasts spilling out—*Crimson save him*, those breasts. *Touch them.*

Bite them. They'd been the center of his attention every night she'd performed. What did they look like beneath the dress? What did they feel like? Taste like?

"What next?" he begged on a ragged exhale.

"Well," she breathed, "from here, touching starts to get more... adventurous."

"Touching," he mumbled and slid his hands down her body, aiming for that place of his dreams. But she slid his hands back up.

She smiled against his lips. "Next time. Hitting a home run might be thrilling for you, but if it's a quick game, it's not fun for the woman."

No idea what she's talking about.

He pulled back with a frown and looked into her eyes. "More kissing?"

She nodded. "The idea is that the more you increase the anticipation, the better the foreplay, and the wetter she is. Then it just feels better for everyone."

Crimson, he felt stupid. "Wetter?"

Melody paused. She seemed to consider, then mumbled something about fucking baseball. She guided his hand under her dress and up her bare thigh. He shuddered at the silky-smooth texture. *Higher. Higher.* Heat. Damp. Wet. *Fuck.* He lost all sense as she pressed his hand between her legs. He groaned into her neck, fully immersing himself in how she felt on his palm.

"Here," she moaned.

Blood rushed to his head, to his cock, everywhere. He felt the damp slide through her intimate undergarments. *That* was where he wanted to be. To touch. To taste. To feast. To fill. A snarl of yearning spilled from his lips as he suckled on her neck, trailed his nose over every inch of skin there, and then pressed the heel of his palm against her mound.

She cried out with a gasp, "*Forrest.*"

Well-damn. When she said his name.

"Melody," he breathed, his fingers tickling up and down her seam, testing the wetness there. "You are already wet there. We didn't kiss enough. What does that mean?"

She made a small whimper and rocked her hips into him. "It means I'm already hot for you, elf."

A surge of arousal laced with pride speared through him. She was like this because of him.

"Teach me what to do next."

"Sweet baby Jesus," she cursed softly. "I'm probably going to hell for this. But there's a special part of a woman's anatomy... If you stimulate it enough, it will bring her to climax."

She melted against him. He held her upright with one hand while the other continued to hunt over her drenched panties for this magical spot.

"I want my mouth down there," he announced.

Melody trembled. "Next time."

But that need insisted he continued. It pulsed at him. He wanted to feel more of her, and while his mouth kept exploring her neck, lips, and décolletage, he finally pushed aside her underwear.

He startled, realizing what he had done.

He paused, his fingers so close to her heat but not connecting. They stood still for a long, ragged breath. Him bent over her, her arching against the cabinet, his hand up her dress, fingers stretching out her underwear.

She covered his hand with hers so viciously that she slapped.

She shuddered against him and kept pushing his fingers, guiding him through her nest of curls, and bade him explore. Swiping through her slit with his fingers, deep into her folds. *Warm. Soft. Inviting.* Just how he'd always dreamed. She pushed him deeper. His fingers went *into* her tight entrance, but only for a second, only to moisten, and then she pulled him out and showed him where she wanted it most.

Right at her apex, he toyed with a little nub.

"This is my clitoris," she whimpered. "This is the part you play with."

"I want to play with it all," he decided.

"Next time."

With her promise sating his demands, he used slow circles to work her, curiously watching her facial expression shift from aroused to downright drugged. The faster he went, the quicker her breath, the redder her cheeks, the more high-pitched her voice.

"And if it dries, you—" She guided his finger back deep inside her, groaning as he filled her again.

"*Fuck,*" he gritted out, his eyelids fluttering at the sensation of her inner walls clamping around his fingers. That was *definitely* another spot he wanted to explore, to learn. He imagined what it would feel like if it wasn't his finger. If it was his cock sliding into her. Moving in and out. He grew impossibly harder and rocked against her hip, crushing his erection into her, chasing his own elusive sensations. "You're so tight. I'm going to..."

"Forrest..." Her moan punched desire through his system. He was losing his mind. Melody used short, breathless words to encourage him. To show him how she liked it. To ride his fingers for her pleasure. And he was lost. No. He was found. He was who he'd never been—someone *seen*.

He rested his forehead against hers and struggled to breathe. Sweat prickled his skin. He felt like he was drowning at the same time as flying.

"Yes, Forrest."

Fuck... my name.

More.

He needed more.

More taste. More everything.

"Sometimes," she panted. "If you're feeling particularly wicked, you can replace your fingers with your tongue."

That was it.

The visual. The scent of her in his fantasies. Him lapping her up as she rode his face like she did his fingers. Pleasure exploded down his spine. Hot liquid spurted out of his cock. He shuddered and gasped and seized as he climaxed.

When he was done, shock barreled through him, and he froze. He waited for her to notice his shame, but she only said, "Yes. Like that, Forrest. Keep doing exactly what you're doing, and Rory—she will..."

White noise rushed in his ears. *Rory.* Not Melody. His chest wrenched tight. *I can't breathe.* She was only doing this to teach him how to please another woman. But while her mind had been there, his had been so into her that he'd made a fool of himself. And she didn't notice.

This was the second time she'd done this.

"Got it," he said abruptly, sliding his fingers out of her. "Until she climaxes."

Melody's brows squished together as she braced herself on the cabinet, chest heaving. "Forrest?"

His shame felt more glaring with every second, and he couldn't. He just couldn't. His mind churned. He turned his back and mumbled something about seeing her later. Then he rushed out of the museum.

He moved so fast and with blinders on that he almost missed the wall of pictures dedicated to her—in the past. His steps stuttered. Melody stood on a stage with thousands of adoring fans, their faces tilted up to her in rapture. She was the center of their universe.

Would she ever be able to share that spotlight with him?

Would he ever be the center of her universe?

Nero's words came hurtling back. *She is a marvel to be shared. She will never belong to one person but to all.* A woman like that didn't see someone like Forrest.

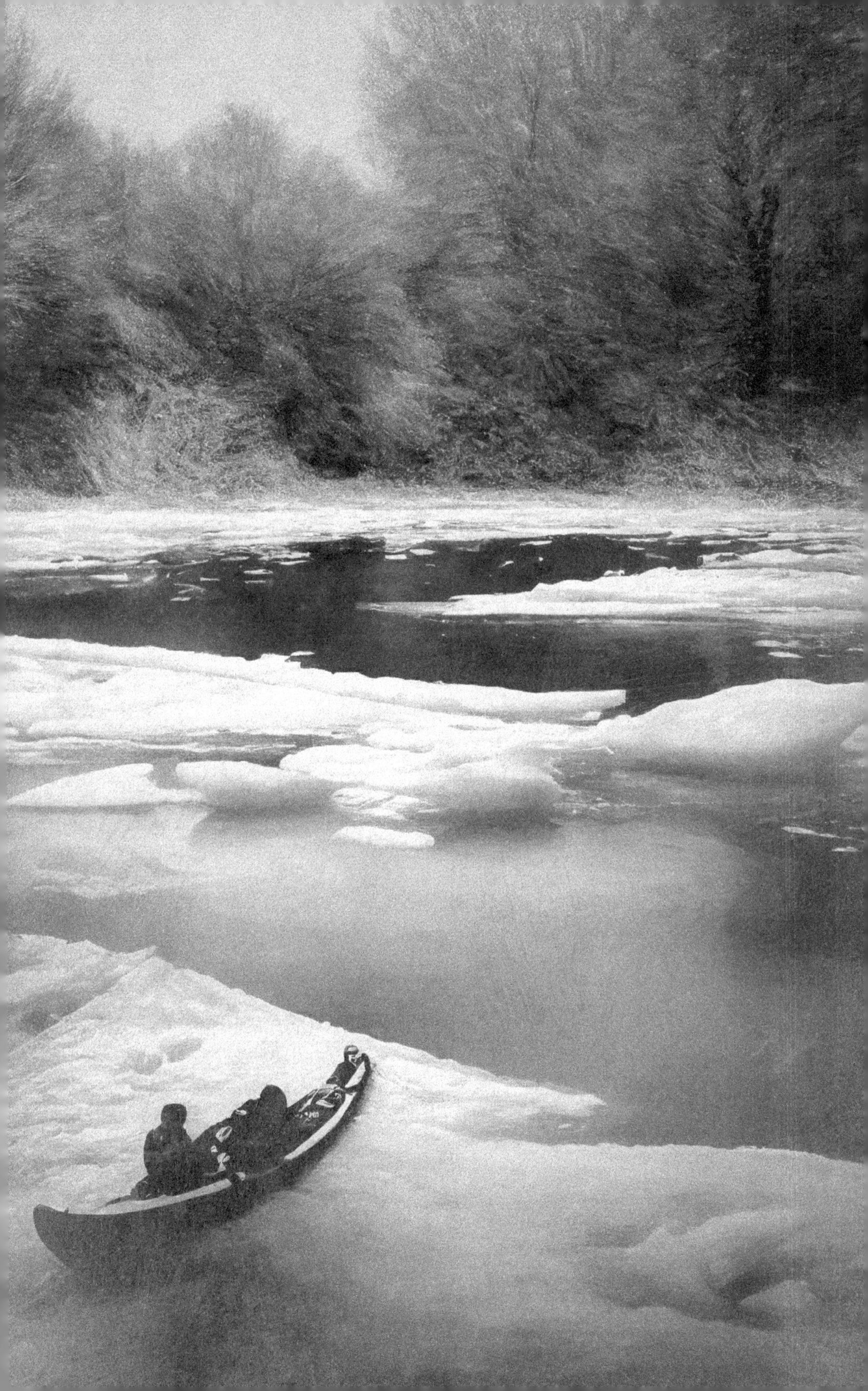

CHAPTER
TWENTY-TWO

Cornelius watched from the deck of his ship for the return of the Reaper hunting party led by the president himself. The ship moored in an icy bay between the Autumn and Spring Courts. The snow and ice made it impossible to arrive at this location by anything other than a portal. It also made it difficult to get home.

Their fuel stocks were low. If this expedition wasn't successful, subsequent raids on the Tainted would be brutal.

He hugged his insulated cape to keep out the biting cold and squinted through the snow glare on the land. Any minute they would return.

He hoped.

It had been days since they'd arrived in this bay, and he was getting impatient. If the party didn't return soon, if Cornelius didn't return to Crystal City, then all his plans would be derailed.

Melody would accept another's belt, and he couldn't have that.

His plan to overthrow the president hinged on having her in his pocket.

The president said he approved of the match, but if he did, then why was he taking so long? Why was he pushing the boundary of Cornelius's loyalty?

Why was he here at all?

Since they'd left for this mission, Cornelius had been suspicious. The fact that the president was here said he'd lost faith in Cornelius to get the job done. They were becoming distrustful of each other. Soon, one of them would snap.

Perhaps it should be Cornelius—now, while he still had enough fuel to return to Crystal City.

"Movement," barked a soldier as he stared down the lens of telescopic binoculars. "Northeast quadrant."

Cornelius's gaze tracked where he pointed. Sure enough, a small group of people in white camouflage suits trudged across the snow toward the shore. The darkly dressed figure they dragged was a stark contrast.

Cornelius gestured to two soldiers standing like dumb dolts watching the approaching party.

"Don't just stand there," he clipped. "Get the harvesting supplies."

They jumped into action, rushing about the deck to drag out the glass containers, needles, and solutions required for the job. Harvesting the fuel had to occur while the subject was alive, or the fuel would leave the body on its own.

Within minutes, the president arrived via dinghy with four Reapers and the fuel source. Cornelius counted the hunting party. Two Reapers were missing. He didn't bother asking why. A death toll on these expeditions was expected, and worth the fuel they reaped.

He blew on his hands to keep warm as hardened Reapers dragged their prize onboard. Cornelius gave the president a quick once-over, checking for injury, half hoping the man had something dire. It would save a lot of trouble if he were. But as usual, Nero was unharmed. Not even a drop of blood on him.

Unlike the Guardian they dropped at Cornelius's feet. From the oozing bullet wounds and gashes, he'd put up a fight.

"Hand me the extraction kit," Nero said to Cornelius.

Cornelius blinked at him. Not only did the president want to be here—amongst the Reapers—but he was going to take Cornelius's job from him. While his men watched? *Insulting.* Seething hate boiled beneath the surface of his skin, but he smiled tightly at Nero and handed him the needle filled with mercury. "Good work, Mr. President."

Nero gave no evidence of hearing Cornelius. He plunged the needle into the Guardian's thick neck, depressed the liquid metal, and then instructed his Reapers to collect the unique balls of energy popping out of the body with quick efficacy.

They hurried to fill their glass canisters before the balls of light entered the atmosphere.

Cornelius stood back and watched as the nameless Guardian's face lost its youth. This one looked almost human if not for the pointed ears. When their harvest was complete, the male wouldn't be recognizable. Not that it mattered. They would dump the body overboard after they were done. The sea animals would eat the corpse.

The bright balls of light were the reason they could activate a

A SONG OF SKY AND SACRIFICE

portal that allowed humans to cross with metal and plastic. The Tinker had created the machine that used the fuel. She was the genius who figured out Guardians were the only Tainted who carried the substances at the same time as using magic.

"Good," the president said as the harvest completed. He gestured to his Reapers. "Prepare to head back out."

"What?" Cornelius grabbed Nero's arm. "You're going back out?"

Nero glared at where Cornelius touched him. He let go. But not of his anger. This would be an inconceivable setback.

"There is another rookie Guardian out there," Nero explained calmly. "We separated the two, could only take down one, but we will go back for the second."

That meant they would be out here for another few days. "But you said we would be back in time for the Phoenix Ball."

"Plans change, Captain." Nero canted his head, studying Cornelius with suspicion. "You wouldn't want us to miss out on another valuable fuel intake, would you? A rookie Guardian is still hard to overcome, but we will lose more than a few Reapers if we must start hunting their elite Guardians."

"Of course not," he blustered and stood back as the Reapers refilled weapons and restocked supplies for another multi-day journey into the snowy wilderness.

He said nothing as they departed the ship. He watched quietly as the dinghy paddled through the cold waters to the frozen shore. But when the hunting party disappeared into the woods, he turned to his crew.

"Fuel the portal machine," he barked. "Prepare for travel."

"Captain?" his First Mate inquired.

They both knew leaving the president would be a death sentence. But Cornelius lifted his chin and said, "We will return immediately once this fuel cache is secure in Crystal City."

This was just the opportunity he'd been waiting for. If they returned a little too late—let's say... *after* the Phoenix Ball's rehearsal dinner—and the president had died in the unforgiving wilds of Elphyne, then the path would be free for Cornelius to rule Crystal City.

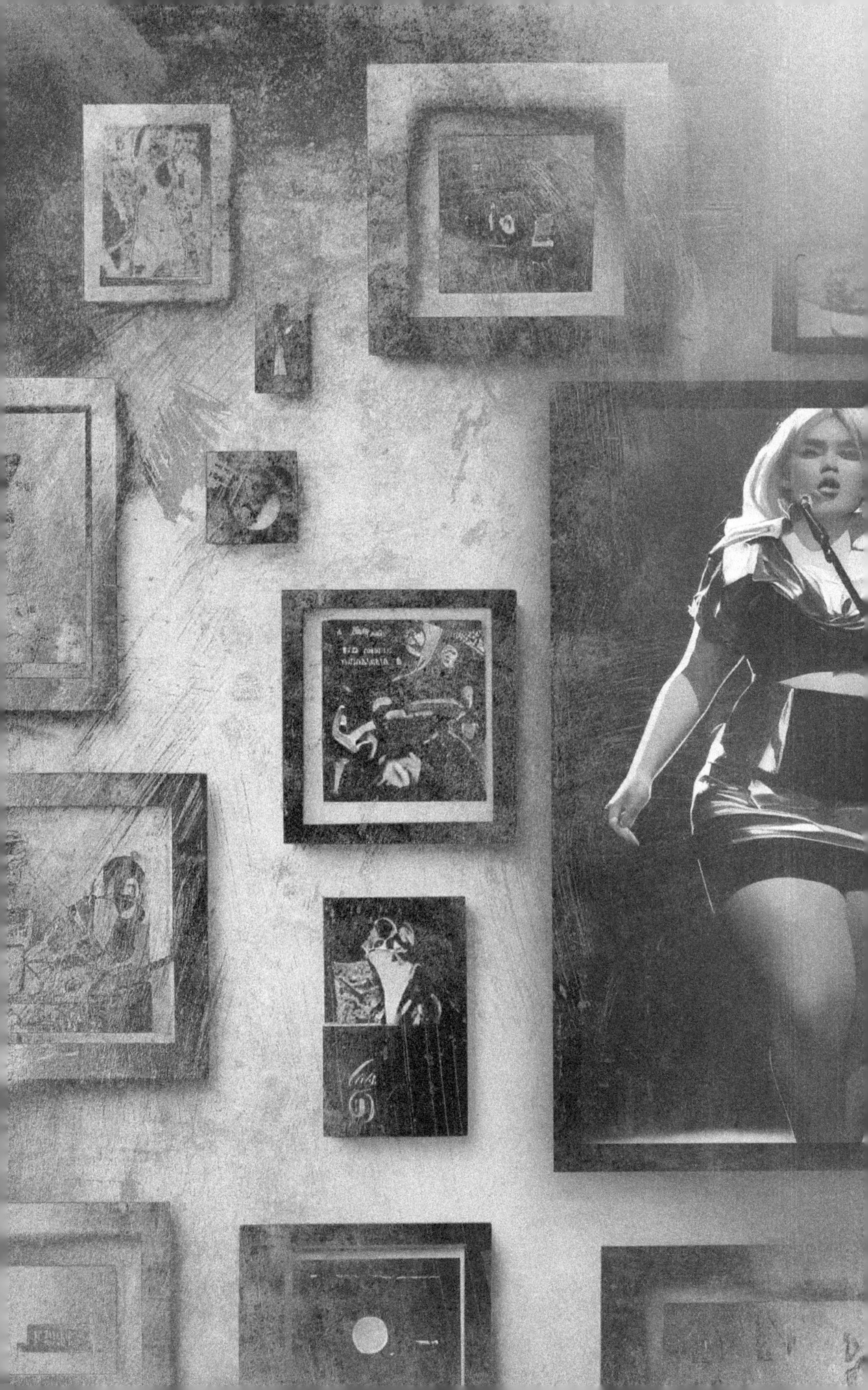

CHAPTER
TWENTY-THREE

Melody pressed her forehead against her apartment window and watched the rain fall. She listened to her band practice behind her—what was left of the band. Days had passed, and Caroline was still missing. No one had seen or heard from her.

They did their best to remain positive. Melody kept thinking that if she stayed under the radar and did as she was told, the Phoenix Ball would arrive swiftly, and Caroline would be returned. It wouldn't matter if she accepted the Captain's belt. They would be free before she had to go through with a wedding.

Melody continued her lessons with Forrest where possible, but he was closed off to practical demonstrations. She couldn't help but feel disappointed, which was stupid. They weren't an item. Never would be. There was only one reason she had let him stick his hands up her dress.

Liar.

She liked it. She should admit it.

Refusing to dwell, she wondered why he'd rushed out of the museum instead. It was out of character for him. He'd been so stalwart in his bodyguard duties. Something had happened that he refused to acknowledge.

Since then, he continued to turn up for his duties, but he brushed her off when she offered unsolicited tips for seducing Rory. He would only slide her an unreadable look and say, "Got it."

Their intimate moment was all she'd thought about, but it didn't seem to cross his mind. All Forrest wanted to talk about was her gift and being connected to the Well. Every morning he escorted her down to the garden, and as soon as he'd been sure no one was in there with them, he gave her lessons—not the other way around. She still remembered him drawing a diagram of elements making up the Well in a sandy patch by the fountain in the garden the other morning.

"Chaos. Spirit. Fire. Water. Air. Earth," he said, pointing with his stick. "We won't know exactly what you're capable of until we test you at the Order. With the taint making everything so unpredictable, we should wait for then. But we can give you a basic understanding of theory now, so if you gain access to the Well, you will have a defense against attack."

Melody frowned at the word attack. She'd stupidly thought once she got to Elphyne, all her troubles would be over. "It's still dangerous out there, isn't it?"

He met her eyes. "And in here too. Nero found a way to connect to the Well where no other can. If we had more time, I'd investigate because it means that you and I could do the same. I would also teach you to defend yourself, so someone like the

Captain can't put you in that position again. But we don't have time."

"The rehearsal dinner is in a few days."

"Yes. You have songs to write and appearances to keep. I have... planning to do."

"I noticed you speaking with Rory last night during my performance." She fidgeted with her dress, hoping he would elaborate on his plans.

He grunted but didn't comment. Instead, he explained which elements he believed her gift was grounded in and, if so, what sort of spells she could cast. Some spells were instinctive, some required Elven glyphs to be written or scratched into surfaces, and some sketched these symbols using hand signs in the air. It all sounded so complicated. Melody could understand why some fae dedicated their life to learning about it at the Order Academy.

Melody lost focus after that. Forrest was doing everything he could to go through with his agreement to take her with him, but beneath it all, she felt like he was pulling away.

That was days ago. Since then, she'd stewed over Forrest's growing aloofness toward her and kept returning to her old insecurities. She was different from who she was in those Hall of Fame pictures at the museum. She caught him staring at them as he'd rushed off. How he'd faltered. How he mustn't have liked how much she'd changed.

She stopped by the pictures on her way out of the museum and wondered what he saw. To her, she was a woman on a stage—arms wide, the world at her feet, a grin on her face.

Melody brought her mind back to the present, and the horrible weather outside.

The rain poured, and she hated it. She used to love it. Each drop was a beat she could harness. But now, all she could hear was gloom. How long could she go without seeing the sun before she went insane?

But these people in this Tower had gone millennia like this. They were so cut off from the world. How could they know what they were missing?

The plucked chords of her band's latest song sounded off key, and she wanted to instruct them but didn't have the heart. Forrest gave Melody new material about monstrous fae during their garden lessons. She still refused to sing about his childhood, but he'd told her of a strange little creature called a wolpertinger. Something between a rabbit and a chicken with antlers. It lured unsuspecting single women in with its cuteness, and once it caught them, it transformed into an adult-sized beast that mated with her.

At first, Melody had been horrified, but as Forrest spoke, she started to feel a little sorry for the creature. Don't get her wrong—it deserved to be despised for its forced mating habits, but she could see there was another level to its tragic existence. There were no females of its kind, and the kidnapped woman died horrendously during childbirth. Even the fae called it an abhorrence of nature.

So, she made the song to the tune of the Police song, *Every Breath you Take*. She thought it was funny at the time she'd thought of it, but now the minor key just made it sad. This 'monster' that kidnapped women was doomed from its birth.

Melody left the window and sat with her friends, "Don't y'all think it's a little sad that this creature is always alone?"

Andrew put down his violin. "It's alone for a good reason."

"Yeah," Timothy scoffed. "Don't go catching feelings for it. Like you wrote in the song, it will snap you up like yesterday's breakfast, and before you know it, you're knitting booties for weird wolpertinger feet. And then you die. End of story."

"But what about the other fae?" Melody asked, testing their reaction. "What do you think of the ones who are kind of like us? I mean, what's so bad about them, except they look a little different? And they basically live forever."

Her band went silent and stared at her.

"Fae?" Andrew asked. "Are we calling them that now?"

Melody sighed. Sometimes she forgot that they'd grown up in a bubble. From the moment they were born, they were taught to hate fae.

"All I'm saying is maybe we should go there and see what it's like before we pass judgment."

"You want to go there?" Timothy gaped.

"I mean, would it be so bad? What if they're good people? What if we can be free there?"

Andrew came to stand at the window with Melody. He put his arm around her shoulder. "Sweet, there's no use hoping for that kind of world. I know you came from somewhere you can choose your fate, and I've fantasized about being in such a world, but it's not like that here. It's too dangerous out there."

"You know they have protectors who kill the bad monsters," Melody said. "They're called Guardians. And there are kings and queens and soldiers. They have palaces and castles. Waterfalls. Trees. Good Lord, they have entire *forests*."

Timothy slipped his arm around Melody too. She put her head on his shoulder. "I guess it might be nice if I weren't so afraid."

"I just want Caroline back," Andrew whispered.

"I know you do, honey. I know."

The rehearsal dinner night came around faster than Melody was prepared for. Tonight would run differently than other nights. She would perform a short set with her band, but then because she would be a participant in the betrothal ceremony, she would also retire to the dining tables before dinner was served and join the rest of the elite.

There would be no propaganda tonight. The actual Phoenix Ball —where the official betrothals were announced, including hers— would be a more formal occasion.

Tonight was the last night bachelors could offer their belt to one of their approved bloodline debutants. Anyone who opted to wait for the Phoenix Ball would have that choice taken away. Not that they had many to pick from. The approved partner list was short and sweet, and one that a woman called Ms. Vanderhall carefully spent the entire year constructing. A mass marriage ceremony would happen, and after the ball, newlyweds could leave together for their first night of marital bliss.

Whenever the Captain suggested Melody should choose him, a switch flipped in her mind, and she disassociated or pretended this archaic practice didn't exist. It wasn't going to happen to her.

Then why did she feel like puking?

Andrew had refused to offer his belt to any approved partners so that he would be allocated one during the ball. Timothy felt the same. Even if Caroline wasn't locked up, she wasn't due to become a debutant until next year. And Melody... she would smile, nod, and do whatever she was told while Forrest chatted up Rory.

Hopefully, in three days...

Her mind shut down. Fear and doubt stopped her from imagining herself with everything she wanted.

"Show me how you like to be kissed," he'd said. *"Show me so that I may learn to be your everything."*

Her small taste of Forrest was so intoxicating it was all she could think of.

That and how awful she'd feel if he and Rory hit it off. But there were two things wrong with that scenario. Would Rory betray the only family she'd ever known in three days of coital bliss, even if he looked as hot as Forrest? And then if she did, if miracles happened, would Forrest want to be with Melody?

Who knows, you might even fall in love. Her own voice came back to haunt her. Bitterness grated through her to the point her mind started to go to dark places—anything to stop that future from eventuating. Even wondering if seducing Rory was still in the best interest of Forrest's plan, and if it wasn't, would he still take her with him?

Would he think the small amount of instruction she gave him was valuable?

Maybe that was why he grew detached from her—he had found another way to save Willow, which didn't involve her. Or perhaps he was going to seduce Rory, and then they would all drive off into the Elphyne sunset looking all perfect and...

Gah! Melody shook her head. She was obsessing, and she knew why. She'd developed strong feelings for the fae, and instead of talking to him and revealing her vulnerabilities, she would instead turn him into a villain... or herself into the victim.

When he picked her up from the green room that evening, she planned to let him know how she felt. But as she opened the door, she was struck dumb. *Sack of potatoes. Sack of potatoes.* She sucked in her gut and tried to make the extra weight disappear by thought.

He wasn't in his usual Tower Guard uniform but a suit that stretched lovingly over broad, muscular shoulders and tapered down to a narrow waist. Even encased in civility, there was something wild about him. Something ready to pounce—just as he had in the museum. He'd become needy, demanding, and aggressive at a point in her teaching.

And she was there for it. Goddamn, she wanted to peel back those layers he kept over himself and expose the primal beast he contained. *"I've spent too much time in the minds of animals,"* he'd said.

She pressed her cool hands to her hot cheeks and smiled meekly at him, hoping he couldn't read minds. She was falling for him. This would ruin everything.

"You look worried," he said quietly as Sid, Timothy, and Andrew went ahead. "Don't be. It will be fine."

Still trying to calm her rabbiting heart, she glanced sideways at him but couldn't determine a thing. "So you're still going to... Rory?"

He gave a short, clipped nod. "I've arranged to be seated with her at dinner."

"Good. That's good." It sucked.

She pressed her lips together and forced her eyes not to burn.

Forrest placed his palm at the small of her back as they walked, guiding her. The heat of his body bathed her.

"You look like a star," he murmured.

Her breath hitched. "What?"

"The center of the universe."

They arrived at the dining hall, and she stopped. They met eyes. She sensed this was a pivotal moment. It would be too late if she didn't say something meaningful to him now. Words caught on her tongue. Nothing came out.

"I got it," he said calmly. "Don't worry."

And then he left her at the foot of the stage. In a daze, Melody hitched her diamanté-ladened dress so she could walk unhindered up the steps. Once on the stage, she gave her band a tight smile and then took her place behind a microphone and faced the audience.

Tonight, the dining hall was set up differently. The tables were smooshed together and lined up in a unique horseshoe shape. Crisp tablecloths covered the lot. No flower arrangements but candles flickered on Phoenix sculptures surrounded by plastic ivy leaves. More would be added during the actual ball, but for now, it served as a practice run. The most crucial decor existed behind Melody on a tapestry—a family tree diagram of the Tower bloodlines. Important families and their descendants. She dared not see if her name was embroidered already.

It didn't matter anyway because the Captain sat directly in front of her at a table closest to the stage. He'd returned early from his trip abroad, wearing his jacket wide, blatantly exposing where he rested his hand on his Phoenix belt.

CHAPTER
TWENTY-FOUR

After seeing Melody to the stage, Forrest wiped his sweaty palms on his pants and surveyed the room. Tables had been moved, but the richly dressed elite were the same. Being the Sacrifice for the Rubrum royals, he'd learned to use his invisibility to his advantage, and that training had stayed with him well into his adult years.

Take time to watch, listen, and process. Never go in before deliberating.

Over the past week, he'd talked to Rory any time he bumped into her, especially in the dining hall where he could drag out conversation. He thought his efforts were in vain until two nights earlier during Melody's performance when he'd made a derogatory comment about not looking forward to the ball, and she sympathized with him.

"*Every year, I have to sit through this nonsense,*" Rory snarled. "*Get used to it.*"

"But you're not forced to participate?"

She went quiet. She seemed to catch her mind drifting and scowled. "It doesn't apply to me."

"Why?" he'd said, unable to help himself. "And how do I get on that boat?"

Her lips curved at his addition, but she only vaguely gestured at the bloodline tapestry being hung up. "My father and I are not on there."

At the time, Forrest had thought it odd, but now he realized why. To pass as wholly human, Nero hid the true length of his time alive and ruling this city. To do that, he had to erase all physical evidence of himself and his bloodline. He must also be controlling their memories somehow. That was the only reason Forrest could think to explain how the man had been in power for generations.

A spell had been cast over the entire city... or perhaps just the Tower, which was why they were forbidden to leave.

No human here knew about Well-blessed humans in Elphyne. Melody hadn't known she had a gift or access to the Well. Most humans had zero access to the Well, even when they stepped foot on Elphyne soil. Forrest had assumed that because he saw Nero ingesting stolen mana, it was how he gained power and immortality, but what if he'd had access to the Well all along? It might not be a lot. It might have faded over time, but what if Nero had been given the same chance as all humans upon thawing from his deep sleep, and he'd ruined it, and that was why he stole mana now?

Many questions hurtled through Forrest's mind, but one in particular. How much of this was Rory a party to, or was she a victim, just like the rest of these people?

Victim was a stretch, he thought, as he surveyed the elite. They ate until their bellies popped buttons and consumed like there weren't starving people outside this very building. Forrest spotted a short, pale head and tensed. Willow was here. He hadn't seen her since the garden and had begun to worry whether she was safe. But there she was, rosy-cheeked and wearing a frilly dress. From her incorrigible grin, she was enjoying herself. She glanced over at him, and her face lit up. He gave a slight shake of his head. Willow pouted but went back to bouncing on her seat.

Next to her, Rory was dressed in unexpected finery. Some of her outfit was hidden by the tablecloth, but he assumed it was a dress from the form-fitting and flattering cut. The copper beads in her hair matched a new set of rings across her knuckles. The shaved side of her head had been recently clipped.

An unsettled feeling churned in Forrest's stomach as he walked toward them. Tonight would be the night he made his moves—whether with Rory or against her remained to be seen.

"May I?" He pointed to a vacant chair as he arrived at the table.

The move was bold. Rory usually sat alone, and there had been no place settings to suggest otherwise. The event organizer had meticulously placed name cards everywhere else. Forrest was meant to be with a group of bachelors.

Rory glanced up from telling Willow to sit still and stared at him as though trying to figure him out. Sitting further down the u-shaped table settings, the highbrow elite in floral patterned clothes looked aghast that Forrest had the gall to approach Rory.

But if he cowered now at convention, he would lose any chance of impressing this woman. Already he felt he should have taken Melody up on more of her lessons in seduction. He feared his embarrassment would come back to bite him.

He said, "Since we're both in the same mind for this event, we can commiserate together."

She blinked. Then shrugged and kicked out the chair next to her. He caught a flash of silky-smooth leg through a slit in the dress. Sitting, he knew he should say something charming about her outfit. She was attractive. But she wasn't the center of his universe.

As if conjured by thought, a powerful voice filled the room in a haunting tune he'd not heard before. The crowd hushed, stopping everything to listen. Forrest knew if he looked up, he'd lose his nerve, so he sat down without a glance at the stage.

Willow bounced on her seat, hardly able to contain her excitement, so he held his hand out and said, "Hello. I'm Forrest."

He'd learned humans had this hand-holding convention for new social acquaintances. Touching palms was odd, but he supposed they would think fae customs were strange too. Having already lived with humans for most of her life, Willow knew exactly what to do. She squealed and gripped his hand, then shook it vigorously before biting her lip with mischief. Suspicion ground through him before he realized why she had the look of an imp about her. She wouldn't let go.

Forrest chuckled as she continued to shake.

"Willow," Rory warned, a flat smile on her face. "What did I say about behaving?"

Willow sighed and let go before moaning, "I can only wear a pretty dress if I'm good."

"And?"

"And you'll show me how to use my pinky finger to attack a giant."

Rory shifted uncomfortably in her seat and glanced at Forrest.

She said to Willow, "I was going to say you might be able to come to the ball."

"OH."

When Willow fidgeted, Rory exhaled and waved her out. "Go on. But you know what happens if—"

Willow made a zipping sign across her lips and nodded. She slid off her seat and ran to a corner where two other children waited. They squealed as Willow made it. Disturbed, Forrest tried not to look interested. He hadn't known Willow had made friends here. He'd assumed the ones she spoke about in the garden were imaginary. He knew he'd made up a few friends and talked to his animals when he was her age.

There were no other children her age at the Order.

"Sorry about that," Rory said. "She's a handful, but she's a good kid."

"She looks happy," he noted.

"I hope so." Something flickered in Rory's eyes, but she stamped it down fast as a waiter walked up and deposited two glasses. Possibly ale. Forrest sniffed. Definitely alcoholic.

The music died, and an announcer took Melody's place.

"That concludes our first performance of the night. Next, may I invite the unbelted debutants to the stage, and we will quickly run through the procedure while the first course is served."

Unable to tear his eyes from the stage, Forrest watched as Melody didn't stay with the other unbelted woman but as she moved down the steps where the Captain waited for her.

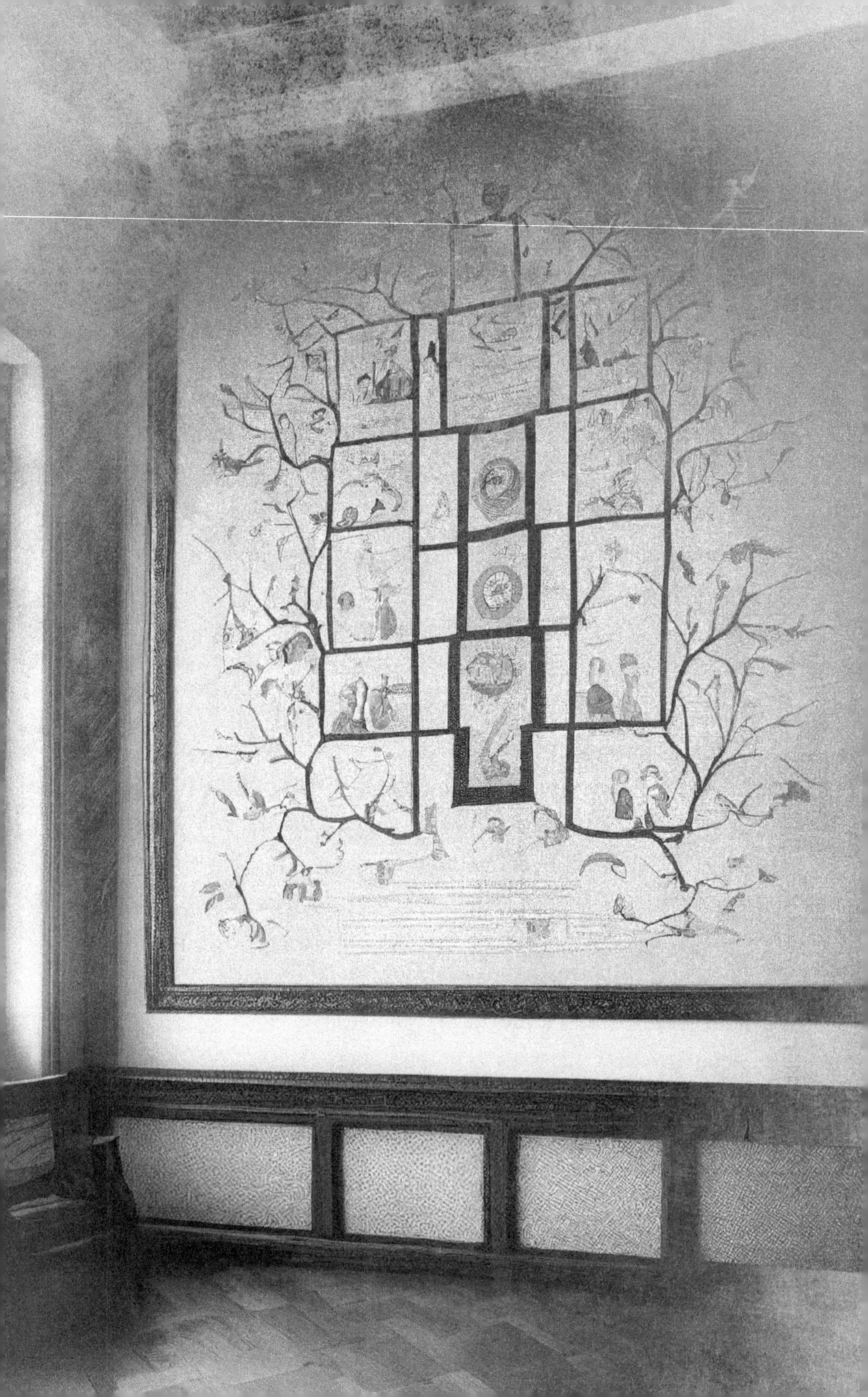

CHAPTER
TWENTY-FIVE

Melody knew from the moment she glimpsed the Captain in the audience that the night would not end well. He wasn't supposed to be back from his expedition.

Why was he here?

And why was he staring at her like she was his next meal?

If she didn't go down and nip this in the bud once and for all, she would spend the rest of the evening suffering for it. She would not accept his belt. He needed to get over it.

But her excuses vanished when she met him on the floor before the stage, and he slid his belt out of his pants. Something about this time gave her pause, and she couldn't place why. He had a certain confidence about him.

"Time for you to accept your fate," he said.

"Cornelius—"

"I'm sure you've noticed I've returned early. Without the president." His mustache twitched as a smile tried to break free on his face.

That simple, self-satisfied action caused her to shiver as dread tickled the back of her neck. She glanced around the room. No Nero. Not that she could see.

"He won't be returning," Cornelius explained quietly. Holding her stare, he held out his belt. "That means I will be responsible for the fate of your female friend in prison. I will be responsible for the rest of your band. I will control everyone. Now is the time to decide, Melody. Which side of that control do you want to be on?"

"What happened to him?"

"Let's just say he didn't return from his hunting expedition." He clicked his tongue in disapproval. "That's what happens when the president fails to trust his soldiers. Something I would never do."

Nero was gone.

Melody should be elated. Shouldn't she? Except the Captain was right. There was no one else to hold him back. He was in control.

She glanced to the table setting she knew Rory was at. Forrest sat there staring at Melody.

If she made a scene now, he would forgo the plan and come over to intervene. This might be his only chance at convincing Rory to side with them. She couldn't get in the way.

"If you want to see your friend alive again, then accept the belt, Melody."

CHAPTER
TWENTY-SIX

"You'll regret it," Rory said to Forrest.

"Pardon?"

"If you let her slip through your fingers, you'll regret it."

The astute woman knew exactly what was on his mind. His face must read like an open book. He should stay with Rory, but the very thought of that lecherous cockroach with his hands on—Forrest sucked in a burning breath. He'd been about to say *his mate*. That's where his mind went. It was how he felt about Melody.

Possessive. Irrationally protective. Obsessed. Eternal.

He'd been enchanted with Melody from the start. He wanted her. Needed her. The snarl of longing built in his body like a rising tide, growing in pressure under his skin. And then the Captain slid his belt out of his trouser loops and gave it to her.

Frozen, watching in horror, he could do nothing as Melody smiled politely and accepted the belt. She tied it around her waist so the ends dangled down her front, then she gave the Captain her cheek. Smug and with eyes that bled entitlement, he pressed his lips to Melody's flawless skin.

Red vibrated through Forrest's vision.

Mine. She's mine.

"Excuse me," he mumbled to Rory and pushed his chair out. Without taking his eyes from Melody, he strode across the room with decisive steps, his instinct driving him. He simply could not allow what he saw to be real. He refused to acknowledge it.

He was beside the couple in a heartbeat, gripping Melody's arm and leaning into her ear as he said quietly, "What are you doing?"

"Remove your hand from my future wife," the Captain barked, and Forrest went deathly still. He knew the precise seconds and moves needed to break that man's weak neck.

His fingers twitched.

He's not worth it.

She is.

Still holding Melody, he turned his back on the man to growl into her ear, "You are not doing this."

She smiled tightly at the Captain and whispered back to Forrest through her teeth, "I have to."

When he made no response, she gave Rory a pointed look and then said to the Captain, "You'll have to excuse my bodyguard. If you give me a moment to explain that I am safe with you, I will meet you at the dinner table."

The Captain glared at Forrest but then schooled his expression before making a short bow to Melody and saying, "Again, my darling. I regret my misplaced original belt. I admit I don't know what happened to it."

The fact the Captain so clearly dismissed Forrest as a threat showed how arrogant he was. Whether it was because Melody called Forrest her bodyguard or whether it was a byproduct of the belt exchange, the Captain was sorely mistaken.

"It's not necessary," Melody said tightly. "This belt is fine."

"Nevertheless, I will find it. And then you will have one befitting a woman of your new station." He paused and flicked his gaze to Forrest before darting back to her. "I will see you *shortly* for dinner."

Forrest barely waited until the Captain was gone before lowering his lips to Melody's ear. "I refuse to share you with anyone else. You belong with me, Melody."

Her breath hitched. "But you... you stopped wanting lessons. In the museum, you ran away."

"I ran because the very *thought* of tasting you made me climax so hard, I soiled myself." He breathed hard through his nose, struggling not to taste her right there, no matter who was watching. "I ran because I was ashamed."

Her chest rose sharply. "Why didn't you tell me? I thought it was me you didn't want. That... that I wasn't desirable."

"Melody. You mentioned another woman's name while I was infatuated with you. I was not okay with that."

Another sharp intake of Melody's breath. Her expression morphed as the cogs turned in her mind. He could see her figure out that he'd dismissed the very object of his supposed seduction to be with her, be damned with the consequences. He thought she might say something harsh, some reminder of his mission, but her lips trembled when she whispered, "I mentioned her name because I was protecting my heart."

Forrest's anger tempered. His eyes softened, and all he wanted to do was kiss her. He wanted her to see him. He wanted her to *feel* for him and no other.

"I don't want her," he said, low and rough. His next words conjured visuals that made him dizzy with desire. "I want my tongue where my fingers were. I want you."

"But you'll sacrifice the mission if—"

"I'll sacrifice the world to be with you."

"I want you too."

They shared a long, intense, and agonizing stare because they both knew they stood in the epicenter of a crowded room. His body heated. Trembled. His desire stoked. Why were they waiting? Her eyes dipped to his lips.

"Are you feeling wicked?" she whispered so quietly that he almost didn't catch it.

If you're feeling particularly wicked, your tongue can replace your fingers. A thrill entered his stomach, tightening everything in anticipation as he realized she was responding to his declaration. Perhaps she'd agonized over every second of her lessons as much as he had.

"I'm feeling more than that," he growled, hardly able to breathe.

"We probably shouldn't."

"Why not?"

"He's watching."

"We can go somewhere private."

"Not for a while."

"Now."

Her face lit up with an echo of his desire. Now. Here. Somewhere. Somehow. But as fast as the notion entered her eyes, all it took was one look over Forrest's shoulder to where the Captain waited, where he watched, and Melody's face deadpanned. Her shoulders slumped.

"We can't." Her step away crushed his heart.

"Don't," he pleaded, hating how his voice sounded so small, so desperate.

One word. That's all he could sacrifice. What he felt was too big for words.

Don't walk away. Don't turn your back. Don't unsee me.

She stopped at his shoulder. Tensed. Looked back at him as he faced her. Like this, despite their body language saying they were about to separate, they were still yearning to be close.

"Caroline is in danger," she reminded him. "The Captain said Nero wasn't returning from Elphyne. If that's true, then…"

"Nero is missing?"

"That's what he said."

"I don't believe it," Forrest replied. "No one else has mentioned it."

"I don't think he's announced it yet."

"Humans lie all the time."

"But if he's not lying, then what?"

Guilt sliced through him. This wasn't just about them. It was about her friends. The mission. Willow. Rory. But whenever Forrest made those excuses in his mind, the roar of defiance inside him was harder to ignore.

Me, it shouted. No more sacrifice. No more them. *Me*.

Fuck everyone else.

Me. He wanted to pound his chest and demand her take note. *Me*.

Forrest didn't care about anyone else for the first time in his life.

The selfish notion burrowed into his mind and devoured all decency and common sense. This was the animal urge driving his sanity. There was no reason in primality. This was his need to be seen. By her, and only her. It built beneath his skin like an itch.

He glanced at Rory's table, and she was not there. Willow probably played with her friends. He couldn't find it in him to care. The organizer directed debutants on the stage before the large tapestry, ensuring they had the space to stitch in the next generation. Another organizer spoke to the inebriated elite at the tables drinking and eating, a clipboard in her hand. And there, waiting and watching as he talked to another military officer, was the Captain.

"Go and sit with your betrothed," Forrest conceded. The word tasted vile on his tongue but also spurred him on. It made him wicked. "And while you're talking to him, I'll be over there, sitting at the table and planning all the filthy things my tongue will do to you tonight when you're sitting on my face." *My* face. *Mine.* "And, Melody. I've had decades to imagine my first time."

"I'll smother you."

That was what she was worried about? Not the suicidal notion he'd just proposed, his demanding words, or the confession he found so embarrassing. Her earlier words came back to him. She didn't think he was attracted to her.

"I *want* you to smother me," he said. "I want to drown in your taste."

He didn't think she'd agree to it. Some dark Unseelie part of him thought she would ignore the fragment of him that needed her most. That's what everyone else had done. But while he stood there, lungs dragging in the air like sand, a slow, mischievous grin spread across her lips, and she nodded.

"Tonight," she declared. "For us. Not her. Not him. Not them. Us."

Us. His mouth watered. His heart thundered. She was as needy for him as he was for her.

Somewhere in a dark, hidden room of Forrest's mind, his reason spiraled. He slammed the door and locked it in. His smile turned criminal as Melody gave him a pointed, sultry look. And then she walked calmly to the dining table. She sat like a queen, ready to face her foe across the battlefield.

He liked confidence on her. She suited it. And he liked even more how she made him feel the same.

Tonight.

CHAPTER
TWENTY-SEVEN

Melody sat demurely at the table she'd been assigned. She thumbed the belt at her waist while the Captain sat opposite her talking to a military man, completely ignoring her other than marking her arrival with a glance.

Dismissed but still in a cage.

She wanted nothing more than to tip the table up and spill everything onto him, to rip the burning belt from around her waist and shove it in his face.

The hardest thing in life, no matter her time or this one, was to hold back everything that made her Melody because it wasn't the right time.

It was never the right time.

Unless Melody and Forrest could convince Rory.

Three more nights before she was officially chained to the Captain. Until then, she had a certain amount of freedom—freedom she well intended to explore. Even if things went sideways, she'd always have the memories of these next few nights with Forrest.

Already aroused to the point of pain, she squeezed her thighs together and averted her gaze from the Captain. She hated her thighs on any good day, but like a horny teenager, all she could think of was what Forrest had said to her.

I want to drown in your taste.

The tone of his voice had been so raw, rough, and on a vibration that pushed all her buttons. An illicit thrill ran rampant through her body as the anticipation of tonight compounded.

I've had decades to imagine my first time.

Forrest's reluctance to continue lessons had nothing to do with not being attracted to her nor her insistence he seduce Rory. He was falling in love with Melody, and he'd thought she felt nothing for him.

It seemed they were both sacrificing their hearts for the good of others.

I want my tongue where my fingers were.

Melody startled as the elite couple beside her burst into laughter at something said in conversation. It felt too rehearsed. Too much like they were trying to get her attention. The Captain smirked as though he'd heard, but the increasing noise made it difficult to hear beyond who was next to her, let alone across the table. The Captain stared at her with secret thoughts spinning as he tilted his head to the military man next to him.

I hate you. She smiled at him. He lifted his glass and nodded as though one would nod to a worthy opponent he'd just beaten in a game of chess. He didn't know half of it. The game wasn't over, far from it.

Goosebumps erupted as she waited for Forrest and tapped her feet impatiently. Searching the room, she tried to locate where he'd gone. He said he'd be waiting at a table, planning things, but he was nowhere in sight.

I'll sacrifice the world to be with you.

Melody shivered as the Captain's voice filtered across the table. The man beside her tinkled his spoon against his glass and spoke loud enough so his voice carried across the table.

"I say, Captain. You're back early from your latest journey." He narrowed his eyes at the Captain. Something about his words hushed all those around the table. Even Melody could see the Captain was uncomfortable as he gestured at Melody and replied.

"A man so well matched as yourself, Phillip, surely understands the importance of this night. The President understands my leaving early to be here."

Phillip raised his brows. "A man so well matched as *myself* understands the importance of industry. And this trip, and now tonight's festivities, have already pushed back delivery."

Melody's ears pricked up. The Captain owed Phillip?

"These things take time," the Captain said, then gave Melody a proprietary look. "But as you can see, I will soon have more influence and the means to expedite."

Melody couldn't look up. Heat scorched her face. This was why he wanted her... control, influence. The Captain had political aspirations and would use Melody just as the president did. A future here flashed before her eyes—a life of emptiness, more than she'd ever imagined.

The couple next to Melody gave her a concerned look. The female had coiffed hair with feathers stabbed into the knot. Probably from the barbed wire net above the city. Probably fae feathers cleaned of blood. The man looked important enough to be one of the businessmen running the city. They were the only ones allowed to leave the Tower. His cheeks were ruddy and bursting from time outdoors. He probably had a kept mistress out there and then returned to an unsullied family, his bloodline dating back to the nuclear fallout.

Phillip and his wife took that as a sign to talk, and she wished they hadn't. Because once they started, then others would come. Sitting there alone was asking for company. It had always been like this—even back in her time. At first, people pretended they weren't entranced with her celebrity. Then suddenly, one would gather the nerve to talk to her, and soon it became an avalanche of requests for selfies and hugs. At least there were no camera phones these days.

"I'm sorry, I just have to say that your voice is magnificent," the woman said to Melody, leaning forward to see past her husband. "I was just saying to Phill, wasn't I Phill, that you have such a unique way about you that just—ooh, it touches the soul, doesn't it, Phill?"

He smiled tightly and nodded.

Someone sat in the empty seat to her right. Melody turned excitedly, grateful for an excuse to ignore having to talk about her performances.

Rory.

Oh, shit.

Rory's face was passive as she pressed a sharp knife to Melody's side.

Why was Rory holding a knife into her gut? Why hadn't the Captain said anything—he saw something was wrong. Bastard. He would let her die.

"Cut the dramatics," Rory whispered harshly.

"What is going on?" Melody asked.

"I just found out Willow revealed her true self to you."

Oh. That's why.

"I'm not sure I know what you mean," she replied, somewhat breathlessly.

"Don't lie." Rory pressed harder, pinching through the dress. "I can gut you right here, and no one would blink an eye. Willow told me while you and your bodyguard talked."

Did she say anything about Forrest's identity? Panic scorched Melody's pulse.

"I saw Willow shift into fae form but said nothing because it's none of my business."

Another press of the knife inward. Melody winced but refused to whimper in pain.

"I won't say a thing," she continued. "Unless you want me to. What do you want?"

Rory assessed her silently, and perhaps something Melody had said hit home because the knife disappeared from her side and landed on the table with the other cutlery.

"I want you to forget what you saw," Rory said quietly. She darted a glance at the Captain, who'd narrowed his eyes at her. "Focus on your new affair with your guard. And if I ever catch word of Willow's identity talked about in public, being my father's favorite won't save you. He'll find another star to shine for him. He always does."

Rory gave a wry smile. Melody thought she might say something else, but a long, tension-filled moment passed. Finally, as

Rory pushed back the chair to leave, she whispered to Melody, "Don't blow it."

When Rory was gone, the couple's female leaned over her husband to ask, "What was that about?"

Melody's mind whirled with emotions. She didn't know which one to stop on first. The belt around her waist felt tight, as though it was saying, "Look at me."

Seducing Rory would not work, even if Forrest and Melody hadn't changed their minds. Rory had noticed they were into each other. And if she'd seen it... then the Captain certainly knew. Melody's eyes lifted to meet her new betrothed's gaze across the table. He wasn't even pretending to be interested in his companion's conversation.

He watched Melody.

He waited for her to do something.

When she could only stare back, the Captain dismissed her again.

No, she thought. *I have things to say.*

The moment she thought it, she knew it was time to use her voice for something worthy.

"Excuse me." Melody stood.

"Melody," the Captain clipped. "Sit down."

"I have to go."

"Sit down and shut up."

Melody walked like a zombie to the stage. This might be her only chance. She was risking everything. Caroline's life. Her own. But something about what happened made the decision snap in her brain. She'd just had a sexy elf proclaim his desire for her. She'd just had a woman threaten her with a knife. She walked away from an asshole. She was still here. Still strong. Still with a voice she could use.

She could no longer be the puppet of this warped dynasty. Someone had to start shouting. It may as well be her. Walking across the stage, she picked up her drumsticks and sat down behind the set. Andrew and Timothy played their elevator-type music. They watched her curiously. This wasn't in the set. Not in the plan.

"I'm taking over," she said to them. "This is going to cause trouble. If I were you, I'd leave and make it clear you're not with me."

They stopped, eyes wide. Music halted. Conversation muffled as everyone turned her way. The woman who organized the event looked up sharply from where she ordered servers around. The Captain stood slowly, fury on his face as if he no doubt readied himself to stalk up to the stage and pull her down by force.

This was it. The moment. No turning back.

Melody clapped her hands to a beat next to the microphone. She pressed the pedal feeding to the gramophone recorder the Tinker had made. It captured her beat on vinyl. Once she laid down the sample track, she set the sound to repeat, so the beat continued in the background.

Then she took a breath.

Thought about if she really wanted this.

Yes.

Melody swallowed, then lifted her chin. She hit the base drum's foot pedal and played a slow rhythm like a heartbeat over the clapping beat she'd laid down.

She leaned into the microphone and said, "This is for all those told to sit down and shut up." *Thud thud.* "It's time to think for ourselves." *Thud thud.* "Do what you want." *Thud thud.* She pulled her belt off and tossed it. "It's time to love who we wanna love."

Andrew recognized the beat first. He picked up his violin and added to the tune. Timothy hesitated, but his expression hardened, and then he hammered out the piano refrain. Melody lowered her lips. She pressed them hard against the microphone and sang about not sitting in silence, not living in fear, and making a noise.

Grinning from ear to ear, she belted her heart out to the anthem, *The Voice* by John Farnham.

When it was done, when the last thudding heartbeat died, she stood up, knocked her drums over, and lifted her chin high. Andrew, God bless him, ripped off his belt and shouted, "Love who you want to love."

With tears in her eyes, Timothy smashed his fists on the piano keys, then picked up the stool and threw it. Andrew tossed his violin. They kissed.

Chaos erupted. Tower guards flooded the stage. The Captain moved, pointing at guards as he owned them, demanding they bring her to his room.

But they couldn't get through.

Everywhere in the room, people argued. They brawled. They threw food. All because, somewhere deep down, no matter how many centuries had passed, Melody's song ran true. It called to a deep, primal desire to be free.

"Run," Andrew shouted to Melody as he punched a guard. Timothy jumped on the back of another, biting his ear.

Melody kicked off her shoes and hurled them at the guards, then she hitched up the skirt of her dress and ran.

What the hell had she started?

CHAPTER
TWENTY-EIGHT

While Melody had been dining with the enemy, Forrest stood by the kitchen door to gather his thoughts. He couldn't return to Rory. That ship had sailed. It had never launched, really. It had always been Melody since he'd first arrived, and now, he needed to see this through so he could make another plan.

So he stood there, as promised, thinking about everything he would do to Melody tonight when they were alone.

Then he saw Rory walk up to her, sit, and argue in hushed tones. He was ready to storm over and take Rory out, be damned with her lineage to Maebh. But as quickly as the argument had begun, that confrontation was over, and Melody suddenly walked to the stage.

The look on her face had turned his blood cold.

At first, he'd been stunned. As always with her, he'd been besotted by her voice. Then he realized what she sang about, and he feared.

He'd heard people talking from his spot by the kitchen while the song reached its crescendo. Some were angry. Some were curious. Some... some shouted their true feelings. The staff were particularly vocal. How they hated being told what job they had to have. How they hated the oppressive betrothals. How they wanted to pick their own love matches, their own lives.

The song finished.

A man bowled into Forrest after being punched. Forrest shoved him off and glanced back at the stage. Melody was gone. His heart jumped into his throat. He needed to find her. Nothing else mattered. He charged through the crowd toward the stage. *Where was she?*

He scanned the dining hall, but he found no platinum blond hair over the heads of the pompous elite. Guards caused a commotion, and outliers joined the band in their rebellion.

But he did see silver.

Willow chased her two friends around chairs, having fun in the chaos and playing tag. She caught them easily and pouted.

"You're too easy to catch." She scowled. "My other friends are better than you."

They poked their tongues at her.

"Willow," Forrest said as he came up to her. "Have you seen Melody?"

Still scowling at her friends, she said offhandedly, "She went that way."

Willow pointed to the exit, then started squealing and chasing her friends again, as though this chaos was the most excitement they'd had all year.

Forrest was ashamed of how quickly he left.

It might have been the perfect time to spirit Willow away. He could have taken her kicking and screaming, and no one would have said a word. But not Rory. And all he cared about was finding Melody. Everything was spiraling out of control. This was not how it usually went down for him. He was the dependable one, but as his quick strides turned into a jog, he started to panic. What if the guards had already found her?

First, he tried her rooms, but they were empty. He thought about back-tracking and checking the green room but decided against it. If she was feeling out of sorts, where would she go? Probably somewhere she felt powerful. Confident. Somewhere she looked at the sky and felt inspired.

The garden.

He was in the elevator and traveling down in seconds, hating how he had no fae sense of smell here. If he could connect to his gift, everything would be so much more. He could track anyone through his creatures. The elevator clanged at the ground level, and he wrenched the brass cage door open. He rushed through the empty lobby—the guards must have been called to the dining hall to deal with the trouble.

Forrest burst into the garden, and the connection to the Well hit him ten-fold. He gasped as he acclimated. With clarifying energy, he was suddenly himself again. The Well still accepted him. It still fed into him, trickling up from his feet to fill him with mana. Soon he would have enough to use defensively. If only there were a power source here, he could refill at a faster rate, but he would have to make do with the natural state.

Melody was here. His fae nose scented her.

He lifted his nose to the breeze at the same time as connecting with the birds around him. Using their minds and her scent, he located her in the maze of hedges. He broke into a jog down the path. With each thunderous step he made, his animal instincts jarred awake. The thrill of the hunt ground through him. His nostrils flared. His adrenaline surged. And then he heard her footsteps quickening.

She was running.

So he chased harder.

He crested a corner and glimpsed platinum hair and a dress before she disappeared again.

"Melody," he called. "Stop running or..."

He'll what? Heaving in ragged breaths, feeling like a huffing Well-hound, he resumed stalking at a slower pace, forcing himself to suppress his wild urges. When she ran, he wanted to hunt. He was *not* feral, despite what his family had claimed he was. He knew that.

Need and concern rolled into one confusing cocktail. He picked up his speed again, and before long, he caught up with her. She panted, resting her head sideways on the hedge wall. Her eyes squeezed shut as she held a palm to her stomach—keeping herself from unraveling. No... tracing her palm over where the belt used to be.

He slowed. "You should have waited for me."

"I was afraid," she replied without opening her eyes.

"I would never hurt you."

"Not of you. Never you." Breathless, she tapped her waist, fingers trembling. "The damned belt thing. I spoke out, and now they'll find me. My mom always said wanting things came at a cost." Her bottom lip trembled. "There's always a cost."

"I'll pay it for you. Just don't run again. Running makes me want to hunt you," he murmured, trying but failing to explain how close he was to losing control.

The impulse to embrace her bordered on insanity. And if he embraced her, then he would want more from her. Every cell in his body wanted to climb into her. One urge was feral, the other soothing. They warred with each other in his mind. Every instinct that kept him celibate all these years raged beneath his skin, done with being leashed.

Her eyes widened as she took him in, no doubt seeing his state. Veins bulged. Fists flexed. Chest heaved.

Everything was changing tonight. His palm landed on her collarbone. He pressed hard, pushing her against the hedge, causing her breath to hitch. Words failed him. Blind desire mixing with relief clouded his head. She was here. He touched her and felt her heartbeat pounding. His fingers slid around her neck. He cupped her nape and dropped his forehead to hers.

No fear in her eyes.

"You ran," he rasped.

"Not from you," she said, her gaze softening, her hands roaming over his chest.

Not from him. He knew that. Deep down, he knew it. But he needed her to say it, and now that she had, twice, their precarious situation became clear. They were doomed. Whatever happened from here on out, he would pull no punches to keep her safe.

"I'll kill them all," he said, eerily calm. "Right here. I'll fill myself to the brim with mana and bring the tower down."

"No!" Her fingers curled in his shirt, gripping tight. "There are innocents in there. You heard them. Some were joining me in their dissent over the forced partnerships. Even if nothing comes of it, we've sown the seed. It will fester and grow until it bursts again. Plus..." Her voice softened, as did her touch. "Willow and Rory still need to come back to Elphyne with you. And then there's Caroline. What if I've inevitably hurt her too?"

Forrest's grip tightened on Melody's neck. She peeled the patch from his eye and scowled at it.

"I hate that you have to hide your beautiful eyes." She trailed fingers over his ears. "I hate that you had to sacrifice so much. You have such a big heart, Forrest. I hate that what I feel is ruining your plans."

"You could never ruin me."

A tingling, sparkling blue light sprung from the ground, causing Melody to cry out in surprise. But Forrest wasn't afraid. He knew what this was. Despite being shocked, he couldn't be more satisfied. The light washed upward like a wave, curling around one of their arms until it settled in a spiral pattern from wrist to shoulder. Melody's emotions barreled into him, striking him.

Fear. Desperation. Want. Need.

It all came from her.

"What's happening?" she whispered.

"It's a Well-blessed mating," he replied, eyes full of awe as he took in their matching marks. He licked his lips, stunned. "I don't know why. I don't know how, but Melody... the Well approves of us being together."

"So, it's not ruin," she breathed.

"No."

"It's... home."

The fear and hesitation he'd felt down their bond disappeared.

Melody's eyes darkened. She gripped his head and drew his lips down to hers.

Kissing her—*his mate*—was the most satisfying thing he'd ever done. She whimpered and curled her fingers into his hair, ripping tiny strands out at the roots in her haste. Still, it wasn't enough. They weren't close enough.

Their kissing turned urgent, mad, and unbalanced. He snarled and crushed her to his chest while his mouth ravaged hers. She ripped at his shirt and slid hands onto his feverish flesh. Those musician's hands, those expert fingers, deftly explored his body. Her throaty moans of appreciation shot straight to his cock. He dropped his face to her shoulder and groaned.

"Mel..."

"Forrest just... I need you inside me. Now. Here. Say yes. Please say yes. Before they come to take us away."

He stepped back. She didn't like that. He felt it down their bond, saw it in her scowl.

"Why did you stop?" she accused. An emotion came down their bond that he never wanted to sense from her again. Self-doubt. Her palm went over her belly in a move he'd seen her use countless times before, and it infuriated him.

Couldn't she see how into her he was?

"Why do you think?" he asked as he took another teasing step back. "Sense the answer down our bond. Focus on our connection."

She canted her head, studying him.

"It's weird. I have feelings that aren't mine. You feel... I don't know. I can't explain it. *That's you?* But it's giving me urges. I want to... I feel... *oh.*" Her eyes widened, and her voice dropped to a lusty rasp. "Wicked."

Forrest's breath quickened as she read his deepest desire. He didn't want to fight his instincts anymore. He wanted to accept them, no matter what anyone thought of him. They should be climbing the walls, getting out of there. He should be finding a way to cut through the barbed nets above them and launching them into the sky in search of freedom. But a part of him feared she was right. They might not get another chance.

Insane desperation spurred him onward.

"We don't need the Well to tell us how we feel," he said. "I've felt like this since I first saw you."

But now she knew him. She felt him. She saw him.

And from the lowering of her lashes, the sultry pout to her lips—she liked it.

Melody grinned, turned, and ran.

He blinked.

Then he grinned, too. He'd initially feared her running from him, but this was trust. Nowhere in her emotions did he sense fear. Just a challenge. A thrill. So, he chased. He enjoyed. He pushed all the pent-up restlessness into his thighs, pumped them hard, and hunted her like a wolf tracks its prey. Like he'd done so many times in the minds of animals, catching her was satisfying. The necessary claiming he'd dreamed of.

Somehow she'd known.

Catching her in the maze's center, he yanked her back to him. He wrapped his arms around her, trapping her against his front. Every heave of her lungs pushed her breasts against him. He shoved his hand up her dress—no preamble. He cupped her between her thighs and squeezed. She moaned.

"You're wet," he rasped.

"Yes."

He dragged down her underwear and slid two fingers into her heat, wetting them himself as she'd taught him. Then he found her clit—swollen and aroused—and he pinched. She dropped her head on his shoulder and melted against him. Overwhelmed by her emotions, she couldn't speak. He knew because he felt every single one. They were joined. Soul to soul. Heart to heart. He would never be unseen again. Never.

Hungrily, he kissed her neck while he worked her clit with his fingers but as soon as the rich scent of her arousal hit him, his mouth watered, and he growled. He ripped and tugged at her panties and then pushed her down to the ground.

"Should we…" She gulped. "Should we be…"

He swallowed her words before they ruined everything. Yes, they should be escaping. But a claiming needed to happen. At least some part. A taste. This urgency drowned out rationality. It made him mindless.

He tossed her skirts over her hips and swore at the alluring sight of her blond, wet curls between her thighs. His erection jerked, and he almost lost control of himself. *Slow down.* He sat back and rubbed his mouth, eyeing her. His aching desire was like a scourge through his veins. He was so hard. He wanted to bury his cock there.

But he had to taste her more.

The need had plagued his dreams, living and awake.

"Hurry," she urged, trying to sit up.

He arched a brow at her impertinence. "I'll take my mate the way I want."

"We don't have time."

He planted his palm on her chest, and then, when she'd laid

back, he slid that palm down her front to spread the curls between her thighs. He was gifted with the glorious pink, glistening sight of her desire.

"Forrest," she begged as he swiped his finger through her slit.

That was it. His name on her lips. He dove down and lapped her up, moaning at her sweet-salty taste. Better than anything he'd dreamed. He went to work with his tongue while his fingers pumped inside her. He sensed down their bond when he worked her right, and he did more.

Her taste made him blind with lust. Every lick of his tongue echoed a tingle in his cock. It had nothing to do with the mating but everything to do with his need for her. Just like in the museum, getting her off made him deeply aroused.

Her back bowed, she pulled his hair, moaned, and writhed and panted his name… because of him.

Melody screamed her release. She let it out. Her power bathed him, zinging across his skin like a lightning storm, bringing every hair on his body standing on edge. He continued to feast on her pulsing core as his own climax punched through him.

Heaving breaths, eyes watering from the intensity, he sat back and gaped at himself.

"Fuck," he mumbled, ears burning. "Melody, look what the taste of you does to me."

She pushed herself up onto her elbows and gave him a sultry look. "I wish I could say I'm sorry. But I'm not. I love that I make that happen."

"I want more," he growled. "But we've pushed our luck as it is."

He wiped his pants as best he could, then looked at her glowing,

Well-blessed marked hand. A sense of dread unfurled in him. "This is going to be hard to hide. We should leave now."

Melody stopped smiling. Her hand touched beneath his left eye.

"Forrest, you have a blue teardrop there."

He touched the spot. It felt the same, still with the ridge of a scar, but blue light glanced off his fingertip. "It's my Guardian mark. It grew back."

"How can we hide that?"

"If you want to stay here, I could cut it out again."

"No, we can't," she said, shocked. "You've sacrificed enough. Besides, I think I've burned my bridges here."

Someone was coming. Too late, the notion came from creatures scuttling around the garden. Pain exploded in the back of Forrest's head. Stars burst behind his eyes. Nausea rocked his body. He tried to lash out at whatever had hit him, but his efforts were in vain. He hadn't refilled enough mana. He stumbled from the dizziness.

"She's right," the Captain said as he hit Melody on the head with the butt of a gun. She flopped unconscious before she could get a sound out.

Adrenaline surged within Forrest, trying to push out the disorientation from his pain. He called every ounce of mana. He felt it building and soaking into him from the ground at an alarming rate, but it wasn't fast enough. He was too weak. Cut off for too long. He fell to his knees, heartbroken as the Captain leaned over him and held up a belt—the more elaborate belt he'd tried to give Melody that first day in the garden.

"I came here looking for this," he said. "I *knew* I hadn't lost the original. I would never take it off unless it was to give her. While she humiliated me in the dining hall, I sat there stewing over that missing piece of the puzzle in my brain. And then I remembered... I'd lost the original here, in this garden." He gave a short, sharp laugh. "I came here thinking I'd find it, thinking I'd prove I wasn't losing my mind, but instead, I found you both together—" He kicked Forrest's blue arm. "Spreading your disgusting taint."

He sighed.

"What to do with you now? Use you to cement my new position here, or use you both to recover my debts?" He got down on his knee to get up close to Forrest. "Some of your kind pay handsomely for a talented human musician such as her. You'll never see her again. I'll make sure of it. And I'll make sure the right person finds you here in all your tainted glory."

"I'll find you," Forrest bit out. "If you hurt her, I won't just kill you, I'll make you suffer."

The butt of the Captain's gun came down on Forrest's temple, and everything went dark.

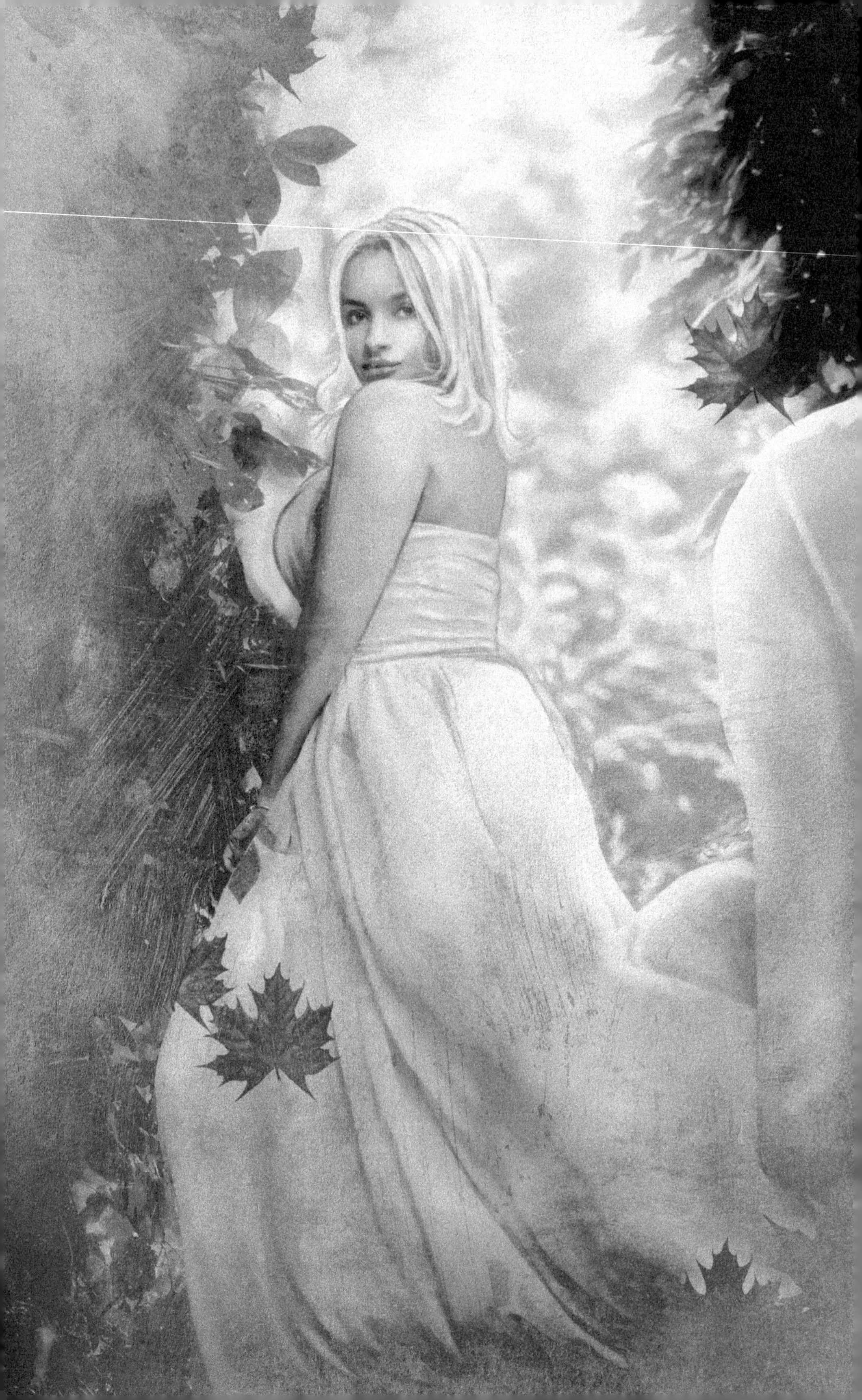

CHAPTER
TWENTY-NINE

Melody woke groggily with pain throbbing in her head. As her eyes opened, the blinding light hurt. It made her feel sick, so she squeezed her eyes shut. Too late. She gagged and rolled to her side and hurled. All that came out was the water she'd drunk at dinner. The salty wind smashed her face, giving her much-needed oxygen. The ground rocked side to side. Seagulls squawked...

Melody gasped and opened her eyes more slowly this time.

She was on a boat.

Blue sky.

Rocking.

Oh, God. She retched again. Her temple throbbed. She grabbed her head and looked around.

The boat was made from wood, curved and long like a giant canoe. A great sail puffed out from a center mast. It wasn't too long. Maybe twenty feet. She'd seen bigger boats in the harbor when she'd been taken on a tour—her only tour—the week after she'd thawed.

It had been Nero's way of wooing her. He showed her the potential, how they fought back the Tainted, and why she should sing for him. But... Why the hell was she on the deck of a Viking-style boat? And why the hell were two people arguing so loudly it hammered in her head?

Scanning up and down, she found them at the helm raised above the deck she was on. They stood before a wheel. The Captain in an outfit she'd never seen him in. It looked fae. But he wasn't. So, what was he doing?

He argued vehemently with a short woman with curly black hair. Melody rubbed her eyes. Wasn't that the Tinker? Yes, she had a set of brass goggles resting on her head. They were the kind that looked like spectacles for magnifying vision. She was dressed in dirty coveralls more suited to the grease monkeys who worked beneath the airships on the dock. Oh no. Was Melody on one of those zeppelin-style airships they'd been building?

There was no blimp above her. Fearful of what she'd find, she glanced over the side—but turquoise rolling waves greeted her. Okay. Not in the air. But no safer. Still here. Still—she caught sight of the blue twinkling on her arm. Forrest! He'd been so focused on Melody and her on him that neither of them had noticed the Captain until he'd hit Forrest over the head. Then her! Goddamned bastard.

Melody tried to get to her feet. *Scream. Use your voice.* But the wind stole anything out of her lips. All she had to do was get in earshot of the Captain, and she would scream her little heart out. But the boat rocked. She careened. Almost went overboard. She latched onto the wooden railing, and splinters pierced her flesh. Rushing air stole her voice as she cried out.

A hand went over her mouth and pressed something wet onto her lips. The smell of it. Chloroform. Melody lost control of her motor function. But she heard two things. The Tinker shouted, "I didn't sign up for this!"

And the Captain bellowed back, "I gave you fresh fuel. Open the portal, or you're joining her."

⚖

COLD.

The second time Melody woke, she was shivering, and the ground moved at a different pace. No longer the giant rocking of a tumultuous sea, but a bumpy rocking. A clip-clop. *Horses.* She hadn't heard horses—or any kinds of other animals—for so long. The gag in her mouth tasted bitter, like the drug that had taken her under. Fumes still entered her eyes and lungs, making her dizzy and faint. But she couldn't remove the gag. Her hands were tied behind her back.

This was not good. Not good at all. She couldn't speak. Without her voice, she was powerless.

Blue sky above her. Glorious green trees whizzed past. They were the kind of green that looked warm, despite the air holding a chill. From the angle of the shadows, the sun was getting low. *Elphyne.* She arched her back and looked over her shoulder. Yes. She was in a coach of some kind. It reminded her of the polished type they used before cars were invented. A man sat in the driver's seat.

The heavy breathing of a horse and its galloping hooves were the only sounds.

He wasn't the Captain. He wasn't human.

The driver was tall. He wore a brown velvet coat. Diamond-studded, pointed ears stuck out from long, russet hair that streamed behind him. Intricate braids lashed about in the billowing mess. She was sure they were meant to look regal, but, somehow, the journey had made the hairstyle nothing short of wild. Tanned skin. Freckled nose.

Recognition—deja vu—barreled through her. It couldn't be Forrest. His ears were round... but there was a certain familiarity about the elf. They went over a bump, and her vision went sideways. She groaned and tried to keep herself from falling unconscious again. Regrettably, she had to lie there and focus on simply not passing out.

The sky, the sky, she told herself. It was the same sky she'd gazed upon from the president's garden. The same sky Forrest would see.

If he was alive.

It was then she noticed she wasn't alone. Another figure, hogtied and unconscious, lay next to her. Black curly hair. Short. Female. The Tinker. No goggles. Melody tried to kick and rouse her, but she wouldn't respond. Oh, God. Was she dead?

The only dead person Melody had ever seen was her mother in the hospital.

The cart slowed and stopped. Melody's throat closed over a whimper. She would not let her mind go to those dark places, so she forced herself to sit up. Noticing movement, the driver twisted to check on his prisoners and grinned. He had a handsome face, but there was a hardness to it—a cruel twist to lips sprinkled with scars.

"Oh, goody," he drawled. "You're awake."

She tried to curse at him, but it came out muffled through the gag. He ignored her as he busied himself, stowing his reins and collecting whatever he'd stashed in the front seat.

Looming before her was a behemoth castle made of stone and twisted trees. Vegetation grew along every crevice of the four towers. Leaves on plants ranged from brown to orange to red. Autumn colors. Melody's stomach bottomed out. The driver's brown velvet coat had a crest—a royal wreath with leaves.

Was this... was this Forrest's childhood home, the Autumn Court?

The coach had stopped inside the defense walls of a multi-acre area filled with a broad range of fae of various vocations. Woodcutters, livestock, soldiers, gardeners, attendants. Fae with wings, fae with horns, and fae like her captor—elves. The place was a hive of activity.

Up on the battlement walls, glaring guards stood watch. The main castle was levels high—perhaps five or ten. Stained glass windows featuring Autumn colors fractured the light around them. Melody glanced behind her to possible freedom but only found a thick forest that looked as ominous as the ones she'd seen in Brothers Grimm fairytale books.

Stone buildings nestled amongst the trees. Smoke came from chimneys. There was a village out there. A big one. It reminded her of where the witch from Hansel and Gretel might live, and she shuddered.

Perhaps escaping there wasn't such a good idea.

"Hey," Melody whispered to the Tinker, but the gag once again muffled. It didn't stop her from trying again. "Wake up."

"Hunter," the driver barked, beckoning to a dark elf with a bow slung over his shoulder and an ax at his hip. The ax looked suspiciously made of bone. "Take that one, will you? I'm not sure what we're doing with her yet."

A tall, slender woman wearing a dark dress stood near the portcullis leading into the castle. Her tawny skin seemed almost glossy in the waning light. The cut of her black bob made her beautiful face severe. A dark ribbon slashing across her neck failed to hide a puckered scar. When she locked eyes on Melody, a pink, pointed tongue darted out to lick her lips. Fangs.

Vampire. She had to be. The only creatures in Melody's songs with pointed tongues and fangs were vampires.

"Wisteria, my love!" the driver shouted as he departed the coach with a gleeful flourish that confused Melody. "I have brought you a gift."

Melody looked around the coach. Empty except for them. *They* were the gift.

"Wonderful," replied Wisteria. "I am starving today, Luthian. And you do know how I prefer the taste of human."

"Oh no." He laughed but gave a considering look to Melody. "While you might want to feed on her, I advise you to take caution. Look."

He came back to hold up Melody's marked arm. Wisteria gasped with glee.

"But that is not the only reason I brought her here." His eyes gleamed with excitement. "She's a talented *human* musician."

Wisteria clapped. "How splendid. We can put those instruments to use again. With all the talk of war and coups, life has become somewhat dull here lately."

"I told you I'd replace the Peach. And I have not one but two we can tap for our special blood elixir." Luthian's chest puffed conceitedly, and he gestured off-handedly. "It was only a matter of time."

"You do look after me." She smiled warmly at her partner. Her expression shifted to cold stone when she focused on Melody. "Let's get the musician inside as soon as we can. I don't like sharing with your family. Your mother has been a prude lately. It's rubbing off on your siblings. And what of the other one?"

"We'll put her in the dungeon for now," Luthian said offhandedly.

His fist closed around Melody's hair. He yanked her over the coach's side. Needles pierced her scalp. Still bound and gagged, she clumsily tried to go over to stop her hair from coming off in chunks. She hit the ground hard and winded herself, eyes watering.

"Get up." Luthian's voice turned cruel. He lashed out for Melody's hair again, but she flinched away and forced herself to her feet, giving him evil glares every inch of the way.

When she got the gag off...

Luthian indicated for her to walk through the portcullis. "That way. And mind the murder hole."

The murder what?

CHAPTER THIRTY

"Wake up, you Tainted bastard."

A hard slap to Forrest's face roused him, but he kept silent, using the moment to assimilate. Everything came flooding back. Melody was his mate. The Captain kidnapped her. Forrest would murder him.

The pain in his head receded as the Well flowed into him at a glorious rate. It was as though it had his back... as though it knew he had to replenish faster than ever before. If this was a boon he needed to repay later, he would gladly take it.

A cold, thin pressure at his throat had him peeling his eyes open.

As Rory leaned over him, copper beads in her hair clinked. Eyes narrowed, thick lashes squished, suspicion and hatred speared at him. He glanced down calmly at the blade in Rory's hand.

"You lied," she hissed. "You're nothing, but a filthy, feral liar, aren't you?"

Fury simmered at her words. He mentally prepared how to use that knife to gut her, no matter the deal with Maebh.

"Stop!" Willow's distressed voice pierced the air.

"He came to steal you away," Rory said, never taking her eyes from him. "I can't allow that."

"I said stop to Uncle Forrest." Willow's face appeared next to Rory's. She pummeled Rory with her fists. "He'll kill you."

Both Forrest and Rory startled, confused. Rory licked her lips, uncertain. Perhaps Willow had seen how this scenario played out in the future. Forrest would take that knife as he'd prepared. He would stab Rory. He would win.

"He just wants to find Aunty Melody," Willow urged.

"That's all you want?" Rory said to Forrest, surprising him. "If I let you go, you'll leave?"

Forrest's eyes darted to Willow, then to Rory. "Yes."

She eased off and put the knife away. "Then go."

"Come with me," he said. "You both need to come with me."

"Willow stays here."

"Rory," he said. "*Aurora*. You're one of us. You're half fae, just like Willow."

She shook her head and pointed the dagger at him. "No, I'm not."

"Your mother was a changeling daughter of the Unseelie High Queen and the Seelie High King." He cocked his head. "Maebh planted her own flesh and blood here to rule the humans. To take them down from the inside. But something happened, and her daughter died. I suspect it was about the time Nero came to town. Probably the death happened not long after you were born. Maybe he saw your pointed ears. Maybe they were cut off at birth, and your mother was killed. Maebh never knew her granddaughter existed. *You.*"

He tossed out explanations without foundation, but it was worth a shot. It made sense. If it was Forrest, and he wanted complete control over this city, he'd get rid of the previous rulers and slot himself into a position he could lord over the next.

"You're fucking lying!" Rory growled through her teeth. "Get out of here before I change my mind."

Forrest swallowed. With each second ticking by, finding Melody would be more challenging. He gestured to Willow. "Come willingly, or I toss you over my shoulder and take you."

"Oh, no," she said, frowning. "You can't do that."

"I think I can."

Her eyes went misty, and she cocked her head. "I mean, you can't take me yet."

"What?"

"I was sad at first, and then my tomorrow friends made me remember I'm going to live here for a while with Aunty Rory. It's my destiny. I have to grow big and strong, or the dragon will get me."

Willow stunned them both. Sometimes she seemed years wiser than her age. But she was still a child—none of this made sense.

"Willow—"

Her little face turned fierce. "She needs me to fix clouds in her head."

"What?" Rory said, her eyes wide at the little girl. "What did you say?"

Willow hid behind Rory and shifted fully into her fae form. Ears elongated. Teeth grew sharper. Eyes became otherworldly and gold. Then she bared her fangs—*at him.* "My friends want me to stay!"

"Who?" he asked. "The children you were playing with? They're not your family, Willow. Let's go. Now."

"You have exactly two minutes before the military comes running through that door." Rory's voice had gone cold and distant.

Forrest wrenched his gaze from Willow and found Rory staring at the minotaur statue covered in feathers. Her jaw worked and then hardened.

"I'm not leaving," she said. "And neither is Willow."

Forrest bellowed his frustration.

Rory shouted back at him, "You're a fool if you let Melody die for this."

She was right. He wouldn't sacrifice the only thing he'd ever wanted for himself. He shoved his fist into the soil and pulled with all his metaphysical might. The ground gurgled beneath him. Vines rumbled and writhed. Roots slithered and rolled. He called on his Elven affinity with nature and demanded it create life. He claimed that boon the Well offered, and he amplified it tenfold.

Every Guardian who'd found himself in a Well-blessed mating had his powers evolve. Forrest hoped the Well would do him the same honor. He hoped it gave him what he wished for.

A tree burst upward from the ground like a warrior's spear, knocking them all to the ground. It reached full height, yet still, Forrest asked for more. He needed it big, so big it punched a hole in the barbed wire net blanketing the city. As it grew, creaking and moaning, he sent his awareness out, hunting for creatures far and wide.

But he found something that made his heart beat again—an echo of Melody in the distance. It came down his bond like a soft lullaby straight from her lips. She was alive. Gathering his resolve, he locked down his bewilderment. To escape, he needed a ride. So he sent his request out into the sky.

See me.

Find me.

To the robins inside the garden.

To the cockroaches and ants in the dirt.

Still, he kept hunting. *Out. Out.* Further. Across the wastelands surrounding the city. Into the dead forest. *Beyond.* He shouldn't have this much range. He'd never gone so far. But the Well kept feeding him mana as though he sat in the center of a watery power source. He hit a familiar mind pattern—a wild kuturi flying free, hunting for food.

Perfect.

He nabbed its mind and forced it to change flight path.

Here.

See me.

Forrest flung his hand out to the tree trunk still growing beside him. He latched onto a passing branch. It yanked him up with it, lurching him into the air. Soil upturned as the roots grew to compensate for the tree's weight. The fountain and minotaur statue toppled. Hedges churned. He was already fifty feet up when the Tower guards burst into the garden—and someone else. Nero. He shouted, pointed, and bellowed at Forrest.

Guns fired.

Forrest threw up his hands to shield himself. Vines and branches grew thick around him, shielding him in a natural cocoon. Bullets splintered the wood. Before the branches completely enshrouded him, he glanced down one last time through the gaps.

His gaze landed on Willow and Rory being rushed inside Sky Tower. To safety.

Good.

This wasn't over between them. He'd tried. He'd given Rory something to think about. One thing was for sure, Rory wouldn't hurt Willow. He knew that in his heart. On a whim, he decided to do one last thing before he left and gave a message to the robins in the garden. The next time Willow visited, she would receive it.

The growing tree hit the barbed sky net. It screeched and wailed with tension. Then it snapped. Wires pinged. Warped twangs sounded. The entire net toppled. Shouts came from below as soldiers raced to get out of the way. But some of them weren't fast enough. The fae-killing barbed wires smothered them brutally, cutting deep with the weight. Forrest watched with satisfaction as they were sliced into pieces.

The screech of a kuturi sounded, drawing his attention back to the sky.

Here. He pressed his will on it. The bird swooped down until its talons pierced a branch below him. He forced himself out of the splintered cocoon, leaped, and landed between its wings. Then, taking hold of the kuturi's mind again, he flew them in the direction he sensed Melody through their bond.

He prepared to fight.

There was only one place in that direction fond of purchasing human slaves. His old home—the Autumn Court.

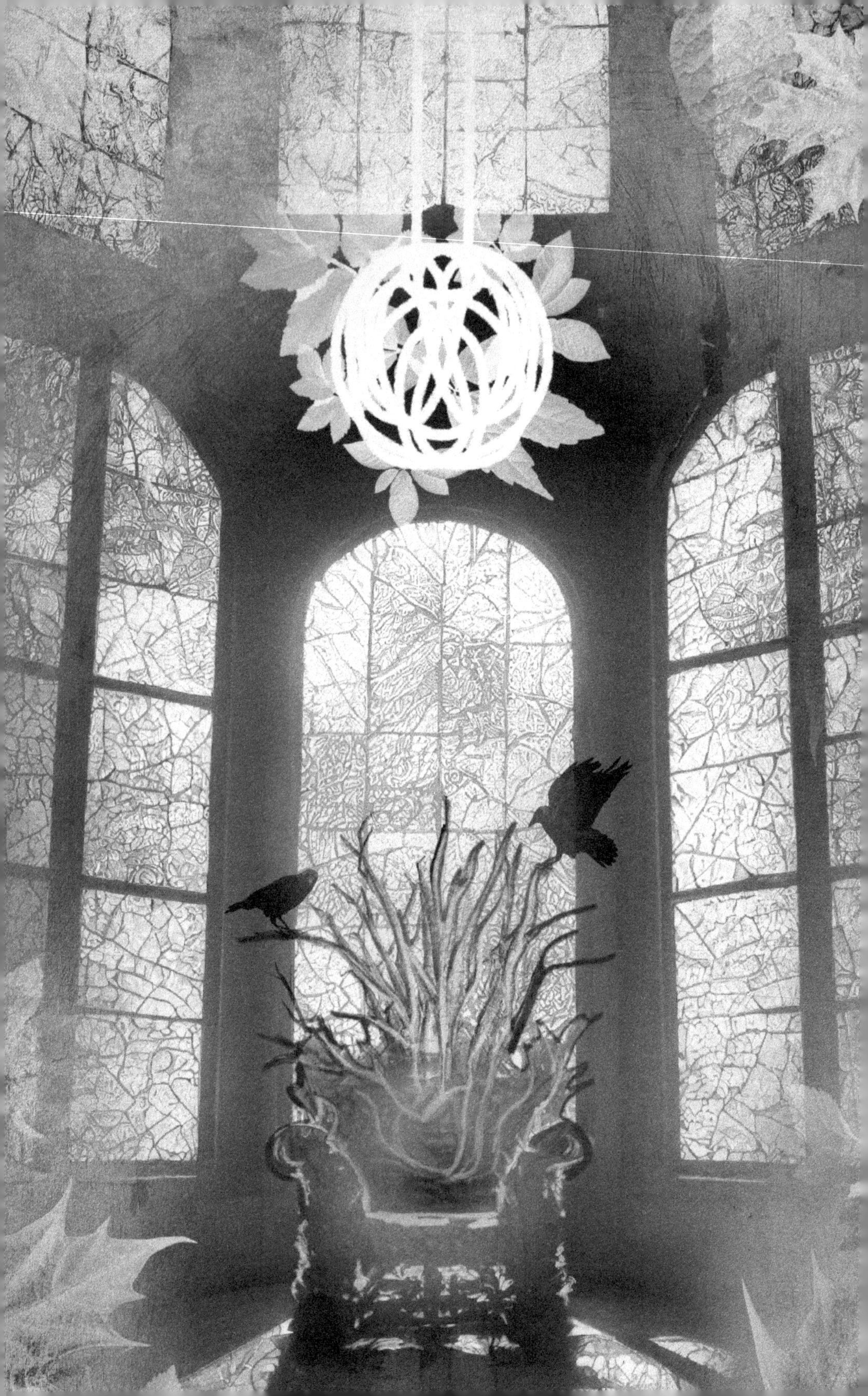

CHAPTER
THIRTY-ONE

Wisteria and Luthian laughed at the horror on Melody's face as she stumbled, trembling, toward the gate. It felt like a walk of shame. Fae stopped what they were doing to sneer and hurl insults. Two black demonic dogs on leashes snapped viciously. Glowing blue acid leaked from their eyes and sizzled on the ground. The kennel master clapped his hands and barked a command as she neared, causing them to back off.

Through the gate, under the portcullis, a dark space existed between the gate and the carved wooden doors of the castle. She glanced up. Guards glared down at her, spears ready to fall like the snap of teeth.

"Didn't I just tell you to mind the murder hole?" Luthian clicked his tongue. "Keep moving, or they might consider you foe."

The murder hole: where unwanted guests were stabbed and no

doubt had other nefarious things dropped on them. Melody rushed forward, heedless of sharp rocks beneath her bare feet, hating how their laughter wrought fear into her soul.

The double doors opened before she arrived, but no one waited inside. When she glanced over her shoulder, Luthian's hand was still in the air, suggesting he'd used magic to open the door. He swung his arm around Wisteria's shoulders.

"On you go," he said to Melody.

A sick feeling grew in her stomach. Walk of shame over. Now she walked the plank. But what kind of royal sharks would be waiting for her?

"Straight down the hall and to the right," Luthian said, clearly enjoying the mystery he forced on her.

Melody stumbled onward. She went directly where he told her, but two steps onto the cold slate floor, a striking female version of Luthian cut her off. Voluminous pantaloons in brown silk rustled as she settled. Small embroidered, pointed slippers peeked out from beneath. A belt at her waist tinkled with glass and jeweled trinkets. Red, curly hair was pinned and braided in an intricate style that cascaded down her back and accentuated her elven ears.

"And what do we have here, brother?" She inspected Melody.

"None of your Well-damned business, Ellwyn," Luthian snapped, then gestured impatiently at Melody. "Carry on."

Melody tried to sidestep, but Ellwyn blocked her. She put her hand to Melody's chest and glared at Luthian.

"You're wanted in court," she said to him. "Important discussions are being had. We don't have time for your dalliances with human conquests."

"She's more than a human," he speared back at her. "She's Well-blessed *and* a talented musician."

Ellwyn's eyes snapped to Melody's arm and widened before darting back to her brother. "Well-blessed? Are you insane?"

"She'll be extra tasty to the vampires."

"And you didn't think to wonder which Guardian of the Twelve she belonged to?" Ellwyn tapped her foot impatiently. "I'm sure you considered that, right?"

After a long, drawn-out pause, Luthian said, "Of course I did. Now, out of my way."

"She can play while we talk for all I care. Just get your intrepid ass into the throne room."

Luthian cursed, then said to Melody, "Ahead and left to the throne room, then." He kissed Wisteria on the head. "Playtime afterward, my love... unless you want to come to court."

"You know how much your mother dislikes me."

"My mother is a bore."

Wisteria pouted but bowed and took her leave. Luthian shoved Melody forward on the cold slate and stone corridor. Sconces on the wall glowed with glass lanterns but no light globe. Little balls of brilliant light buzzed inside, casting the illumination. Were they fireflies?

Once through the cold corridor, the castle surroundings turned from brute, ragged rock to honed smooth stone and carved luxury. Grand tapestries on walls depicted battle scenes and glorious feasts. When she looked closer, she found secret indulgent sexual escapades or torture weaved in—wickedness in the darkness.

An emblem with the Autumn Court crest—a wreath of leaves in

different colors—also had Elven glyphs with what Melody guessed was a motto. Farther down the hall, the motto was in English: *In Decay we Harvest.*

Despite the shift in interior design, the rock and vines gave the decor a simple reminder that these people were dangerous. They entered a throne room through ornately carved doors, and Melody was overcome with sound.

Loud voices all around were raised in argument. Lords, ladies, and royal advisors were on the outskirts of a hall with high ceilings. They spilled onto the slate floors before the thrones and parted to make way for Melody and her captors as they walked forward.

A king wearing a crown of richly colored autumn leaves and thorns sat on a podium at the end of the room. His queen and children were by his side—five children plus an empty chair. They dressed in the same velvet brown that Luthian and Ellwyn wore. Many had diadems, tiaras, or coronets. Each had twisted branches, vines, and leaves woven into the jewel-encrusted structures.

This was Forrest's family.

The one that had shunned him. They'd treated him like nothing... worse than something they hated. And the queen—his mother. How could she have done that to her child? Melody's fear melted away into hard loathing.

"Finally," shouted a stocky prince from his seat. His short brown hair matched a bushy beard falling to his chest in a braided point. "You test us with your tardiness, brother."

The king lifted his black-gloved hand, and silence descended on the room. Two crows on his throne of twisted vines and branches cawed. The queen barely glanced at her arriving son, and when

Melody looked more closely at the seemingly young woman, she found ghosts in her eyes. It would make her character either cunning and fearsome. Or cold and empty. Melody couldn't decide. Only time would tell.

"Take your place, Luthian." The king waved at the doors. "Close the door. We have matters of state to discuss."

As guards closed them, Luthian strode toward the royal podium, dragging Melody behind him. "I have a gift to loan the court. Something to make these proceedings a little more entertaining."

His siblings groaned as if their brother constantly interrupted these events with his "entertainment." The king's eyes hooded as he watched Melody approach. She shuddered with dread.

Like Forrest and most of his siblings, the queen had long auburn hair. Hers was brighter and entwined on top of her head, with the ends fanning like flames beneath her crown. But the fire in her hair didn't match her pale expression, so when interest gleamed in her eyes, Melody wasn't sure whether to be afraid or happy.

"What do you play?" Luthian asked Melody.

She tried to speak, and he reached to remove her gag. Elation washed through her until the king snapped, "No singing. Just music."

Luthian clicked his fingers, and a server dashed forward from beyond the watching crowd. A gut-strung violin-type instrument was placed into Melody's hands. Her brows lifted. The craftsmanship was incredible. Carved, ornate, and with a horse-hair strung bow. She itched to test it out, wondering how the sound differed from her usual metal-strung instruments. But she lowered her hand and lifted a stubborn chin.

Defiance bled out of every cell in her body.

"I was hoping you'd do that." Luthian grinned. He waved a hand, and a jolt ran through Melody as though she'd been zapped by touching a charged electrical wire.

Instantly, she was compelled to fit the violin's chin rest beneath her jaw. Her hand moved of its own accord to bring the bow across the strings. She was helpless to stop.

"Play," Luthian demanded. "Something good."

She did.

Her hands moved, her fingers set chords, and music filtered into the large, cavernous room with all the grace and dignity she wanted to refuse. Melody glared at Luthian as he made his way to the front, stepped onto the podium, and took the empty seat to the king's right.

The stained-glass windows she'd glimpsed from outside gave everything a slightly burnt tint. It was as though she'd landed in hell. The people in the crowd were demons to her.

Some wrote down proceedings. Some had books. Many wore fashion like the princess with the pantaloons. The males wore waistcoats and tailored jackets instead of flowing blouses. All six of Forrest's siblings sat on the podium with bored expressions on their faces. Three females. Three males. The one who'd blocked them—Ellwyn—sat to the immediate left of the queen. She stared at Melody with apparent interest echoing her mother's.

If Melody could get her gag out, then she could... what? Tell them that Forrest was her mate? The son they never wanted to acknowledge? Scream and use her gift to peel the skin from their faces? Try to force them to do her bidding? There were too many of them. All these fae would have their own magical gifts. Would hers hold up against them on her own?

Melody's fingers flew over the violin, pouring out a song pulled from her memory. She wasn't sure what it was. Maybe something made up. Her body moved on its own accord.

There was nothing so frightful than having her will taken from her.

Her mind turned to the Tinker. Maybe she was somewhere. Maybe she had gifts she didn't know about. Maybe she would come. But Melody had barely said boo to the woman at Sky Tower. Even if she could escape... why would she come to rescue Melody?

Which meant Melody had to get out by herself.

But how?

Get the gag off. Scream. Run. And then where would she go? Deep despair hit her as she realized Forrest was most likely dead. He was the only place she wanted to be. He was her home. Her everything.

As she played until her fingers hurt and her despair deepened, the court went into session again. They spoke about her as if she didn't exist, talking over the sound of the music. Forrest had endured this for years as a child. Her heart ached for him.

But just as the ache wrapped its suffocating embrace around her chest, another set of emotions trickled in.

Hope. Calm. Certainty.

The emotions certainly didn't come from inside Melody. She was too distraught. So, if the feelings weren't hers, they must belong to... courage surged in her. She looked up, eyes wide, and blinked away the tears.

Forrest was alive.

Certainty. Calm… Anger.

Fury.

Vengeance.

He was coming for her. He was confident he'd find her. And he would rain down hell on them. She had no doubt. From that first time he'd lost his temper at the Captain, Melody had always been his weak spot.

Her elation started to turn to trepidation. This would be a blood bath.

The Autumn Court discussed vehement plans for defense and attack against their enemies—particularly the Seelie High King—Melody tuned out and focused on finding a way to get her gag out. When Forrest turned up, he would need her help. Whatever magical geas Luthian had placed on her body didn't extend to her mouth.

She had one advantage here. Luthian didn't know her gift was based in her voice. The gag in the mouth was coincidental. It must be. The Captain didn't know about it either. He'd just wanted her quiet. The Tinker also had a gag in her mouth.

Okay. This is good, she thought. *I can surprise them.*

As surreptitiously as she could manage, she rolled the gag by rubbing it against the violin at her neck. The chin piece provided a ribbed surface she used to catch the fabric. No good. It hurt her neck to move so counteractively to the playing. Next, she tried biting the cloth, but it was thick and tasted horrendous. Maybe she could use both in tandem. Poke her tongue at the gag, rub her cheek, repeat.

"That bastard Seelie High King is putting the pressure on our borders," someone shouted. "What are you doing about it?"

"We only need to hold him off for a little longer. Maebh is weak.

Once we claim her territory, I will receive her tithe from the Well, and my power will grow. *Then* we will handle the Seelie High King because I will be the new Unseelie High King."

"My father is right," Ellwyn said. "Maebh is not fit to rule. Her people see that. Her time is up."

"But no one can get past her demogorgan—not even the Guardians." An elf with wild hair stomped his long wooden staff carved with patterns of twisted crows. "How do you plan on defeating it if they can't?"

"I won't need to defeat it." The king stood. The crows on his throne cawed like heralds. "It will come to us when we take the Winter territory. What's hers will be mine."

Excited murmurs rippled around, but then the man with the staff said, "Only if you can separate Maebh from her monster."

"We have a plan."

"And when will that be actioned? When we're out of food? When our sons and daughters die from the pestering Seelie *floater* at our borders?"

"And then there is the taint in the Well," another councilor called out. Melody couldn't see who. Her eyes were filled with water. Her fingers blistered as she was forced to shift into playing another song seamlessly. "I tried to scry this morning and ended up almost being trapped in my vision." A pompous scoff. "I'm two hundred years old. I have *never* been trapped in a vision."

The king waved them down. "That's for the Order of the Well to deal with. We're lucky if you think about it. While they're focused on that, we can focus on harvesting in decay."

"But if we can't access our mana, we can't protect ourselves."

"He has a point, father," said Ellwyn. "Perhaps it is time to reach out to our youngest brother."

The crows behind the king cawed as he furiously snapped at his daughter. "He is not, and never has been, your brother."

At the mention of Forrest, Melody shouted behind her gag. She tried to stumble forward, to convey somehow that Forrest was her mate. Maybe Ellwyn was the only one in the family who would side with Melody. But she did nothing.

The queen stood. Her eyes narrowed on Melody.

Melody took it as a sign of hope. She tried to nod to the Well-blessed marks on her arm and shout, "*Forrest*. He's your son!"

Maybe some of her gift leaked out. Melody would never truly know, but the queen stepped off the podium.

"Dear," the king sighed with frustration at his queen. "Return to your seat. Leave the human alone."

But she walked straight up to Melody with zombie-like strides. She stopped before Melody and watched her play with an increasing look of anger.

"Like I said," the king said to the councilor who'd asked about the taint. "It is an Order matter. Send an emissary to the Order and demand an explanation from the Prime."

With her eyes, Melody pleaded to the queen. A spark of something flared in her angry eyes. Recognition? Pity? The queen laid her hand on Melody's, and a cool zing flowed from the contact. The urge to play died.

Melody whimpered in relief. Her fingertips screamed from blisters. Blood trickled down her hands, making them sticky. But she was lost, staring into the eyes of her mate's mother as she cupped Melody's face and wiped away her tears. It was exactly what

Melody's mother used to do. The queen trailed her touch down to Melody's Well-blessed marks.

"Mother," Luthian warned. "That's my human. Get your own."

"Enough," the king snapped. "Get back to your seat, Brinwa. *Sit down.*"

"Yes," the queen—Brinwa—said, lifting her chin. "I've had enough."

Luthian slowly straightened. He glared at his mother, but she stepped before Melody, protecting her. Guards were called to remove Melody. The queen wasted no time and pulled Melody toward the back of the room, away from the front doors, probably to a private exit. They pushed past those crowding the podium. Suddenly, people were everywhere.

Being pawed at by a stadium of fans had nothing on this. Fae everywhere wanted to touch Melody—not because of her talents but to stroke the glowing Well-blessed marks on her body for luck. Seeing what happened, the queen waved her hand, and a blast of hot air forced people away.

"Mother!" Luthian warned again.

Quickly. Adrenaline surged through Melody. She dropped the violin just as two guards came for her. One guard caught her hand as she reached for her gag, wrenching her arm at a painful angle. But her other hand was already pulling it down.

Fresh air rushed into her lungs on a deep inhale.

The guard's eyes widened as if he sensed the danger. She glared at him and was about to say *"Let me go"* but didn't get a chance. The carved front doors opened with such force that they shattered against the walls and fell off their hinges in a splintered mess. Fear froze Melody's heart when she heard beastly snarls filter over the crowd. Unable to see the doors, she knew who'd arrived and tried to force her way to him.

Forrest.

"What are the Well-hounds doing out?" barked the king.

"I let them out." Melody glimpsed her mate's head above the crowd blocking her view. She tried to shove them away so she could see more. Forrest was as dangerous and lethal looking as the acid-leaking beasts before him. He wore the same outfit she'd left him in but had windblown cheeks and hair. He set his sights on his father. "Where is she?"

"Here," she croaked. But her voice was raspy and soft.

The siblings turned to each other with surprise. The king stared unfazed at Forrest. No—he stared through Forrest. Like he wasn't there.

The bearded prince leaned forward to eye his siblings down the line. "Did you hear something?"

Luthian scrunched his nose. "I'm not sure what you mean."

"Must be the wind," the king retorted before settling his gaze forward again, looking *through* his youngest son as if he didn't exist.

Beside Melody, the queen gasped. Tears brimmed in Brinwa's eyes. It looked like her puppy had been killed—or her son. One she might still love. Melody's heart wrenched in her chest. How sickening of them. How cruel.

"My mate," Forrest snarled, unaffected by their behavior. "I can feel her here."

The king stilled. The struggle on his face to keep his cool was evident. "The wind must be powerful today."

Snickers and laughter erupted around the room.

"I'm in no mood for games today," Forrest said. He took his hands out of his pockets and pushed up his sleeves.

The king's eyes dipped to the blue marks on Forrest's hand, then a look of complete disappointment traveled over his composure as he spat at Luthian, "What have you done this time?"

But Luthian wasn't cowered. He looked his father in the eye. "I didn't know it was *his* mate, but now that I do, it's even more satisfying."

It.

He kept calling Melody *it*.

Yet she could have sworn she detected jealousy in Luthian's eyes as if this new nugget of knowledge infuriated him. Tension in the room thickened as the dogs snarled and stalked forward. The king raised his hand. The dogs stopped, sat, and then wagged their tales.

Did the king have the same gift as Forrest?

"Do you think you have the power to defeat me?" He scoffed at Forrest. "I am a *king*. Even a Guardian has no—"

The king choked. His eyes glazed over like he was falling asleep with them open. His arm snapped out to the side and his fingers wrapped around Luthian's throat. He squeezed until his son's eyes bulged.

"Where is my *mate*," Forrest snarled again. But his words echoed from the king's mouth.

Melody could have run forward, but something held her back. A thought. A realization that the people here were just like those in Sky Tower.

"You have a voice," Melody said to Brinwa. "Use it."

Melody's hesitation cost her. A guard took hold of her arm and covered her mouth. She struggled against him as a chorus of gasps cascaded about the room. They'd come to the same conclusion Melody did. Forrest had taken over the king's mind as he did with the animals.

Choking and spluttering, confused, Luthian struggled against his father's firm grip just as Melody struggled against the guard. The king wasn't aged and weak. His body was as youthful as his sons—appearing not a day older than thirty. For Forrest to have dominated like this, he must be powerful.

"Stop it," Ellwyn shouted, panicked. "She's over there with mother."

Forrest turned Melody's way, and sweet relief washed through her. But the guard's grip tightened. His fingers dug into Melody's cheeks.

A surreal moment washed through her—it was as though she looked at Forrest through a mirror. He was close but so far away. Close, but never accessible. And then Queen Brinwa latched onto the guard's arm. The acrid scent of fire and sizzling flesh came a second before the guard's scream. He let go and stumbled back.

Melody ran to Forrest. Her mate. *Home*. His arms enveloped her. *Safe*. While the court of powerful fae, princes, and princesses watched, he checked her over.

He whispered, "Are you hurt?"

"A little," she said, her bottom lip trembling. "But I'm okay."

She touched his stubbled jaw, hardly believing he was here. So like the avenging Viking that had stolen her attention when he'd first walked into the dining hall, he was everything and more.

His fingers trembled on Melody's chin. *Fury*. His gaze latched onto her bleeding hands. Shit. Nerves bundled tight in her chest, strangling her lungs. This was not good.

"Which one." His voice became guttural, animalistic. Bloodlust entered his eyes. "Point out who did this to you."

Luthian's lips curved in a wry smile, and he signed his own death warrant. That smug sneer hit Melody's buttons, and a surge of loathing washed through her. Years of cruelty showed on Luthian's face. Forrest felt her reaction and knew Luthian was to blame. In the span of a crow's beating wings, *he knew*.

Something snapped within him. Melody felt it like a twang of energy echoing down their bond.

The crows on the king's throne cawed and squawked. They flapped their dark wings in a fury and pecked Luthian's eyes. His blood-curdling scream broke Forrest's hold on his father's mind.

The crows stopped pecking. There was nothing left of Luthian's eyes but bloody gashes and red tears. One of the siblings helped him, but everyone else took to their feet with menace over their battle-ready faces. Every member of the court around them had stern expressions. And the soldier who'd tried to halt Melody was slowly sliding his sharp bone sword out of its sheath.

"*Stop*," Melody exclaimed, power coating her demand.

The guard didn't just stop. His head exploded. Blood and brain matter went everywhere. All over Melody's face. All over her front. Into the crowd of watching, screaming gentry. Melody exhaled. Gasped. Gulped. Tasted bitter tang.

Fanned her hands in panic.

Retched.

"I didn't mean to," she blubbered, covering her sticky mouth. "I didn't mean to."

"It's okay," Forrest calmly said, tugging her back to him. "It's the taint on the Well." *Comfort. Home.* He wiped the blood from her face and looked deeply into her eyes. "He had it coming."

The king bellowed his rage. "How *dare* you?"

He raised his hands as claws and wind whooshed from nowhere. The crows that had pecked Luthian's eyes out shot into the air and multiplied into tens, hundreds, until the room filled with squawking black storm clouds.

"Kill them."

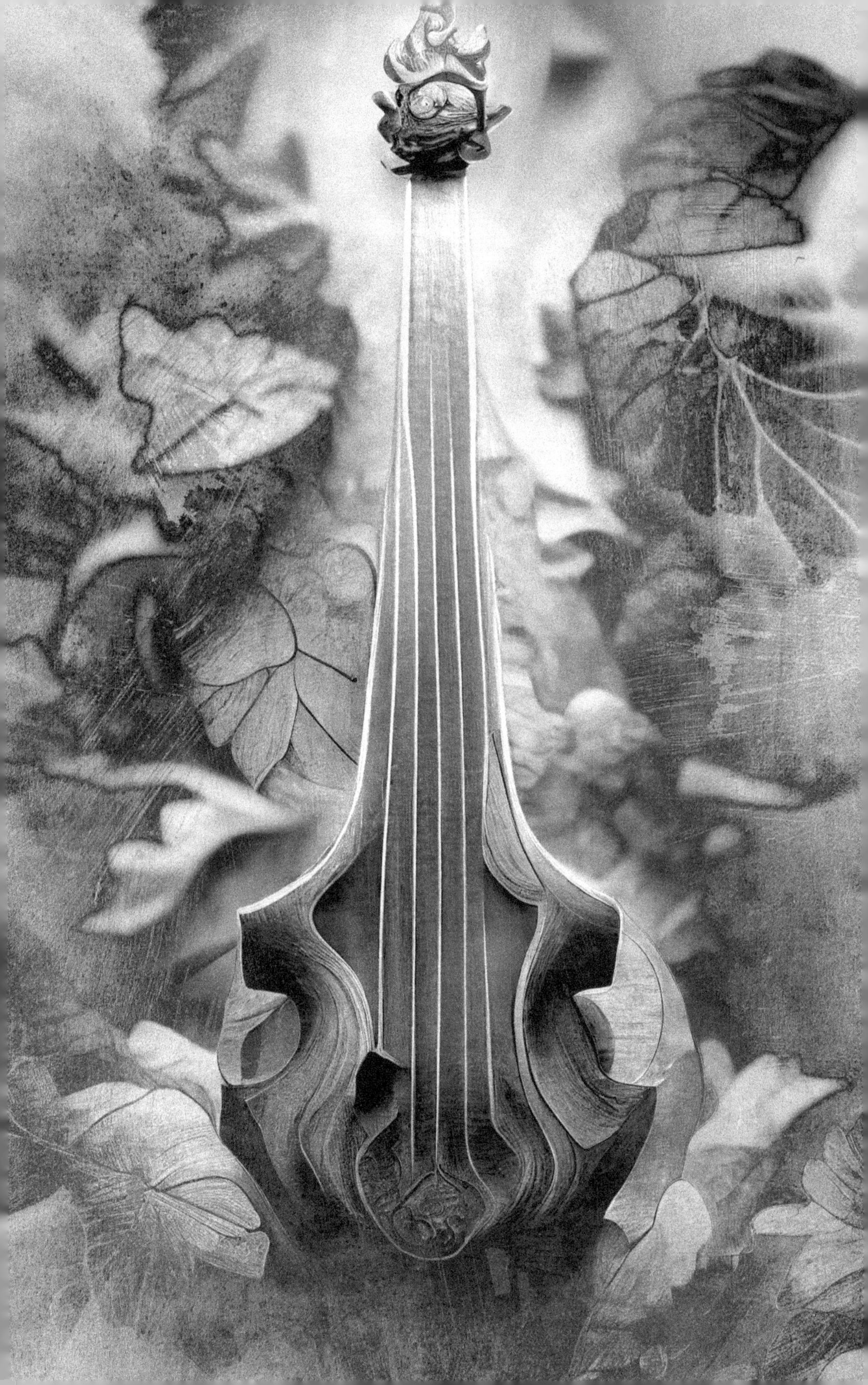

CHAPTER
THIRTY-TWO

Forrest had Melody in his arms.

Nothing else mattered.

Not the hurricane of feathers with sharp beaks descending on them. Not the primal survival instincts snapping into place. Not the deep satisfaction of having ruined Luthian's eyes or the damage he might have done to his father's mind.

In the epicenter of the feathered storm, he kissed his mate. Deeply, passionately, and without a care about the world crumbling around them. She sensed his calm. She *saw* him. And as she responded to his kiss, he knew she understood that he'd wrested the minds of every single crow from his father. They flew around them not to attack but to protect.

Melody pulled back with wide eyes. "Forrest, I'm covered in blood."

"I don't care." He smiled. "You taste the same on the inside."

His smile died as responsibility kicked in. He flicked a switch in the crows' minds. Although it killed him to do so, he halted them. The birds plummeted. In one last act of mercy, he ended their lives before they hit the ground.

He'd always been able to control animals, but the Well-blessed bond had given him so much more. Entering his father's mind had only scratched the surface of the newfound power he sensed in his future.

The thud of feathered bodies hammered like war drums. Seconds later, manabeeze floated from corpses as their magical essence left them to rejoin the Cosmic Well. Forrest had just killed his father's army of crows in the blink of an eye. But it had cost him. His mana stores were depleted. He'd borrowed from his mate. Now he was virtually empty.

Melody had no idea what he'd done, and she rocked, unsteady on her feet from the aftereffects of his taking. He gripped her arms, stopping her from falling as glowing balls of light floated up around them in a lazy dance in the air.

"You're okay," he said to Melody, holding her steady. "I borrowed your mana. The dizziness will pass."

Understanding flickered across her expression as she met his eyes.

"We have to leave while the manabeeze circle," he muttered. "No one wants to be hit with those during battle."

Every fae in the room, including his father, held steady. They hated it, but they wouldn't make a move. The unpredictable taint on the Well could do anything, could trigger an accident, and they were all too selfish to act. Melody's expression darkened as she glared back at his family. Hatred and fury billowed down their bond. It left a bitter taste in Forrest's mouth. He knew what she was thinking.

"Forget them," he said. "The floaters aren't worth the mana."

She saw the pleading look in his eyes. He meant it. Now that he had her in his arms, they weren't worth it. He'd already forgotten them just as they'd forgotten him. He'd rather spend his energy on her.

He should hate them. Should raze them all to the ground for how they mistreated him as a child. How they mistreated Aeron because every time they ignored Forrest, they turned their cruelty on Aeron tenfold. He'd copped the brunt of their attention. He was three years younger than Forrest, and he'd been beaten, flogged, whipped, and humiliated more times than Forrest could count.

Forrest should kill them all for that.

But hurting them would make him just as cruel. All he wanted to do was take Melody home. To his joy, she reluctantly nodded, and they turned toward the exit.

Melody moved a fraction of a second after him. He sensed her mood shift. Felt her stiffen. She whirled to face the podium and screamed like a banshee. Her voice became a weapon. It sliced through the air with sharp intensity. One of his siblings had fired an arrow from their bow—he didn't even have a chance to see who before the stained glass shattered above them. Shards cracked and fell like lethal snow. Every single one of his siblings cringed and cowered. Blood oozed from their ears as they all whimpered in pain.

The arrow never hit.

It never pierced Forrest's chest, but it wasn't because of Melody's scream. Forrest's mother had stepped between him and the podium, protecting him. The arrow protruded from her shoulder.

"Mother!" he bellowed, rushing to catch her as she fell limp to the ground.

In his strong hands, her thin body felt like a brittle twig. Her crown toppled and cracked onto the slate. She turned toward him, face ashen, but when their gazes clashed, she whispered, "I saw you, my son. Always did."

Silent tears leaked from her eyes. Trembling fingers touched his hair lovingly. But she had no strength to tickle his scalp as she used to. The arrow was deeply embedded in her shoulder, and blood oozed at an alarming rate. Forrest's hand hovered over it, unsure what to do. Pull it and risk more blood, or...

"Forrest," she rasped, urging him to respond.

She'd said his name.

"I know you did," he croaked. "I remember."

And he could thank Melody for that. In a roundabout way, seeing what happened to her reminded him that his mother was a victim too.

Perhaps it was his words, or maybe it was the slow thudding steps of his father drawing closer, but his mother's eyes turned from hazy to sharp. Her jaw hardened. Her fingers wrapped around the arrow shaft, and when the king of Rubrum City stood over them with a sneer on his face, she pulled the arrow out of her flesh with an agonizing wail.

"You and your soft heart, Brinwa," the king taunted. "This blood is your own doing."

He leaned down to claim the arrow. Brinwa's bloody teeth

bared, and she shoved the arrow straight into his heart. The king swayed in shock.

"You always had a touch of Seer in you," she said as he collapsed on top of her. "But it's your heart I pierce this time."

Forrest shoved his father off his mother as their siblings raced down. Everyone else in the room knew not to get involved. This was royal politics. This was for them to act upon.

Ellwyn kneeled by her mother and placed her palm on the bleeding wound.

"I'm healing you," she said. "No matter the risk from the taint. Hold on."

Brinwa's hand latched onto Forrest. He gripped tightly back. Then Melody joined in.

"You did it," she said, smiling. "You used your voice."

The gravity of her words dawned on Forrest. Melody must have said something to his mother—just like the song she'd sung in Sky Tower. She'd inspired another to stand up for her beliefs. He looked at his mate with awe-filled eyes.

Nero had called her his harbinger. But she wasn't one of doom. She was one of great change.

"And I have more to say," Brinwa said through clenched teeth, patting Melody's hand before looking around at the family crowding her. "This needs to happen now."

Wincing, she pushed everyone off her and claimed the king's crown. He gurgled and reached out for help, but no one offered. Not even the children that had been so vocal against Forrest. They ignored the king, just as he'd bade them ignore Forrest. And while Forrest wished this new turn in his family's loyalty was because of his arrival tonight, he knew at least it was partly for his mother.

Brinwa straightened her spine, placed the crown on her head, and held her chin high.

"In decay, we harvest," she said and walked unsteadily to the throne. Most of the manabeeze had now hit the ceiling and escaped through the broken stained windows. She sat on the throne just as the king's lifeforce popped from his body in glistening white balls of light. "We reap," she said, "no longer from the suffering of others, but despite it. That is the true nature of the Autumn Court. We will prevail." Her eyes landed on Forrest decisively. "All of us together."

"Long live Queen Brinwa," Forrest bellowed.

His cry was echoed amongst the court. No one dared to claim treason. Brinwa now contained the power afforded through a royal tithe from the Well—a boon for protecting its integrity in Elphyne. She was mighty, and she had just proven her alliance with a representee of the Order.

"My son," she replied as her court continued to echo his proclamation. "You have been gravely offended by this court. Please accept our deepest apologies."

A public confession. His debt would never be denied. But he only bowed and said, "I wish to leave with my mate. That is all."

Brinwa's gaze darted to where Luthian cowered, clutching his bloody eyes, and her brows lifted. *Are you sure?* She seemed to ask. This was Forrest's chance to exact more revenge, but as before, Luthian wasn't worth the trouble. No one would heal him—like they didn't work with Aeron's hearing, the risk from the taint was too much. Brinwa's wound still oozed, and he sensed she would wait for it naturally to heal.

Now that Forrest had seen a head explode from a complication with the taint, he was sure Aeron had to stop waiting for his hearing to be fixed. Forrest cared too much to risk damage from another healing attempt. Aeron needed help through this new hurdle in his life.

It was time to go home and be with family.

"The Tinker," Melody said. "She was another human sold to Luthian."

Forrest slid his gaze back to his mother. "Will you free her into our care?"

Brinwa nodded and gestured to a guard, who whispered into her ear. When she straightened, it was with regret on her face.

"It seems Luthian's prisoner has already escaped."

"We'll find her," Forrest said to Melody. She looked concerned but nodded.

"I will also send Ellwyn out with a party of trackers. The prisoner will be found and returned to you at the Order." Brinwa dipped her chin and said, "You are free to go. I would offer you a portal stone, but..."

"It is not necessary." Forrest gave a shrill whistle and immediately heard the beating wings of the kuturi that had brought him here. "We have a ride."

"Then may the water flow again next time we meet."

"Come on," Forrest said to Melody. "Let's go."

His beautiful banshee queen smiled and nodded. Blood on her face made her look fierce, and he was in love with her all over again. She took a crunching step and whimpered quietly. Glass cut into her feet.

Forrest scooped her up. Careful not to hit any wayward manabeeeze, he carried his mate out and didn't look back.

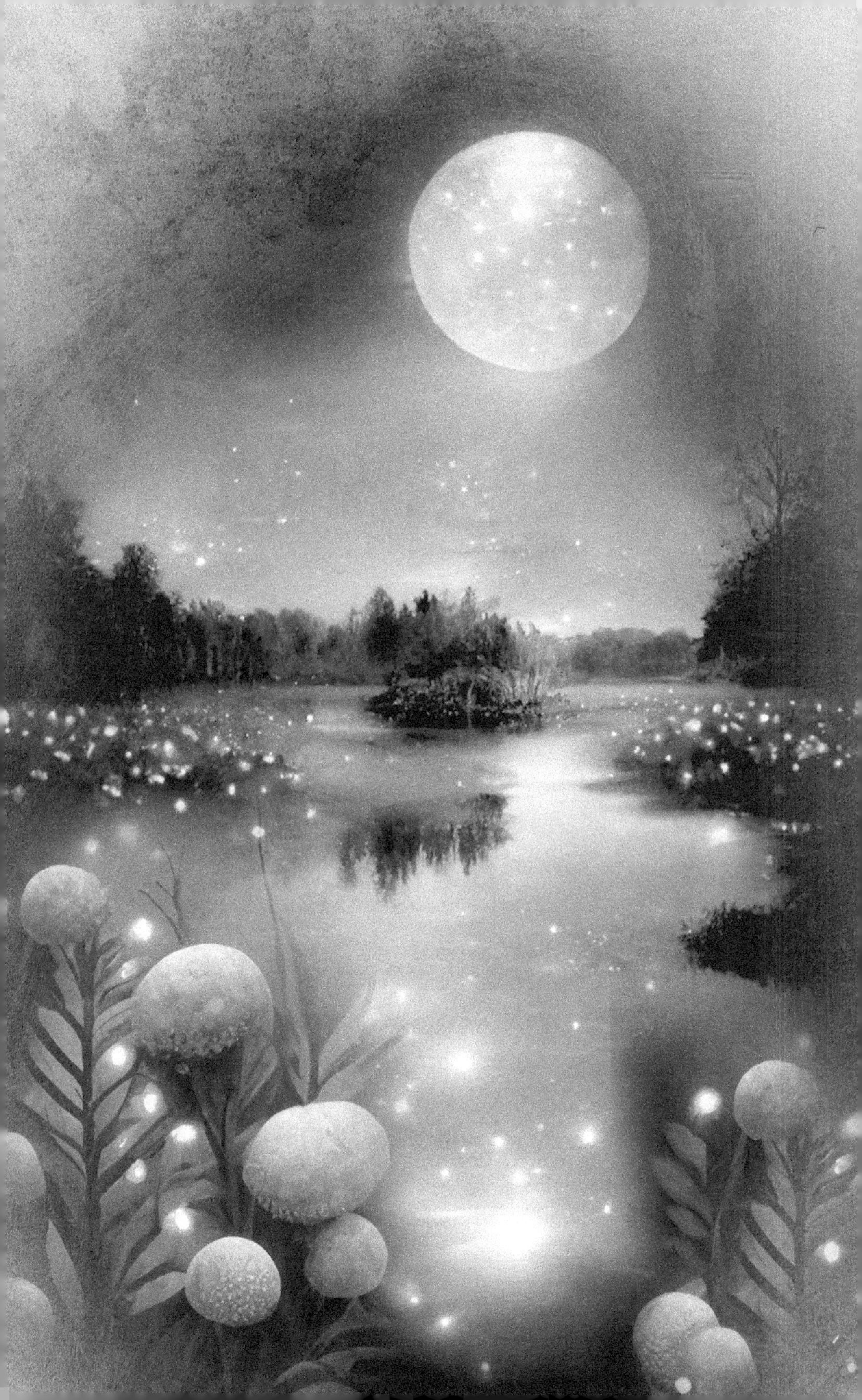

CHAPTER
THIRTY-THREE

Melody leaned her head against Forrest's chest as he carried her from the castle into the courtyard that was once bustling with people. Night had fallen, and most of the fae who'd milled about were now gone. Only soldiers kept watch, and none of them cared about the majestical beast flapping its wings, eager to get out. Part eagle, part lion.

The demonic hounds trotted behind Forrest but whined when they saw the kuturi—a creature Forrest told her would fly them home. To the Order of the Well.

"This is Misima," Forrest said to her.

"You know his name?" She looked at it, hesitant, and bit her bottom lip. "Sorry, is it a boy or girl?"

The creature huffed and clicked its beak. A Well Hound yapped in warning. Forrest gave it a stern look and probably said something mind-to-mind because both dogs swiftly padded away.

"Yes, this kuturi is male," Forrest replied, his eyes crinkling at Melody.

He put her down and then held out his hand.

"You want me to climb up?" She hesitated. It was about the size of a large stallion, but it had to fly with its own weight... and them.

Forrest's brows lifted. "You're offending him."

"I am?"

He chuckled and tapped his temple. "He's telling me you're taking too long to climb onto his back. He thinks you don't believe he is strong enough to carry two measly fae, which offends his sense of virility."

"Oh." She stepped forward, then held back. "But are you sure? I mean... the two of us?"

"Melody," Forrest admonished, his voice deep. The kuturi clicked impatiently too. "Do you trust me?"

He climbed onto the back of the kuturi and held out his hand again. That notion she'd glimpsed of him the first time they'd met had nothing on this. He was his namesake—the very element of wildness. He fit so perfectly in this world.

"It's a valid question," she shot back rather inanely. "I have no idea—"

She squeaked as he tugged her up, adjusting effortlessly to hold beneath her arms and swing her onto the back of the creature before him. She nestled between his powerful thighs and leaned back against a solid wall of strength. Maybe this would be okay.

"I can sense your trepidation." His arms came around her to grip the kuturi's feathered neck.

"Ya think?" She leaned forward with him. "We're about to launch into the sky—at night. No seatbelts, no saddle."

"I won't let anything happen to you." His voice was hot in her ear, and it warmed more intimate places she didn't care to admit. Not now. Not still covered in the blood of a fae she'd accidentally killed. Forrest said, "Now, hold here, and here, and squeeze your thighs."

Lord, she was putty in his hands when he spoke like that.

"If heights worry you, don't look down," he continued. "The Order is a few days of travel by kuturi, and we will circle Rubrum City first to look for your companion."

He made a *ki-ah* sound, and the kuturi's enormous wings flared wide. It bounded on lion's paws, then leaped into the air.

Melody's stomach dropped as they lifted. A thrill pulsed through her veins, and she grinned. She held no fear as they surged through the dark sky. It made no sense. She should be screaming, horrified of falling into nothingness—into a world she had no clue about—but she wasn't.

For months she had stared at the sky from the Tower and wished for this very thing. Freedom. At a loss for words, perhaps for the first time in her life, she stayed silent and took in what she could, but it was hard to see anything below them. The night was a murky blanket covering even the largest detail.

"We won't find your companion tonight," Forrest said, as though reading her mind.

"Do you trust your mother to search for her?"

"Yes," he replied. "Fae can't lie, remember. She is not the type to find a loophole. She is queen now, and there is a lot she's suppressed over the past few years. I wasn't the only one suffering in this family. I got out young. I sense what she said in the throne room has been thought about for a long time. Whatever you said to her made an impact."

"I only told her to use her voice."

"Sometimes, one final push is all we need to tip the bucket."

"I hope the Tinker escaped. I hope she has a gift to protect herself."

Silenced passed for long minutes as they both ran out of words. Melody grew sleepy as they flew. A little itchy from the blood crusted over her skin. A little grossed out.

"It's about time I showed you something good to sing about," Forrest said with a smile. He piloted the kuturi so they turned.

"A bath?" she replied, voice full of hope.

His chuckle was a warm rumble against her back. "Close enough. If we change kuturis, we will fly through the night and day and reach the ceremonial lake tomorrow evening. It's a source of power. We can stop there to clean you up and refill."

"Refill?"

"My mana," he explained. "While you seem to have a near limitless supply, I don't. I can't always borrow from you. Not only will it disorientate you, but a Guardian cannot rely on another, even his mate. I must always be ready for battle. I want to be at maximum capacity when I explain to Rush why I left his daughter behind with the enemy."

His words sank into Melody with dread. In all the chaos, she'd forgotten about his purpose for being in Crystal City in the first place. And she'd forgotten about her friends. What state would they be in now? Were they alive?

Sliding his hand around her middle, Forrest hugged her. "It will be okay."

Her throat closed up. How did she get so lucky finding him? The soft touch of his lips at her nape said he felt the same way. Much in this life wasn't fair, but they had each other. They would never be alone again.

Lulled by wind, the rhythmic beat of wings, and the warmth at her back, Melody fell asleep. She'd been so comfortable, so filled with trust, that she didn't even notice when Forrest switched out the kuturis—twice. When she woke next, the sun was high, and the animal beneath her was black and white and slightly slimmer than the first.

"Just a few more hours, and we'll be at the lake," Forrest said to her. "I'll hunt, and you can bathe. Then we'll carry on through the night until we get to the Order."

Melody's stomach growled by the time the sun set and they swooped lower. Sleep had allowed her to last without food, but now her hunger made her feel faint. Her muscles ached, and she was so busting to relieve herself that she feared she wouldn't be able to hold it in. At least she had slept—Forrest hadn't. When she'd queried it, he mumbled something about Guardian training and that he would be fine.

The few hours went past painfully slow. Melody was about to demand they land somewhere so she could go to the toilet but then glimpsed glimmering blue, purple, and yellow lights beneath them in the twilight. As they descended, more twinkling lights came into focus.

"What's that?" she asked, pointing down.

"The ceremonial lake."

"The glow? Are there people down there?"

"Usually not unless there is a tribute initiation. The glow is the plant and aquatic life. It's a place rich in mana, and the connection to the Well is strong. The water is a source of power, which means bathing in it will restore our personal wells at an advanced rate. Here we will rest."

Anticipation and wonder filled her. No one had told her of such marvels about Elphyne. Forrest took them down and landed the kuturi on the lake shore. It halted, kicking up sand and puffing with labored breath.

After helping Melody down, he said, "Wash in the lake, and I'll find water and hunt. I'll join you in a minute." He started to move but turned back with a warning look. "Don't stray far from the shore. The further you head into the forest, the more poisonous the plant life. And the further you swim into the lake, the more the Well Worms won't think twice about dragging you into the deep."

"Well Worms?" *Lord Almighty.* What other dangers lurked in this beautiful place?

"The worms judge those who want to be Guardians." He paused. "It's an experience no one wants to repeat. Most don't survive the process. So, unless you want to float and bloat, be quick. I won't be long."

"Got it."

She found a private spot in the trees to relieve herself, wincing the entire time at her aching and stiff muscles, but she couldn't complain. Forrest was out there, running without sleep, finding food and water for them. The air was surprisingly warm as she tiptoed to the water's edge. Almost balmy. She was surprised to find the water also warm. Hot springs must exist beneath the surface. The journey here had been cool but bearable. It was so different from the wet and miserable Crystal City.

A physical feeling trickled down from her head to toe. It was like her entire body exhaled. The wind brushed her face gently, lifting her hair like a lover's caress. She raised her face to the moon and smiled at the welcoming feeling bathing down on her.

As she tested the water with her toe, the bioluminescent algae—or whatever it was—swirled around her feet as though happy to meet her. So pretty. Like stars she could touch.

Swallowing her nerves, not wanting to seem like a complete chicken, she quickly submerged herself into the shallows. She gathered sand to scrub the worst of the dried blood. Since she'd been covered in it, she immersed fully clothed and refused to acknowledge what washed off her in droves.

Within minutes she felt restored... revitalized. She had no idea if her inner well was refilling, or if she even needed it, but noticed her fingers weren't sore anymore. The blisters were mostly gone, and the soles of her feet didn't sting from the cut glass. When she checked, the wounds had closed over, and scars had formed. The water—and perhaps just existing in this magical realm—was healing her faster than before.

Sighing, she floated on her back and stared at the sparkling sky.

A splash had her turning. Forrest arrived, and—she sucked in a breath—he was taking his shirt off. Melody's mind blanked as she drank in the sight of him. Even under the starry night, the toned musculature of his body was riveting. Broad shoulders—the kind of shoulders that should be illegal... narrow waist... abs she could cut herself on. The Well-blessed mating mark twined down one arm from his shoulder to wrist. The unique pattern echoed on her skin.

Again, she wondered how she came to be so lucky. Why her, out of everyone from her time? Why did she get picked to freeze in time and wake up with these gifts?

He caught her staring. A small smile lifted his lips. "I like it when you look at me."

"I'll look even more if you take off your pants."

Her eyes widened. Did she just blurt that out loud? His smile spread.

She liked that she made him happy. Clearly, she did. Whatever he saw in her, she could always trust that smile. Sadly, he left his pants on as he submerged and joined her. He used his shirt to wash before wringing it out and putting it back on.

"I've set up a campfire by the shore and have skinned a rabbit." He splashed his face.

"That was fast."

He gave a nonchalant shrug. "Doesn't take me long to hunt."

Of course. He'd be able to sense and trap any animal close by. He'd probably be able to make them walk into his dangerous arms.

"Plus," he continued, "a patch of berries, herbs, and nuts grow around the dock where the tributes are held. The less we cart from the Order, the easier it is for events."

"How long will it take you to refill?" she asked, hoping she sounded casual, but the memory of his naked torso made her hungry in more ways than one.

Her skin felt tight over her bones. She buzzed with the need to touch him.

"A few hours, give or take."

"Hm."

"If I stay submerged, it will be faster, but we need to eat."

With that, he scooped her up and walked them onto the shore.

"I can walk," she said with a smile. "My feet are healed."

"I like holding you."

They were still smiling as they sat down by the warm campfire by the trees. Forrest fitted the game he'd hunted to a spit roast made from sticks. He'd done all this in the minutes she'd been bathing and floating in the water. She drank greedily from a rolled leaf he filled with water drained from leaves on a tree.

"I still can't believe you did this so fast," she said, licking her lips.

"I had help." He stretched his legs out.

"Help?" she looked around. "I thought you said no one was here."

He smiled tiredly at her. "Sprites told me which trees had the most water stored from rain."

"Sprites."

"Harmless elemental beings. Some are made of fire, air, water, earth... that sort of thing. They're timid things sometimes and only show themselves to those they trust. Sometimes they're more trouble than they're worth, but if you can get on their good side, they help." He checked on the roasting game as he spoke. "But don't mix up sprites with pixies, who are vicious little things."

Her brows puckered as she recalled what she knew about them. "I thought pixies were our size."

"They are," he replied. "But they can shift down in size and love causing mischief with their tiny fangs. Sometimes it's easy to confuse them with sprites."

"I have so much to learn about this place."

"I will teach you." His eyes met hers over the campfire. "Give you lessons."

Lessons.

That one word sent a flush of heat to her face. *His hands up her dress, between her legs, so eager to learn.* If only she'd known then that this was how it would turn out. She wouldn't have let him stop. Wouldn't have said another woman's name. From the flush to his cheeks and the way he looked away nervously, she knew he'd remembered the same thing.

Clearing his throat, Forrest removed the game from the fire and broke off some meat for her. They both ate greedily.

Afterward, she stared into the darkness around them. She felt nothing but calm assurances down their bond. It was soothing to know that Forrest wasn't worried. She shouldn't be either.

But everything that had happened bubbled up. His family. Would they really hunt for the Tinker? Timothy, Caroline, Andrew. What had become of them? Willow—why hadn't Forrest come back with the girl?

"What about Willow?" she asked. "What happened?"

"She didn't want to come," he mumbled, now staring at the fire. "Said it was her destiny to be there. I did everything I could to convince her. Rory refused to come, even though I told her who she was. But you'd been taken, and I had only minutes to get out of there before the guards arrived. Even if I managed to knock both unconscious, taking them with me would have been impossible. I made a choice."

She bit her lip, letting his words soak in. He'd mutilated himself to get into that place. But he'd left it all behind to come after her. A rush of love so strong and deep crushed her. Forrest held his breath as he no doubt felt it travel down their bond. He beckoned for her to join him on his side of the fire.

She was there in an instant, leaning into him for comfort. It felt like the world stopped at that moment.

She was safe here.

She had everything she never knew she wanted.

But she'd left so many behind.

"What do you think happened to my band?"

His brows knitted together. "When we see Silver and Shade, I'll claim a debt they owe. Silver will smuggle your friends out."

Relief sagged her chest, and she almost wept. "Really?"

"Of course." He touched her cheek gently. "I'll fight for your happiness, Melody. You're my mate."

She fell into his arms and sobbed. He stroked her hair and held her close.

"I'm sorry," she said. "It's just so overwhelming. I can't believe we're here."

"Never apologize for your tears," he whispered. "They mean you care."

She cupped his face and kissed him. He opened his mouth and let her taste him. When their tongues clashed, a raging desire so thick and urgent filled her. She became breathless in seconds. Needy in less.

Forrest's hand speared into her hair. He gripped tight and pulled away with his breath laboring. For a moment, she thought he was going to say stop, but his eyes—oh, how his eyes drank her in —*butterflies in her stomach.*

"On your back," he said, eyes smoldering. Melody never moved quicker than she did at that moment. He climbed over her, braced his elbows on either side of her head, and whispered in her ear, "That's my girl."

She went all gooey from his praise. He ran his palm up her thigh, over her crumpled dress, until he cupped her breast with a groan of appreciation. He nipped at her lower lip and tweaked her nipple through the thin, damp fabric. She arched into him.

"I want to resume my lessons," he decreed quietly. "I want to please every inch of your body."

When he spoke to her like that, all deep, ragged, and needy with a lick of boyish eagerness, she was done. Dead. His.

"What was next before I stopped the lessons?" His frustration at himself hit her in a hot wave.

"Well," she said, heartbeat quickening as he kissed down her neck. "I suppose we started with first base... but then somehow skipped to third. I guess it's time for a home run."

"I have no idea what you're talking about, but please don't stop. I love the sound of your voice."

A throaty sound slipped out of her as his hand dipped between her thighs. She rocked into him. His fingers were at her underwear, beneath, and rubbing between her folds. He coated his fingers with her desire and explored leisurely at his whim. He watched her come undone with fascination.

"God, that feels so good." She ran her hands down his muscled back as she lowered onto the sand... no, not sand. Softness bloomed under her back. She craned her neck and found flowers there now. "Forrest, look."

His fingers paused between her legs, his eyes glazed over with a frown as he took in the new garden bed. "I'm not doing that. Are you?"

"I wouldn't know how." She shook her head and gasped as more flowers bloomed around them.

"It must be the Well," he said, working her again with his fingers between her legs. "We're blessed."

Melody sat up.

Forrest's frown deepened. He stopped and pulled back. "Is something wrong?"

"Not at all," she said, a smile stretching her lips. "It just occurred to me that there's another lesson I want to teach you, and it's *you* who should be lying down, not me."

He sat back cautiously. She wanted to giggle at the nervous energy emanating from him.

"You're going to like this lesson," she promised.

His brow arched.

"Do you trust me?" she asked.

He shot her an amused look but then nodded.

"Take off your shirt."

The instant eagerness and arousal injected into his expression was all the permission she needed. She planted her hands on his chest, urged him down, and helped him remove his shirt. He was tense all over and studied her every move.

She explored his magnificent torso, noting when he made little male sounds of pleasure. She kissed him—starting at the base of his throat, trailing her tongue around his Adam's apple, and then moved south. When she got to his waistband, he sucked in a breath and held it.

She glanced up, caught his eyes—saw the simmering need, the caution, the hope. She smiled against his skin, and her tongue darted out to trace along the waistband, licking through his sprinkling of hair, searching deeper as she felt the hard bulge where his shaft began.

He groaned and exhaled. "Mel..."

"Shh."

But he couldn't. He sucked in deep breaths and exhaled. Panted. Skin pulled taut over muscle. He gripped her hair tightly. "I'm so fucking *hard* for you."

"Good."

She unbuttoned his fly and peeled open the placket. She found the silken tip of his erection and gently bit it, silently saying a prayer to the heavens. With a muttered curse, he thrust into her mouth, demanding entrance.

When she opened, he cupped her face with a hitched breath. Feeling empowered, she tugged his pants down his hips to gain better access. She took him in hand.

"Show me how you like it."

He licked his lips. "I don't know how I like it."

She lifted her gaze to him and found trepidation. "No one has touched you like this?"

He shook his head.

"You are my first, in every way. Except kissing." He blushed. "I kissed someone once."

"Oh, Forrest, my darling. The things I'm going to do to you. Show me how you want it?" She squeezed his shaft. "Soft, hard, rough, gentle."

He thrust into her, and she caught that wild look about him.

What had he said in the garden? He liked the chase. He wanted the hunt. He liked to let his inhibitions go.

"Do you want to fuck my mouth?" she asked coyly. "Or do you want to chase me through the woods, catch me, and then have your way with me?"

Heat flared in his eyes. "Yes. All of it."

Opening her lips wide, she swallowed him, taking his length deep down into the back of her throat. He grunted, groaned, and pulled her hair. After a long-held breath and an encouraging word from her, he flexed his hips. Melody bobbed on him, taking him as deep as she could before coming off and gasping for air. Her throat could do wonders, and she was glad to share them with him. Before long, his pace increased to a frenzy. He snarled and lifted her up his body with effortless care until she lay flat against him, her legs straddling his waist. He crushed her in his arms.

"Put me in," he demanded huskily.

"I shouldn't be on top. I'm too—"

"Stop offending me, or I'm going to—*Crimson*." His hand went down her back, scrunched her dress, and yanked her underwear aside until he felt her aching, needy entrance. With his other hand, he guided his cock through her juices, eliciting a melting whimper from her lips.

"There," she mumbled. "Push in."

He thrust and entered her slowly but stopped. She sensed panic as he met resistance. She pulled herself off him and then sheathed herself again.

"Sometimes you need to move a few times," she whispered.

"You're so tight," he muttered. "So..."

He was all virgin male, stuttered breath and urgency. But he was a fast learner. He pulled out and pushed in harder. She rocked at the force and gasped at the sensation of him filling her. He stretched her ass cheeks so he could open her further.

He didn't wait for her to adjust. He planted his feet beside him, knees bent, and pistoned his hips, hard and fast, grunting with a kind of determination that made Melody feel needed to the bone. She had never been on top. Never had someone who wanted her up there. Hit after hit, he wound her up, unfurling bliss, boosting her confidence. Soon she was riding him as much as he drove into her.

Their lovemaking turned to raging need. He kissed her everywhere he could reach. He lifted her dress clean off her head. He drew her full and aching breasts into his mouth and mumbled beautiful praise along with curse words she'd never heard before. It was as though he couldn't decide which way to feel.

She climaxed first, burying her scream into his sweaty neck, muffling her sound as best she could. He seated himself shortly after, hugging her tight, trapping her against his torso with the force of his emotion. A long, satisfied groan tore out of him.

Puffing and needing to see his face, she straightened. Wonder was all over his expression—from his fever bright eyes to the blush in his cheeks, to the way he still tried to touch her all over. It all made her feel loved.

She rocked her hips in small motions to wring the last of her throes from him. He trailed his hands over her full breasts with heavy-lidded, affectionate eyes. "I'm the luckiest male alive."

"Mm." she smiled lazily. "Happy first time."

A bashful look overcame him and then hunger as he toyed with her breasts. "First of many, many more."

She kissed him on the lips, positively preening under his tribute.

And then she made her own kind of prayer, worshiping his body with her hands. Gloriously soaking up all the hard slabs of muscle slick with their lovemaking efforts. And to think, when she'd bumped into him that first time, she had no idea she would be in this position. She'd been in awe of that strength. She'd made a fool of herself touching his biceps.

She tried to climb off him, but he grumbled and held her planted on him.

"I should get off you," she murmured and tried again. Now that the rush of endorphins receded, she was acutely aware of her nakedness. Acutely aware that he was a hard slab of perfection beneath her, and she was... well, still not comfortable.

"Why?"

She scoffed. "You know why. I'm—"

"Incredible. Amazing. Beautiful." He kissed her. "Mine."

"Too heavy."

"Why do you keep worrying about that?"

A flush of annoyance washed through her, and she climbed off him. She reached for her dress. "The Captain called me a sack of potatoes," she grumbled. "And Nero forced me to eat until I got fat. I'm not comfortable with the way I look. I spent half my life caring about my appearance. It's not something you can just erase, even if you're telling me I look fine."

He propped himself onto an elbow and glowered. She felt his wrath but knew it wasn't directed at her. He scowled into the darkness, probably dreaming up all the ways he would find the men who'd harassed her. That wrath grew thicker.

"Just forget it," she mumbled as she dressed.

"I hate that he's so far away, yet he's still infecting your happiness."

"As I said, it's fine."

From the rough way he dressed, and the irritation spearing down their bond, he would not forget. She'd just ruined a perfect moment with her self-doubt. This was his first time, and she'd made it all about her.

Maybe she just needed a cigarette.

"Forrest," she sighed. "I'm so sorry. I wanted your first time to be everything you dreamed of." She threw up her hands. "I didn't even let you chase me."

His laugh was genuine and from the belly.

"Believe me when I say that was perfect." He touched her cheek. "I didn't hurt you, did I? I sort of... trapped you there."

"Honey, you can trap me any time, anywhere."

His expression sobered. "I have no words to describe how whole you make me feel. I just wish I was the same for you."

"Oh, Forrest." She threw her arms around him and held him tight. "My body image issues are about me. About what that evil man made me do and how another man made me feel. Before this time, I was confident in my skin—no matter the size. I want that feeling back."

Forrest's eyes softened on her. "They hurt you in more ways than one. For that, I am truly sorry."

Like lightning, it hit her. That's what she'd needed to hear all this time. Not someone telling her she looked fine or beautiful when inside, she felt wrong. She'd wanted someone to *understand*. To listen. To sympathize. She'd been fed accolades and compliments all her adult life, but she'd stopped listening to them. But here, now, hearing Forrest say he understood her pain...

This was everything her mother had always promised her.

Companionship. Compassion. Connection.

Tears welled in her eyes, and she said, "Thank you."

"You're in Elphyne now. With me. No one will tell you what to do again."

"You're right," she said. "I guess things have moved so fast that it will take a while for my brain to catch up. But we have time, right?"

"One thing the Well rewards you with is time," he said with a stifled yawn. "And with someone to share that with, it is the truest blessing."

She kissed him gently and marked his drowsiness. "Hun, you give new meaning to the saying *rode hard and put away wet*. You should rest."

"No." He made a valiant effort to stand but ended up laying down. "We should get going. Sleeping in the wilderness is not good without permitter mana stones."

"Not sure what they are, but you can tell me next time. I'm not tired," she stated. "I slept all night. I'll keep watch."

"Maybe just an hour." He laid down and gave her a last warning look. "Don't let the moon climb too high. Wake me if you're afraid. Of anything. Just an hour."

When she stroked his hair, he gave her the oddest look accompanied by a sense of loss. She debated removing her hand, but he bade her stay. When his lashes drifted closed, she sang a lullaby she'd learned during her time on Broadway. Within seconds, he was asleep.

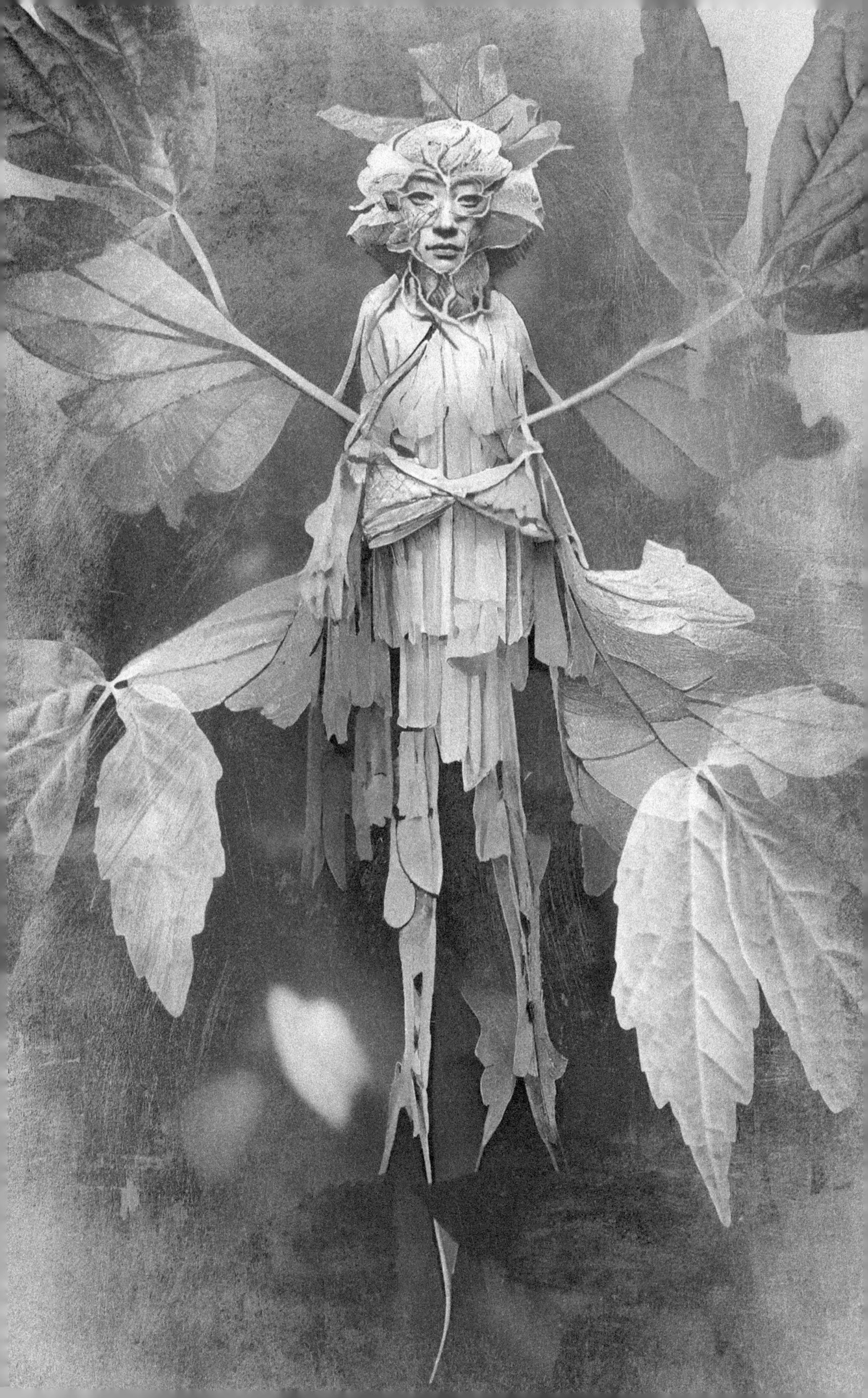

CHAPTER
THIRTY-FOUR

Forrest woke to the sound of singing. At first, he panicked. He hadn't wanted to sleep until they were at the Order. He didn't want Melody to fear another thing in Elphyne on the off chance that he wasn't enough for her to stay. The fear had slid into his nightmares.

He sat up, worried, but she was still next to him. The voice was hers.

"Hey," she said in that husky timbre he loved. She continued to hum her song with her chin resting in her hand. Woodland sprites played in her hair, and she loved it. It was written in her face, her lazy posture, and all down their bond.

He narrowed his eyes to check they weren't pixies and, once satisfied, smiled back at her.

"How long was I out?" he asked.

"Not long." She reached for him and whispered, "Look what's in my hair."

"I'll get rid of them."

"No!" Her eyes widened. "They were too afraid to come over for such a long time. Now listen to them."

He peered closer and noticed they weren't just playing. They were twisting strands of platinum hair into braids as they hummed the same song. He'd never had the chance to study woodland sprites up close.

"What do they look like?" she whispered.

He settled in next to her. "Their little bodies are made of sticks. But they shift and roll like they're not solid. Their wings are like the membranes in leaves."

"So magical." She smiled. "They're so gentle too."

He wanted to let her soak this in, but with each passing second, his restlessness increased.

"We have to go," she stated. "Okay. But what do I do?"

He helped her to her feet, and the sprites fluttered away. Her disappointment was notable, but then she rallied. "Plenty more time for exploring later."

⚖

NOT LONG AFTER, they landed in the training field before the house of the Twelve. When Forrest had left a few weeks ago, the unlawful party the crows had thrown was messy. Not a glimmer of evidence of that party remained.

He glanced warily to the dark house where the Six lived. Since it was night, they would be awake. Possibly out. Possibly looking for another soul to sup on.

He tightened his hold on Melody as he helped her off the kuturi, then sent his gratitude mind-to-mind and slapped the wild beast so it flew away.

He took her hand.

She gave him a nervous look.

"It's my fault," he said. "Whatever happens from here, the fault is mine, not yours, for leaving Willow."

Her lips firmed, and he felt a stalwart sense of loyalty from her.

"For starters, you did them a favor. You said it yourself. Second, I'm not leaving you. I'll face this with you."

He gave her a quick kiss on the lips.

The front door burst open, and Clarke rushed out. She'd either predicted he'd arrive, or they'd heard. Rush was immediately behind her.

Clarke ran down the porch steps but faltered as she hit the lawn. It broke Forrest's heart to see the initial hope in her eyes turn to agony when she realized Willow wasn't there. She whirled and ran into Rush's arms. He crushed her head to his chest, his brows furrowing.

Forrest tensed, ready for the sharp words of a hurting parent, but Rush only stared at the mating marks on Forrest's arm, then at Melody's, and nodded toward the house before taking his mate inside.

Forrest exhaled. "He's not going to kill me."

"He'd better not," Melody said fiercely. "My voice is ready. That's all I'm saying."

Forrest took Melody by the shoulders and said, "I love you."

"I love you too." She smiled back and touched his cheek. "I meant what I said. I'm not leaving you."

Looking into her eyes, feeling her resolution, he believed her. She tried to straighten her dress and sucked in her stomach.

"You're beautiful," he said softly. "Like the stars."

"Stop it."

But she smiled, and he felt her confidence bloom through their connection. She would get used to Elphyne. Soon it wouldn't just be sprites hanging on her every word. It would be all of them. He guided her up the steps and into the dimly lit house. A somber atmosphere greeted him inside.

Melody clung to Forrest. They stopped at the open threshold of the living room. Two long couches faced each other. A third was pushed up against a wall. Most seats were filled.

Caraway—the newest and largest member of the Twelve—stood against a wall and folded his arms, watching the people on the couch warily. His muskox horns curled from the top of his head.

"All a bunch of Vikings," Melody whispered in awe.

He gripped her hand possessively, and she smirked up at him as she squeezed back.

"This is half of the Twelve," Forrest said, gesturing at the Guardians and their mates sitting about the living room.

Aeron was notably not there, nor was Indigo or his mate. Probably still at Helianthus City helping Haze and Peaches with their newborn. Shade, however, sat with his arm slung around Silver's shoulder. Thorne occupied another couch with his mate Laurel. Leaf sat with a dark, judgmental look, but Forrest had no idea if it was directed at him or the others.

He sensed there were words said before he'd entered the room.

"What happened?" Rush asked before Forrest could introduce his mate.

"Where is she?" Clarke demanded, her voice shaky.

Forrest shrugged. "You probably know. She didn't want to leave."

"Know?" Rush gaped. "Why would she know? And Willow is six. She doesn't get a choice."

When guilt flashed over Clarke's face, Forrest knew his gut instinct was right. That warning the Sluagh had given them weeks ago meant more to her than she let on. Forrest had tried to take Willow, but she didn't want to leave. If they attempted another rescue, who was to say they wouldn't make matters worse?

"How about a thank you," Melody snapped at Rush. "How about a—we're sorry you had to chop your ears off and risk your life. Hun, you have no idea what we've been through to get here. I mean, look at the state we're in. *Look*. We flew all night and day to get here. How about a simple, *are you okay?*"

Everyone stared at Melody, shocked. And she hadn't even used power in her voice. Pride swelled in Forrest as he looked at her.

Silver tried to hide her smile but failed. Like the other women there, they'd all probably dealt with their mate's temper at one time. Forrest was grateful he wasn't like that with Melody. He hoped his anger was never directed at her.

Clarke burst into tears and cried, "I'm so sorry. This is my fault."

"It's not your fault," Rush said, scowling. "It's hers."

He pointed at Silver. Shadow peeled from Shade's body like wisps of menacing smoke. He bared his fangs at Rush in retaliation. Silver just rolled her eyes, unperturbed at the possessive behavior. Elves were nowhere as protective of their mates as vampires or wolves, but Forrest understood. He drew Melody tight to his side.

His action softened her tone but didn't stop her continuing reprimand.

"I don't know y'all from a bar of soap, but, quite frankly, I didn't think coming here would be worse than where I've been. Forrest spoke highly of y'all so much that I had it in my head this would be like heaven." Melody's jaw worked as her patience was tested. "Forrest has the biggest heart of anyone I know. He tried his damnedest to please everyone, but it's not possible. And it's not his fault, so a little respect from y'all wouldn't go astray." She patted her throat. "Sorry. When I get cross, my accent gets thick."

Leaf, who'd stayed silent, said, "You did what you could, Forrest. We are glad you're back in one piece and with a Well-blessed mate."

With his mate's head still crushed to his front, Rush had the decency to shoot Forrest an apologetic look. It took a long hot minute of tension before Forrest spoke.

"Melody is right," he said quietly, raising his marked arm. "And as you can see, there were a few surprises while I was there." Melody squeezed his hand as he continued. "Rory has taken Willow under her wing and seems to have the sole responsibility of her guardianship. She was not mistreated. I asked Willow on multiple occasions. There was a private garden connected to the Well where they trained. Willow was in good spirits most of the time and called Rory Aunty." He took a deep breath. "When my bond triggered with Melody, we had to leave. Even if we could hide it, there was a military man there who—" Melody shuddered, and Forrest didn't want to continue, but they needed to know it wasn't just about Willow. "He had an unhealthy obsession with Melody. Nero used Melody's talent to sling propaganda. She's a musician."

"Holy shit," said Laurel. Her palm slapped her face. "You're *that* Melody. Holy *shit*. Silver—you know her, right?"

Silver's eyes narrowed on Melody. "Yeah. I used to listen to your last album on repeat when I worked. I had no idea you were living in the Tower. I'm so sorry. If I'd known, I'd have found a way to get you out too."

Melody tensed, but her scowl dropped. "Thank you for saying that."

"Are you okay?" Silver asked. "It's not a picnic in there."

"I had it better than most... but I might need your help getting some friends out."

"Absolutely," Silver said. "Whatever we can do. I can start tonight."

Melody's relief hit Forrest through their connection.

Rush cleared his throat, bringing the focus back to Forrest. Rush was doing his best to remain calm. This must be hard for them.

Forrest said, "The Captain wanted Melody to mate with him—"

"Marry," Melody corrected him.

"Right. Marry," he said. "But she refused him. So, when he saw our mating mark, he kidnapped Melody and one other. Sold them to my brother, Luthian. Within seconds after I realized my cover had been blown, Rory turned up, threatening me. There was no way I could hide my bond mark. I had to escape there and then. I had to find Melody." He looked at Shade, who knew about Haze's mate's blood being used by Luthian as a drug for vampires. "You know what he's like. I had to go."

Shade nodded.

"You mentioned Rory..." Leaf suggested.

"I told her about her heritage, but she refused to listen."

The front door slammed wide open. A gust of cold wind came in with three leather-clad, dark-haired warriors—the crows. None looked happy.

CHAPTER
THIRTY-FIVE

Aeron felt the loud shudder of the front door slamming through his bones. He stared into the quiet darkness. It had been weeks since the demogorgon screamed in Aeron's face, and still, he heard nothing. The silence was worse than anything he'd ever experienced. It left him with nothing but his own dark thoughts.

He lay still, debating whether to go downstairs.

As often at these nocturnal hours, it was usually the vampires causing a stir in the common areas. But as soon as he tried to pass off the excuse, he knew it would be wrong. Shade was rarely here now, but instead living at Rush's cabin with Silver. Indigo and Violet were in Helianthus City with Haze and Peaches.

Aeron put his hand on the wall. Sometimes he could sense vibrations below. He pushed his mana into the walls and increased his awareness. He'd always understood the way things worked. And what he didn't know, he did his best to learn. So, he'd instinctively become curious when he figured out he sensed vibrations more without hearing. Any chance he had to test the effect, he took. Multiple pulses came back to him. The living room was fully occupied.

Hyper curiosity had always been a flaw of his. Since the moment he'd been plucked from his mother's dying arms and tossed into a royal family who treated him like shit, he'd been wondering why. Why. Why. Always *why*.

No answer satisfied him. Ever. But he kept searching.

He tossed his covers off and lit the candle by his bedside with his mana. It sputtered and sparked with a flash. By the dim light, he dressed in Guardian leathers that had been in a pile at his bed. He'd used them today to accompany a rookie Guardian to gather samples of mana-rich earth around campus. The Mages in the Academy studied every possible angle to identify this taint on the Well.

Without his hearing, his usefulness to the Order wore thin. But after he'd finished wallowing in his misfortune and fucking any female who offered, he'd tried his hand at doing something proactive. No matter what he did, he was left with a bitter taste on his lips.

Still seeking answers.

He braided his long brown hair and carefully made his way downstairs. He had to exercise caution now in everything he did. Especially at night when the light he relied on to communicate was almost gone.

He walked to the living room door and stood at the threshold, taking in the scene. The crows had just arrived. They'd left the front door open. Everyone was arguing. That much was evident. Rush and Clarke were back. Thorne and Laurel. Silver and Shade.

Caraway. Leaf glanced over from the couch, then turned to the crows walking into the crowded room.

Aeron straightened as his eyes tracked to a familiar auburn-haired elf.

Forrest. And... a blond woman. Human. Aeron narrowed his eyes, immediate distrust simmering in his blood. Who was she? Then he saw the blue marks on her hand holding Forrest's. She was his Well-blessed mate. A pang of—something—in Aeron's chest as he realized what this meant.

Forrest, the only family worth Aeron's time, would be busy with his female. Aeron would be more isolated. These were selfish, self-destructive thoughts. But they were there. Already feeling stupid for coming down, he turned to leave, but Forrest spotted him.

His eyes gleamed, and he strode over, gripping Aeron hard on the upper arm. His mouth moved rapidly. Aeron almost punched him, but Forrest quickly hand-signed his apology and beckoned Caraway. The big shifter brought a piece of paper and a charcoal stick. Forrest made him write down what was being said.

As usual, Forrest was looking after Aeron, as he'd been doing so since Aeron was three. Aeron didn't deserve him. Especially not now as he watched Forrest's mate talk and realized all he wanted to do was hate her.

She'd done nothing wrong.

When she glanced at him and smiled warmly, he dropped his gaze and shifted to stand next to Caraway as he scribbled madly, trying to fill Aeron in on what had happened.

CHAPTER
THIRTY-SIX

With the new guests' arrival, Forrest gave another rundown of the events and where it left them. He added information about Nero's mana-holding ability in desecrated areas.

Cloud's expression morphed from pissed to furious and disgusted within minutes.

"You left the child with Aurora?" he spat. "What kind of idiot are you?"

Forrest felt Melody's defenses rising again, and he squeezed her hand to encourage her to stay. He knew how to handle Cloud.

"As I mentioned, neither were willing to leave. Rory seemed to take on a protective role for Willow. I'm sure she will be safe enough."

Lightning crackled in the air. The living room suddenly became stifling.

"Protective role?" Cloud hissed. "*Protective?*"

Cloud's crow brethren suddenly looked nervous. Even River tried to assuage Cloud, but he shook him off. This was doing nothing to ease Rush's and Clarke's nerves. Forrest was ready to take Cloud outside until he calmed down.

"There is a statue in the center of his precious, private garden," Cloud stated, suddenly eerily calm. "A chained minotaur. Correct?"

He nodded. Had Cloud spent time in the garden while trapped in Crystal City during his youth? Melody glanced warily at Forrest, confused.

"It is covered in tar and feathers," Cloud gritted out as his wings materialized behind him, full and bristling but with scars. "Whose wings do you think they were hand plucked from?"

"Yours," Melody said, eyes wide.

"And who do you think did the plucking?"

"Nero," Forrest said.

"No, fuck face. Aurora did it. And she did it laughing while I bled rivers down her fingers."

Stunned into silence, everyone did nothing as Cloud pushed past and stormed out. River and Ash followed, shooting Forrest disgruntled glares as they went. Forrest scrubbed his face. Now it made sense why Cloud hated the woman so much. It also made sense why Rush looked like he wanted to murder Forrest.

"You left my child in the hands of a fae-killer."

Forrest's mouth opened and closed. He had no words. He was never more pleased to have Leaf stand than in that moment. The Cadre of Twelve team leader said, "I've let this go on for long enough."

He gestured at the front door, and Legion walked in, surprising them all. The tall Sluagh was the leader of the Six and looked like death warmed up. Long, black hair hung from a widow's peak like a silken waterfall. Dark suit. Tattered wings draped behind him like a dreadful king's mantle. Eyes that seemed to take in everything.

They landed on Forrest, then skated right off him, bypassed Melody, and landed on Clarke. It was Leaf who announced Legion's purpose for being there.

"I've had an interesting conversation with Legion," he said.

"No shit," Thorne mumbled.

Leaf glared at him before folding his arms and saying to Clarke, "Are you going to tell everyone, or shall I?"

Once again, guilt stamped over her features.

"What's he talking about, princess?" Rush bowed his head to Clarke.

Her eyes, already red from crying, glimmered with renewed tears. "I..."

"Clarke," Rush said softly. "You can tell me."

She buried her face in his chest and sobbed. Rush gathered her into his arms. "Someone better start talking soon."

"You all know the Six have their own Seer, Varen. And the Order has Dawn," Leaf explained solemnly. "They both concluded that Willow's destiny remains in the human city for the next few years. Any attempt to remove her will unleash more destruction and suffering on this world." His gaze settled on Clarke. "You knew, didn't you, Clarke, yet you insisted on sending someone to retrieve her."

"What's he talking about?" Rush asked Clarke.

She pulled back and wiped her nose. She tried to talk, but then her bottom lip came out, trembled, and when she glanced at Forrest, she broke into tears again.

"Oh, babe." Laurel stood up and rushed over. "Is it true?"

"I'm so sorry," Clarke said, switching to hug her girlfriend. "Oh, God, it feels like I'm always saying sorry." She took a deep breath and exhaled. "I'd hoped I missed something in Willow's future while she was there because I can't see Nero's future. He's a void. I hoped we might change things if Forrest just went and looked for himself."

"You were warned, Clarke O'Leary, Mother of Destiny," Legion said sternly. "We won't warn you a second time."

His wings vibrated with a buzzing sound that filled the atmosphere like a swarm of manabeeze. The skull beneath his skin became prominent. Then it lit up like someone held a candle behind his bones. He paused, staring at Clarke for a long minute that suggested he spoke mind-to-mind with her, and then his visage flickered out of existence. He was gone. Completely.

"What destiny, Clarke?" Rush asked, frowning. "What has our little girl got to do with anything."

Leaf answered for her. "More than any of us will ever know. In light of this information, the Prime has forbidden any more resources to be wasted on rescuing a child who can't be rescued. From now on, we will devote a hundred percent of our efforts to clearing the taint on the Well. Is that understood?"

"Fuck you," Thorne growled. "Righteous ass. You don't know what it's like to leave a child behind."

Or to be the child left behind, as Forrest knew Thorne had once been.

"I know more than you think," Leaf shot back. Threat pulsed in the room like a tangible thing until Leaf sighed and dropped his shoulders. "We have multiple Seers saying Willow must remain on her current path. For the fate of the world. Rush, you know it must be this way. You all do."

Rush scrubbed his face, looking more resigned than ever since Willow's capture.

"I spent fifty years in limbo," he said to Clarke. "Cursed and away from my son so that I could bring you safely to the Order to join our fight." He sent Thorne a grave look. "We both know how painful it was. We hate the Prime for making it happen. But we also know we wouldn't be here today if it had never occurred. We haven't beaten Nero yet. Maebh is still causing us grief. But we are stronger. We are growing. If the Well has given you these visions, we must trust them."

"So you're okay with this?" Clarke's accusation barely came out.

"Of course I'm not," Rush replied. "Of course we want Willow here, by our side. Isn't that what all parents want? But, princess, we gave birth to a girl destined for great things. It will backfire on us if we hold her back."

Forrest went to the kitchen, filled a cup of water, and returned it to Clarke.

"What's that for?" she asked with a sniff.

"I left a message for Willow—told her to contact you using her blood connection anytime she's in the garden. If you have water nearby at all times, you can be sure you won't miss her call."

Hope flared in Clarke's eyes. Rush gripped Forrest's arm as he moved to return to Melody.

"Thank you, Forrest."

That was another debt Forrest chalked up. He nodded, knowing he would claim both his and Shade's to help Melody's friends escape the human city. He glanced at Silver, and she was already on her feet approaching. Shade's shadows circled their bodies as they walked closer.

"I'm going to reach out to my contacts tonight," she said to Melody. "What can you tell me about your friends?"

"They were in my band. Timothy and Andrew should be fairly easy to find. But Caroline was taken a prisoner as an incentive for me to do as the president wanted."

Forrest said, "There was an ex-Reaper there. His name is Sid. He might help."

Shade visibly bristled when he answered, "I don't want Silver talking to him."

"It's not your choice," Silver snapped back.

"Do you like it when I talk to my past lovers?" Shade's brows winged up.

"Lovers, as in plural. I had one, and you mangled his hand. Give me a break." To Melody, she said, "Don't worry. If we can get to them, we will."

Melody glanced at Rush and Clarke. "Would your contacts be able to smuggle Willow out too?"

"Maybe in time," Silver replied. "But after what Leaf said, I don't think we should."

Shade's shadows engulfed them, and then they were gone.

"I need to explain all this to the Prime," Leaf said as he stood.

"Wait," Clarke said. "Before you go, there's something I should tell you. And Aeron."

Caraway glanced up from where he scribbled notes about the conversation for Aeron. An uneasy feeling settled on Forrest.

The shame on Clarke's face warned him something was off. Had she kept information from them?

She took Rush's hand as she spoke. "I knew your mate was in there, Forrest. I should have told you before you went in. I also know where Aeron's and Leaf's mates are. Aeron's is a woman in Crystal City with black curly hair. I see her with goggles on her head all the time, so maybe she's an academic? And Leaf... yours will wake in a few years. I know the location. We'll have to be ready to unearth her before—"

Leaf held up his palm, furious. "I don't want to know."

Then he walked out.

They all blinked at his reaction. Leaf, of all people, knew the tactical advantage of having a Well-blessed human in their ranks. But he'd dismissed it with anger.

"Forrest, hun," Melody said. "I think she's talking about the Tinker. There were no other women in Crystal City who were from my time."

"The Tinker isn't in Crystal City," Forrest said, turning his attention back to Caraway as he scribbled down the details for Aeron. "She was kidnapped by my brother but has since escaped. My mother has sent a hunting party after her and promises to return her unharmed to us."

Aeron read what Caraway scribbled, and his expression darkened.

"We'll find her, don't worry," Forrest said.

But like Leaf, Aeron didn't seem to want to know. He sat there brooding, stewing, and then suddenly stood up and walked back to his room.

"I'm sorry," Melody said to him quietly and touched his arm.

He patted her hand. "We'll still find her, even if he's not ready for her."

A bright blue glimmering light shot up from the cup in Clarke's hand. Within seconds Willow's smiling face came into focus in the reflection.

"Willow?" Clarke exclaimed. "Look, Rush. It's Willow!"

She shot Forrest a grateful, teary glance and then grabbed Rush so they could sit down at the couch with Thorne and Laurel.

A rush of peace washed through Forrest, and when he heard Willow's first words, he knew he'd done the right thing in leaving her there. She didn't admit it, but she'd seen the same future as the other two Seers. And if Forrest cut his ears just so that Willow would know how to contact her parents, then that was a worthy sacrifice.

"I'm okay, mom. I'm playing with my tomorrow friends."

With the last few day's travel catching up, Forrest took Melody's hand. "Come on. We'll let them have some privacy."

He didn't think he had it in him to stay awake to show Melody his room, but he managed to find some food and settle them both in before completely dropping in a heap. Melody sang a song as she bathed, and he laid down on the bed watching her lazily, pleasantly, and happily.

Her song was about an invisible boy who grew up as a hero, and he knew, no matter what had gone wrong and what had gone right over the past few weeks—how Melody saw him was all that mattered to him.

Forrest had done all he could for other people tonight. The rest of the night was for him and his mate. He would face tomorrow when it came, but he wouldn't be facing it alone.

EPILOGUE
A WEEK LATER

Forrest woke to pitch-black surroundings and a feeling of being watched. His heart thudded in his chest. He patted the bed beside him.

Melody mumbled in her sleep.

"It's fine," he said. "Go back to sleep."

Within seconds her breathing evened out. She was here, as she had been for the past week. And she wasn't going to leave. They'd already had word from Silver that their extraction of Melody's band was successful. Her friends were due at the Order tomorrow morning. Apparently, the chaos Forrest had created in the city with his exit was the perfect opportunity to get in and out unnoticed.

Distance from that place was both positive and negative. Melody needed her friends. She felt awkward here. But she was healing, just as he was. He hated how much damage those men had done to her self-esteem. Regaining familiarity will be good for her.

Ridding her of those demons would be even better.

Willow, however, still firmly insisted she stay in Crystal City. Clarke tried to convince her every chance they could to come home. But even Forrest had to admit her parents were coming to accept their child's position. They seemed content with regular contact with Willow, and somehow, Rory kept letting her communicate.

Whatever Legion had told Clarke would stay between them, but it had convinced her to stop trying to forcibly remove Willow from Crystal City.

Scraping at the window.

Forrest jackknifed up.

"Fuck," he bit out, tossed his blanket off, and went to the window by the bed. He pulled the curtains closed before falling into bed. "Damned west-facing window."

He'd drawn the short straw when choosing a room at the house. Sluagh liked west-facing windows. He had no idea why. Before he closed his eyes, an impulse made him peek through the curtain again.

His breath hitched. Standing outside in the dark, a pale figure stood out in contrast. The male had his face tilted to Forrest's window as if he'd been waiting. Forrest had never seen him before. White, short hair was slicked back from a strong forehead. Skin so pale it seemed white. Severely handsome face. Dark suit. Tattered white wings. A ghost made flesh.

Not a ghost.

There, beneath his left eye, twinkled a blue Guardian teardrop.

Sluagh. And one of the Six.

Yes. The deep masculine voice whispered in Forrest's mind. Below, a wry twist formed on the male's lips.

"Who are you?" Forrest mumbled, knowing the Sluagh would

understand. He was probably rifling through Forrest's mind right now.

Emrys.

"What do you want?"

A deeper twist to those lips. *To give you the vengeance you seek.*

Suddenly Forrest was assaulted with images in his mind. He wasn't himself. He was someone else... somewhere outside the Crystal City walls. Forrest shut his eyes so he could concentrate.

Was this a memory?

Or was the Sluagh feeding Forrest this information from one of his brothers?

The night peaked as Nero watched his soldiers tie the Captain to a tall wooden pole outside the city walls. No protests came from the traitor's mouth, no unearthly wail, but only the unbearable heartache they loved well.

"Do you know, Cornelius," Nero said as he closed his eyes and listened. "Do you know what happens when a heart aches in the middle of the night?"

"This is a mistake," the Captain said through beaten and swollen lips.

Nero backhanded him, shutting him up.

"I am talking now," he said. He straightened his suit and brushed his hair with his hands. "You almost cost me everything. But you weren't to know I had a prototype for a handheld portal device. Pride was always your downfall, Cornelius."

The man on the pole canted his head but said nothing.

"Now where was I... oh yes, a story." The president paced before the prisoner. "You're not the only one who knows how to use the fae. During the great war your ancestors lost against the Tainted, you imbeciles gave

me one precious piece of insight. The Sluagh can be summoned by sacrificing a soul with so much heartache that the temptation is irresistible to refuse. All I need to do is ensure they face west." He leaned toward the prisoner. "You asked if the mission to find fuel was punishment. But you see now, don't you? This *is your punishment.*"

The images in Forrest's mind ended. He glanced outside. Emrys beckoned Forrest.

I will take you there.

Forrest looked at his sleeping mate, then back at Emrys. Forrest had pulled his punches and let the water roll off his back all his life, but he'd never had someone like Melody before.

When he was a child, he'd always wondered if, deep down, he was Seelie because he didn't fit in with his family. But now, looking down at Emrys, he didn't have a single doubt in his mind. He dressed and went downstairs to meet the Sluagh on the lawn.

Up close, Emrys was even more pale and frightening. Black glyph tattoos slithered over his skin, ducking and weaving in and out of view. Galaxies were born and died in his dark eyes.

"What about the taint?" Forrest asked. "Won't that affect the travel?"

Sluagh could skip distances similarly to how Shade traveled through shadows. They called it flickering. Emrys offered his hand out to Forrest.

"We *live* in the taint," he said, using his voice.

Emrys flickered them to the dead woods near Crystal City. Forrest was too far to see clearly across the miles to the wall, but he vaguely worked out a dark blob where a pole had been erected.

Do you want to go closer? Emrys whispered wickedly into Forrest's mind.

Forrest had the sense this particular Sluagh had a devious streak. And the minute he thought it, Emrys read his mind and smiled.

"Why are you helping me?" Forrest asked, unnerved.

Silence.

"Okay," he said. "Don't answer that, then."

Emrys turned his head to the city and narrowed his fathomless eyes. *Do it now.*

That was all the permission Forrest needed. He called any wild creature in his vicinity and sent it hunting toward the wall for its next meal. Animal after animal heeded his call. It didn't take long for the Captain's screams to rent the air—even across the distance.

"Let's go," Forrest said.

You don't want to watch?

He blinked. "No. But if you do..."

Emrys appeared torn.

"I don't need to," Forrest said. "I have what I came for."

Emrys took Forrest's hand and flickered them back to the field before the Twelve's house. When Forrest turned to hand sign his gratitude, Emrys was gone. Forrest looked at the Six's house across the field, checking to see if he was there, but the structure stood dark and quietly formidable as it always had.

He might never know why the Sluagh had helped him. But he wouldn't look a gift horse in the mouth. Forrest returned to his bed, tucked himself in, and hugged his mate.

He'd always worried his animal instincts would hurt the ones he loved. That was the real reason he stayed celibate for so long. But the truth was, that wild disposition finally had a purpose—to protect.

When he fell asleep, it was sound and deep in the knowledge he'd ticked that final task off his list. He most certainly did not dwell on what the Sluagh might ask in return for this favor. If he did, they might come calling to collect.

Even if they did, the sacrifice was worth it. Melody would never fear that man again.

Need to Talk to Other Readers?

Join Lana's Angels Facebook Group for fun chats, giveaways, and exclusive content. https://www.facebook.com/groups/lanasangels

ALSO BY LANA PECHERCZYK

The Deadly Seven

(Paranormal/Sci-Fi Romance)

The Deadly Seven Box Set Books 1-3

Sinner

Envy

Greed

Wrath

Sloth

Gluttony

Lust

Pride

Despair

Fae Guardians

(Fantasy/Paranormal Romance)

Season of the Wolf Trilogy

The Longing of Lone Wolves

The Solace of Sharp Claws

Of Kisses & Wishes Novella (free for subscribers)

The Dreams of Broken Kings

Season of the Vampire Trilogy

The Secrets in Shadow and Blood

A Labyrinth of Fangs and Thorns

A Symphony of Savage Hearts

Game of Gods

(Romantic Urban Fantasy)

Soul Thing

The Devil Inside

Playing God

Game Over

Game of Gods Box Set

ABOUT THE AUTHOR

OMG! How do you say my name?

Lana (straight forward enough - Lah-nah) **Pecherczyk** (this is where it gets tricky - Pe-her-chick).

I've been called Lana Price-Check, Lana Pera-Chickywack, Lana Pressed-Chicken, Lana Pech...*that girl!* You name it, they said it. So if it's so hard to spell, why on earth would I use this name instead of an easy pen name?

To put it simply, it belonged to my mother. And she was my dream champion.

For most of my life, I've been good at one thing – art. The world around me saw my work, and said I should do more of it, so I did.

But, when at the age of eight, I said I wanted to write stories, and even though we were poor, my mother came home with a blank notebook and a pencil saying I should follow my dreams, no matter where they take me for they will make me happy. I wasn't very good at it, but it didn't matter because I had her support and I liked it.

She died when I was thirteen, and left her four daughters orphaned. Suddenly, I had lost my dream champion, I was split from my youngest two sisters and had no one to talk to about the challenge of life.

So, I wrote in secret. I poured my heart out daily to a diary and sometimes imagined that she would listen. At the end of the day, even if she couldn't hear, writing kept that dream alive.

Eventually, after having my own children (two firecrackers in the guise of little boys) and ignoring my inner voice for too long, I decided to lead by example. How could I teach my children to follow their dreams if I wasn't? I became my own dream champion and the rest is history, here I am.

When I'm not writing the next great action-packed romantic novel, or wrangling the rug rats, or rescuing GI Joe from the jaws of my Kelpie, I fight evil by moonlight, win love by daylight and never run from a real fight.

I live in Australia, but I'm up for a chat anytime online. Come and find me.

Subscribe & Follow

subscribe.lanapecherczyk.com

lp@lanapecherczyk.com

- facebook.com/lanapecherczykauthor
- instagram.com/lana_p_author
- amazon.com/-/e/B00V2TP0HG
- bookbub.com/profile/lana-pecherczyk
- tiktok.com/@lanapauthor
- goodreads.com/lana_p_author